Birthright

(A Luo Tragedy)

Other Books by Joseph Alila

Fiction

Sunset on Polygamy
The American Polygamist
The Thirteenth Widow
The Milayi Curse
The Wise One of Ramogiland
Sins of Our Hearts
Whisper to My Aching Heart
Not on My Skin
The Choirmaster
The Luo Dreamers Odyssey (From the Sudan to American
Power)

Poetry

Thirteen Curses on Mother Africa
Rateng' and Bride

Birthright

(A Luo Tragedy)

CONTENTS

Chapter 14
Daughters Unite a Grieving Family
142

Chapter 15
Atieno, a Troubled Soul
149

Chapter 16
Dreaming on the Sinai
156

Chapter 17
Dorka's Angst
162

Chapter 18
The Untouchable Pearl
169

Chapter 19
Battle by the Graveside
175

Chapter 20
You Never Will Marry Olisa
183

Chapter 21
The Odongos, a Healing Family
188

Chapter 22
Aura Leaves Hospital
195

Chapter 23
Cigarette Dialogue
202

Chapter 24
Elizabeth Teases Thim Lich
206

Chapter 25
Elizabeth Graces Aura's Return
210

Chapter 26
Owinyo the Peacemaker
215

CONTENTS

Chapter 27
Okulu Wronged and Bitter
221
Chapter 28
Okulu, a Victim of a Father's Silence
226
Chapter 29
A Man Rules Okulu's Home
233
Chapter 30
Abich Catches a Big Fish
245
Chapter 31
You Are Hurting Me!
252
Chapter 32
All Have Changed
261
Chapter 33
Odongo Breaks His Cruel Silence
265
Chapter 34
Aura Charms Away New Tension
272
Chapter 35
"Okulu Son of Odongo"
275
Glossary and Notes of Luo Words and Phrases
279

1

An Uncommon Crime

JUMA WAS RUNNING for his life. He had been running in darkness for about two hours. In his northward flight across the land, he had gone through a series of bushes and grassy patches most of the way, wading through swamps, and swimming across large streams. His whole body ached because of impact wounds from encounters with thorny bushes and entangled creepers. Simply put, Juma was sore, muddied and wet, having swum across the last stream as recently as five minutes before. The miracle so far, in Juma's ordeal, was that his feet remained intact. No thorn, rock, nor tree stump had punctured his feet, even though he had been running in the dark over a rugged terrain spotted with countless thorny acacia trees.

His clothes had not been as lucky as his feet. Hardly any clothing remained on his slender body; only odd bits of cloth remained hanging on his slender frame. His faded-blue cotton pair of shorts had not survived during his brief-but-perilous journey. What was left of the shorts mostly covered his rear. A few strips of dark cloth remained of what was a black-and-white shirt, which spotted large irregular holes on so many fronts that some of our day's image-conscious professional wrestlers would have envied him.

Juma had been hearing his pursuers most of the way. Then, half an hour before, he stopped hearing the howls from their chase dog, which happened to have been his own dog, Grace. He recognized Grace because when she howled, she sounded more like a fox than a dog. He recognized his persistent pursuers by their voices. They were Okulu, his stepbrother and the man after his neck, and the pair of first cousins, Judas Oremo and John Odemba, playing interested-observer roles. He heard them twice before when they approached large streams and spent time arguing over which path to take at Y-junctions, with Grace sending mixed signals to them. Judas was Juma's dear friend. Juma believed that Judas was the one holding Grace. The presence of Grace and Judas in the chase made Juma less nervous. He understood that both members of the dog-man pair were loyal to him and were there to warn him whenever the pursuers were too close. John Odemba was the oldest man among the pursuers; he was a reasonable man, and his presence in the team reassured Juma.

The pursuers' voices and personalities had been very clear to Juma throughout the initial stages of the chase. However, as the night progressed, more voices joined the murderous choir running after his life. There too were more dogs howling in the chase initially; then it was back to one dog barking and hardly any human sound.

Just over two hours into the chase, Juma emerged on top of a small ridge, in a part of the land he never visited before and only saw on clear, mist-free days. Ahead, he could see a prominent light sitting on the middle reaches of a lower ridge. The light twinkled like a little star in a dark sky. A dog barked ahead, making him a little jittery. He froze where he stood to admire the single light ahead, thinking that his pursuers had leapfrogged ahead of him and were waiting in ambush. He ignored the threat, judging that the dog was at least a mile ahead of him.

Reassured, Juma slowed down to a jogging pace, choosing where to step for the first time after hours of running. He realized that he was running parallel to a wide path to his right. He also realized that he was entering a moderately populated area with clusters of fenced homes, with an occasional light making it through the tall euphorbia fencings around the homes.

Someone was cooking sweet potatoes; another was cooking some fish. That freaked Juma, with the aromas reminding him of the mother he left only a few hours before. When he last saw her, she lay helpless on the dusty ground near her open-air cooking place, writhing and groaning in pain after he had a mere exchange of words with her. Absorbed in thought about his mother's condition, he sat on a stone in the middle of a bushy area. The persistent smell of food gave him some assurance that he was among human beings, some of whom could listen to him and buy his side of the story.

The wind changed direction and hit him with the stench of warm waste; he thought he was sitting in the middle of an overused school latrine he had graduated from a month back. Someone could have been relieving herself or himself in a thicket close by, so he thought. He decided it was time to move on before he risked landing in the hands of some villager outside seeking cover to answer to nature's call.

As Juma stood up to leave, a bird that had been resting in one of the trees made a querulous noise, startling him. Juma shouted, "Ma!" before he resumed running, thinking that his pursuers were nearby.

A man shouted, "Who is that?"

The man's voice sounded muffled, as if he was talking with his mouth full of food. Juma fleetingly felt homesick, thanks to the idea of someone eating food, but he kept running northward.

The man coughed repeatedly, cursing himself for talking with food in his mouth. His breathing normalized, the old man did not bother following up on the source of the sound of distress, dismissing it to be from some youthful lovers going by his home. The old man often heard such youth go by his home the whole night. He in fact was eating some cooked corn-on-the-cob, while listening to his radio, and he was in no mood to stand up and investigate any indirect threat to his home.

Juma kept running northward through the bushes; he was alert, clutching the half-a-pound hardwood club with which he had left home, hoping he never would use it.

As far as he could recall, he had raised the club to defend himself against Aura, his mother, who had approached him, threatening to hit him with a cooking stick. However, Juma knew he had not hit his mother; neither had she delivered her blow against him. He was certain Aura fell down after a round object hit her on the head.

Juma and his mother had quarreled over food. He had demanded food from her, shouting, "I want food."

Needless to caution that Juma was a spoilt child and the spoiling authority was his father, who treated him like a small god because of his being the lastborn child from his bag of arrows.

By that tragic evening, Juma had shouted at his mother, perhaps for the millionth time since he learnt to open his mouth. Well, Juma was the last born of his mother and of his father, and more.

Maria Aura, Juma's mother, hated the new manly voice she was hearing from her son. He sounded like his father, the man she loved dearly. On that account alone, Aura was not ready to hear the same sound, from another man, giving her orders; she didn't expect it from her own son. Her son and last child had become a man; she was thrilled for that. Her son was a good pupil in school; she cheered him on. Now he was a man, and she was barely forty-six years of age! He was a child she conceived at a time when she thought all her eggs had expired. Juma was a special child in her heart, but the thought that her son soon would be shouting at someone's daughter to give him food, the way he had done to her all his life, was unacceptable to her. He had to stop.

Juma was mature-fourteen years of age and had just graduated from middle school with a Perfect A! He knew he was heading to a top National School, most likely Alliance Boys School, which was his first choice. Juma was spoilt and now he was famous, and he had become an object of much public adulation that came with the fame. Fame, praise, parental love, academic excellence, and adolescence had entered into Juma's head, he had started acting up, and his mother did not like his "big-man" antics.

"I have no food, Juma."

"Ma, I want food!"

"Juma, I won't give food to a man who does not work."

True, Juma had not been to the fields in two weeks and there was a reason for that. The examination results had been out for two weeks, and Juma was one of the top students in the nation. He was still celebrating with his friends over his perfect score, and he had stopped helping his mother in the fields. All he did was sleep, party during the night, and sleep.

"Give me food!" Juma shouted louder than the previous times.

"Do you think you are a man? You, a mere thing, I dropped the other day, to keep shouting at me? I'm going to shut that mouth for you," a worked-up Aura of Tanga said. She had been cooking some *ugali*, and at the spur of the moment, she jumped up from her stooping position, and she was about to hit Juma with the cooking stick, when something hit her on the head. Then she was collapsing as her feet gave way.

Juma, who had raised his club to counter her mother's cooking-stick attack, saw her collapse into a heap; then she was kicking, writhing, groaning on the ground and breathing with difficulty. She still clutched her cooking stick in her right hand.

"Ma, what happened to you?" shouted Juma.

Juma thought a lightning bolt had struck his mother, but the evening sky was clear all round, only the reds and oranges of the afterglow of the sun that had just set behind the lake lit the western skyline.

"Help! Help!" Juma started shouting for help.

The first person to answer to Juma's call for help was Okulu, his elder brother. Okulu emerged from behind a granary, not far from the fireplace where Aura had been winding up her evening-cooking routine.

"Juma has killed Maria!" shouted Okulu. He shouted so loudly that the whole village of Kougo received the message clearly. He started shouting even before he reached the scene of crime; and when he reached where Aura lay, groaning and writhing in pain, he simply walked past her, almost stepping on her head.

It soon downed on Juma that Okulu was not available to help Aura. Juma quickly understood that Okulu was there to incriminate him.

For a moment, frozen in utter helplessness, young Juma just stood there watching his suffering mother; the suddenness of the tragedy unfolding before his eyes had unnerved him. Juma had a club in his hand, but the horrid scene that confronted him, with his mother on the ground groaning like a deer under the dual weights of a hunting dog and a hunter's spear, had so overwhelmed him that he never thought of attacking Okulu, a man twenty years his senior.

As Okulu entered Atieno's house without checking on Aura's condition, an alarm sounded in Juma's head, jolting him awake from his brief reverie. *Why is Okulu calling me the killer without bothering to check on my mother's condition? Why had Okulu not stopped to help? Had Okulu planned to harm my mother then call me the killer?* Juma wondered.

Even in his panic mode, Juma quickly read wrong in his stepbrother's behavior. Juma was a young man, yet not a young man in the birthright politics in his father's home. Juma was Odongo's "spiritual eldest son" according to his Luo people's lore and marital law, upstaging Okulu (his stepbrother), a decades-older man. Therefore, Juma knew he was an object and a target of envy from some quarters in his father's home.

Juma quickly confirmed conspiracy in the evolving tragedy. He knew his mother's life was in danger and so was his.

"Ma! Ma! Who hit you on the head?" Juma shouted, shaking his mother up in the semidarkness, hoping to get a name, but she never answered and continued to groan.

Alone, his mother dying from an assailant's blow to the head, and with his father, who could have listened to his evidence, away in Tanganyika, visiting with Aura's people, Juma knew he was in grave danger in the approaching darkness.

I have to escape, he judged.

Heading toward the euphorbia fence to take strategic cover, Juma heard other people shouting from all directions; he hoped they were coming toward his father's home; he needed them. He intended to remain around his mother until a couple of villagers arrived, after which he would run for his life.

Atieno had listened to the worsening situation in the home from the safety of her house, where she would remain for the night. Since Okulu left her house on a scouting mission, Atieno had listened keenly to the shouts between Aura and Juma. Then she heard Juma cry for help. Atieno's heart darkened.

"It is happening! Finish him off, Okulu; he has tormented you for too long," Atieno whispered, aroused, violently stirring her pot of warm blood meal. Out of curiosity, she briefly peeped through a crack in her door and saw a warm red color of the setting sun fill the bay (part of which was visible through her door) with shades of red, orange, and violet. She flinched in shock. "Leave me alone, Aura; let it be you and your son!" Atieno cursed in excitement, nearly toppling her pot of blood. "So Okulu has done it," she cheered up, thinking that Okulu had taken care of the boy of privilege who had denied him their father's stool.

Then Atieno heard Okulu cry out, saying, 'Juma has killed Maria!' She felt greatly relieved, believing that her co-wife, the woman who, for decades, pricked her heart with thorns, was no more.

"So it has happened? Okulu has taken care of you Aura the usurper from Tanga. Aura, feel it in your flesh, even if only briefly before you die! You have been inflicting that pain in my heart for eternity. Feel the might of Okulu's hand. When your foolish husband arrives, your privileged son will be rotting in jail, and you will be a long-dead thing," Atieno whispered, stirring the rest of the blood meal, which she had intended to cook for her grandsons Luke and Mark for the next day's lunch.

Now, Atieno's daughter-in-law, Juanita, was a born-again Christian who never tasted any meat products, leave a lone blood meal. However, as long as her sons, Luke and Mark, visited their grandmother's house, they were free to help themselves to meats and blood meal.

Atieno changed her culinary plans. "The boys' blood meal has to wait, now that Okulu has bloodied his hands and needs ritual cleansing," Atieno whispered.

Just then, Okulu ran into the house, surprising his mother.

"How soon; you did not finish her off?" she asked, whispering anxiously.

"I think I did; she cannot survive," Okulu said trembling.

"But I can still hear her groaning," Atieno argued in whispered words, feeling disappointed, even though she could not shout because she could hear people gathering around Aura.

"Ma, I have done what you told me to do!" said a nervous Okulu, shaking uncontrollably and pacing the floor.

"Why are you shaking like that?" Atieno asked, in rage.

"It is her groaning, Ma; it is too loud. I have killed a woman," Okulu said rather loudly for Atieno's comfort.

"Smarten up! Drink that, it should help fortify you," Atieno ordered, and closed the door, while handing over a calabash of special herbal brew, whose use was popular among warriors of a century before. She had fortified the herbal formulation with a generous amount of alcohol and some blood meal.

Okulu drank it in one quick sustained desperate act; thanks to the darkness, he would never know what he had drunk. The natural narcotic in the cultic brew elicited a violent sneeze from Okulu; it brought immediate relief to him.

"How do you feel?" Atieno asked.

"Better," Okulu said. His head felt lighter, and he had a strange mental clarity and courage that could have confronted a lion.

"Okulu, listen to me; this is not about me; it is about you and your future," warned Atieno. "Where is Juma?" Atieno Nyomulo asked.

"I don't know, Ma."

"You should know. Go after him. You must get him before he talks to somebody in the village," Atieno whispered harshly.

"Ma, this is getting scary; I have done my part," Okulu complained

"You haven't completed your work; she is still alive," Atieno whispered.

"I did what I was supposed to do," Okulu said, pacing about restlessly.

"Give me that club; get a spear; you need it," Atieno said, snatching Okulu's club.

"I didn't use the club, I used a stone," Okulu said.

"I thought you were smarter than your father. No wonder she is still alive," Atieno said, castigating her son.

"I'm sorry," Okulu apologized.

"Go after him, now," Atieno ordered.

"O my head aches; o her groans, they are too loud!" Okulu complained, feeling the side effects of the narcotic brew.

"Be a man. Go finish the job," Aura said, pushing out

Okulu.

As Okulu emerged from his mother's house, a spear in his hand, shouting, "Juma has killed his mother," he could see an elder standing around where Maria Aura still lay. Okulu's heart sank. He made an immediate about-turn to reenter his mother's house, colliding with her in the doorway.

"Watch where you are going, before you stab yourself, you coward," Atieno whispered sternly.

"There are people around the body; I can't finish the job," Okulu said, once inside the house.

"Sh . . . ! You are a half-baked moron like your father. Give me the club; I'll go and finish her myself. Go and look for Juma. You must stop him before he talks," shouted Atieno, pushing out Okulu into the fast-approaching darkness.

"Atieno, what will I do? I knew Okulu would mess up and not finish the job," she muttered, making a quick retreat after seeing people around her fallen co-wife, who was still groaning on the ground.

"Juma, run!" Aura shouted once then continued to groan, her strength waning. She had mustered just enough strength and gained some presence of mind to utter those words.

Even with her failing strength, Aura understood that Juma, her little boy, was in danger; she knew he had been in danger since his birth. With her husband away, Aura knew that Juma was alone and a target of Atieno's murderous scheme, of which she, Aura, had become a victim.

Panicked, Juma withdrew from his mother, retreated through a gap in the euphorbia fence, and hid but still kept his mother within view.

From his post, Juma saw Okulu emerge from Atieno's house, a spear in hand, and still shouting, "Juma killed Maria!" only to beat a quick retreat. Then moments later, Juma saw Okulu reappear from the house, still carrying a spear in his right hand. Juma did not want the armed stepbrother anywhere near his mother. He judged she was safer in the hands of his uncles. To distract Okulu from approaching Aura, Juma did something unusual: He shouted, "Okulu!" thus inviting Okulu's attention before he took off, knowing that he could outpace Okulu, who was two decades older.

Okulu reacted predictably; he started chasing Juma.

"Don't kill him, Okulu! Bring him back alive; the law shall take over from there," an elder shouted.

Okulu met two of his cousins, Judas and John, outside the fence.

"What happened, Okulu?" Judas asked.

"Juma has killed his mother," Okulu responded pacing about restlessly.

John looked at Okulu suspiciously; he saw a nervous man.

"Have you been drinking, my cousin?" John asked.

"No," Okulu replied, looking about wildly.

"Where is Juma?" John asked.

"He ran in that direction; we have to get hold of him," Okulu said pointing northward with his spear.

"John, wait here with Okulu, I'll be back," Judas, the youngest man among the three men, said. He was not sure of what he was hearing and seeing. Aura was groaning loudly nearby, and Okulu continued to accuse Juma of her murder without any concern for the victim's condition. Moreover, Okulu, the accuser, definitely had alcohol in his breath. Judas resolved to check on Aura's condition, even if she was dying.

Juma was Juda's dear friend, and he, Judas, did not understand how Juma could have killed a loving mother who lived every minute of her day for him. Second, Judas knew enough about the perpetual conflicts in Odongo's home to have doubted Okulu's words on any day. However, the evening was no ordinary day in Juda's young life; he was in the middle tragic crisis. Here was Okulu, a relatively old man, with alcohol in his breath, accusing his stepbrother of murder Aura who was hurting, and nobody appeared to be anxious to administer any first aid.

Reaching where Aura lay groaning in pain, young Judas asked, crying and overcome with grief, "Who did this to you, Mama Juma?"

"She can't hear you, Judas; she is badly hurt," shouted Elder Owiny. "Go and help Okulu chase the killer."

"We need to take Maria to Macalder Hospital," Judas retorted. "Juma is going nowhere; he'll be back on his own."

"Judas, listen; help Okulu capture Juma. But don't harm the boy," Owinyo ordered his son.

"Dad, I don't believe Juma did this to his mother," Judas opined.

"We will find out who did what, but go right now; make sure Okulu does not hurt Odongo's little son," Owinyo ordered.

Aura stopped groaning, raised her head and said, "Judas, go and protect Juma," and then resumed groaning.

The sight of Aura down on the dusty bare ground, groaning helplessly, touched Judas greatly; yet he felt relieved after hearing Aura's voice.

Judas left the scene immediately, Juma's dog, Grace, behind him. The poor dog had heard the owner's name mentioned variously; she had been asleep just before the chaos but was now awake; she too liked Judas who traveled often with Juma, her master.

Outside the euphorbia fence, Judas found John and Okulu where he had left them. Okulu was still shouting his outrageous claims, with John calming him down and asking, "Okulu, tell me as clearly as you can, which direction Juma went?"

"How many times have you asked me the same question? He ran toward Wachara, in Bwai South."

"Let's go," Judas said.

"Where are you going with that dog?" Okulu asked, wondering whether it was wise to have Juma's dog in the search for her owner. *Grace could warn Juma about my location*, Okulu argued within his mind.

Sure, there was a dark and murderous spell over him, but Okulu had the presence of mind to understand who was friend and who was foe. The big bitch known as Grace was his foe.

"It would help sense where Juma has stepped or passed through; she is his dog," Judas argued.

"Don't try to be too smart with me; I passed the same KCPE test you and your friend have passed; that was many years ago. I'll be the boss in this search; you got that, boy?" Okulu warned.

Judas found Okulu intimidating; the spear the latter carried made him the more dangerous. Judas had picked up a machete as he stepped into the dusk, and he believed the machete was the more appropriate tool for the slash-and-run chase ahead. He too was a big boy; Okulu was not going to scare him off the search for a dear friend. "Grace, let's go!" Judas ordered, picking up a running pace.

"John too found Okulu's behavior unusual. *Had Okulu harmed his stepmother?* John wondered in silence, with Okulu jogging behind him.

In Cousin Okulu, John sensed a nervous and dangerous man, who even was talking to himself in between occasional shouts of 'Juma has killed his mother.' John knew that Okulu had a bone to pick with him. The bone the cousins shared was one Juanita, Okulu's wife. John had left permanent footmarks in Okulu's home, having fathered both of Okulu's children, something that was the subject of constant whispers and knowing winks within Thim Lich Village. Therefore, John understood that, given the opportunity, the inebriated, nervous man jogging behind him would not have hesitated to harm him. John let Okulu jog past him, and he would maintain the same cautious and watchful posture the whole night.

Therefore, Okulu started the hunt with two men whom he knew to have doubted his claim that Juma had harmed Aura, the latter man's own mother. Moreover, the two men were Okulu's cousins but they never were his comfort friends. Judas was Juma's friend and therefore Okulu's enemy by default. John repeatedly had violated Okulu's marriage, while responding to a sanctioned 'cultural noble calling.'

As the trio of Ougo grandsons started the chase, their target, Juma, was running cross-country, headed northwest, following no beaten path. He knew the landscape well as a herdsman. The land would be familiar to him for at least two miles.

Two hours later, Juma entered some bushes to rest. He was in alien territory but that was secondary to immediate need, rest. He never before was that tired, thirsty, and hungry. However, alleviating hunger and thirst had to wait. He had not heard them most of the time, but he knew the dog that sounded like Grace would be on his scent again. He needed to rest before his brother's group again hits on his trail with the dog.

While Juma was resting on his back among the bushes, he realized the trouble he would be in, should Okulu succeed in convincing people that he, Juma, had hit his own mother with a club.

Okulu could claim that he had hit my mother by accident, or that he had thrown the stone to stop me from hitting my mother with a club; that could leave me in trouble, Juma wondered.

Judging that facing his father belonged to the future, he realized he had to survive the night chase before he could tell his story. Second, he prayed that his mother survived and talked.

Juma's mind returned to the immediate, like which of his sisters lived nearest. However, he had not visited either of them in recent years, and he would have to ask his way around to reach their homes. He knew that one lived in Homa Bay and another in Gwasii, but the information was worthless because either location was expanse. Moreover, he could not recall the brothers-in-law's names. Second, the sisters lived in distant places that necessitated that he traveled by bus, and he did not have even a cent in his pockets.

What sister would welcome the murderer of her mother to her home? Juma wondered. If his mother died, the sisters would know within hours, and if she survived, it would not stop his persecution as a disobedient child unless she came to his defense. Whatever happened thence, Juma realized, would only make him notorious; he concluded his Alliance dreams were as good as dead. *No, I'm not going to visit any sister,* he said in his heart.

Juma was becoming too casual as the night aged; he even had stopped to rest, forgetting that he was the hunted. *If Okulu is still chasing me, he and his team must be at least two miles back. They perhaps have lost my scent because I had followed no beaten path,* he said in his mind.

2

Ada, a Balm amid Peril

A WAVE DROWSY WAVE made a couple cycles through Juma's tired mind and body. "No sleeping here; not now," he mumbled, resisting sleep, when the wild reminded his of his vulnerability as the hunted. Hardly half an hour into Juma's rest, a rodent cried helplessly at the mercy of an owl some ten steps to his left, reminding him of his perils as the pursued and hunted.

Worried, Juma resumed walking northward, startling the owl, which took off with its prey. Moments later, he was wading through a small stream oblivious of the dangers he faced. Emerging on the other side of the stream, he encountered a footpath going uphill. He decided to walk in a northerly direction but remain a few steps parallel to the footpath.

He was aching and itching all over, having waded through the saline waters of the last stream. One hundred yards later, he hit a grassy area with few bushes here and there. Ahead was the outline of a small home inside a low euphorbia fence. There was a single source of light in the home; the light never flickered in the evening breeze.

His aches worsening as he felt relaxed on account of the promise of human company ahead, Juma decided to seek refuge in the home.

A dog started to bark at him when he was still fifty yards out. He froze.

"Jomo, shut up," a woman's voice called on the dog to behave.

Juma was determined to seek refuge in the home; and

the dog would not deter him. What had driven his escape so far was fear; he feared Okulu and the duo of cousins, John and Judas, whose minds, Juma then believed, Okulu had poisoned with lies. Now all Juma felt he needed was an ear that could listen to his side of the story. He needed a person he could witness to about the tragic event he was part of a few hours before.

The more Juma reflected upon the tragedy, the more he was convinced that Okulu intended to put him in trouble and lock him out of Alliance High School. *How is my mother now?* Juma wondered as he passed through the gate and entered the one-house home.

"Who is that?" a feminine voice called out, emerging from the only house in the home, training a flashlight on the intruder.

Her name was Ada, and she knew that whoever had been approaching her home was not Pastor Aaron, her husband, who normally rode a bike fitted with a headlight. The idea of him riding a bike along narrow rural paths in the dark always freaked her out. She believed the headlight only made her husband an easy target waiting for some bad person to waylay.

'If anybody wanted to waylay me and kill me, they would do it, even if I switched off a spotlight. The Lord clears my path, but it is okay that I see where I step,' Pastor Aaron often argued, dismissing Ada's concerns.

"Who is that?" Ada asked again, standing her ground as Juma inched forward.

"I'm Juma," Juma said, tightening his grip on his wooden club.

"Jomo, shut up!" Ada commanded her dog, which was itching to attack Juma.

"Juma, where are you from?"

"Kadem."

"*Jakadem,* come in!" Ada called out, trying to make an immediate friendly impression on the boy. Then she was flashing him up and down with her flashlight. Juma felt naked for the first time; his clothes had large holes they hardly covered his sensitive parts.

"O my! O my! You have scratches all over your body. Come in and do not talk yet. I have to get hot water for you to clean up your wounds," Ada said mournfully. She realized she was a witness to a young face in big trouble.

Whatever trouble must have been grave because Kadem was a couple of miles away? She hoped to inquire about his problems, but she first had to provide for his basic needs of food, water, and comfort.

Juma entered the house, wondering whether he was walking into a trap.

"Sit right there on the wicker chair to your right," directed Ada.

Juma sat down wondering where he was. The grass-thatched house was neat and well furnished; it even had a bookshelf full of books, a number of which were Christian books, including several different Bible versions and Church Hymnals.

Is this a pastor's home? Juma wondered, standing up to survey the house.

The source of the light Juma had seen from the river was a hurricane lamp, which meant that it had a protecting glass shield around the wick. For the lamp to have been visible, the door had to have been open. No. Looking around he saw a glass window with a curtain facing the gate.

Why is the curtain not in place in the night? Ada is expecting someone home soon, and the person needs the light to guide him home; maybe the pastor is not home yet, Juma reasoned, pacing about, thinking of his security, and even checking other escape routes. There was an unlatched door to the back of the house, through which the woman had passed to go and get water for him. Juma mused how the nighttime ordeal had turned him into a sleuth like some he had met in some of the novels in a teen series he read regularly.

Ada came back from the back of the house to find Juma pacing about restlessly.

"Are you okay?" Ada asked.

"I have to go," Juma announced.

"No. You are safe here, my child. I do not know what happened wherever you came from, but you walk with a special light around you. You'll be okay," Ada said. "You, bath water is ready. Pass through this door. There is a fenced bath to your right; it has a lantern inside. The clothes in there are yours to keep. Follow me," Ada commanded.

Even though she had no children, Ada kept the

secondhand clothes to give to the needy that often walked into her home. Often, her husband, Pastor Aaron, received the clothes from the mission office as donations for the poor in his church.

As Juma bathed in the outside bath, Jomo the dog stood watch outside; it did not bark for the duration of his sanitary exercise.

What next! What would I tell her? Juma wondered as he reentered the house wearing a fresh set of clothes.

For dinner, Ada gave Juma cooked peas and corn-off-the-cob mixture. She watched as the handsome boy ate sparingly. Ada had not asked yet, but she knew the boy was running away from trouble.

"Juma, tell me exactly where you are from in Kadem," Ada demanded after the boy was through with his dinner.

"Thim Lich."

"How old are you? Ada asked.

Juma fiddled with his fingers, wondering what her expectations were.

"I'm sixteen years old," Juma said, exaggerating his age.

"Is your father alive?" Ada asked.

"Yes."

"What is his name?"

"Odongo," the boy said.

"Is your mother alive?" Ada asked.

Juma did not respond. The question bothered him. He left behind a mother who was hurting badly. He was old enough to know that his mother, Aura, was so badly harmed she could have died after he left home.

"Juma, is your mother alive?" Ada repeated her question, eying the young man in the face, challenging him to open up.

"Yes," Juma said looking down, betraying some guilt. Tears rolled down his face. That he had raised a stick against a mother who loved him haunted him, even though he was certain that he had not hit her. He felt responsible for her fate because the battle in his father's home in recent years had been about him and Okulu. The contentious issues were land, wealth, and what his mother called *duong'* (eldership: the right to a father's stool and spiritual leadership); and those fighting it out in words were his mother and stepmother. That evening, Juma felt that Okulu had taken advantage of the confusion during the quarrel between him (Juma) and his mother over food to harm her.

"What is her name?"

"Aura," he said breaking into a muted sob.

"Juma, why are you crying?" Ada asked, having realized that the boy was nervous about answering questions about his mother. "What had happened to your mother?

"My mother is hurt," Juma said.

"What or who hurt your mother?" pressed Ada.

"Something hit her, maybe on the head, when she was quarrelling with me." He was sobbing again. "Someone has killed my mother."

"She will be okay?" Ada said reassuringly.

"You know that she is okay?" Juma asked.

"I know; the God I worship protects the helpless," Ada said. "Now tell me, where was your mother when you saw her for the last time?"

"She was groaning, lying down on the ground, while my stepbrother, Okulu, shouted, 'Juma has killed Maria.'"

"Who is Maria?"

"Maria Aura is my mother. She warned me to run. I have been running since the sun set, with Okulu and his friends chasing me with dogs."

And he is so young; God help us. He can't be a killer, Ada prayed. "Was your father home?" Ada asked, imagining the long distance the boy had traveled; she dreaded the swamps, rivers, and bushes the young man had gone through to save himself.

"No, he is traveling in Shirati, Tanzania."

"Who else was home with your mother?"

"My stepmother, known as Atieno, and some elders who arrived just before my mother ordered me to run."

Where is Aaron? He normally is here before eight o'clock news, Ada wondered. She decided her husband would have to ride back to Thim Lich with the boy and wheel the woman to some hospital. She had concluded that Aura was a victim of a rivalry between two co-wives turned tragic. "Your mother needs urgent help," Ada declared.

"I want to go back to help my mother," Juma said.

"No, Juma; you can't go now; you could get hurt."

"She needs me. I could sneak back without any notice."

"Do you have any siblings?" Ada asked.

"I have two sisters; they are far much older than me. They married and left home."

"Mm . . .! Can you tell me something about yourself," Ada asked, trying to keep the restless boy engaged, praying that her husband arrived soon.

"I'm the last-born of my mother and father," Juma said, pacing about the floor.

"No. Who are you? Are you in school?"

"I finished middle school; I'm waiting to join high school!" Juma said emotionally. What he saw was a dark future with no prospects because his dear mother could be dead. Second, he feared that Okulu, who had hurt his mother and branded him a killer publicly, was out to get hold of him and dump him in some jail, hoping to ruin his chances of going to Alliance High School.

"Why were you quarreling with your mother?" Ada asked.

"I was asking for food," Juma started to say, before Ada finished the sentence for him, saying, "And she could not give it to you because you had not been helping her with the animals and in the farm."

"How do you know that?" Juma asked, wondering whether Ada had read his mind.

"What each member of your group does is to party and dance and sleep and confuse girls; I know that," teased Ada, wondering, *Where is Aaron?* She was running out of questions to keep the restless boy engaged.

"I'm sorry, I met some wrong friends," Juma said.

"Yes, the usual wrong friends; I guess they must be saying the same about you whenever their parents catch them misbehaving," Ada chastised the boy, who had returned to his seat.

"I'm sorry," Juma said.

"How many times have you said that to your mother, only to misbehave again?" Ada asked mockingly, believing that she had created a comfort zone between the boy and herself. She picked up a Bible from the shelves and was about to move the lantern, but stopped. The lantern was supposed to help guide her husband home across the monotonous terrain of ridges, with no distinctive features.

She had to align the lantern with the glass window facing the main gate, and she never disturbed the lantern during the night as long as her husband was not yet home.

"I know you have clearer vision than mine. Can you read Ephesians chapter six, verses one to four?" Ada said, handing over the Luo Bible to the distraught boy.

Children, obey your parents in the Lord for this is right; Honor thy father and mother which is the First Commandment; with a promise, that maybe with thee and thou may live long on Earth, Juma had recited without opening the Bible, his youthful verve alive for the moment.

"Good. Repeat it aloud," Ada urged the boy, but Aaron's continued delay bothered Ada. She worried that the boy could start thinking about his mother again.

Juma repeated the recitation, but he would struggle through the last stanza, as the thought of his mother from whose lap he recited the memory verse as a little boy who had not known how to read revisited his mind. He could hear her loud groans.

"Thank you, Juma. Do not worry about your mother; she will get well. Do you see yourself in that reading?" challenged Ada.

"Yes. I have been disobedient at times," Juma acknowledged.

"How many times this week has your mother reminded you about farm duties but without much success?"

"Many times," Juma said.

"The same *Paul's Letter to the Ephesians,* chapter six, verse four (King James Version) tells fathers: *Fathers, provoke not you children to wrath, but bring them in the nurture and admonition of the Lord.*"

"Amen!" Juma quipped unprompted.

"Tell me, has your father or mother failed you? Have they provoked you to anger?" Ada pressed on, believing that the boy had some positive Biblical foundation.

"No."

"Do you love your mother and father?"

"Yes."

"So why do you do things that provoke your parents to anger?" challenged Ada.

"I'm sorry," Juma said mournfully.

"You must be a spoilt child, Juma."

Juma did not respond in words; he kept fidgeting

uncomfortably, wondering how Ada knew that he was a spoilt child.

"Who is your father's first wife?" Ada asked.

"My grandmother told me that my mother is the first, even though she is younger than Atieno, my stepmother."

"I see. It is about birthright that your home is at war! Let's pray," Ada mumbled, then offered a brief prayer for "the unfortunate woman and her young son;" she prayed for "peace and harmony in all polygamous homes."

"Juma, look at me. Wipe off those tears from your face; a young man who is still looking for someone's daughter to marry should not walk with tear marks all over his face. Have faith, your mother is in God's hands."

Juma wiped off the tears, embarrassed, but felt lucky that his father, Odongo, who was in the "men-don't-cry school of thought," was not around to see the tear marks streaking down his face.

"Juma, you have a mother who loves you and goes to the farm alone in the morning as you sleep because you have to eat. You break her heart when you come home in the evening and demand food. That is why she quarreled with you."

"Yes, Ma'am."

"Did you hit your mother with a stone?" Ada asked, with her eyes on the boy.

Juma did not say a word. He kept looking down, clutching the Bible. Juma knew that he did not hit his mother with a stone, but he had behaved in a manner that angered his mother, allowing someone else to harm her. He felt guilty because he had angered his mother, eliciting her wrath; and the Bible in his hand had spoken loudly to that. He had not hit his mother with a stone, but he had exposed her to the assailant's stone. Thus judging, Juma looked at the Bible then at Ada, whose eyes locked with his.

"Juma, tell the truth; you have a Bible in your hands; you cannot lie while holding the Bible," Ada cautioned, believing that the boy had beaten his mother with some object. "Did you hit your mother with a stone?" Ada challenged.

"I did not hit my mother with anything. I asked for food. She said she had no food for me because I am lazy. I repeated, 'I want food.' She shouted back, 'I have no food for a man who does not work.' I shouted again, 'I want food!' Angered, my mother stood up with the cooking stick she was using to cook *ugali* and raised it to hit me. I jumped backwards, raising my stick to block her stick; just then, a round thing hit her on the head, and then she was falling down toward me, as I jumped backwards. I . . . I . . . ."

"It is okay, Juma; don't cry, she will be okay," assuaged Ada.

"I cried for help. Just then, Okulu, my stepbrother, emerged from behind the bushes, shouting, 'Juma has killed his mother.' My mother was groaning on the ground, as I stood around shocked. I felt helpless; I couldn't even cry. Okulu did not even stop to help; he hurried to his mother's house, still shouting that I had killed my mother. As . . . my . . . ."

"It's okay, Juma. What happened next?"

"As my uncles and cousins arrived, my mother shouted, 'Juma run away.' I ran away, as more elders arrived and gathered around my mother, knowing that she would be safer with the villagers around.

"What did you have in your hand as your mother talked to you?" Ada quizzed, looking for any inconsistency in the boy's testimony and body language.

"I had this club, Mama," Juma said.

"Only?" Ada asked, doubting whether the boy was capable of delivering a mortal blow with the club.

"Yes."

"Did you raise you stick against your mother?"

The boy hesitated, looking at the Bible in his hand.

"Juma, did you raise the stick against your mother?" Ada repeated the question, wondering why the boy was silent. Even more intriguing to her was that the boy always hesitated and looked at the Bible before answering her questions; yet he did not appear to have told her any lie. She wondered how often the boy lived by the Bible.

God, why is such a young boy of faith like Juma in the raging flame of polygamy? Ada wondered, begging for understanding. *Yea, sins of the father! God did not intend that a man should live with two women,* Ada rumbled in silence.

"Yes; I raised my club to block her cooking stick from hitting me," Juma explained his action.

"She threw the cooking stick at you?" Ada posed a deliberate question, trying to find inconsistencies in the boy's narrative. She had decided she would defend the boy with her skin, but she needed to be certain about his credibility.

"No, the cooking stick did not even reach my stick. She fell down, with the stick still in her hand."

"It is okay, Juma. I can keep the Bible," Ada said, satisfied with the boy's repeated account. She understood that Juma was an only boy and a lastborn child. She knew that such children, when they arrive late in their parents' lives, tend receive too much love, spoiling love, particularly from the mother. Such children take their occasional quarrels with their mothers to be daily bonding rituals. Ada understood that, even as the mother pained during the annoying tantrums every sunset as the boy returned from the fields with the animals or the daughter returned from the river with a pot of water, the games reminded the mother of the last umbilical link she cut with a child. Finally, the pain of living through the adolescent protests reminded the mother of the first cry at birth, the pain at birth, and the fact that the child of yesteryears was grownup yearning to be free to join the world.

Ada looked at Juma and saw a boy-child of yesterday on a mother's laps; yet now, he was a man, had a deeper voice, and perhaps was talking to girls already, and in deep trouble. She pitied the pain that had driven Aura to get into a quarrel with her son. Ada was such a lastborn child, though she had not experienced the joy of motherhood. She remembered how delicately her mother had treated her, shielding her from most house chores.

Juma surrendered the Bible, a little relieved, but the thought of his mother kept weighing down on his young soul. He wanted to head back home and face his stepbrother, but he felt tired, disoriented, and lacked the will to start a night trek. He recalled that his flight path had started east for a half mile, then north for a couple of miles, and then west for half a mile. Juma did not know where he was and how far he was from home. He was in alien territory, and he was too young to have known his new location. That he had followed no beaten path completed his disorientation.

"Juma, you should lie down and rest until morning; then Pastor Aaron will take you home."

"I can't sleep here," Juma tried to protest, but he would not finish his statement.

Jomo the dog was barking excitedly. At first Ada thought that it was her husband, Pastor Aaron, on his way home. However, Jomo continued to bark, warning Ada that strangers or wild animals were about her house. Then two dogs were barking at each other.

There was another dog outside. Grace! Juma's heart sank in anxiety; he stood up ready to flee. He had recognized the other barking dog; it was his own bitch.

Grace and Okulu are here! Panic filled his heart. In Okulu, he sensed peril; the image of his mother writhing and groaning in pain revisited his mind. In Okulu, he felt fear in his heart and saw danger outside.

Outside, the three intruders, led by Okulu, Juma's stepbrother, too were in peril. The big dog, Jomo, was closing in on them, chasing after Grace, the smaller dog.

Then Jomo stopped twenty yards out. He was still barking, but he was a bit reassured; he had sensed his owner, Pastor Aaron, who had just crossed the river and was approaching still pedaling his bike, his headlights on. However, the strangers had not realized Aaron was approaching from their rear, because they were in a forested area.

Jomo continued to bark, and so did Grace. Here was a stalemate between two dogs: one waiting for his owner to back him up and the other wondering why the male dog detested her and was blocking her from reaching her owner, who was hiding inside the home ahead.

"Okulu, let's move on, he may not be in this home," Judas said.

"He is here; Grace can't be wrong," Okulu argued.

"Okulu, we have company!" John said.

"What company?" Okulu asked.

"There is a light approaching from the river," John said.

"We are three people; he or she is one person," Okulu said, raising his spear. Since the chase started, he had tested his spear, whenever someone approached or whenever he needed to challenge the two men accompanying him in the chase.

Concerned that the glass window had attracted the strangers, Ada thought of closing her glass window with its wooden shutter, but stopped when she realized that her husband was approaching from the opposite ridge.

Juma was on edge. "That must be them," he warned.

"How do you know?" Ada asked.

He wanted to say, "*The other barking dog is Grace, my dog,*" but said, "I feel it in my heart. I have to go."

"Stay where you are and nobody will harm you. This is the house of a servant of God," Ada said reassuringly.

Okulu and his team had faith in Grace the dog; she had redirected them to odd routes the boy had taken, even when a broader path should have been a more logical route. For example, the boy had avoided bridges, preferring to swim or wade through some rivers and streams. In the present case, the single light in the fenced home had been an attractive beacon the moment the boy crossed the river. Grace had lost his scent before the bridge; she then picked it up fortuitously upon checking the bushes after the bridge. Taking cover in the home was the most natural thing a fugitive could have done, reasoning that his or her pursuers had lost interest in the chase. He thus decided to hide in full view like a rabbit.

Okulu was a worried man. His life hung on how believable his version of events would be. He knew the boy would tell his story; he had resigned himself to that. He had thought of eliminating the boy should he were to reach him first. However, he was not sure that was possible with Judas around. Okulu knew that Judas had been suspicious of him the whole evening. Then there was the uncertainty over the strength of the opposition in the home. Okulu wanted out but he feared the tag quitter.

Hardly an hour into the chase, Okulu had stopped to relieve himself in a bush. Judas, who had followed him, found him cursing and talking while he relieved himself. 'How did I fail to finish her off,' said Okulu.

"You should sing, Okulu? I almost walked over you," Judas faked a complaint before disappearing behind a bush to relieve himself too.

Judas had picked on Okulu's runt; and he would warn John to watch out.

"We must protect the boy, even if we have to tie up Okulu," Judas had said.

"But Okulu is armed," John said.

"We are also armed," Judas observed. He is not a man you want to follow you in this bush; he could take you out, for any reason.

Okulu was worried that Judas had heard him. He had been increasingly worried about the boy. Thrice, since the chase began, he had advised that Judas returned home with Grace, believing that the dog alerted her owner and fugitive, Juma, whenever the chase team was a mile of his location, thus allowing him to escape.

"Okulu, leave Judas alone; you and I are too old to keep up with the dog. Second, having the dog is better than hunting in the dark without knowing if we are on the right path," John would argue, thwarting every effort Okulu made to dismiss Judas and Grace. Their purposes were never the same; Okulu was hell-bent on getting a chance to eliminate the boy; he saw John, Judas, and the dog as obstacles. He wanted them out of the hunt, but he too needed their instincts.

Judas and John saw Okulu as a suspect in the attempted murder of Aura; they too understood that he meant to hurt Juma.

Aaron had stopped cycling while still fifty yards out, but the spotlight he always traveled with was still on; he now trained it on the three strangers ahead. Earlier, he heard Jomo barking as he came down the opposite ridge, riding his bike. Now he understood why. Three men were ahead, blocking his path. One man carried a spear. Aaron resumed riding toward the men. Fifteen yards out, the men stepped away from his path, two to his right, and one to his left. Aaron read ambush in their reconfiguration. Second, they did not appear to be locals. He stopped riding but did not dismount from the bicycle.

Aaron was a man of God, but that had not precluded him from arming himself for self-defense while on the road at night, given that he lived in a sparsely populated forest area. Strapped to his bicycle was a sheathed sword that doubled as a walking stick. His mind raced to the walking stick, but a voice warned him, saying, "Aaron, you are not a man of the sword; you are a man of words."

Aaron decided to break the silence; he could call out the strangers and tell them to lay down their arms. If that failed, he could call Jomo the dog to attack the strangers. He abandoned the latter option because the strangers also had a dog that had prevented Jomo from advancing. His only choice was to call a bluff on the strangers.

From inside the house, Ada could see that her husband was still cycling home but at a slower pace. Just then, the light stopped advancing. She panicked. Her husband was in danger. Behind her, the worried boy was pacing about the living room, talking to himself.

"Juma, go to the bedroom and stay there," Ada ordered.

Juma did not move; entering the woman's bedroom was not something he would have done unless it offered the only exit route to the outside. He knew he could escape through the door to the outside bathroom; he had to do that soon.

"Did your pursuers have a dog?"

"Yes. I know it is my dog."

"It is your dog?" Ada asked, saying in her heart, "*What luck!*" She read danger; she judged correctly that the people outside believed in the dog known as Grace. If the dog said that the fugitive boy was inside the home, they were bound to believe in her senses.

"Yes, my dog Grace," Juma said still pacing about, looking around the house, scanning to find a weapon, like a spear, he could use to defend himself. If there was a machete, the owner had hidden it from view. There definitely was no spear in the room. *How does a man live in a home without a spear?* Juma wondered in silence.

There indeed were a spear, a machete, and farming implements. However, Pastor Aaron, a man of faith, who considered his house a temple of God, was not the man who could have bothered to defend it with a spear; he left it to the Angels to defend it. Therefore, he kept his spears by the granary. For a man who never went hunting, he often wondered why he kept the spears at all. Apart from his dog, four cows, and six bulls, and Ada's fowls, he had no other domesticated farm animal, and the idea of defending them never crossed his mind. Even when Jomo alerted him to something unusual in the home, like a bull loitering in the home, it never crossed his mind to arm himself before he ventured outside, a major point of contention variously visited in his two-person home.

The Aarons had no child, so whenever Ada chastised Aaron for venturing outside "unarmed like a child," she always rubbed him the wrong way. 'Ada, you don't need to remind me that we have no child!' he would complain. 'You know I didn't mean that, darling! If anything, I have failed to please you with a son. And don't go there again, dear,' Ada would rumble on before she ended her witnessing with, 'Can we pray?'

"Stay put, whatever happens, my husband will not allow them to come in," Ada had reassured Juma.

"My brother is a bad man; he could harm your husband," Juma warned.

"He is a bad man? What else has he done?" Ada asked.

"I was a small boy when things happened, but I heard that either he or his mother killed my grandfather."

"Stay put; they will have to kill my husband and I and all of the Lords armies to reach you," Ada reassured the boy, but he had an escape plan.

Juma did not want to stay in the house and risk Okulu sweet-talking his way to get him. *No. Not again*, he resolved.

Juma still remembered how as a five-year old, he almost drowned while Okulu watched smiling. He still saw that smile on the older stepbrother's face, while he gulped a mouthful of river water. Juma had tumbled into a flooded local stream while playing sharpshooter, throwing pebbles at fast-moving floating leaves; then he suddenly was drowning. A woman passing by pulled him out of the water before he could take in a second gulp of water.

The woman, a neighbor at home, had chastised Okulu, saying, "How dare you? Look at you! How dare you play with the life of Aura's only son? I'll let your parents know about this reckless behavior.'

Okulu, then a twenty-five-year old, had responded to the woman, saying, "I was teaching him how to swim."

"Liar, I would have called you a witch, but Odongo, your father, is from a good seed."

"Are you abusing me?" Okulu had protested.

"You cannot scare me the way you threatened Juma's life. I repeat, your father is from a good seed; I'm not sure I know from whom you got your strange behavior," the woman had repeated her line of attack, refusing to back down.

Okulu had walked away, head down in shame. Juma remembered that Okulu had reported the matter to Aura, and the woman too had reported the matter to Aura, and he, Juma, became a center of attention for a period of time, when his mother never allowed him to go near any large body of water. He could not remember if Okulu, then a married man already, ever received any word of caution from anybody over the incident.

Driven by the fear for his murderous stepbrother, Juma resolved to escape as soon as Ada stepped out of the house. He was not going to let Okulu lay his hands on him.

Ada locked the front door, went through the back door and then ordered Juma, "Lock this door. Open it only when you hear my voice. I'll be back." With that, Ada hurried toward the gate; she was unarmed.

Juma let Ada go then locked the door; he would walk out through the same door a short moment later.

3

Showdown on Mikumu Ridge

"WHOEVER YOU ARE COME BACK to the light and drive all your spears into the ground," Aaron challenged the strangers.

"Who are you?" Okulu asked; he was the lone man to the left. He had a spear.

"I'm a pastor of the Lord, and you are blocking the path to my home. Come back to the road."

"Where is your home?" Okulu asked.

"It is the home of light and hope; it is the home whose beacon of hope has attracted you in the night like a moth to a light. And you are not the first strangers to have staggered their ways into my home."

"If this is your home, I want to warn you that there is a killer hiding inside it," Okulu warned.

"That does not surprise me, Mister. My light brings home robbers, thieves and even killers. They all come to seek forgiveness in the home of light. My home is a temple of Light," Pastor Aaron continued to play with metaphors of hope, faith and light, hoping to mollify those he could have called 'the men of darkness.'

"Sir, we have no time for your sermon; call your wife, or whoever is in there, to bring out the killer," Okulu demanded.

"Young men, come out into the light, surrender your weapons; then we can call the chief to arrest the killer," Pastor Aaron responded.

"You are wasting our time. Go and bring out the killer," Okulu demanded; he was growing nervous.

At the very moment in time, six neighbors to Pastor Aaron emerged from the bushes to his left and right. They had heard Jomo bark, before they saw Pastor Aaron's light. They had been comparing notes around a fire in the headman's home, which was a couple of hundred yards from Aaron's home. Then another dog that sounded like a fox was barking too. Then they heard competing voices, one of which sounded angry and belligerent. The other voice they recognized to be Aaron's voice. Concerned, the headman, one Oloo, hurriedly left for Aaron's home, his security team with him. They had listened to the exchange between the Pastor and the stranger on the left before coming out in the open. Each man carried a spotlight.

"Pastor Aaron, do you need help?" Oloo asked.

"Oloo, is that you?" Aaron acknowledged the headman.

"Who are the armed men ahead?" Oloo asked.

"I don't know them, but they claim that they are after a killer; they further claim that the killer is hiding in my home," Pastor Aaron explained, even as the headman already had a good measure of the issue at hand.

"Strangers, who are you? Where are you from?" Oloo asked.

"We are from Thim Lich, Kadem," Okulu said.

"If you don't know where you are, this is Apuoche in Bwai. I am Oloo, the Village Headman. If indeed there is a killer in that home, I will arrest him and lock him up. I will hand him over to your chief within a day. At this time, it is advisable that you go your way. Okay?"

"We need him now," Okulu declared in the collective, even as he wondered why Judas and John were not participating in the exchange.

"Whoever you are there to my left, you are violating a legal order to disperse. Leave with your men," Oloo ordered.

"Okulu, let's go; the headman will do his part," Judas advised.

"If you are cowards, I'm invading the home alone," Okulu retorted angrily.

"I dare you, Mister Okulu," Oloo challenged, making the order my personal on Okulu, latching onto the cue from Judas. As if prearranged, Oloo's men switched on their flashlights, training all of them at Okulu and his men.

"Okay, we leave you alone," said Okulu, heading west. John and Judas crossed the road to follow him. Okulu believed that Juma must have escaped from the house already, most likely heading northeast along the Mikumu Ridge. He intended to head west, go by the house, and then head northeast.

"Go in peace," Pastor Aaron said.

Jomo started barking and charging forward at the departing strangers, with Grace answering back, though under a short lease from Judas.

"Jomo, stop," ordered Aaron.

A quarter of a mile later, along Mikumu Ridge, Okulu's team stopped to decide their next move.

"Okulu, where are we going?" John asked.

"Look at the dog; she is telling us that it has sensed something," Okulu said, in a rare public acknowledgement of the utility of Grace.

"It could be a rabbit," retorted Judas.

"No; he must have passed here; that was a human path on the grass," Okulu said, flashing at disturbed dried foliage. His spotlight was low in battery, so he used it only when necessary.

"Okulu, what is wrong with you? We left the boy back there," John said. "And the only reason I could not have recommended going in to grab him is that he is the house of a Servant of God. It is not right to continue chasing a man who has taken refuge in a Pastors house."

Grace was barking and dragging Judas along a northerly slope.

The chase was on again, but the three men were tired and hungry. They went down a valley; hit a sugarcane field, leaving with a cane each, as Grace emerged with them on the opposite ridge.

"He must be close," Okulu said.

"No. It is the wind coming toward us from the north. He could have passed here thirty minutes ago," John observed.

"Let's run faster," Okulu said.

"I don't believe you can run," Judas, the youngest of the trio, challenged mildly.

"Do you want him to escape?" Okulu retorted.

"Stop quarreling, if you want to get hold of Juma," John intervened, standing between Okulu and Judas.

"No, I don't want Juma to get hurt running through sugarcane plantations, heading nowhere. I want to return him to his father," Judas said, moving on after restless Grace, who was dragging him along, anxious to reach her fugitive owner.

"Aaron! Aaron! Are you okay?" Ada called her husband moments after the Thim Lich men had left.

"I am okay, Ada."

Ada did not say another word; she was relieved. She had listened to the exchange between the strangers and the locals, and she had concluded that Headman Oloo was on top of the situation.

"Juma, I'm Ada, open the door for me. Open the door!" Ada called out. She had rushed back to her house ahead of the men.

Ada received no response from inside her house.

"Juma, open the door."

There was no response. She would enter the house through the backdoor, which was open. She knew Juma had escaped.

Just to confirm her suspicion, Ada walked into the small house, looked everywhere, and she did not find Juma. The boy had escaped; she had only unpleasant options. She knew, Oloo and Aaron would demand to know where the killer boy was.

Will I accept that the boy was here and had escaped? Or should I deny that he was here? Ada wondered. The former option could annoy the headman who would blame her for having allowed a fugitive to escape.

Ada was a dedicated wife of a Pastor of the Lord; that required that she told the truth.

Lying could save the boy's life. Yes, a lie can save a life, buy enough time for the faithful to achieve a Devine goal. Rehab of Jericho shielded Joshua and his fellow Hebrew spies in the Promised Land. And Abraham perhaps lied about Sara, his cousin and wife, in Egypt, calling her my sister, Ada pondered, visiting her Biblical foundation in life to search of a justification for the decision she had to make.

If she told the truth, the headman would mount a search for the boy, who stood accused of a crime, rightfully or wrongfully.

Ada decided that she would reveal that the boy was there before, but only if the Village Headman would be willing to detain the strangers overnight. However, here, she erroneously was assuming that the headman and her husband were coming in with the strangers.

"Ada, open the door," Pastor Aaron called.

Ada opened the door.

Elder Oloo and his men entered the house cautiously, with Pastor Aaron closing the rear.

"Where is he?" Pastor Aaron asked.

"Where is who?" Ada retorted.

"Where is the boy accused of killing his mother?" Pastor Aaron clarified.

"God, thank You for the late-night guests and the time You have availed to us to praise You. Amen," Ada prayed.

"Elder Oloo, take a seat; and you boys, sit wherever you like; I'll give you water to drink," Ada instructed, filling up an aluminum pot with water, planning to prepare tea.

"I guess Juma is the boy they were looking for," Aaron said. He had heard her call out the bearer of the name to open the door for her.

"Yes," Ada replied, collapsing into her chair. "He was here, but he has left, and he is no killer."

"Ada, that is for the law and the judges to decide. My work is to take him to the Chief of our Bwai Location, who would then send him to Kadem to face the law," Oloo said.

Aaron made a brief inspection and confirmed that the so-called fugitive was nowhere in the house, before reporting, "The boy is nowhere in the house."

"He escaped after I came out to check why Jomo was barking," Ada said.

"Oloo, the boy is in the Lords hands, but I don't like the men chasing after him; particularly the one they call Okulu," Aaron said.

"Oloo, I wish you had at least one man who could track down those killers before they reach the boy," Ada suggested.

"I'm just a village headman; I have no police of my own. As you say, he is in God's hands."

"I can track them down." The volunteer was Allan Muga, a middle-aged man, a hunter, and a man who understood the wild. "What I don't like is the fact that they are traveling with a dog."

"That is the hunted boy's dog," volunteered Ada.

"That could help me in tracking the boy," Allan said.

"Allan, leave them alone; God will protect the boy," Pastor Aaron said.

"Oloo, thank God, Pastor Aaron has not listened to your frequent advice that he marries another wife. In case something happens to me, I wish to share with you what the boy told me. It is a story about polygamy, rivalry between two women over their husband, and a struggle over the future of the man's livestock wealth."

"Ada, I'm sorry if I have been too hard on you by insisting that you get help in taking care of your husband whose demands as a man have not waned. Sara looked for a helper, who would give new life to Abraham's home, and the Old Testament patriarch was less faithful than Pastor Aaron here; and Sara's action did not stop God from blessing her, an old woman, with her own seed," Oloo argued, attempting to support his belief in polygamy on a Scriptural base.

"Oloo, let's leave that debate for tomorrow; there is a desperate boy out there running for his life, with a murderous bunch of men after his head?" Ada suggested.

"I welcome the debate, if it will be over tea and a lot of food. Pastor here will be the referee; I'll come with my Bible," Oloo responded in kind. "I agree with the pastor that the boy is in God's hand, but I'll keep my ears open for any news about him. I have to go, the pastor has had a long day; he needs to shower. If you want to whisper to him what you know about the case, he will fill in my council in a few days."

"The invitation is open; the pastor does not need to be there when I entertain you," Ada said, enjoying the lively rural-folk talk.

"Did you hear that, Pastor Aaron?" Oloo asked.

"I did, and it is only fair that, as she entertains you, I'll be spreading the New Word from house-to-house in your home. Then we will see who is the greatest loser," Aaron threw in a challenge.

"*Spreading the word?* What word?" Oloo wondered aloud.

"The same word that was with God at the Beginning," Aaron upped the theology a bit. "When I am done with your home, you will have only one wife; which one it will be, is not for to you to choose."

"Oloo, leave the pastor alone, he is talking in tongues," one Okelo said.

"Oloo, do you now understand why I have never thought of leaving the pastor?" Ada asked.

"You are right, Ada, he has sweet words, but that does not explain why he has failed to convince another girl to come and help you care for him," Oloo said, maintaining his stand against monogamy.

"Well, I now understand why you are the headman of this village," Ada said.

"Let's leave it at that. Pastor Aaron, we expect you to brief us on the matter of the boy in a day," Oloo said, leading his men out into the night.

4

Origin of Atieno's Woes and Wars

NOW THAT AURA'S ARRIVAL in Thim Lich was at hand, Ougo called Odongo to his hut for a man-to-man talk about Luo marriage ways that the men and the women they marry must adhere to if they intend to live in peace and spiritual harmony in one home.

"Odongo, now that Nyatanga (Aura) is coming, know that she will not enter the house Nyasakwa (Atieno) has polluted. Our traditions dictate that Nyatanga is senior to Nyasakwa; therefore, Nyatanga cannot sleep in Nyasakwa's house. Take Nyatanga to your grandmother's house until you construct a house for her," Ougo instructed his son, avoiding calling his daughters-in-law by their names out of respect to them; he instead called them by the names of their respective places of birth (Sakwa clan, for Atieno; and the country of Tanganyika, for Aura).

"When shall the Luo move away from their simple worries?" asked Odongo, grumbling.

"Check your tongue, Odongo! You created the mess by allowing the woman you call your wife to stay. Now you must live with the inconvenience," warned Ougo. The mess was Odongo bringing home a woman ahead of Aura, his boyhood bride whose bride wealth he long settled.

"Atieno is my wife; she has my son," declared Odongo with very little emphasis on the words.

"Rawo, you have chosen a life of battles; I don't envy you, but you must live with your wives the way our ancestors designed it. Nyasakwa is the junior wife, and the boy you call yours becomes a junior son when Nyatanga gets her son," advised Ougo, not hiding his hatred from Atieno and the child he considered illegitimate.

"He is my seed," said Odongo, lamely without any force behind his words.

"Tell me how. All we hear is that she became pregnant when someone waylaid her. How is Okulu your son?" challenged Ougo.

"I have things to do before I travel to Tanganyika," Odongo said, bolting out of his father's hut; he could not explain how Okulu was his seed, short of acknowledging that he was the unknown man who violated Atieno in her youth.

"Wake up; your hanger-on wife (Atieno) must know that the owner of your home (Aura) arrives in a few days. About your son, I don't feel my blood flowing in his veins," declared Ougo in anger at his son's audacity to stand up on him. Part of Ougo's anger that evening was at Atieno whom he never forgave for having married Odongo, when she did, ahead of Aura.

"He is my son."

"I know you have tasted the maddening honey that attracted many men to her skirt, but be prepared for battles from the woman who walks like a man (Atieno) when Nyatanga arrives with her pot of butter. You must be firm in doing what is right. Your obligation in each of our rituals will be to Nyatanga first. Whenever there is a ritual, never go to Nyasakwa's house before you spend a night in Nyatanga's house and eat in her bed. You must plow Nyatanga's farm first, and celebrate the event accordingly, before you plow Nyasakwa's farm."

"Can we talk this when Aura has settled and had her children?" lamented Odongo

"Nyatanga might not have any child if you don't observe our ways. I'll be watching, Nyasaye (God) willing. You can go," Ougo said in disgust, dismissing Odongo.

Atieno indeed fought many battles against Aura and the Ougo clan. Overall, she fought the bedroom battles well, years later giving her husband a son, Okulu, and four daughters (Alal, Arua, Olga, and Abich). When her daughters would marry, they brought untold wealth, in the form of dowry, to Odongo. In short, Atieno was a stable and secure woman economically. However, the sore in her heart was always Okulu. A decade into her marriage, Atieno remained convinced that she was not a favorite of her husband because of Okulu. Whose son was he? She was not sure because she conceived him at a time when gold miners in Macalder swarmed around her and bit her like wild African bees. In the madness brought about by the location of the gold mine close by, she even became a victim of rape.

So, ten years into her marriage, Atieno still was looking for another son, with whom to please her husband, and no more children were coming. Atieno blamed Aura, her co-wife, for her procreative bias. Atieno believed that she never saw enough of her husband because of Aura's bed of charms. She often joked that she had a *half-a-night* husband. Indeed, Odongo never spent a whole night in Atieno's bed since the day Aura landed from Tanganyika ten years before. To Atieno, getting another son under such conditions was unlikely because her husband always ended by her bed at the wrong time in her menstrual calendar. When he visited, it often was to assuage her during crises, and mostly for half a night.

One had to pity Atieno's situation. First, she was fighting for her husband's heart under protest and with her aggression directed at him; whereas Aura fought the same battles with tact and soft words whispered into her husband's ears after carefully prepared and delicately presented dinners. Aura never allowed Odongo by her side while he or she was angry, and she prayed for him every night.

Adding to Atieno's disadvantages was her inferior position as a second wife in a bigamous home, in which rules of spiritual as well as general conducts favored seniority. In such a home, the first wife led in the plowing, planting and harvesting seasons, and she had the priority to celebrate each event with her husband, leaving him a shell of a man for the other women to mine for love. As a second wife, Atieno only could breach the code of conduct and jump the queue at the risk of dire spiritual consequences. She could not do that for she feared inviting the dreaded *chira* curse into a home. Even if she tried, her husband could not have agreed to join her in the illegal dances. Therefore, Atieno grudgingly drank the dregs Aura left of her husband's heart at odd points in her fertility cycle, giving him the beautiful girls.

Always feeling victim to what she called "Aura's strange bedroom etiquette and charms," Atieno would extend her marital wars, beyond bedroom access to her husband, out into the farmland. Often fighting with rage, some of her desperate acts bordered on witchcraft.

The first such act was a blatant religious violation, whose effects would reverberate across the land to Tanganyika—Aura's land of birth. Atieno confronted the aftermath with a cold heart. If she could not get a son, so shouldn't Aura. That was Atieno's resolve.

One September day in 1956, Atieno deliberately sprayed the beans she was planting in her farm into an adjacent farm belonging to Aura. Now, there are no holier places for a Luo woman that her bed and her farm. Atieno's secret act was a violation of another woman's shrine. Any Luo adult of her time could have found her act utterly disagreeable.

When the beans matured, there was irrefutable evidence of what Atieno had done: her red-bean variety had found its way into a section of Aura's white-bean farm! Odongo, Aura, and the rest of the Ougo home were in uproar against the violation.

Noticing the unforgivable violation, Aura raised the matter with Odongo, who would confront Atieno.

"Atieno, why did you plant your beans in Aura's farm?" Odongo asked.

"You saw the beans?" challenged Atieno.

"Yes."

"Why has Aura failed to complain to me?"

"Did you plant the beans?" demanded Odongo.

"Some naughty bees are responsible for the mischief on the farms," claimed Atieno.

What an answer. Odongo was stunned. He ran to his mother for a resolution. Apudo in turn ran to Ougo's hut to break the news about the strange event.

"She is a witch! She is out to destroy Aura's house!" charged Apudo, Odongo's mother.

"I have taken note," Ougo said tersely, shutting off any father dialogue over the matter.

Listening to her husband's terse response, Apudo knew she had said enough, even as she wanted the matter resolved in the presence of all parties concerned.

The matter did not end there. It found its way to Ougo's dispute-resolution chair, before which Atieno would maintain that bees were responsible for the mix-up in the farms.

Ougo would quash the matter after cautioning Atieno to watch her strange ways. "If you don't change, this village will start calling you a witch!" Ougo had said in disgust, escorting his warning with a stream of brown tobacco-chewer's saliva.

"Have I not been called worse things? Have your people not called my son a "stranger," in the land of his father? Have they not destroyed my son's chance to see his seeds in this land?" Atieno had challenged her father-in-law, before walking out in disgust. From that moment on, Atieno lost the trust of her father-in-law and mother-in-law.

Like every wise father-in-law, Ougo let Atieno's challenge pass.

Turning to Aura, Ougo implored her saying, "Nyatanga (Aura), hold dear to your Christian beliefs. Nothing will happen to you or your children." The reassuring words could have passed without notice, except Ougo was a practicing Luo traditionalist and not a Christian.

After the brief exchange, Ougo dismissed the gathering prematurely, struggling to suppress any feeling of anger. It was not right for a father-in-law to quarrel with a daughter-in-law in the presence of her husband. Such quarrels often turned deadly, if the man's son lost his temper and hurt his wife. Moreover, a Luo man cannot beat his daughter-in-law, however provocative she is! It is taboo!

A few days later, Ougo said, "Odongo, find out what bothers your wife. If she needs another child, give it to her."

"I think it is the normal jealousy between women," Odongo reasoned.

"No. She wants a son from you! If you don't solve her problem, she is going to hurt someone," Ougo warned.

"But I gave Atieno the first son," Odongo declared to his unbelieving father.

"You know that is a lie; there is no Ougo's features in the boy," Ougo declared. "Odongo Rawo, what Atieno did in the farm of Nyatanga was the act of a witch. She intends to bring harm to Nyatanga. If you don't know, a woman's farm is like her bedroom, another woman cannot violate it."

The matter would grow new legs years later. Aura, a young woman and a mother of two twin daughters, stopped giving birth, however regularly she tried. Odongo's mother would direct much verbiage at Atieno amid Aura's struggles to conceive.

Aura would struggle for seven years before she again could conceive, thanks to the intervention of some herbalist from Tanganyika. She was as thin as a stick. The word *chira* (curse) and bewitched dominated feminine chatter about Aura, and each pundit blamed her condition on overt and covert actions of Atieno. Few saw Aura's brush with infertility as the case of a woman who raised twin girls, when she should have discarded one of them; that her religious convictions would not allow her to undergo ritual cleansing provided fodder for her antagonists!

At the height of the crisis, and just when she had lost hope of ever conceiving a child, Aura flew off to Tanganyika to complain to her parents and seek medical intervention.

Gor, Aura's father, consulted with some wise man, who gave him some herbal medicine to give to Aura. Ayiera, Aura's mother would explain to her daughter how to use the herbal medicine:

"When you see the first signs of your monthly period, brew these leaves and roots in hot water, ferment the brew for two weeks, and serve it to the father of Rachel and Leah on the fourteenth day at sunset, just before he visits your bed.

"This batch is for you, brew it cold, and take the unfiltered brew, daily, from the onset of your monthly period until the morning of the fourteenth day. Your husband must remain on his brew for fourteen days, and he must remain faithful to you for the entire one-month duration of the treatment.

"How will I make sure that he does not visit Atieno's bed during that month?" Aura asked.

"Make sure that he never strays. Wake up, Aura; he is your husband. You know what he loves to eat. Convince him to pretend to be sick during the treatment," explained Aura's mother.

Aura left her father's home for Kadem, wondering how she would detain a man she shared with another woman for a month. Reaching home, she embarked on her new mission within two days.

Odongo, who thought she had left never to return, embraced her emotionally.

The treatment worked, and Aura became pregnant on first attempt.

During Aura's pregnancy, Atieno often told other women that the former woman would never give Odongo the son for whom he and his father (Ougo) had hoped. Her disagreeable remark became the more frequent as Aura's pregnancy advanced.

Atieno would earn the label "witch" from many angry listeners to her rant. "Atieno, my daughter, whose behavior are you copying. Aren't you ashamed that the whole village calls you a witch? It is unheard of for a woman to bemoan, ridicule, or be sarcastic about another woman's pregnancy. Yours is a first. To our Luo minds, the journey to childbirth and out is akin to dying and resurrecting. In that journey, there are the possibilities of both mother and child surviving it or not getting out of it alive. There is the chance of the mother surviving but with a stillbirth; there is the chance of a child surviving but with the mother dying. Why do you wish that to happen to Aura?"

"Leave me alone; I have enough of my own burdens. Let Aura struggle with hers," warned Atieno.

"Atieno, why are you at war with Aura while she is pregnant? Has Odongo not given you many beautiful daughters, some already married?" Atigo, Atieno's own mother chastised her, when her behavior and utterances reached her chair.

"Ma, you had one husband and never shared him with another woman. You do not feel my pain; you cannot feel my pain. Ma, you don't know how it feels like for a man to leave your side at midnight and not return because some loose cow, real or imagined, had broken through the shed," Atieno said, her veins standing out.

"The same Odongo covered your shame when you became pregnant in your father's home. I can feel your shame, if that is what you mean," Atigo fired back.

"You cannot feel it; the moment that woman gives birth, and it will be a son, that is the day the Ougo family will push Okulu out of their land; then he will be our shame; you and I," ranted Atieno with much passion in her eyes. She never backed down against anyone who attacked Okulu's parentage, something her mother appeared to have hinted at in her message.

"What has Odongo not done to Okulu? He took him to a boarding school. You have all the wealth you need; you know no poverty," Atigo rose in defense of her son-in-law.

"Ma, you had no woman playing God over you, every season, controlling when you can plant, plow, and harvest your fields, and see your husband. I do. Okulu has the support he has because he has beautiful sisters who have brought him wealth," charged Atieno.

"Why fight a man who has given you all the daughters you needed? Why the fight with your co-wife, when all we know about her is that she has a good soul? Your daughters, Alal, Olga, and Arua have nothing but praise for Aura," Atigo observed.

"Ma, I have to go; mine is a life of battles. I don't need your help," Atieno said, defeated; she was surprised that her mother could not appreciate the value of the battles, she, Atieno, fought every day.

"Leave me alone; I don't know how to quarrel with a man," said Atigo in anger.

"Lucky you; you married a loyal monogamist," Atieno said in disgust; she had nowhere to turn to for a sympathetic word, but to despair she would not.

"Don't talk about the dead in pejoratives; he was the best father the world ever saw," Atigo cautioned.

Then Atieno was crying like a child on her mother's shoulders; her mother had touched a soft spot in her heart, her late father.

Such tough words characterized visitations between Atieno and her mother, particularly after her father, who used to empathize with her situation, died.

Then ten years since Aura entered the Ougo home, she gave birth to the boy child, Juma son of Odongo, and the whole Ougo home was beside itself, though in dichotomous manner, with some celebrating while others dreading it.

"Odongo has a son!" Owinyo announced to Dora, his first wife, on the morning after Aura delivered baby Juma, a boy. Owinyo was in a celebratory mood.

"Yeah, Odongo has his own son!" Dora said sarcastically, sharing in Atieno's tribulations.

"*Odongo has his own son?* What about Okulu?" Owinyo asked in rage, even as he understood what his wife meant, and the person with which her sympathies rested. Very few people in Thim Lich would talk about Atieno's problems without disagreeing over their positions.

"Where have you been, Owinyo, my husband?" Dora asked, aiming to annoy her husband, who was one the Ougos who tried to be neutral over the feuds and marital matters in Odongo's home.

"What do you know that I don't?" asked Owinyo.

"Atieno came to this village with a child of her own; she named him Okulu. What kind of name is that? This village never heard such a name before," Dora wondered aloud.

"What if Odongo fathered him in the bush?" Owinyo asked. He had asked the same question whenever the matter of Okulu's birth came up during a conversation with friends.

"That is not what I have heard. Atieno, herself, doubts whether Odongo fathered Okulu," Dora said.

"Well, I am a man like Odongo," Owinyo said. "I always wonder if all my children are my seeds."

"And you think some of your sons are not yours?" Dora retorted.

"I didn't want to say that; you forced me to say it," Owinyo said, happy that he had made his point. How could a man of his time have known if a child was his? A man who bothered about such matters would have died of heart attack before his time; or he could have killed his wife and children on mere suspicion.

Such was the talk about Okulu when Juma was born. The talk divided the villagers into pro-Atieno and anti-Atieno camps. The only word the village used sparingly was *kimirwa* (bastard), in reference to Okulu, because there was a level of uncertainty about whether or not Odongo fathered him.

As Ougo predicted, the battle in the Odongo's home

would rage on for decades before what pundits would call the Aura-Okulu tragedy engulfed it. There were the struggles for seniority between Odongo's two wives, Aura, the younger-yet-senior wife, and Atieno, the older-and-yet junior wife. Once Juma was born, the women started proxy fights on behalf of their sons, Juma, the younger-yet-senior son and Okulu, the older-yet-junior son. This last type of battle was over birthright and inheritance due to the sons. Okulu was Odongo's first child and son, even though his paternal lineage was unclear to many. Second, Okulu was twenty years older than Juma, who was the spiritual first son and the designated inheritor of their father's stool.

Atieno detested her and her son's inferior positions in the Odongo home. To add insult to injury, Atieno was eight years older than Aura, Juma's mother. When Atieno arrived in the Ougo home to prepare her nest for her husband, Aura was still a mere child in her father's home in faraway Tanganyika. It would be another year before Odongo brought Aura home to take up her place as the principal wife.

Much as Atieno complained about how her son and herself were denied their seniorities, few in the Ougo home and beyond sympathized with her complaints because the contested issue had a spiritual foundation: life in marriage in a traditional Luo home was a religious affair, with each woman's house and farm as holy shrines.

Had Atieno traveled across the land, she could have met sages willing to empathize with her situation, and even some who could have ranked her above Aura. The difference in opinion was natural because the Luo peoples had come a long way and assimilated other cultures and religions whose doctrines had shaped their ways of life in urban homes away from the rigorous demands of Luo customs.

No doubt, to be a first wife and yet not be one haunted Atieno. That the woman playing seniority over her was the generation of her eldest child, made Atieno's anger the more justified.

Now, compound Atieno's seniority blight with a son conceived out of wedlock and her marital life became one hell of a journey. Now, early in that life's journey, it suddenly was apparent that the son would become a man of questionable virility. Okulu indeed became an impotent man could not procreate, and Atieno blamed Okulu's condition on the actions of a human hand aiming build Aura's house. All these turned Atieno's jealousy against Aura venomous.

The anger would become murderous since the news that Juma had excelled in his KCPE exams and would be heading to some important school reached Thim Lich Village. Atieno immediately read a power surge in Aura's house; her worst dream had come true; the little baby of yesterday had become a man ready to go places. Then village fences were abuzz with Juma going to places with strange-sounding names like Alliance High School and Mangu High School. Inflaming her jealousy and a sense of doom for Okulu was the incessant chatter among those in the younger generation, who were saying that Juma would be going to such faraway places as England and America.

Before the news of Juma's enhanced academic promise and the sudden projection of power from Aura's house damped Atieno's spirits, there was a more damning event in Atieno's life with stress. Odongo had just forced Okulu to start his own home. Okulu's new home was less than a hundred yards from the home of Omulo (Atieno's father).

First, Odongo's act was a significant misstep because he should have constructed a home for Atieno and her son, Okulu, and left Aura in her home. Odongo had not done that, he instead continued to pursue a unity agenda, chasing a unity that did not exist and never had existed in his home.

Second, in locating the home close to Omulo's, Odongo made an expensive political blunder, onto which his detractors were quick to latch to his detriment. They read a man rejecting a son, saying, "He is not my seed; he came with his mother; I have returned him to her people."

The village euphorbia fences were abuzz with busybodies imbibing beer and revisiting the matter of Okulu's parenthood, saying, "Odongo has retuned Okulu to his owners." The same gossip reached Okulu and Atieno, and they felt more abused than ever before. Like the pundits, Atieno read rejection in Odongo's act; she judged that Odongo had returned Okulu to her people.

The important pointer Atieno and her friendly pundits had missed or ignore in Odongo's action was the fact that he as his father had stood in the area where Okulu built his home, and holding his staff of authority, he pointed at the exact spot where Okulu constructed Juanita's house. Only a Luo man's biological father or paternal uncle could have done that. Here was a man whose actions were screaming loudly, saying, "This is my son!" and listeners were hearing, "This man is not my son!"

Blinded by anger brewed over a lifetime, and the fresh rage over the audacity of the man she married to have washed her dirt in public, Atieno decided to hit back at Odongo where it mattered most: Eliminate Aura and stall Juma's academic prospects. She intended to have Juma incarcerated, even hang!

"Kill him! Or kill his mother and call him the killer!" That was Atieno's instruction, having served Okulu an oath blood and intoxicants.

"Ma! We can't do that."

"Okulu, it is about your future, it is about your children's future; the fight now is yours; I have done my part. If he lives, that boy will drain your luck until you are left begging for fish at Macalder Fish Market."

Now, Okulu had done an incomplete job; both Aura and Juma could live. Atieno's house had a major problem in her hands: Aura was not dead, and Juma was on the run, perhaps talking and pointing accusing fingers as he went.

5

Becoming a Man

WHEN JUMA TURNED FOURTEEN YEARS of age, he overheard a scary conversation between his parents; the conversation was about him. It was one evening during his senior year in middle school. He was hanging about his mother's house at dusk, having returned from a meeting with friends. Juma had thought of talking to his mother over something, however, he realized that his father was home talking to her about him. Juma knew that it was wrong to hang around his mother's house with the aim to listen to her conversation with his father. However, Juma would not resist the urge to listen because his parents were talking about him.

"No way, Juma is but a child; I will not allow any woman near him soon," said Aura. If this statement from his mother was alarming, what his father said next was not new to his ears; Juma had grown up listening to the same refrain from everyone in the village.

"But Juma bears the burdens of the spiritual *elder son*. Just as this is your home, it is his home too. He has a hut already; he gathered materials and built the hut alone. He is a man, what else does he lack as a man?"

"My husband, Juma is a child; he is not ready to breathe a woman's breath every night."

Juma had heard the same argument a few weeks back, even us he could not understand that kind of adult talk. However, he shared his mother's general point of view: He agreed that he did not understand girls at all. If he knew anything about girls, it was from general biology that said that women gave birth after receiving one component of life from the man. However, how he would find that act of procreation challenging was not clear to him, a virgin. Maybe, his mother was not talking about sex or the literal sharing of the same air under a blanket with a woman. However, the discussion was taking an uncomfortable turn for his ears. Juma thought of moving on, but it was tempting to continue listening to the conversation.

"Aura, my lover, when I married you, you were no older than Juma, and we have done very well," Odongo said.

"You miss the point, my husband, a woman is always older and wiser than any man; she can feed a houseful of in-laws at a time when a man of her age would not know from where to gather food. Yes, you were older than I was in age, but I grounded you as a man, at a time when you were running scared of Atieno," Aura said.

Now, Juma found his mother's argument interesting for she was speaking about responsibility. In the world he lived in, girls generally were more responsible than boys were; girls often took care of their immediate siblings without seeing them as rivals, something boys rarely did. The girls Juma knew cooked for their families, drew water from the river, and gathered firewood from the forest by their early teens. Juma agreed that girls matured earlier than their male age mates did. The other part of his mother's answer was usual talk; she always maintained a cautious "war" posture toward Atieno, even when either woman invited the other to share a meal. *Strange!* Juma thought.

"I can't argue against that," Odongo said, something Juma found to be a reasonable stance. Yes, his mother managed her house, and Juma often wondered whether his father was a factor in running the home, other than his announcing such decisions as what bull to sell for school fees.

"Save the cattle wealth you want to waste on a wife and sell it for Juma's school fees. You know that he could be in secondary school in a few weeks," Aura implored.

"I already planned for his fees; he can go to school and have a wife here at home. I will take care of his wife," Odongo said.

Juma found his father's position scary. He was a virgin, and he did not understand his father's fanatic insistence that he, Juma, married a wife.

"Listen, *Nyanyuok* (Luo: he-goat*)*, I understand your concern, but I'll not allow my baby to become some old woman's husband," Aura protested mildly, suddenly injecting a romantic word into their discussion.

Juma shared his mother's point of view that he was a baby. He too was old enough to realize that his mother's tone and language had changed noticeably. He felt guilty for his intrusion into his parents talk.

"Aura, my dear, it is my call to make. My son is a man already," Odongo said.

I don't feel I'm a man, Juma said in his heart, hurrying away to his hut. Although Juma was only a fourteen-year-old virgin, his mother's use of the he-goat metaphor to describe to his father had warned him to move on. He felt guilty of having tapped into his parents' conversation, and he cared about the future, with a woman.

"What do you want me to say then?" the soft-spoken Aura challenged her husband. Meanwhile Juma had moved on out of his sonic range.

"Nothing," Odongo grunted.

"Okay, your meal is ready; if you are giving away my baby to another woman, what do you want me to do? Can this old body get a replacement?" Aura lamented, choking with emotion and desire. Even Aura doubted whether she could conceive and give birth, again. Getting Juma was hard enough, at a time when she was younger. Now she was in her mid forties.

Having left his parents to their devices, Juma went to his hut and slept, scared, imagining that his father would follow him to demand an answer to his question. Juma wondered how he would react if he came home one night only to find a woman in his bed.

That was not the first time Juma heard his father say that he, Juma, should get a woman to marry. Odongo had broached the idea to Juma a few weeks before. It was a few days after Juma sat for his KCPE examination, and he was at dinner with his father, when suddenly the dinner turned sour.

"Juma, I said that there is a woman, a young girl, I want you to marry. What do you say?" Odongo had repeated the question, having had no response from Juma, who was dining with him in his hut.

Juma did not answer. He had a lump of *ugali* and some boney pieces of fish he was chewing in his mouth. Because of the nature of the subject his father was demanding an answer on, and the stress it caused him, Juma, munching the food became too complicated a task to complete. So worried, Juma had trouble swallowing the food; the stress had broken the rhythm of the otherwise effortless ingestion process.

Odongo was watching as his son struggled with the boney food; he understood that his son was struggling with the concept of marriage; he knew the boy was not ready for marriage.

But whoever was ready for marriage? Odongo mused. He let the boy clear his plate without demanding an answer from him. Then as he watched closely, he realized the boy was choking in silence.

"Juma, do you need to drink water?" Odongo asked.

"Yes," Juma said, anxious to leave his father's hut.

Marriage! Juma had exclaimed in his heart once the food safely reached its destination, without misdirection into the respiratory tract. His interest was education.

Juma immediately staggered out of his father's hut; he was in fear. The question about marriage had disturbed him greatly, shocking him to his toes. He frankly had no answer to it.

Since the bothersome day with his father in the latter's hut, Juma started accompanying other boys to dancing parties during the night.

Odongo watched Juma, monitored his activities, and concluded that it would be a short while before he (Odongo) saw a daughter-in-law. He understood that his young spiritual first seed was becoming a man fast, even venturing out into the darkest nights alone. A few weeks later, Odongo silently left for Tanganyika. His mission was to get a young girl Juma could marry. Odongo intended to pair up his son with a wife before, in his words, 'the boy left for the corrupting ways of Nairobi.'

Odongo did not explain to Aura why he was going to Tanganyika; he wanted his son to transition into married life as quietly as possible before his antagonists, within the Apudo-Ougo clan, offered their demeaning opinions about his premature move to pair up Juma with a woman to marry. Aura had taken the visit to Tanganyika as one of the business trips her husband often made to her land of birth, where he had many friends.

Meanwhile, for a child who had not known the ways of men and women, Juma found the possibility of early marriage worrisome, and he found the idea of him marrying a woman both alien and remote, even as he had a father who lived with two wives. The dance parties had yet to change his perspective on life. For one, he had no girlfriend; second, he did not know what he would do with a woman. Third, he was a boy, whose sole interest was books and play with other boys. Yes, his voice had deepened in recent months, and some crops of hair had popped up in some hidden corners of the body, something that made him a subject of ridicule around communal swimming-and-bathing sites along the River Kuja, but that was all the proof there was that he was a man.

Juma's mind was not ready for marriage, even as there was a particular girl spreading her net over him, calling him, dear this and dear that on the dance floor. However, he never had warmed up to her, leaving her baits untouched. That was as of a few weeks back, just before Odongo went to Tanganyika. Now, Okulu's tragic action against Aura had changed Juma and put his plans in doubt. Besides his father's plans on marriage, Juma had looked forward to a life as a brilliant student in Alliance High School. He knew both prospects were in jeopardy. He was a fugitive in the middle of somewhere alien, sharing the nightlife in the wild with hyenas.

What rapid change I have experienced; I am indeed a man, braving the wild alone. Maybe I have lost my place at Alliance High, but when my tribulations are over, I will go back to my father and say, 'Give me the wife you have been bothering me about,' Juma chanced a moment to muse about his future, even as he was in the wild.

Juma was not sure about his location, but his guess was that he was somewhere in the land of Bwai or Nyamwa. The laughing hyenas reminded him that he was close to Ruma Game Park, with its many wild animals. The possibility of being close to a wild-animal park hit him hard, but he was tired, his mind was begging for sleep, and while his body ached all over, his eyelids drooped, feeling heavy on sleep; not even the sound of hyenas would prevent his tired body and mind from succumbing to sleep. He slept deeply, but only for a short while.

6

From Hunted to Savior

JUMA SPRANG AWAKE from his brief slumber; he had been sleeping for close to an hour. A dog was barking close by as part a chorus of baking dogs in the distance. As Juma became fully awake, he realized that the dog was not barking at him. It instead was barking at hyenas that were laughing in the distance, perhaps enjoying the last remains of someone's goat.

Juma's path of flight since Ada's house had been northwest along Sirime Ridge then north toward Det Market. Because his adversaries had a dog and flashlights, he had been able to adjust course whenever they seemed too close. When he finally stopped to rest, he was in a highly populated area around Kobama Chief's Camp. That he was in a populated area gave him some peace of mind. It meant that his scent was just one of the hundreds of scents Grace would have to analyze at once. Thus reassured, he coiled and crawled under a thicket to rest, and fell asleep until the barking dogs awakened him.

Fearing for his life, Juma sprang to his feet, wondering whether to seek refuge in a nearby home to his right. He shelved the idea, when he sensed that the sounds of the hyenas were growing fainter with time. Moreover, he had a bigger problem from which he had been running: he perhaps had killed his mother! It did not matter that he had not thrown the stone or club that hit her on the head. He had created a situation that an enemy of his mother had exploited to do harm to her; he had been a disobedient son, and his disobedience had harmed his mother, so he reasoned.

Over the last fortnight, Juma had been the talk of the village; he was the boy with whom every girl wanted to share a talk, and he was the boy every grandmother called 'my smart husband,' with pride. That had changed in an instant; he was a hunted man with a tag of mother-killer over his head, thanks to a scheming brother. He was a fugitive running for his life in the middle of the night.

Juma was a young man, but he had read many books. He had studied the Bible well, and in his moment of need, he thought of Daniel, Joseph, Jacob, Abel, Isaac and Solomon, all men their fathers loved; he thought about their unique circumstances, looking for some "teaching moment of faith" onto which to hold. Juma had heard of how his mother (Aura) should have been the first woman Odongo brought home as a wife, but he had not done that. He heard how Odongo instead had eloped with one Atieno of Sakwa and made her a wife before he could consummate his childhood marriage to Aura. He often heard that Odongo never lived in peace since because his wives always were at war against each other.

His mind still wandering, looking for something to hold on to, Juma recalled the Biblical story of Jacob and the rivalry between his wives, Rachel and Leah, who were siblings. The rivalry between his mother and stepmother paralleled that of Rachel and Leah. He recalled the story about how Jacob had worked for seven years to marry the woman he loved, his cousin Rachel, only for his father-in-law and uncle, Laban, to insist that that he, Jacob, must marry Leah, his older cousin, first.

Yes, he, Juma felt like Joseph, the son of Jacob and Rachel, whose life stepbrothers had kept in peril in a deep hole only for them to sell him to traders in a caravan to Egypt, where he would live a life of twists and turns and lows and highs—a life of wisdom, treachery and power in Pharaoh's Palace. Now, here was Juma in the wild, living at the mercy of hyenas because he was running away from his false accuser and stepbrother, Okulu—a grownup man who had harmed Aura (Juma's mother) seriously. Joseph's story gave Juma some hope. He prayed that the villagers had taken his mother to the Hospital.

Juma put these thoughts aside. There were many voices from the direction of his last stop. He sat up, all-ears, where he was in the bush, listening for any familiar voice. He identified none. The voices grew louder, moving closer. He realized that the voices were coming from a group of people walking along the broad livestock path about twenty-five steps to his right.

No. They were not his pursuers; he realized they were boys and girls, perhaps night revelers on their way to a party. In good times, Juma could have trailed them to their destination and whiled the night away, but the times were not good; even his high-school dreams had left him, and in their place was an antsy void—a timeless suspense whose end he had no control over. Moreover, his clothes were in irregular strips hanging on his aching body. He was in no shape for any party.

Juma let the party group go by before he started moving parallel to its general direction. Yes, there was loud music coming from a home farther down the ridge; a skyward beam of light gave its location away. He let the revelers alone. Ahead, he saw a light on top of a hill; he estimated that the hill approximately was two miles away, excluding the height of the hill. His heart skipped a beat and a reassuring feeling hit him for the first time that night; he had had the same feeling each time he saw the same light from several ridges back. *What is it with the light that it so tickles my heart?* Juma wondered. *I'm going to the source of that light to find out what it is,* he said in his heart, hastening his pace, going downhill.

The light had awakened a popular religious lyric in his heart. In his hour of need, the young man had remembered that even amidst darkness and despair, there would always be a beacon of hope, a small light on a watchtower on a hill, beckoning the hopeful to come home. It was a message his mother had preached often, and to which his young soul rarely had paid any attention. Now he remembered it while in the middle of a dark night in an alien land; he remembered the message while running for his life, trading paths with hyenas. Even the near-miss experience at Ada's house had not dampened his positive outlook about the light ahead, which had grown brighter. He decided to go to the source of the light.

Avoiding the partying home to his right, Juma headed straight downhill. The bushes cleared, leaving a grassy rolling slope. Moments later, he stopped dead; he had moved too soon and fast, and he was too close to the receding group of party girls and boys. He let them go then resumed walking, increasing his pace, anxious to cross the valley ahead and in haste to reach the light on the hill yonder. He could not explain why the light attracted him.

The cloud cover that had hidden the rising moon, so far, rolled eastward, giving way to moonlight. Juma became nervous because the "ten-o'clock"-position moon had made him visible to anyone within one hundred yards. He cowered in the tall grass, scanning around for any other night travelers within sight. There was no one all round. Stooping low to remain covered by the yard-tall grasses, he started moving again.

Ahead was a small patch of trees. Farther ahead was a bushy valley. Before that were fields under cassava and potatoes crops on the red sandy clay soil. Juma hurried, moving from field to field. The last field before the bushes was of knee-high young cassava trees. Here and there among the cassava trees thrived mature off-season groundnut plants. He reached down and uprooted three of the groundnuts. Under ordinary circumstances, he could have hesitated before uprooting the groundnut plants, but the circumstances were unusual. He was hungry. As he stopped to eat some of the crunchy nuts, he realized how tired he was. He too was sleepy. The light ahead still urged him to trek on, but he too loved the nuts. He headed for the cover of the bushes ahead. He intended to eat the nuts then lie down for a brief rest, the light on the hill ahead forgotten for a while.

In the bush, he plucked off all the nuts on the plants, feeling his way around, from nut to nut. The first plant provided a fistful of nuts. He made a move to pocket the nuts for future use, but he soon realized that he had no functioning pocket; the tortuous journey had ripped open both side-trouser pockets. His donated imported sports pants (thanks to Ada) had no back pockets.

The night had been full of surprises, and so, the lack of functioning pockets on the pants was no surprise to him, except their torn state made him realize how naked he was. He sat down in the bush and enjoyed the nuts. Yes, three more nuts eaten and his throat started to crack with thirst, but it had to wait until the house on the hill. The inviting light was still visible, even from among the clusters of trees down the valley.

He was thinking of his mother again; he was thinking of her food, of her love, and of her gentle ways with him.

Juma was not a bad boy; he was a spoiled child; needless to add, he was a special child, and the last-born of his mother — coming after two girls. A ten-year gap separated him from the twin girls. His father admired him like a piece of jewelry, for he was his spiritual first son and the last of his children.

Juma thought about his father; he imagined how the night could have been different had his father been around that evening. Now separated from his father, Juma figured that Okulu was having the upper hand, telling everyone that he, Juma, was a murderer. Juma expected his father to be back in Thim Lich in two days, and he, Juma, intended to be there to tell him his side of the story.

But how will I reach my father while Okulu is hunting for me with dogs, as if I am a rabbit? Where is Okulu now? Juma wondered from the cover of the bushes.

A dog was barking in the distance; it had the distinctive familiar foxy style of barking of Grace.

Grace! Yes, that is Grace, my bitch. That is Grace! Okulu is still using Grace to track me down!" Juma said in his heart.

"Run!" Aura's last spoken command to Juma rang in his ears. He started running in the general direction of the light! The bushes were becoming thicker, grassier, and wetter; the ground was getting stickier with mud.

The stream; where is the local path across the stream? Juma wondered, running northward in full panic mode. He made a ninety-degree turn and headed east along the river. The party at the home half a mile above him was still on, and the light provided a welcome illumination of the river below; the moon too was up in the east. He guessed that it could have been well past two o'clock in the morning.

Juma had guessed right; there was a broad and distinctly defined path from the party home leading northeast toward the stream. He hit the path at full speed downhill. Grace was still barking in the distance as Juma neared the narrowest part of the stream.

"Help! Help!" A voice twice called out from the direction

toward which Juma was heading. He had crossed a branch of the river from the southern side, and he was now on an island of dry land, thanks to the January drought. The path had narrowed to a two-person lane. Tall leafy papyrus grass dominated the section of the river valley. There was a bushy sponge-wood bush every five or so yards.

"Help! Someone, help!" the voice called again, as if anticipating Juma's arrival?

Juma slowed down. The river valley was unusually quiet. He wanted it that way; for a querulous crane or heron disturbed from its sleep could have been a disaster to his escape plan. Even the voice calling out for help was reducing his chances of eluding Okulu and Grace. Okulu could think it was from him, Juma, calling for help. Juma did not want Grace anywhere near the river. Even if he, Juma, hid from view, she could nervously seek him out. He resolved to reach the source of the voice before he or she messed up his morning.

Juma pushed aside any thought that the voice ahead was from a victim of python attack. He hurried forward at a walking pace. Grace was still barking on the previous ridge, but she was on a path running east across the ridge, while he was crossing the river, and he was heading north.

The reassuring light was still teasingly visible, flickering on and off, beckoning him to hurry up. The light looked nearer now that he was in the valley; the light appeared to hang precariously on the hill yonder.

After twenty steps more, his outdoor sense warned him of trouble ahead. As he walked, the land moved up and down underneath his feet. The experience shook him to his core. "*Anete! Quicksand! Quagmire! Volcanic! hot salt,*" the words screamed danger in his mind. Juma had walked in such areas, whenever he took livestock around natural animal saltlicks.

"Help! Help!" the voice called out again. Now that Juma was closure to source of the distress, he judged that it was a woman's voice!

Juma felt a sudden flashback, and he was getting emotional; the woman's cry for help took his mind back to Thim Lich eight hours earlier. Juma remembered his mother groaning helplessly, and yet he had not helped her because the same murderous man, now on the ridge yonder, was threatening his life.

"Run! Juma run," Juma remembered his mother's whispered command to him to run in order to save his life. He had obeyed his mother's command that he left the scene when she, herself, needed urgent help, and he had run for his life.

Damn! I should be moving faster, Juma cursed himself for wasting valuable time thinking of his mother. Jolted to attention by Grace's sound, Juma's mind came back to the present: a trapped woman was calling for his help. Then Grace was barking on the previous ridge, reminding Juma that Okulu's threat was still about and real. The image of a fallen mother groaning in pain revisited his mind, warning him of the difficult choices he faced.

Ahead, the woman cried one more time, "Help!" then followed a loud silence, except for Grace whose sound seemed to be growing louder.

"Has she gone under? Python? No, let it not be," Juma whispered. He had met a python before, but that had swallowed a small goat, and his fellow villagers had no trouble chopping it off piece by piece without due concern for the goat. Moreover, he, Juma, had neither a machete nor a knife. A hardwood club was not going to subdue a python. "No, let it not be a python," he whispered in prayer, moving closer to his destination, testing the stability of the ground as he went.

"Help!" she called again. "She is still alive," Juma whispered, still moving forward cautiously, his fears somewhat subsided. That he was moving away from a dangerous brother, who hardly was a mile away from him, ceased to bother him. He had resolved to do what he could do to save the woman's life, due in part t his mother's command to him to run for his life, a command he kept hearing in his ears.

Juma was an accomplished river and lake swimmer, but this was shallow stream flowing in an unstable volcanic area. Whoever was crying for help was not fast drowning, about that he was certain. So his swimming skills were irrelevant. From experience, he knew that the woman was sinking inch by inch, whenever she moved. A year before, he had watched one of his mother's cows sink in a similar manner. She survived only because there were many herdsmen about the saltlick, who joined hands and pulled it to safety.

"Help! Help! Help!" the woman begged.

Juma was there! He hardly was ten steps away from her. He could vaguely make out her upper body breasts up; the rest of her body was beneath the surface. She could have been in a black top and no headscarf.

Juma assessed the situation: both of the woman's arms were still above the white salty quicksand crust.

What if this woman is a witch who slipped into the mud on a night errand, while harassing night travelers? Juma wondered, his grandmother's nighttime stories revisiting his youthful mind, but he pushed the thought aside.

No you have to act, an inner voice urged Juma forward.

"Whoever you are, help?" the woman pleaded.

Juma paused for hardly a minute, wondering whether, in attempting to pull out the woman, he too would sink. He stood two steps away from her. He was on firm ground, though it shook, whenever she wriggled. A head, past the victim of Nyogunde quagmires, was a narrow dark area running east to west, which Juma guessed to be the northern arm of the stream. There was a white narrow wooden footbridge running across it. *Good,* Juma said in his heart.

He walked across the stream, testing the narrow wooden footbridge. It took him hardly a minute to cross to the northern end of the stream. Good! That was useful knowledge, incase he had to run across it with Grace and Okulu in pursuit.

"Help!" the woman called out, wondering what the stranger was trying to do. Her name was Elizabeth; she was hardly seventeen years of age.

"I will help you. Do not panic; otherwise, we both sink. Stay put, I'll be back in a minute," Juma instructed.

Elizabeth could have been out of her senses in panic, but the man's voice was manly and reassuring; it was too deep for the age of the man she was seeing in the moonlight. He too sounded polished, as in "educated and learned." His smell was sweaty, raw and rough in a manly way. She held her peace, believing that the manly boy knew what he was doing.

"Thank you! Thank you," she whispered excitedly.

"I'll be back and I love you, too!" Juma replied, moving

away from Elizabeth.

Elizabeth cried softly, understanding that she was in danger, and she might not live to know the bearer of the gentle-yet-manly voice.

Elizabeth's fateful night had been long. She had left home two hours before to go to a party across the river. She was alone, having missed her company from a nearby home by minutes. She had crossed the northern branch of the river, walking on a white wooden footbridge. She was supposed to have stuck to a narrow path among sponge wood bushes for the rest of the way across the fifty-yard river basin. Hardly a few steps along the path she had walked countless times since she was a five-year old girl, the unthinkable happened to her: a bushbuck hurtled across the path, hardly a yard from her.

Fear and panic sent her jumping to the right, where she landed, legs first, into a warm salty quagmire. She was sinking, yelling for help, and groping for anything to hold, but there was nothing, within reach, onto which she could hold to prevent her from going under the earth. She was sinking, and the more she struggled to get free, the deeper she sank. She sank up to her waist in the first minute; she then sank to her shoulders in five minutes. Then a voice told her, *Elizabeth, stop kicking about, if you want to live.*

She stopped kicking about immediately. She waited for an hour, shouting, "Help," once every few minutes.

After what seemed forever, she felt the earth tremble, as if there was a distant earthquake. No. It was not an earthquake. *Sound of footsteps,* she thought. Someone was coming toward her, but whoever he or she was hesitated on hearing her calling for help. Since then, the man had reached her location and was organizing how to rescue her.

"I might live!" she whispered repeatedly, holding her peace as she awaited the man's return.

Juma had seen a sponge-wood tree with a sizable branch a few yards back. Walking quickly, yet cautiously, he reached the tree, held the branch that just filled his closed palm and yanked it free. The branch could have been three arm lengths. Without bothering to trim branch of leaves and secondary branches, Juma cautiously dragged it back to the young woman, wondering if it was strong enough for her to hold on to as he pulled her out.

"Hold this firmly here with both hands. I'll pull you out from the other end. Don't kick about and don't touch my arm; if I need to hold your hand, I'll hold it. I surely will," he instructed and warned her, his scouting command skills unmistakable in the night air.

"I love you; if that happens to be the last word from my mouth as we sink together, stranger, let it be," she said exuberantly, sailing in a new boat known as hope. She had a sense of hope she never had before in her young life.

"Whoever you are, please don't be too excited as we do this," Juma said, and without wasting time, he pulled her out in one quick attempt. It took him hardly half a minute to accomplish the task. He had surprised himself; all over sudden, he was a man who had beaten great odds, swimming across rivers and running through thorny bushes; yet he had mustered enough courage, skills, and strength to pull out the woman from the mud.

"Whoever you are, you shall live long," Juma said, muting his own excitement

"Thank you; I love you!" Elizabeth responded. Then she was crying hysterically on his shoulders, hugging him and kissing him.

Juma's adolescent hormones could have been running wild like hers, but his life was still in danger, and he understood that. His heart sunk in fright. With Grace still barking on the adjacent ridge, he read danger, and he did not need the loud sobs or any form of celebration. At that moment, Grace and her handlers could have been half a mile away downriver and approaching from the east, having followed the party revelers' path to their destination.

"I have to go!" he whispered, prying off the hot body smearing him with mud.

"No; you saved my life. You can't leave me here; I'll go wherever you go!" Elizabeth said.

Juma was a virgin, but his father (Odongo) was anxious that he married at fifteen years, for reasons of heritage. He, Juma, was Odongo's spiritual eldest son. Juma had abhorred that kind of talk from his father. Now, here in the middle of the night, he had saved a bird whose first act was to claim him as her own.

He noticed she was fully dressed. She had some canvass shoes on her muddy feet.

"Hurry up! I have to guide you out of here," Juma said. They had crossed to the other side of the stream.

She washed her legs; minutes later, she started to fiddle with her dress, trying to wash it while it was still on her body.

Juma noticed Elizabeth's discomfort and walked a few yards then hid behind a bush to allow her to sanitize herself.

Grace was barking again, but she was farther west of Juma's location, but still on the opposite ridge; her sound was growing faint too. For most of the previous hour, Judas maintained a disciplined hold on the dog's lease, believing that Juma was somewhere in the valley.

That is good! Juma judged in his heart, believing that his pursuers had missed him by as short as a hundred yards.

"Who are you? How handsome! What happened to your clothes?" Elizabeth asked. She had refreshed and was holding him again, her wet clothes dripping saline Nyogunde water into his many open wounds. Juma's skin itched in so many places that he felt miserable in the woman's hands.

"Nameless! That is my name," Juma had a moment to joke amidst his salty agony; Grace's barking too was getting fainter with time, bringing needed relief. He felt his chances had improved, perhaps due to Judas's help. Then there was the developing feminine trap around him, holding him skin on skin.

"Nameless? You must have a name. Even the barking dog across the ridge must be having some name," she said motherly, reminding Juma of his mother's condition earlier in the night.

Now, that hurt Juma. "Yes, I have no name," he said.

"Can we stop for a moment?" Elizabeth asked.

"Okay," Juma volunteered.

"Can I lean on you, just for a moment?" Elizabeth asked leaning against him in the process. Then she was praying. She prayed for about three minutes; she prayed about the "lover" who saved her; she prayed that wherever he was going, might his path be clear.

Juma said Amen, when she was done. How strange! He wondered. He had not been as prayerful during the night of his greatest peril in life the way he normally did. It had taken meeting the young woman to refocus his spirit that had been wondering aimlessly, following his body blindly, and running to nowhere the whole night. Even Mrs. Aaron's Biblical Devotionals had failed to settle his loitering spirit.

The cocks were crowing from different ridges, reminding him of his mother's condition and the events that caused her harm. Juma had spent a night in the wild because he was running away from Okulu. That was new, but during the last month alone, he twice had reveled until daybreak, something that had brought much angst in his mother's heart, leading to too much quarrelling between them because, as a night reveler, he had no strength left to go to the farm. Their quarrels led to the tragedy of hours before.

Maybe my hurting mother needs me by her side now. And here I am in the hands of this alien woman late at night, Juma said in his guilt-laden heart.

"Say something," Elizabeth said, still leaning against her superhero. They had been standing in silence, each engrossed in private thought. The young man was revisiting the tragedy in his home and his role in it. The young woman was getting used to the touch of her superhero, wondering how close she had come to going under without a trace, hardly a fortnight after burying her father.

"Let's go," Juma suggested to the woman, anxious to get away from the valley above which Grace still hovered, with Okulu dangerously close by. The woman was still leaning on him.

"Where are we going?" she asked.

"Take me where you came from before you ended up in the muddy river," Juma said.

"You don't want to know my name? Hold me. Are you shy? " she asked, then tiptoed and kissed him. He did not resist her advance. She was deliberately harassing him, trying to find out if he had known any woman. She was lucky that he had matured tremendously the last eight hours; he at least could talk. However, he, like most fifteen-year old boys, found her manners intimidating.

"Can we go to that home on the hill?" Juma asked.

"Which home on the hill?" Elizabeth asked in surprise, setting him loose, a little, his left hand in her right hand.

"The home where the light flickers on and off in the wind," Juma said.

They were walking again, hand in hand.

"Do you love dark-skinned women, my Arab friend?" Elizabeth asked, deliberately ignoring the man's request that she took him to the "home of light." She instead was intent on getting under the alien's skin, so that he could identify himself in anger.

"Stop it, I'm no Arab," he whispered harshly.

"You are angry at something; I know you are," she said looking at him in the eye. They had stopped for a face-to-face conversation, with her trying to read his face in the moonlight.

"Okay, let's keep going. We will talk in better times," Juma said.

"Which better times?" Elizabeth asked, wondering whether the boy knew that she had lost her father. *Is he a relative of my father? Otherwise, why is he going to my father's home?* She debated.

You'll know tomorrow."

"You don't want to know my name, Mister Nameless?" complained Elizabeth.

She was trying to be nice to the man who had saved her life, but he was as cold as the head of an axe before sunrise. She knew something serious was amiss with the stranger. She had kissed him twice and received no emotional response.

"Let's reach your home first, then I will try to know you," Juma said, annoying Elizabeth.

What was it? He has some airs, as if he knows he is destined to greater things. He has such a way with words that allows him to look down somebody without sounding rude. Who is he to delay knowing me? Elizabeth wondered. As the only girl in the village to have stepped inside a high school, she was the golden girl in her area.

"You'll try to know me?" Elizabeth wondered allowed.

"Let's take this path," Juma ordered, startling Elizabeth, because the path the stranger was pointing at was a dead-end animal track.

"That is not a path. Leave me alone," she complained,

resisting him. He was dragging her along, and she was resisting, thinking that he could be a bad man.

"Okay, I want to reach that home on the hill as fast as possible," Juma said in a pleasant tone.

"Easy, my husband, I'll take you home," said Elizabeth teasingly, but worried that they could be blood relatives; yet she had hoped that she would marry the man.

"I know where I'm going, and don't shout, I'm not a bad man," Juma remarked. The whole conversation had slowed him down, and noise and stagnation was not good for him, a man escaping from danger.

"If you are going to the home where that light dances in the wind, then follow me! It is my late father's home. I am sorry, but that is his funeral bonfire! We buried him two weeks ago. That is the reason I am still around this village; that is why I almost died crossing a river, going to a party, doing what Grandma had warned me not to do. I should be in Ogande right now!" Liz said choking with emotion, with the memory of her father revisiting her soul.

"I'm sorry," Juma said. He had stopped dead, wondering, in silence, why he was attracted to a home in mourning.

"You don't have to be sorry, my young friend," Elizabeth said rather carelessly.

"I'm no young man!" Juma flared up; he had stopped moving.

"Keep talking; I love your voice; it is reassuring to me. But you must tell me why you walk in such torn clothes."

"Take me home, whoever," Juma said; he was anxious to move on.

"Elizabeth. That is my name," volunteered Elizabeth, believing that he would follow her example and reveal his name.

"Take me home, Liz," Juma said, going informal, intending to warm up to her.

"You have no name?" Elizabeth asked, as Juma resumed walking northeast, leading the way along the path.

"You'll know it once I have had some sleep," Juma said.

He wanted to tell her his name. However, he could not because of the storm that had been threatening him from the other side of the river.

Grace was barking among the cassava fields, but each successive bark was fainter than the previous one, as if she was heading back. *She must be running uphill with whoever is handling her. Good!* Juma said in his heart, thanking Judas and Grace.

Grace had sensed Juma's scent at the spot where he had hit the broad livestock path, but she had chosen to go against the downhill wind, essentially heading away from the hunted man, who happened to have been her owner. Okulu was baffled, wondering why the dog had turned around. Judas let the dog do her will, even as he knew that Grace was simply going against the wind and away from Juma's direction of progress. John looked on bemused as Okulu cursed at the dog. John suspected what was going in the dog's head.

Judas and John welcomed the journey home.

Elizabeth had realized that the stranger who had saved her hesitated, even stopped, each time the dog barked, but she was too infatuated with him to have said anything. Moreover, she was struggling to analyze every word from his mouth, trying to find out who he was. Even more intriguing to her, was that the young man switched from speaking in *DhoLuo* to polished English once he heard that she was in some high school. The condition of his clothes bothered her. It was still dark, but she noticed bruises on him in the moonlight

The cocks were crowing, as Juma and Elizabeth negotiated the last steep climb into her home. "Where are you from? Who are you?" Liz had asked for the last time.

Silence. Juma did not respond immediately. He was tempted to say that he was a graduate from a middle school and was heading to Alliance High School, but desisted; he intended to protect his anonymity until his situation resolved. He believed the resolution to his problem would be in the home on the hill whose funeral light had been attracting him for miles. Then he would wave his Alliance credentials to claim the girl.

"Mister, you saved my life, and I love you, but who are you?" Liz asked, sounding desperate, wondering how she would introduce him to her grandmother.

"You'll know in the morning," Juma said, thinking of what would happen at the home ahead. He knew the woman's people would treat him like a hero, for having saved her from going under saline valley, but he also knew that they would want to know who he was and why he had bruises all over his body. Even then, he wanted to maintain his anonymity until his father came for him.

"Are you worried about something happening across the river?" Elizabeth quizzed.

"No," Juma replied.

"Why do you keep looking back then?" Elizabeth asked, watching him closely.

"It is the party over there," Juma offered a believable explanation.

"You can't go there the way you are; I don't want any girl to see you like that. Moreover, it is almost daybreak; the party must be ending soon," Elizabeth said.

"I agree," he quipped as they neared the home, which was fenced with a low stone hedge. He had stopped, and was looking at the girl's face in dawn's light. He thought she was a little older than he was, though they were of the same height.

"Why do you look at me like that?" Elizabeth asked, feeling uncomfortable under his searching stare, now that they were closer to her home.

"Well, I want to know you better," said Juma.

"Not here; not in this home; everyone is mourning," Elizabeth said, remembering what her grandmother had told her about how she Elizabeth would remain out of bounds to men for a while.

"I know," Juma said absent-mindedly, assuming that it was about Luo traditional stuff.

It was the dawn of a new day; Juma could see her face more clearly. There was something he found repulsive about her behavior. She touched her nose frequently as if he, Juma, smelled horribly. Juma found that annoying. She reminded him of his father who had a similar habit. In fact, Juma had grown up believing that his father always delectated a horrible smell from him, however much he, Juma, scrubbed himself in soap and water. Now, here, in an alien land, Juma meets this girl with a similar behavior, even as she adoringly called him, "My husband."

"There is my father's grave and here is the log fire whose light guided you home," Elizabeth said, wondering, how she would present the nameless, bruised man in rugs to her mother and grandmother. The man had to be presentable, even if he had saved her life.

"I'll pray around the grave, before you show me where to sleep," he said, hoping to catch some sleep, in case he needed to move again.

"You don't have to; it is an old grave now," Elizabeth suggested, fearing that the man's spiritual engagement with the death of her father would evoke emotions of loss in her heart.

"I will," he said, kneeling down to pray.

Elizabeth stood idly, fighting another fit of emotion. Tears were rolling down her face. She was emotional at the thought of what nearly happened to her in the Nyogunde valley hardly a fortnight after burying her father.

"Thank you, Elizabeth; I can sleep anywhere now. Wipe off those tears, or I'll move to the next home." Juma said, having completed his prayer.

"You saved my life!" she mumbled, fighting the urge to wail for a father she lost recently; and she also was thinking of her own life she nearly traded early because of a party across the Nyogunde. Then it was a full-blown wailing, with her repeating, "You saved my life!"

Juma stood by, idling, shifting from foot to foot; unsure of what else to do to console Elizabeth.

"Olisa! Olisa! What happened?" Grandma, who rarely slept, asked emerging from her house.

"Elizabeth, stop crying, your father died two months ago; stop crying! Grandma, I told you that this child should have returned to school yesterday," Dorka said emerging from her house, dressed in her late husband's red cotton shirt. Dorka already was running toward Elizabeth, alarmed on seeing her daughter in mud-soiled clothes. Next to Elizabeth was the light-skinned stranger in badly torn clothes.

What is this about? Dorka wondered in silence. She stopped moving, trying to understand what had happened to her daughter and the man. Elizabeth was calling the man a savior, but what Dorka was seeing was a man who could have passed for a herdsman for hire.

Overcome with emotion, Dorka was tempted to embrace her daughter, who was coming toward her, but she, Dorka, stopped, when Grandma shouted, "Dorka, do not risk embracing Olisa while you still walk in Ochieng's clothes."

"Wulululu! Wulululu! Wulululu! Olisa, what happened to you? Who is this man?" Grandma asked.

"I don't know who he is, but he is my Angel! He saved my life; I had sunk up to my neck in the Nyogunde, when he came from nowhere and pulled me out off the quagmire," Elizabeth said between mournful sobs.

"O, my only child!" Dorka cried.

"Who are you?" Grandma demanded from Juma.

Silence. Juma did not respond; he just stood there, looking down, shifting on his feet.

"Where are you from?" Dorka asked.

Silence; there was no word from Juma.

"Is he deaf? What happened to his clothes?" Dorka asked Elizabeth.

"Ma, he is not deaf! However, he might be in trouble. Leave him alone for now; let my Angel sleep," Elizabeth said between sobs.

"Olisa, I told you to avoid parties until your father's grave has settled," Grandma chastised her granddaughter.

"I'm sorry, Grandma," Elizabeth said, leaning on Grandma.

"Stop wailing, think of what your special guest will eat. He needs some clothes too," Dorka said, between her mournful stanzas for her departed.

Juma stood idle, looking on as Elizabeth cried on her grandmother's shoulder.

Dorka was dancing, heading out of the gate, and wailing in poem about one Ochieng,' whom Juma understood to have been Elizabeth's late father, who had died hardly fourteen days before.

Juma did not like the noise his presence had created. It only needed a few nosey villagers coming out to find out what clansman had arrived from some distant urban center to mourn Ochieng' to blow off his anonymity. Before he knew it, Okulu would be dragging him away to Kadem.

Maybe I should have not insisted on going to the graveside to pray. Now I risk inviting Okulu and company across the river, Juma debated, cursing his luck.

"Follow me, my grandson!" ordered Grandma, dragging away a brokenhearted Elizabeth. Now that things started to settle down for Juma (Okulu was on his way to Kadem and would not bother Juma for a while), Juma realized how scantily clothed he was among three alien women. He was anxious to enter a house and dive under a blanket.

Caught within the sad crosscurrents of the three women's loss, Juma experienced a flashback to the tragic situation surrounding his mother. *What a night!* Juma's heart exclaimed, as he and Elizabeth followed Grandma to her house, which was the appropriate place for him to lie down and sleep in the absence of a hut for boys in the two-house home.

How is my mother now? Juma wondered in silence, bending low to enter Grandma's house.

Moments later, Juma was on a mat, fighting to get some sleep as reality dueled with dreams for his young mind. Juma recalled a night that started with her indisposed mother fighting for her life, urging him to run for his life. He since received no information about his mother's status. Now here he was in the hands of three grieving women, in an alien land, having extracted one of the women from a quagmire. How strange! Juma wondered.

7

Birthright

THE CONFLICT IN ODONGO'S HOME was not over his wealth; both Atieno and Aura had livestock wealth, thanks to their well-married daughters. Atieno had daughters Arua, Alal, Olga, and Abich, all grown-up women who were well married in both livestock and monetary wealth. Aura had the twin-daughters, Rachel and Leah, both of whom were married to rich men, who had given Odongo many heads of cattle. Odongo's kraal was teeming with livestock.

Juma's birth caused turbulence in the order in Odongo's home, and that turbulence was not over material wealth each son would inherit; it was over future spiritual/political leadership in the home, which included who would inherit the father's staff and stool. In old times, that eldership in a Luo family dictated such mundane things as who had a right to what part of an animal carcass, to the touchier issues of religious observances and land ownership. Therefore, as Juma grew up from a toddler to a sheep-herding boy to a young man with a deeper voice, the house of Atieno Nyomulo looked on warily. That Odongo invested inordinate amounts of his time, energy, and material on the boy sent alarm signals in the house of Atieno. Atieno and her children knew Okulu no longer was the man of religious import in the Odongo home.

Juma was the best-dressed kid in the village. When he reached middle school, Odongo sent him to a boarding school, arguing that the village culture was not good for a modern boy. Odongo could have been right: Okulu had fumbled through high school with a trail of young women behind him. Odongo was not going to allow a similar fate to befall his bright youngest child. Juma would graduate on top of his class, with perfect *As* in all subjects examined. His anticipated direction was Alliance Boys. Now, all that was in jeopardy and Juma had become a fugitive.

When the message of Juma's excellent-graduation grades reached Atieno two weeks before, her head spun with rage, and she had to vent her anger against her husband.

"You don't eat my food these days," Atieno remarked, delivering cold milk and cold potatoes to her husband in his hut. It was a few days after Juma's record-setting performance in KCPE examination became public.

Odongo looked at the potatoes for a moment before saying, "You know that a man cannot live on potatoes and milk alone." His message could have been louder because giving a lakeshore man sweet potato and milk is akin to giving him grass and water, for his Creator did not design his tummy to handle potatoes; he worked best on fish, fish, and fish every day of the week.

"You can't be serious," Atieno said, on realizing that her husband had chosen to belittle her food.

"I'm serious. I'm growing old; I pass out the milk as soon as it hits my stomach," Odongo said, wondering why Atieno gave him a dinner of potatoes and milk, a meal meant for herdsmen.

"Don't joke with me; is milk disagreeable to your stomach only when it comes from my gourd?" Atieno said. She was hurting because of her husband's stinging slur against her food. She regularly scoured her milk gourd, and for her husband to have insinuated that her cultured milk was substandard or full of rancid rancor was a slur she could not stomach. However, Atieno had missed her husband's point. She had visited his hut for reason's she was yet to state; she should have come with a more-inviting dish—a dish that initiated intimate talk—and not just milk and potatoes.

"I have not said that," Odongo responded after drinking several mouthfuls of the milk, in an attempt to smother the effect of his earlier slur.

"So your son is going to Alliance," Atieno remarked,

knowing that she would get an immediate reaction from Odongo.

"*My son?* Juma belongs to the whole home. Atieno, please work to unite this home," Odongo whispered in suppressed anger.

"I'm in no mood to join your unity talks! I hope your celebration with you lover is over by now."

"What are you talking about?" Odongo asked, visually appraising his wife from face to toes.

"You have two wives in this home," Atieno stated the obvious, but that was the point. Odongo operated, as if Aura was the only wife he had in the home.

"I know that," Odongo responded, wondering why Atieno had not found it easier to have come into his hut and said, 'I love you and I miss you,' instead of invoking the name of Juma and his mother into her desire to date her husband that night.

"You don't appear to know that," Atieno said, bolting out of Odongo's hut, hoping that her husband had understood the purpose of her visit.

At age fifty years, Atieno was older compared to Aura, the spiritual first wife, who was forty-two years old. Atieno wanted Odongo by her side, that night. She was not going to allow Aura to continue to celebrate over her head.

Odongo would heed the warning; he would visit Atieno's house that night, for the sake of peace and balance in the romantic engagements in the home. He had other ideas in mind that he hoped to test during his romantic safari in Atieno's house. He intended to portray Juma as a child of the home and not just Aura's child. What better way for Odongo to demonstrate that his home spoke with one voice than for him to sell at least a goat from Atieno's house during his fundraising effort to get money for Juma's school fees at Alliance Boys High School.

Odongo knew Atieno would protest such a move to sell her goat, but he was going to do it anyway because it was the right thing to do. Odongo knew the Ougo family would applaud his gesture because conquering a national examination was like conquering an enemy, and the honor for such a feat went to the whole home that raised the conqueror. For the same reason, Juma's adventure into a high school would be like going into a fight with a giant on behalf of the whole Ougo family. Odongo was a man who tried to run his two-wife home as a united unit, but there always was too much squabbling over rank and privileges.

If that night, all Odongo wanted to preach was peace in the home, hoping that selling the goat would be a significant diplomatic coup (against Atieno's ire), whose net effect would be the reconciliation of his wives, he was wrong. Atieno had her own issues she wished settled in the short term.

Later that night, when Atieno thought Odongo's heart was tender, she said, "I need my own home."

"Why do you need your home?" Odongo asked.

"I need my home; I'm tired of Aura playing lord over me," Atieno complained.

"How does she play lord over you?" Odongo asked, even as he knew that she meant the religious dictates on life in a Luo home, wherein the first wife is the priestess and queen.

"You know that I can't plant my fields before she plants her field; I can't bring home my green corn from the fields before she plants her fields; worse still, you cannot sleep in my house before you sleep in her house. I want my freedom. Yes, she is the first wife, but I want my home, in which I peacefully can retire as the only woman."

"She did not make the rules, our forefathers did. Besides that, why have you failed to visit Aura, since the news that Juma passed KCPE reached this village?"

"Since which year have Aura and I been at peace? We are in a war to our graves; she denied me seniority, and when she gave birth to Juma, she denied Okulu his birthright. Why should you play the reconciliatory husband? You are not a fair reconciler; you have always been on Aura's side. Odongo, give me my home where my grandchildren can visit me without worrying about *chira,*" Atieno pleaded with her husband, citing c*hira,* the dreaded Luo curse.

"I want to have peace in this home," Odongo said.

"Keep off my fights with Aura; I never had a son who could qualify to go to Alliance Boys High School. Give me my home in the name of peace," Atieno demanded.

Odongo was not ready to split his wives' residences yet, but he never before heard Atieno state the source of her anger so clearly. He had a hunch that Juma was in danger. However, Odongo's immediate project was to get Juma a wife before he left for Alliance High School. Odongo's fixation with giving his young son a woman had to do with the boy's principal position in the home as the first son of the first wife. Additionally, Odongo feared the ways of the modern women his son would meet as he explored the world.

Building a home for Atieno had not been a priority for Odongo. He had planned on a five-day trip to Tanzania. He dubbed it a business trip, but it was not. Like his father before him, Odongo was going to visit a friend to put in place a marriage arrangement between the friend's youngest daughter and Juma. The marriage sealed with a few heads of cattle, Odongo was to come back to Kenya and take his son to Alliance High School after the young man received his wife. He needed a peaceful atmosphere for things to work according to his plan. Yet Atieno was unknowingly creating a new battlefront over birthright.

"I asked you a question, where is the answer?" Atieno demanded.

"I have to check on the kraal; Grace is barking out there," Odongo had responded. He didn't like Atieno's aggressive style and attitude of 'I'm the oppressed woman,' and he wanted out of her bed.

"It's only midnight; are you coming back?" Atieno asked, knowing that would not be the case.

"I have not said that," Odongo said calmly. He was not the shouting type; he often let his actions speak for him. He always walked out of Atieno's bed whenever she introduced Aura and her son into a conversation, and the act of walking out of her bed in the middle of the night hurt Atieno badly and only made her ire against Aura the more intense. In this manner, Atieno indeed was the abused and oppressed woman.

Atieno's issues are not new; they have lived with me since she stepped into my life, Odongo argued, while inspecting his expansive cattle kraal.

Odongo would not be coming back that night; that Atieno knew. Since the light-skinned beauty, Arua, entered the Odongo home, more than thirty years back, Atieno could count the number of times her husband spent a full night next to her. Atieno believed that Aura of Tanga had sprayed a love potion on everything Odongo touched. Eleven o'clock, Odongo would be in Atieno's bed, and he would be out at midnight; he would be in at midnight and out at three o'clock in the morning, which was the latest time he ever stayed in her bed. He always left to go and secure the loose bull that had breached the enclosure and was violating a neighbor's field of millet; he always left to go and scare off the hippos (out of River Kuja and Lake Victoria) before they ruined the corn in his farms. He never came back to Atieno's bed after such excuses.

Atieno was the second wife, yet one of the unusual ones. Like most second wives, she was supposed to own her husband's heart, but she didn't. One, she was older than Aura, the first wife, by eight years. Second, Aura was the softer-powered woman who touched her husband's heart without even opening her mouth. Don't be mistaken; the long-necked Atieno, daughter of Omulo from Sakwa, was not ugly; she was beautiful but overaggressive. She too had evoked the ire of the whole Ougo home against her when she made a claim on Odongo's heart the day she arrived in Thim Lich. When Atieno arrived in Thim Lich, she already was pregnant, a matter often winked at; the derogatory word *illegitimate* often was mouthed about her son, Okulu, even in her hearing. Because of these issues, she embraced a combative attitude in marriage to protect her son.

8

Atieno, the Wild Flower

MANY YEARS AGO, Ougo son of Odongo, Odongo Rawo's father, paid bride price toward the acquisition of a particular bride for Odongo. The bride's name was Maria Aura of Tanga. Aura's father (Gor) was Ougo's friend, and the duo wished that their children married as a way to cement the friendship permanently. This was a childhood engagement, with Aura being nine years younger than Odongo. Over the years, Ougo would take cattle to Gor in advance of a future wedding date. When Aura was still a ten-year-old child, Odongo was a hot nineteen-year-old man dating local girls. His body's hormonal chemistry was fast pushing him toward marriage.

In the 1940s Kenya, education was not a priority. Returnees were coming back from the Second World War, and they were spreading a modern perspective to life among the populace. So not to allow his son to miss the caravan to modernity, Ougo tried to put Odongo through school, but the latter could only reach Grade AB before he dropped out due to poor scholarship, what with all-night partying with girls and an advanced age. By the time Odongo dropped out of school, he could read and write and that ensured him work as a clerk in Macalder Gold Mines. A modern man with money and his ancestral animal wealth was a rich man few women would have passed in the 1940s. Odongo was such a man.

With weekend partying with beautiful women, all of whom were available from among alien communities that had gathered around Macalder Mines to work, Odongo was not willing to wait for Aura, a distant fruit in Tanganyika, to mature. He violated a woman under the cover of darkness; he felt ashamed about it, and he lived in denial with it; thirty-five years later, he still could not muster the courage to acknowledge the violation.

Thus overcome with secret guilt, one evening in 1946, Odongo brought home the woman; her name was Atieno from Sakwa Clan. Tall, light-skinned, and long-necked, Atieno's beauty impressed Apudo, Odongo's mother instantly. Even then, something troubled Apudo: her experienced eyes informed her that the beautiful woman Odongo had brought home that October evening in 1946 was pregnant. Apudo wanted answers from her son, but she was not going to spoil his celebration, so she let him be with the woman until morning, arguing that the woman was pregnant already, and nothing worse could have occurred during the night party Odongo and his cousins had arranged for the woman.

"Odongo Rawo, what is going on?" Apudo had asked Odongo, who had taken a seat in her house early the following morning.

"What do you mean, Ma? I have brought home a girl; that is all," Odongo had responded casually.

"You have brought home a woman and not a virgin girl," Apudo said firmly, as she offered a large calabash of a hot, high-energy cereal drink to her son, who had left a woman in his hut!

"Ma, I don't know what you are talking about," Odongo had said coolly. He was not aware that the woman was pregnant. But even if the girl were pregnant, which she was, that would not have bothered him because they had known each other for more than a month. Second, he was laden with toxic guilt for he anonymously had violated Atieno six weeks before.

The developing child could be mine, judged Odongo. That was his private contention as he enjoyed the revitalizing cereal drink. However, Odongo could not declare that he had violated Atieno, by force; he feared for his life, knowing that the crime was punishable by death.

"Has she come to stay?" Apudo asked, coming down from her intense mood. She had realized that she was talking marital ethics to a modern man to whom having a child out of wedlock was no big deal. Even then, Apudo needed to establish whether the developing child could have been Odongo's seed, and she was trying to gain such intelligence without raising a storm.

"She just told me that she is going to be my wife," Odongo said casually, before reengaging his vessel of the hot cereal drink.

"When did she say this?" pressed Apudo

"This morning," Odongo said.

"Mm! So when she arrived yesterday, she came as a visitor, hoping to go back?" mother asked son.

"Yes!"

"Mm!" Apudo released a sigh of distress.

"What is wrong with her having decided to stay, if I love her?" Odongo asked.

"There is nothing wrong; I just wish to know. But for how long have you known the woman you call Atieno?" Apudo asked.

"One week," Odongo responded. He had told a lie; he had known Atieno for more than three weeks.

"*One week?*" Apudo asked rhetorically.

"What is wrong with that?" Odongo asked

Apudo had issues with Odongo's declared wife: Atieno was pregnant, and the symptoms of pregnancy were too prominent to remain hidden for long.

Is it possible that a one-week pregnancy could produce such strong symptoms as spitting and vomiting? I do not think so. As a practical matter, had Odongo known the woman, as a man to a wife, before last night? These questions rushed through Apudo's mind, but she did not put them to her son. Apudo resolved to keep them to herself until she would share her concerns with Ougo, her husband, who already was enraged about Odongo's deplorable act. Second, she resolved to dope the woman's porridge with herbal brew that would minimize her nausea and other early pregnancy symptoms, and thus save Odongo from public ridicule, should the woman decide to stay on as his wife.

"There is nothing wrong, Odongo," Apudo said, not believing the timeline Odongo had given her. "I guess your father will fight against your marriage to the woman you call Atieno. Why did you do this to us, knowing that Aura, your first wife, is not home yet?"

Even for a modern man, Odongo's demeanor over the

matter of his responsibility for Atieno's pregnancy was too casual. That annoyed Apudo.

"I know that Ougo is not happy about the woman; he passed by my house without saying good morning to Atieno, who was basking in the sun outside," Odongo said of his father's reaction to Atieno's presence in the home.

Ougo knew Atieno was one of the daughters of one of the aliens that had invaded the clan since Macalder Mines started gold production, but he had ignored her that morning, and she had complained to Odongo about the encounter.

"Do not argue with your father over the matter; I will handle him," Apudo ordered, knowing that it was a bad omen for parents a man to send away the first woman he brought home and declared to be his wife, for any reason other than witchcraft.

Even as Apudo advised her son to avoid a quarrel with his father over the future of Atieno in the home, she already had talked to her husband about the matter, and as responsible parents, they had celebrated their son's passage

"Ougo Ngech, Odongo has a woman in his warrior hut," Apudo had informed her husband the previous evening. He was sampling a dish of fish stew and ugali she had delivered to his hut.

"I know that," Ougo had responded.

"Are you coming to my house tonight?" Apudo had asked her husband who had another wife (Anyango) besides her.

"Is she his wife?" Ougo had asked.

"I don't know, but we should not take chances with Odongo's life," Apudo reminded her husband, Ougo; their oldest son was Owinyo.

"He must be warned to keep off her chest," Ougo instructed.

"How could anybody do that? Our son is a single man and there is nothing standing between him and marriage," argued Apudo.

"Go and tell that woman to go," Ougo demanded. "She does not match Aura of Tanga's beauty. Her dark skin does not match Aura's light skin that sparkles in the noontime sun, and Aura's smile never sets with the setting sun!" Ougo praised Aura the daughter of Gor, his long-term friend.

"My husband, Aura is not your sister-in-law to deserve such praise from your tongue; she is supposed to be your daughter-in-law. Moreover, she is not here yet. Besides, she is but a child, who could change her mind when she becomes a woman with the freedom to choose," Apudo cautioned her husband. Ougo's over exuberance about Aura had bothered her. She felt that Ougo needed to be sober over the evolving situation, because unlike Aura, who was tens of miles away in Tanganyika, Atieno already was in the home.

"Aura loves Odongo," Ougo said.

"How do you know that? She saw Odongo five years ago when she was a ten-year-old child. I'm not going to chase away a woman I can see in my home, in the name of waiting for a little girl I have not seen," Apudo argued.

"You'll see Aura soon."

"I hope so, but Odongo Rao has a great catch in his net. Ougo Ng'ech, the youth are still partying over Odongo's catch; I washed your blanket, come home," Apudo praised and pleaded with her husband to come to her house because tradition demanded that Ougo, the father of the bridegroom, be in Apudo's house that night.

True, Ougo was not a happy man. He would protest quietly when it became apparent that the woman he referred to as "Odongo's girlfriend" was there to stay on as Odongo's wife.

But who could have blamed Ougo? Aura had been his pet project for years. When Atieno walked into Odongo's hut, Aura was a beautiful fifteen-year old. She was five feet eight inches. Aura was not exactly short, but she was smaller and shorter than Atieno of Sakwa, who was a bigger and taller woman. Atieno projected the image and promise of one who would become the mother of big fighting men, who could have carried heavy shields and javelins into wars of decades before. These superior physical attributes of Atieno had not passed Ougo's notice, but he was not ready to allow Odongo to welcome another woman into his home ahead of Aura.

Ougo unwillingly would play his role as the father of a newlywed man as Odongo settled with Atieno. Atieno would become Odongo's wife before he settled her bride price. Her pregnancy would become public quickly, something she heard whispered about as she mingled with other women during their daily chores.

When Odongo found Atieno in his hands, marrying her was not in his mind. His fiancé and his father's pet project, Aura, was fifteen years of age and still in the land of Tanganyika. Odongo was having a good time; he was a mine clerk, a man of rank with money to spend. He believed that he had another five years before Aura could join him. Sure, he had a distant feeling, if any, for Aura, yet he knew he was destined to her bed. However, with his hormones running wild, and a distant bride he had seen only once in her childhood, five years before, his feelings for her had faded. All he saw were the local girls whom he could not marry because they were members of his clan. Then Atieno entered his world one dark night and changed his marital future. Atieno came from Sakwa; her father had migrated to Macalder Mines area to run a shopping store. They lived hardly a mile from the Ougo homestead on a piece of land Ougo had sold to her father.

In the pervasive partying atmosphere of the late 1940s, Atieno would lose her innocence, become rebellious, partying with various men in the wild, while dancing to accordion and *nyatiti* (eight-stringed Luo harp) music every night. The adage, *a bird in hand is better than many in the bush*, well captured Odongo's feelings as he succumbed to Atieno's harassing spells on the dance floor, even as marriage to her was not in his mind because he was engaged to Aura. With time, Odongo could not hold the temptation to reach out and grab the low-hanging fruit in his neighborhood. Things happened one dark night as Atieno and a girlfriend walked from Macalder Market. Odongo and a male friend were waiting in ambush for Atieno and her girlfriend. Things happened fast; the men vanished into the anonymity of dark night, leaving behind two violated young women. Atieno and her friend would walk away in shame, not knowing who had violated them.

The incident left Atieno a sore victim, and perhaps pregnant. A few weeks later, she realized she was pregnant, and she did not know which man had contributed to the pregnancy or if the anonymous rapist was responsible. She sought her mother's counsel.

"Atieno, what kind of woman are you? How can you fail to tell which man impregnated you?" her mother had asked on learning that she had a wealthy boyfriend named Odongo Ougo, a gold mine clerk and the son of a famous father endowed with much livestock wealth.

"I'm sorry to say that I don't know, Mama. I had a couple of boyfriends before I met Odongo," Atieno said. What Atieno did not want to explain and revisit was the manner in which she met whoever fathered Okulu. She was a victim of rape, and she was ashamed of herself. Moreover, she did not know the man who rapped her. They were two girls walking in the night, and they became victims of two young men who waylaid them.

"Atieno, I don't want to hear those words of doubt from your mouth. Never again should you utter them, not even in your heart. Of course, the man from Kadem will be your husband immediately. You have his child."

"Do I just walk into his father's home uninvited?" Atieno wondered.

"You have his child in you. Your father would kill me if he discovers that you are pregnant out of wedlock because you have been dancing with gold miners from Kadem and Tanganyika. You have to go tonight. And don't come back before the Odongo carries his son!"

"Ma! It will appear as if I'm a loose-and-desperate woman," Atieno had mourned her fate.

"I don't think you are desperate; how can you be desperate with your father and mother alive? It is not about being desperate; in this land, you must be smart. Now, gather your clothes and keep them ready; I'll send them over once you settle down."

Meanwhile, guilt was weighing Odongo down. He proposed to Atieno the next time they met. Within six weeks, Odongo walked Atieno to the Ougo home. He knew she was not a virgin; what he had not known was that she was pregnant. Odongo would remain silent over the violation of Atieno, while he continued to live with her as a husband.

Omulo, Atieno's father, visited the Ougo home on the third day. He had come to confirm that Atieno had found a nest for her anticipated child. In fact, Atieno had declared that she was not going back to her parents. Ougo and

Omulo were there as witnesses. Omulo had not insisted on bride wealth, which was a 'wink-wink' sign to those in the know that he was aware that his daughter was pregnant. What that meant was that no bride wealth would exchange hands until Atieno was through with the rough journey to motherhood.

Even as Omulo left Ougo's home without mentioning the matter of bride price, Ougo was not aware that Atieno was pregnant, which was odd in a village where news never rested on people's tongues.

Immediately Omulo left for his home, Ougo wanted to send a delegation to take livestock to the former man's home. He had thought of what to do in the circumstances and had concluded that Odongo should marry Atieno but as a second wife. Ougo thought it was fitting that Odongo paid some bride price to her parents.

He shared these thoughts with Apudo, his wife. "I have some five heads of cattle I want Odongo to take to Omulo of Sakwa in recognition of the fact that his daughter has made her bed in my home."

Apudo did not respond to her husband's proposal immediately. She was shocked to learn that Ougo was not aware that Atieno was pregnant. It was midmorning, and Ougo had come to her house to make the announcement. The man yawned twice during the dead moment, warning Apudo that it was advisable that she fed him first. Taking her time, she went to her outside kitchen to warm up some late breakfast for her husband, as she thought about how to break the news to him about Atieno's gynecological condition. No livestock exchanged hands when the bride was pregnant, full stop. Apudo was anxious to let Ougo know about Atieno's pregnancy, but she knew that he would want to know when his son's wife became pregnant and whether Odongo was responsible for the pregnancy.

Once Ougo was through with his breakfast, Apudo addressed him by his adoration, Ng'ech (A large lizard), saying, "Ng'ech, you know that you can't take animal wealth to Omulo yet."

"Why, when their daughter is here in my son's hut?" Ougo asked, wondering what game his wife was playing.

"I wish you wait until Aura of Tanga arrived in this home before you release your wealth to Omulo," Apudo said, playing to her husband's weaker side.

"I don't get your point. Why should Odongo live with someone's daughter without paying bride price?" Ougo asked.

"Aura is Odongo's first wife; you know that. He ate off her hands first, and you have sent countless heads of cattle and goats to Gor, her father. I want to see her here first, before you pay bride price toward another man's daughter," Apudo explained.

"What if Omulo returned here, demanding that we either release his daughter or pay bride price?" Ougo asked.

"We can wait for that to happen. Meanwhile, I want Odongo in Tanganyika soonest possible. Gor and his family will know about this unfortunate event soon, and I don't want them to hear it from none other than Odongo himself, because they will be asking whether he still loves their daughter. Odongo should be the one answering that question, with Aura in his hands," Apudo explained her stand.

What she said made a lot of sense, but her interest then was not how fast Aura arrived home. She was determined to keep the lid on Atieno's pregnancy for a little longer.

Listening to Apudo talk, and reading her face, Ougo thought she was telling him to use his head.

Omulo had left without complaining about Odongo having eloped with his unwilling daughter. Second, Omulo had not raised the issue of bride price, which Ougo found to be unusual. But Ougo rationalized that Omulo had not followed protocol because the latter was on of those Christianized alien who handled marriage issues less formally and more liberally. Ougo found it amusing that his wife was trying to convince him to delay releasing bride price to Omulo. Unknown to Apudo was that Ougo already had a hunch that their son's wife was pregnant (she was spitting a lot and this behavior had been getting worse by the day). However, Ougo had not asked for an explanation for Atieno's behavior, fearing to hear the unthinkable news, that a daughter-in-law was carrying a child that was not his blood. Now, here was his wife indirectly telling him that Odongo's new wife was pregnant after hardly three days in his home.

"Apudo, when are you going to tell me that Odongo's wife is pregnant?" Ougo asked, having decided to face the issue head-on.

"So you know that she is pregnant?" Apudo asked, cursing mildly for having made a fool of herself before her husband.

"Yes, she is pregnant," asserted Ougo, studying his wife's reaction and cursing his poor instincts.

"Well, that is the more reason you cannot release bride price to her father at the moment. Second, Aura will not be here for another year. It is not proper that a man marries two women in one season."

"I agree," Ougo said on a heavy heart. He knew his son had started marital life on the wrong foot. Several scenarios flashed through his mind. What if Atieno is carrying a boy and he is not Odongo's blood?" Ougo asked, still struggling with issues about bloodline, power and tradition in silence.

"Ng'ech, my husband, I know what is going through your mind. The woman is here, and she is pregnant; we can block our ears to the world and wait to accept our grandson, if she is carrying a grandson. Alternatively, we can join the doubters, pundits, and slanderers in the village gathering, and throw mud at Odongo and his wife and call her son names, if she is carrying a son. I choose to shut off my ears and join hands with my son in embracing his wife and child. As our wise say, silence often is the way of the wise," Apudo stated her stand now that she knew Ougo was aware that Atieno was pregnant.

"Apudo, you have spoken wisely. No one has a right to insinuate and speculate about who fathered the baby Odongo's wife is carrying in her. I keep my peace," Ougo said, even as Odongo's marriage to a pregnant woman saddened him. That an alien seed would carry his name bothered Ougo.

"Ng'ech my husband, talk to Odongo over Atieno's condition, encourage him, and remind him of our wish that Aura arrives here at the appropriate time," Apudo implored her husband.

The day Omulo left Ougo's home, leaving Atieno behind, Odongo realized that he was a married man. The following day in the evening, he was in his father's hut in response to the old man's demand that they should meet for father-to-son talk.

"Odongo, why have you disobeyed my orders? You have a beautiful bride in Tanganyika, then this scandal," Ougo asked his son.

"What scandal?" Odongo wondered in silence. He did not speak immediately.

Yes, Odongo agreed that Aura was beautiful, but he could only remember her faintly. He had met her once during his Tanganyika trip five years before; he could only imagine how she looked five years later.

"Do you know that the woman is pregnant?" Ougo asked.

"Pregnant?" Odongo asked, feigning surprise. Though Atieno had not told him that she was pregnant, he had learned it from his mother. He too had heard it from some idle talker. He was a mineworker, so he missed much of idle-local talk, but his wife was the subject of much gossip already. She was pregnant hardly five days into his bed.

"Yes," Ougo replied, reading the young man's body language.

"Is that a problem?" Odongo asked.

"It can be a problem to some people," Ougo said, wondering what his son meant. Was he hinting that the child was not his?

"I guess she is pregnant with my child," Odongo said, allaying his father's fears. He knew that to be the case, except he feared the consequence of going into details of dates and events about why he believed the woman carried his child.

"Let's hope so," Ougo said after a long look at his son in the eye. What he saw was certitude and firm resolve.

"Thank you," acknowledged. He was averse to joining in any criticism of his wife, so he did not respond to his father's remark. He wished his parents embraced his wife and moved on. He loved her, pregnant or not, of that he was sure.

"Son, you will be traveling to Tanganyika soon. Aura must be here within a few months," ordered Ougo.

"Is it appropriate for one man to marry two wives in one year?" asked Odongo.

"I don't know, son, but I'll consult with elders. Meanwhile prepare for the journey to Tanganyika," directed Ougo.

"I will."

"Odongo Rawo, know that I am with you as you start a new life as a married man. You can go," said Ougo.

As the saying goes, time wears even rocks; the same would be the case with Atieno. She ground it out against the Ougos, fighting each day to win her place among them. She would win the battle of recognition as a wife within the Ougo home, even as the Ougo family had raised their eyebrows when she arrived and declared that she would not go back to her parents, who lived a mile away. Then the Ougos would twist their noses, when she started to spit out saliva like a challenged cobra within a week of her arrival.

Out in the village, the rumor mills were churning out such questions as, 'Did Odongo not marry the woman just the other day? Is she pregnant already? How fast?'

For the sake of their family's honor, the Ougos would advance plausible theories about Atieno's early signs of pregnancy. Within the family, the Ougos grumbled about 'a pregnancy out of wedlock,' but they protected their family honor in public.

Seven months later, Atieno gave birth to Okulu to whispers that increasingly were uneasy.

"How soon? Atieno has delivered a *kimirwa* (an illegitimate son)," the midwife, who guided Atieno, when the latter gave birth, would whisper to her husband the day Okulu was born.

"I heard that it was a premature birth," said the midwife's husband.

"No. That was a nine-month baby," observed the midwife.

"Hmm!" the midwife's husband sighed, as if saying, 'That child was conceived out of wedlock.'

It did not take long before the words "illegitimate child" and *kimirwa* (bastard) left every villager's mouth whenever he or she mentioned the name of Odongo or Atieno, his wife, or that of the newborn son.

Whenever Atieno heard such remarks about her son, she would not back off; she fought back with stinging words and appropriated deeds.

"How many men in this village never tasted the honey

in the flower in the field? And how many planted their seeds before bringing their ripened fruit home?" She often challenged any man or woman who questioned the fatherhood and ancestry of her son. Her message: *Your son, brother, or grandson, named Odongo, fathered this child in the bush.*

Atieno would win that battle of words, but she lost the battle for people's attitudes toward her and her son. Okulu would forever be a bastard in the minds of the residents of Thim Lich. It was up to Odongo to step up and explain how the child was his. He could not, even after thirty-five years of life with Atieno!

9

Aura, a Bride before Her Time

AGE AND DISTANCE HAD MITIGATED Aura's chances. Odongo needed to travel only one mile to reach Atieno, who was then in her early twenties. To reach Aura, Odongo had to travel half a day. He had seen her only once before.

Five years ago, Odongo took some ten heads of cattle to Gor, Aura's father. Aura was then a bare-chested girl; her fruits were just starting to form, even as she was maturing fast. Even though Aura was his bride, Odongo, who was a nineteen-year old then, had nothing to say to her, a mere child of ten. *How odd!* Odongo thought. However, childhood engagement was widely practiced, and Odongo would play along, crossing his fingers that, when the girl became a woman, she would be his.

Now that Odongo had his father's orders to get ready for another trip to Tanganyika, he remembered the journey he made five years before, not for anything spectacular about Aura, who then was a mere child, but because his father had since spent a fortune toward her bride price and was planning to spend more.

Aura had been part of the duet of girls Odongo's prospective mother-in-law (Anna Ayiera) had sent to deliver food to him and one Genga, his cousin. He remembered the very words he used in his salutation of her.

"My wife, how are you?" Odongo had asked Aura.

In response, Aura had giggled, covering her face before dashing out, her cousin behind her. On that occasion, she wore a skirt embroidered with multicolored beads and a separate top of the same design. Ayiera, Aura's mother, had spent an inordinate amount of time scrubbing Aura's body clean with hot bread in warm cow ghee. Aura sparkled like a polished red gem in the sun. It was 1941 in North Mara, Tanganyika, and by the standards of the times, the young girl was properly dressed for the occasion.

"Odongo, you have a jewel in your hands; don't go and wait for too long in Kenya. If you went to Kadem and waited for six years, someone else will have drunk from her hands," Genga remarked after the girl left the hut, abandoning them with food; she had not even dispensed the water for the visitors to wash their hands.

"Let them try; I have protected her in an invisible fence of charms," Odongo boasted, serving Genga water to wash his hands. "Genga, I always told you that it pays to be humble; I'd wash your hands a hundred times if Aura ordered me to do that," joked Odongo.

"I envy your position; I hope you wait long enough to allow her to learn how to cook *ugali* and risk losing her to another man," Genga replied in kind, while serving water to Odongo.

"I'd do anything to bring Aura home," pledged Odongo. Then morsels of hot buttered millet bread took over the highway to the stomach, switching off the conversation between the men from Kadem.

The concept of husband to wife was still something of a joke to Aura. Her paternal grandfather jokingly called her 'my wife,' a reference she knew to be a joke.

Then a few weeks before, Aura overheard her father tell her mother that some people from Kenya were coming to visit her (Aura). That had been interesting. She remembered that there was another Kenyan known as Ougo, an older man, who visited her father regularly. On each visit, the man brought some animals for his father.

Unlike Gor's other guests and clients (Gor was a minor wizard), the man known as Ougo never failed to talk to Aura. He called her, "My daughter-in-law," and never failed to give her a gift on every visit. Then five years before, when Aura was ten, the man known as Odongo and his friend Genga came to visit her. Aura heard her mother Ayiera call the two men *oche* (sons-in-law). Her mother gave her food to deliver to the two guests, saying, "Aura, behave maturely, and not childishly, when you deliver food to your guests."

When Aura delivered the food, the man known as Odongo said to her, "My wife. How are you?"

Aura found the reference amusing, and something worth giggling about, because it was no different from what her grandfather called her, "Aura of Kowak, my wife" (she was named after her paternal grandmother).

Safely in her grandmother's house, never to see the Odongo again for another twelve hours, Aura recalled how her mother had spent a lot of time polishing her up with hot oiled bread before she sent her to take food to Odongo and Genga. She wondered what was so important about Odongo that her mother had to scrub her clean before she appeared before him.

The following morning, Aura's mother again scrubbed her clean, dressed her in her best clothing, hoping to send her to say goodbye to her fiancé, but that would not be. Aura escaped from home only to return after Odongo and Genga had departed for Kadem.

Even back then, Aura was beginning to ask questions; she wondered what was going on that her mother had spent hours beautifying her.

Years flew by; Aura turned eleven, twelve, thirteen, and then fourteen years, and with each passing year, her family's reference to Odongo as her future husband or soon-to-be husband became more frequent.

Meanwhile, her friend Ougo from Kenya (they indeed were friends who exchanged gifts daughter-in-law-to-be to father-in-law-to-be!) would keep pace gifting and bringing more livestock to her father. Aura was beginning to wonder when her father would tell her to go to Kenya, which she knew to be a different country.

From the fourteenth year on, Aura was a woman seeing certain secretions every month. Her grandmother and mother started giving her specific instructions about personal hygiene. They taught her about her moral responsibilities as a young woman, warning her against any games with boys, cautioning her against being alone with boys.

From the fifteenth year on, Aura knew the day to join

her fiancé was close. She was thrilled, yet anxious, because she did not comprehend leaving her mother and father to go and live with another man in a distant place. Whenever her mother and father were alone, Aura heard them mention Odongo's name repeatedly.

Aura felt the urge to join her generation in parties, yet her mother had put strict limits as to which cousin oversaw her social activities, because her parents did not want to risk losing her to any man before Odongo sealed the deal.

"Grandma, when will this wedding be?" Aura asked toward the middle of the fifteenth year.

"It is up to the Kenyans to decide when to take you away," Magi Aura said. That was true. It was not a matter of how many more cattle Odongo needed to bring to satisfy Gor. Ougo had paid enough heads of cattle to bring home three-to-four wives for his sons! Gor was getting increasingly uneasy, the longer the Kenyans took to collect their wife. Yet Ougo was still bringing more cattle, saying that Aura was worth it.

Then one day, a mournful dark cloud descended upon Gor's home. Anna Ayiera, Aura's mother, had returned from Shirare Market with some unpleasant news, and she had called Gor to her house for an urgent briefing.

Having served her husband some nuts and porridge, and the latter was through with his snack, Ayiera said, "I have unusual news to share with you."

"What is it, Ayiera? You never sounded so sad before," Gor asked, alarmed.

"It is about our friend Ougo's son; he has married another woman," Anna had whispered as if the message was toxic.

On hearing the news, Gor was beside himself with anger. He did not talk for a while. He trembled in fright, sweating profusely. The news indeed was unusual because Ougo had never slowed down the pace of bringing cattle to Gor. Had the boy found his daughter unappealing? But how could Odongo have reached such judgment about a woman he had not seen since the latter was a child of ten? Gor wondered. Gor sensed that something was not right, yet Gor could not have doubted his wife's words and sources.

"Say something, my husband; we share in Aura's problems," pleaded Ayiera.

"How can Ougo do this to me?" Gor asked in anger.

"My love, I have no answer to that; I am here with you. I am simply narrating what I heard from a Kadem woman I met at the market in Shirare. I trust her word."

"Is there any way of confirming the news?" Gor asked

"My love, don't shout; Aura is only a child; she won't care that a man, named Odongo, skipped her and married another woman," Ayiera argued. Yet she understood that, if true, the news from Kadem could be a life-changing event for her daughter.

"Where will I get all the livestock to refund Ougo?" Gor asked rhetorically, knowing that he would not have met another man and friend as generous as Ougo of Kenya. The latter had given the wealth far and beyond his son's marital obligations to the bride; and Ougo did it to honor a long-term friendship with Gor.

"My love, Aura is alive; she is worth more than the heads of cattle Ougo gave you," Ayiera said.

"Ayiera, my love, you are right, Aura is but a child; how I love her and want her married to the right man who would love her; that is all I have always prayed for God to give her. And now, we have this strange news!" mourned Gor.

"I believe that, if Odongo is the right man, he will be here soon. It is possible that the woman in his house now is some desperate soul looking for a place to rest her head," Ayiera observed, trying to believe her words; praying that Odongo would wake up from the woman's charms and run to Tanganyika to receive Aura, the woman he really loved.

"I hope so. Ayiera, I hope so! Then it is not proper to go to Kadem and confront Ougo and his son?" Gor asked, knowing that Ayiera would say "No."

"No. Gor, the man I married, is not cheap. You cannot do that!" Ayiera said.

At that very time, Aura entered her mother's house with a pot of water. She had heard a bit of the conversation, but she would not say a thing as long as her father was around. She was mature fifteen with hardly a month to turn sixteen. She too was turning out to be a tall sparkling beauty. She was the more beautiful after a scrubbing stint in the lake.

"Aura, go to Magi's house and tell her that I need some salt," Ayiera said. Aura knew that was a lie. Magi never gave anybody salt late in the evening. Aura understood that her mother (Ayiera) was telling her that she needed to be alone with her father for an unspecified amount of time.

Magi Aura was Maria Aura's grandmother. Ayiera had named her daughter Maria to differentiate the two.

"Why is my father sad like that? Is there some problem, father?" asked Aura. She loved her father. Her father loved her too. They never quarreled. If they disagreed, it never was in words.

"Your mother's supper is late. O Aura daughter of Chieng', you are beautiful. I do not know how much more cattle I have to demand from the Kenyans before I could allow you to say 'Yes' to them," Gor mourned over his daughter's unfolding fate.

"Tell the Kenyans that I have changed my mind," she joked back. That had been Aura's verbal line over the last two years; she used it whenever Ougo brought home more cattle to Gor, and the latter joked that she went with Ougo to Kenya immediately. Aura loved her soft-spoken prospective father-in-law who treated her as if she were a pet, whenever he visited, which was at least four times a year.

Aura vaguely recalled how Odongo, her suitor, spoke, but if he sounded like his father (Ougo) and was generous like him, then he would be a fine husband to her. All the news from Kenya had been good to her ears. Odongo had a modern job; he was a white man's clerk, counting pieces of gold. Now that she was beginning to view men with a woman's perspective, she longed to see him again, talk to him, and sample some of his gold.

"I would side with you, if you did! I love you, Aura!" Gor said, speaking sincerely. Weathering the initial storm, and now watching his beautiful daughter leave for her grandmother's house, Gor resolved that whatever happened in Aura's relationship with Odongo, it would not be at her expense.

"Aura, hurry up, your father is hungry," Ayiera said again, her eye locking with her daughter's.

Aura hurried away; she was a little guilty, and she never felt like that before; maybe it was due to some of the body secretions she was beginning to see.

"Gor, my dear, this matter remains between the two of us until the Kenyans arrive here, and I hope they do soon." Saying this, Ayiera was aware that the Kenyans would be on the way. She had met an agent from Ougo with the message that Odongo would arrive in her home in exactly one market week. Ayiera did not want to alert Gor about the message yet. She wanted as much silence over the matter as possible until Aura was safely inside Odongo's heart, which was not possible unless they met physically.

"I'll be in my hut for supper," Gor announced.

"You will eat here," commanded Ayiera, something Gor never ignored. He obeyed.

"What is special?" Gor asked returning to his seat.

"You are grieving; I cannot allow you to be alone," Ayiera reminded Gor of his unsettled heart.

"I was not planning to go anywhere," Gor said without contesting Ayiera's claims about his emotional state.

"I know; but do you know how lonely I will be when Aura leaves, which I want to be soon; she is Odongo's first wife, whatever Kenyans say. She has to be there immediately to take her place," Ayiera spoke, a streak of tears down her face for the first time since hearing the unsettling news.

"Wipe off those tears, Ayiera, my love. I'm alive," Gor said, consoling his wife.

"They are for you; no man should suffer a fate as yours. Aura has belonged to the Kenyans for as long as I can recall. No one will stop her," Ayiera said, mournfully. She was speaking deliberately to soothe Gor's pain. There were two unresolved questions: One, what if the Kenyans abandoned Aura? Should that happen, how would Gor get the animals to refund Ougo?

Gor had brothers who had benefited from some of Ougo's livestock, each man bringing home a wife as a result. In case of divorce, Gor's brothers would have no obligation to refund Ougo's wealth, not because they did not care, but because they were poor. These matters weighed heavily in Gor's heart as he sat in Ayiera's house, looking down most of the time, overwhelmed by the hand fate had played him.

"Those are the rules," Gor said, but he knew the rules could be broken, of course with consequences.

"Your soup is ready, my love; if you want to rest after the meal, your bed is made," Ayiera said, a milking gourd and string in her hands.

"What is the food celebrating?" Gor asked.

"Your daughter is a woman; her grandmother reminded me about that today. Your jokes with her should end, because she no longer is a child," Ayiera said with a wink. Ayiera judged that the situation demanded that they, as Aura's parents, remained cool-headed as they managed their daughter's expectations, if her Kenyan suitor found rest in another woman's arms.

"O women!" Gor whispered.

"I'll be milking the cows outside. Don't leave; I will be back," Ayiera announced, leaving her house, having tied down her husband with food, words, and expectations.

Gor ate then retired for the night; he did not bother to inspect his home before going to sleep. He needed to think matters through while alone in bed.

Things did not seem right to Gor. Why had Ougo delayed demanding that Aura joined his son? Why had Ougo continued to give him more wealth if he, Ougo, knew that his son was untrustworthy? The whole night, Gor groped for answers to such questions. He had none.

By morning, Ougo decided to leave for Tanzania; he had in his possession three cows for Aura's mother and one cow for Aura's grandmother. He played diplomat well, soothing Ayiera's angst with prime cows and reassuring Gor that Odongo would wed Aura the following season.

A year later, Odongo assembled a team of men and took fifteen heads of cattle to Gor in North Mara, Tanganyika. Ougo considered the livestock a fine his son had to pay for the latter's deplorable slight of Aura's hand. Gor received them well. The little girl Odongo saw six years before had become a beautiful young woman of mature sixteen.

Odongo had not known this, but his in-laws knew that the purpose of his journey was to take away his bride. Odongo received a kingly treatment. When on the final day, Odongo appeared before Gor (Aura's father) and his council, he, Odongo, only answered one question, which was, 'You Kenyan's, which of you is Odongo son of Ougo?'

"I am the one," Odongo responded.

"Aura do you accept Kadem as the land of your children?" Ougo asked his daughter.

Gor's question had taken Aura aback because she had no child yet. She smiled without saying a word, but she had nodded in the affirmative; that was all Gor wanted.

"Aura, your guests have a long day tomorrow; go and show them where to sleep," Gor instructed his daughter, after Odongo had paid a salutary monetary amount to the mother-in-law. The Luo call this salutary money *Ayie* (I accept your daughter and thank you for raising her well). *Ayie* (I accept) is a latter-day-post-colonial Luo marriage invention introduced to take advantage of a monetary economy.

Aura had been dreaming of this day. For six years, her mother had talked about the impending wedding constantly. Now a mature sixteen-year-old girl, Aura vaguely remembered Odongo, the man who was to become her husband and the future father of her children, but she knew she loved him.

When, a year earlier, word reached Tanganyika that Odongo, the suitor Aura had grown up dreaming about, had married another woman, Aura had cried for a week.

"Aura, it is not right that you cry over a man's hand. It is normal among our people that a man marries more than one wife," Grandma Aura (Aura's Grandma) had reasoned with her.

"Grandma, Odongo was supposed to be my husband; he has been my husband since the day I was born; that is what you used to sing to me. Now, what hope do I have when he is in another woman's hand?" Aura had lamented, yet she loved the man she vaguely remembered.

"Aura, the law of our land says that you are Odongo's first wife. It doesn't matter how many women he marries," Grandma had argued.

"What first wife? I was supposed to be his only wife," said a tearful Aura.

"Child, stop crying over a man. He is not dead. Go and bathe; you have cried enough," Magi Aura had chastised her granddaughter.

Now, a year had passed, and as Odongo and his team retreated into the bachelors' hut (Luo: *simba*), Aura was at peace. A day before, her mother had instructed her to go with her husband.

"Aura, do not let go your husband. Tomorrow is market day in Shirare. You will go there and wait for your husband," Ayiera had advised her daughter.

"Won't Baba be offended if I leave without his permission?" Aura had asked concerned, yet her heart pounded with the urgent desire to secure a place in her husband's home and heart.

"No, your father has nothing to complain about, even if you elope with the man from Kadem. Listen, Aura, you have your place to defend in your husband's home. There is someone lodging there already; go there and assume your rightful place," urged Ayiera.

That night, Aura would not move an inch from her husband's side. They talked at length, often in each other's hands.

"I don't believe that I'm here with you. Why did you break my heart?" Aura asked, looking at Odongo in the eye, her soft face and glistening moist eyes overwhelming him in the lantern light.

What a beauty! Odongo said in his heart. "It was an accident, Aura," he said in tremulous voice, determined to mollify Aura's stricken soul.

"What caused the accident?" Aura asked, her eyes locked to his; she was not looking for a lie; she had forgiven him the moment he stepped through her father's gate to claim her hand; she was imagining a future with him.

Damn, I am becoming emotional, he cursed in silence, his left eye suppressing a teardrop. "The two of us had not known each other's hearts well. Then this woman unexpectedly swooped out of sky like a kingfisher going after a fish in water, grabbed me in her claws, and started pounding on the gate to my heart; day and night, she pounded on my heart, until she found a little crack and squeezed in through it," Odongo whispered. If he had placed himself in her hands, Aura literally tightened her grip on her suitor.

"Aura, forgive me; the accident happened because you

were far away. Will you forgive me?" Odongo asked in his characteristic tremulous voice that made him the more likely to evoke any listener's empathy.

"I know you were in my heart all the time. Perhaps, I have never been part of your heart," Aura challenged, looking her suitor in the eye.

"You're in my heart, Aura," Odongo pleaded tearfully, hoping to seal her trust.

"But you are not saying it well enough," challenged Aura; she was enjoying as the man shed tears in her hands, making her feel the more loved.

"No words can express my love to you; your beauty has overwhelmed me. I love you," Odongo said, his voice even more tremulous.

"What about the other woman?" Aura asked, avoiding mentioning Atieno by name, a habit she would maintain in her marital life.

"I have a lot of room in my heart for you," Odongo replied.

"I want to believe that the room in your heart is large enough for me; I need the space, and I hope the other woman knows that," Aura warned from the security of her suitor's arms.

"I have reserved most space in my heart for you," Odongo said, wanting to believe what he said, even as his father often reminded him that a stable polygamous home demanded that the man demonstrated impartiality and fairness to his wives.

"I wish to believe you. I'm going to sleep. I know you'll not see me in the morning; go well, I have forgiven you," Aura announced trying to wiggle free.

"But I'm taking you home now," Odongo said resisting her move.

"I'll find my own way there," Aura said.

Aura planned to use an alternate route to Shirare and be there ahead of Odongo and his cousin. In this plan, her mother would ensure that the Kenyans took a slightly delayed breakfast.

"I won't leave without you," Odongo said.

"See you in Shirare," Aura teased.

"Shirare?"

"I love you," Aura said, flashed a smile and left.

Odongo remained in a dreamy state of mind, hoping to

meet Aura in Shirare.

Aura arrived in Kadem Thim Lich to a hearty welcome. Ougo was so happy he personally instructed Apudo to cook the best meal for the bride. Apudo was beside herself with excitement that she killed a goat for her. For a week, people feasted in honor of Maria Aura of Tanga. However, one heart was not happy. Aura's arrival blighted Atieno's heart.

For the past year, Atieno had lived under the cloud of Aura's impending arrival. Atieno had heard about Aura's beauty from men who had seen her. Odongo never spoke about Aura, but even he retreated from Atieno, even in bed, whenever she mentioned Aura. It was as if the Aura was kind of a goddess to her husband. Atieno knew her husband still loved her, but she felt that the said Aura was her father-in-law's very soul.

Then Atieno gave birth to Okulu, a boy, whose birth her husband's parents did not celebrate. She had a feeling that her husband's parents had rejected the boy. Then she started to hear whispers about Okulu's parenthood. 'Is Odongo the father of the boy? How fast? Atieno only arrived here a few months back,' so the whisperers wondered. She feared for her son's future in the Ougo home.

Then she was uncertain of her son's fatherhood. She had known other men in her short life as a woman. She even had been a victim of an anonymous rapist just before she married Odongo. She could not say for sure that Odongo was the boy's father. Feeling besieged, she chose to fight for the name of her child. He was an Odongo, full stop.

"I have to go to Kuja, take care of your grandson with legs like yours," she often said to Apudo, in the hearing of other women.

"What kind of talk is that, Atieno?"

"I'm in a hurry, Ma," she would say running away, her water pot in hand. Yet she was satisfied, having fired a warning shot against anybody who could have had the audacity to question the ancestry of her son.

"No one is going to get away with calling my son a stranger in this home. He is your son," Atieno often cautioned her husband, whenever the latter warned her to respect his mother.

"Okulu is my son; I'm sure of that," Odongo would assert in response.

"Let your parents know that," Atieno would demand.

"Do they doubt that he is my son?" Odongo would ask.

"Look, my dear, the women in this village are questioning as to whether you fathered Okulu, and your mother has not warned them to desist," Atieno always challenged her husband.

"Which woman doubts that I fathered Okulu?" Odongo would ask.

"I don't want to name names, but every woman in the river whispers about my son."

"Know that I love my son. And I love you," Odongo would say to end the discussion, his bag of guilt weighing down on his heart, always wondering if Balak, the man with whom he executed the heinous crime against two young women, finally would talk. Balak never talked for fear of reprisals. He already died, and the secret with him.

For years, Atieno lived a tense marital life, even as she would give Odongo four beautiful daughters. Her discomfort was over Okulu's rank in the Odongo home.

Okulu was, at the time of the heinous crime against Aura, a married man with a wife and two children. He had his home one-mile away from his father's home.

For twenty years, Okulu was the only son in the Odongo home. Odongo had thrown every earthly good and time at him. Yes, Okulu had spent some years in the modern social club known as a formal school. He had graduated out of high school with an ordinary PASS, and at the time he committed the heinous crime, he was working with the local veterinary services department.

Fifteen years before Okulu and Atieno conspired to take Aura's life, an important event blessed Odongo and Aura: Aura presented Odongo with a son named Juma. Odongo was so happy he killed a goat and then another goat for Aura, reasoning that his "elder son" needed to suckle good milk from his mother's breast.

The boy named Juma, though born twenty years after Okulu's birth, instantly was Odongo's spiritual elder son, the owner of his stool. Spiritually, Juma was Odongo's senior son because his mother, Aura, was Odongo's formal first wife. Atieno, Okulu's mother, though older in age and was the first woman to enter Odongo's bed, was subordinate to Aura, because Odongo had paid Aura's bride price years before he met Atieno.

Juma's birth had caused Atieno much angst, and she had not hidden her trepidation against the boy, right from his birth.

"If I were you, I would have killed a cow or a bull for the first son!" Atieno remarked while inside Odongo's hut. Odongo had just killed the second goat to feed Aura, the recovering mother of his new son.

"What kind of comment is that? Okulu is my first born and my first son," Odongo had responded, balancing a calabash of cereal on the floor. The audacity of Atieno to have raised so sensitive a matter as the ancestry of their son surprised Odongo. He knew that there was a level of uncertainty about the biological father of Okulu. He wondered why Atieno, Okulu's mother, was trumpeting it twenty years after his birth. *Does Atieno know that I violated her?* Odongo wondered.

"You know that is a lie," Atieno charged.

"Unless you know something I don't about Okulu's birth," Odongo fired back in anger, saying what he shouldn't have said, given the guilt he daily struggled with during their marriage.

"Are you accusing me of unfaithfulness?" Atieno asked. She was beyond herself in anger. Yes, Okulu was a developing fetus in her womb when she entered Odongo's bachelor hut; yes she wasn't sure as to who impregnated her; yes there were loud doubts with the Ougo Clan as to whether Odongo fathered Okulu, but to hear the charge from her husband's mouth after twenty years of their marriage, devastated her. In anger, she had forgotten that she was the first to have injected Okulu's paternal ancestry into the discussion.

"Save me the acrimony on a day when I am happy to see another son," Odongo complained.

"Yea, celebrate the birth of your eldest son?" Atieno had hissed.

"Atieno, I didn't make the rules," Odongo said in disgust at the circular blame-game; he was anxious to see Atieno out of his hut. He was not in a fighting mood.

"What rules? Was I not the first woman to enter Ougo's

home as your wife? Did I not break your virginity? What rules? Did I not give you a son as the first born, hardly a year of entering the Ougo home? Tell me the rules you are talking about," Atieno rumbled on, laying claim to her seniority and Okulu's paternal birthright; she was a woman fighting an old war the old way; she was fighting it verbally and loudly.

"Well, if Okulu is my first child and eldest son, then what are we arguing about?" Odongo asked, trying to diffuse the tension between them.

"Then what are you celebrating for, when this child comes after you have seen seven other children?" Atieno asked, challenging her husband, who felt exasperated because of her in-your-face challenge.

"Nyomulo, stop; I don't count the number of my children; and I won't allow you to count their number," Odongo warmed, whispering the words at a slow deliberate pace. He was annoyed, and whispering was his way of signaling his anger.

"*Nyomulo?* Do I not have a name? Call me Atieno, if you have lost all feeling for me," complained Atieno

"Feelings are mutual; you kick a man out of your house often, and he loses feelings for you permanently."

"Liar! What did you do when the other children were born? You killed nothing for me; you didn't even kill a hen in celebration," Atieno challenged her husband.

"I didn't have wealth then," mumbled Odongo.

"Now you do! Are you not the father of my many daughters?" Atieno said, raising the stakes in her sarcastic rhetoric.

Yes, Atieno was a mother of many daughters; Atieno demanded respect from Odongo because her daughters had brought wealth to him, through the generous hands of her sons-in-law. Atieno had four daughters and one son. Aura had two daughters and now a son. Odongo had livestock wealth because of the generous hands of his sons-in-law. He had to walk a thin line in his disagreements with his wives because he owed his wealth to their daughters. That was Atieno's message to Odongo.

10

Aura Survives

AN HOUR HAD PASSED since the tragedy that nearly killed Aura. She was arriving in Macalder Health Center on a stretcher. A number of villagers led by Owinyo had been making foursome turns at the stretcher. Aura's final destination would be Migori Hospital.

Aura was in intense pain, but conscious; she knew who had hurt her. Once during the journey to Macalder Aura had mumbled, "Okulu, why do this?" essentially pointing at her assailant in Owinyo's hearing. She had seen Okulu aim at her with a big stone, but she had no chance to call him out, because she was then lunging forward to hit Juma with a cooking stick after an intense argument with her young son.

During her journey to the hospital, Aura remained guarded in what she could say because she could hear some of her detractors among the clansmen exchanging places at her stretcher. The domestic politics in her home had divided the village residents into two camps: one camp shared in her tribulations in the hands of Atieno, while a smaller group of villagers opposed her, whatever the contentious issue of the day. Second, Odongo, her husband, was away on a business-cum-social trip to North Mara, Tanganyika, and she wanted to reserve her testimony for him. Third, she was badly hurt and could hardly talk; she had said enough given her circumstances.

Aura was conscious when the villagers decided that Owinyo was the one to accompany her to Migori Hospital. She had smiled in agreement because Owinyo always was the fair arbitrator whenever Atieno opened up a new line of attack against her. As the firstborn in the Ougo home, Owinyo always played his moderating role firmly but fairly.

Even in her delicate mental condition, Aura was aware that Atieno never came to her side, or if she came, she had remained silent. Moreover, no one brought up Atieno's name. Aura felt scared, wondering whether Atieno and her son were one in a scheme to kill her.

One Genga had run ahead of the stretcher-bearers and alerted the health workers to get ready to receive Aura. Thirty minutes after her arrival at the health center, the medics had looked at the nature of her head wound and decided that they could not handle her case. They took measures to lighten her pain then referred her to Migori Hospital.

Then started the bumpy taxi-ride from Macalder to Migori, during which a nurse known to Aura, volunteered to join Owinyo on the trip. The nurse had given her a painkiller at the health center, and Aura would be in and out of deep sleep most of the way. She dreamed a lot during the ninety-minute ride, and Juma was part of all the dreams.

In one episode, Aura saw Juma holding a Bible and kneeling down as a large woman held his head, while offering him a prayer. In another dream, Grace (Juma's dog) was barking, on shore, as Juma swam away across a river, holding his club across his mouth.

The scariest dream was of herself falling into a bottomless pit, crying and shouting, 'God, you can't do this to me before Juma marries a wife!' She landed at the bottom of the dark pit, only to realize that she was stuck to the neck in mud and was crying, 'Help! Help!' Then Odongo emerged from a bush to her right and pulled her out to safety.

Two hours since leaving Macalder, and after a journey through dust storms and then rain along the way, Aura finally was in Migori Hospital. Hospital staff rushed her to the Emergency Ward. She was in a deep, dreamy sleep. Aura would dream that she was in a large white room; around her were men and women in white robes. One carried a butcher's knife, his mouth and nose covered with a white cloth. Then he was cutting into her head. She blacked out in the middle of the dream.

Doctors stabilized her and observed her the whole night. The following morning, the doctors, with the help of reinforcements from Kisumu Provincial Hospital, performed the surgery.

"Juma! Juma! Where are you?" Aura mumbled; it was a few hours after the surgery.

Owinyo was outside the ICU where Aura had been recovering.

"Who is Juma!" the nurse asked Owinyo.

"Juma is her son. Why?" Owinyo asked.

"She is calling his name; he must be a special child," observed the nurse.

"Will she survive?" Owinyo asked.

"Of course, she is out of trouble," the nurse said reassuringly.

"Can I see her?"

"No. You cannot see her yet. When will the husband arrive?" asked the nurse.

"I don't know," Owinyo said. Owinyo always worried about Odongo and his habitual journeys into Tanganyika. 'Odongo, my brother, please stop your frequent journeys to Tanganyika. You are the head of your homestead; you must be there to adjudicate disputes in your home and perform seasonal rituals in time. I am your elder brother, but I can't run your home,' Owinyo recently warned Odongo to slow down his business trips, believing that old age brings increased responsibilities in a man's home.

Odongo had mumbled something about the need to straighten a few things before Juma went to school.

.Owinyo found it inappropriate to ask another man how the latter was going to straighten his affairs. Owinyo assumed that his brother perhaps was going to consult some psychic in Tanganyika. He was wrong.

Now this: Aura was in the emergency room, and Owinyo had to play the role of her next of kin because Odongo was in Tanganyika.

"He better come back soon; she could be out of here within a week," the nurse said

The first night of recovery would be full of nightmares: 'He almost killed me . . . Run! Run, Juma! Run, he is coming at you! Uuwi! Uuwi,' tumbled out Aura's mumbled words during a dream session.

Apparently, even in her sleep, her brain had internalized the identity of her principal enemy, the man who almost killed her, except she was reluctant to call him by his name. Even in surgical sleep and anesthesia, Aura remained cautious, protecting what she knew about the assailant, distrusting those around her.

Odongo heard about the tragic news about his wife and sons at Shirare border; he was on his way back from North Mara, Tanganyika, where he had been on an extended visit among Aura's people. Odongo's Tanganyikan visit had not been productive, though; he had not found a suitable woman Juma could marry.

The bearer of the message was a cereals trader in a donkey caravan from Kolal in North Kadem. She was Aura's friend, and she always stopped to rest in Aura's house before resuming her journey to Tanganyika. Therefore, Odongo believed her account about the tragic event in his home.

Hurrying away from the bearer of the message, Odongo wondered whether he could have averted the calamity in his home, if he had not whiled his time with his old friends in Tanganyika.

He immediately boarded a Polo Piach bus bound for Migori, where Arua was recovering from her head injuries at an Intensive-Care Unit (ICU) in the District Hospital.

Hurtling along rough roads in the old bus that plied cross-border routes between Shirati, in Tanganyika, and Kisumu, in Kenya, Odongo recalled the wise words Ougo, his late father, had whispered in his ears the day Aura walked into his home. 'Odongo, you are a young man married to two very beautiful women. I want you to be a fair husband. Do not fall into the trap of ignoring either of your wives. If you heed my advice, you'll have a long life.' These words spoken from the mouth of Ougo Ng'ech, one evening in June 1948, constantly revisited Odongo's mind, as the bus hurtled toward his destination.

Reviewing the sad news back in his home, Odongo wondered whether he had not lived his marital life according to Ougo's dictum. He believed he had tried his best, except Atieno felt so wronged that she never relented in her war against Aura. In the process, he, Odongo became a victim of hate. He began to hate Atieno, even withholding love advances toward her. He had failed Ougo's test of fairness.

"I guess you are Mr. Odongo," a nurse asked him at the reception where he had gone to inquire about the whereabouts of a patient going by the names Maria Aura Odongo.

"Yes, I'm Odongo; how is she?" he asked anxiously, the uncertainty bearing down on him.

"She will live to tell her story," the nurse said.

"Where is she?"

"I'll guide you there. You must be absolutely quiet, though; she still experiences nightmares."

"Nightmares?" Odongo asked absentmindedly.

"Yes; she dreams about some woman who is after her life," the nurse said before signaling Odongo to keep quiet. "Sh . . .! We have arrived; don't talk; don't cry. Also note that we had to open her head to push back a part of the skull that had pushed in against brain tissue," the nurse whispered.

They had reached the ICU and were standing outside a no-go glass chamber, inside which Arua slept on a bed, tubes protruding out of various parts of her body.

"Will my wife walk and talk again?" Odongo asked; he had heard that she could not talk.

"We will know that tomorrow when the expert from Kisumu arrives here to remove some of those tubes."

"Is she awake?"

"Put on this mask," the nurse named Meg said, fixing a mask over Odongo's mouth and nose. "They will feel uncomfortable for the first few moments,"

The nurse led the way into the secured room, in which some machines blinked on-and-off. The room was quiet except for a whirring sound from one of the machines.

Aura had been all ears when she first heard a voice like Odongo's voice. Then Odongo walked into the room after Nurse Meg. "O my love; you came? Where is Juma?" Aura asked attempting to sit up.

"No, stay still, Maria," the nurse said. "It is good to hear your voice. I knew you could talk; now I know the man who unlocks your heart," joked Nurse Meg.

"Where is Juma?" Aura mumbled.

"He is well?" Odongo lied, tears rolling down his face.

"Where is my baby? I know you are lying."

"Maria, stay still, Juma is okay at home," said Odongo, overcome with emotion, on seeing his wife, who was alive but on life support.

"Have they killed him? They were chasing him like a dog when he left home at dusk."

"Maria, Juma is fine."

"Is he preparing to go to Alliance?"

"Yes," Odongo said, lying. He was a little relieved; Maria could talk and move her legs and arms.

"Your son almost killed me; he then started chasing Juma as if my little child was a dog," Maria said, straining, tears rolling down her face.

"Ask God to forgive him; don't say anything more," Odongo whispered to signal Aura that she was talking too much in the presence of a stranger.

"You still are the man I married, a cool-headed man, who is never bothered in the middle of any storm. For many years, I have been telling you that your home is on fire, and you would not listen; now this," rumbled Aura.

"Aura, keep quiet; you are still unwell," Meg warned.

"Meg, forgive me, but I love this man; I have loved him since I learnt to say his name. We have lived a good life; yes, I love my husband. I promise to walk, again, for him. Meg, will you tell the doctor to release me tomorrow?" Aura asked, idolizing her husband.

"I will, Maria. Now you must rest," Meg said, resetting the bed sheet to cover the patient.

"I know you care, Meg. Keep me safe," Aura acknowledged.

"Well, your husband is here to stand guard," Meg said.

"You are a nice girl, Meg. Make sure he gets food to eat," Aura instructed.

"I will, Maria. Here are your pills," Meg said, putting two purple pills into Aura's right hand.

"I don't need them; they make me sleepy. Now that he is here, I don't want to miss a moment with him," Aura protested. "But I'll take them because I don't want to disappoint you."

"I'll show him where to get food."

"You know what, Meg, if you have no husband, I can marry you for my man, the old way," Aura joked.

"Sorry, I have my boyfriend. Okay, swallow the pills;

they are different; they will not make you sleepy. Good!"

"I need no more injections," Aura said, remembering the previous day's routine.

"There are no more injections; the doctor has said so. I'll show your husband to the canteen. If you allowed me, I'll show him a few dance spots in town, when the sun goes down," Meg joked.

"Well, he is in your hands for now," Aura said, smiling.

"Don't attempt to stand up yet; I'll be back with the doctor," Meg said, leading Odongo out.

"Has she been talking like that?" Odongo asked once they were out of earshot.

"No. But I knew she could talk, except she was keeping quiet deliberately. She has been suspicious of everybody. I am the only one who can give her food," Meg explained.

"Why you?" Odongo asked.

"Like Aura, I'm from Kowak in Tanzania," Meg said.

"Oh!" Odongo exclaimed.

"Who is the man she calls Okulu?" Meg asked.

"*Okulu?* Why do you ask?" Odongo asked aloud, wondering what else Aura had said to the nurse.

"Whenever Maria had her nightmares, she would shout, 'Juma, run, Okulu is coming to kill you.'"

"He is my cousin's son," Odongo told a lie.

"He is not your own son?" Meg asked.

"No. Why?"

"Who is Atieno?" Meg asked.

"She is my brother's wife," he told a lie. "Why do ask?" Odongo asked.

Meg looked at him suspiciously. She was ashamed of herself because she deeply had delved into the Aura tragic story, trying to understand how a man related to her or her husband ended up bashing her head so ruthlessly. Meg knew that professional ethics discouraged such a deep nurse-patient engagement. However, in Aura's case, Meg refused to care about ethics because she loved the patient.

Smiling, to regain Odongo's confidence, Meg explained, "Aura keeps calling the name during her nightmares."

"Who brought her here?" Odongo asked for the sake of keeping the conversation going.

"A man named Owinyo brought her here. He said that he was her brother-in-law."

"Where is he now?"

"He left earlier today. The patient didn't want him around anymore."

"Mmm!" Odongo sighed in distress, wondering whether Owinyo had sided with Atieno in the present case. Odongo knew that Owinyo and Atieno were pals of a kind. Apart from the cigarette joints, the duo often shared, and the beers they drank together, Odongo knew that Atieno always consulted Owinyo before mooting any idea to him, her husband.

Most famously, Atieno had colluded with Owinyo to push John Odemba (Owinyo's son) into Okulu's home where the man would leave vibrant seeds in Juanita's bed twice before. By the time Odongo understood what was happening, Juanita's first child was calling him Grandpa. Since then Odongo would watch in muted pain and embarrassment as Owinyo's seeds flourished, right under his nose, in Atieno's house. Odongo muted his displeasure because everyone knew that Okulu was impotent, and since Juma arrived too late, Odongo had no other son who could have raised Okulu's head. John Odemba, Okulu's cousin, was the best next alternative, and Odongo had to live with that reality, even as Atieno and Owinyo had secretly worked behind his back to guide John to Juanita (Okulu's wife). Heavier still in Odongo's heart was his well judged belief that Owinyo and their late father (Ougo) had worked in cahoots to render Okulu impotent, thus ensuring that the latter man's seeds would not see the light of day within the Ougo clan! Odongo understood that the late Ougo died believing that Okulu was not Odongo's blood. Odongo believed that destroying Okulu with his alien seeds was not a big deal to Ougo's mind that cherished his male bloodline.

"My brother-in-law, you are lost in thought, anything the matter?" Meg asked after about two minutes passed without any response from Odongo, who was lost in his own thoughts.

"No. Meg, I have a request to make," Odongo said.

"What is that?"

"I will leave here tomorrow morning; I have to go home; I need to see how things are there before coming back."

"I believe the police will come here to record a statement from you and your wife. They have been coming here daily, but we have been turning them down," Meg volunteered.

Odongo was about to say that he wanted to go and hunt for Juma and Okulu, but said instead, "Can the police come here first thing in the morning?" In fact, Odongo did not want the matter resolved within the criminal justice system.

"We won't allow them in before the expert from Kisumu releases your wife from the ICU. Moreover, we want you around her," Meg explained.

"Why must I be around her?" Odongo asked.

"There may be some people out there trying to do further harm to your wife. Some woman dressed like a nurse tried to enter your wife's room last night."

"Who was she?" Odongo asked, visibly moved, wondering how far Atieno's many tentacles could have gone to harm Aura, if she, Atieno, ordered them to do so.

"She escaped when the night nurse in the room challenged her."

"Hmm!" Odongo sighed in distress, wondering whether Atieno had released all her children against Aura and her son.

"What do you want to drink, as for food, it will be egg-sandwich until you return to your land of milk, meat, fish and honey," Meg announced, taking her liberty with culinary preferences of men from the great land of Adem.

"Any soda," Odongo said, producing a twenty-shilling note.

"I don't want to touch your money and risk trailing you around like a shadow," joked Meg.

"I have a sweet enough tongue; so I don't need a love potion to convince you to be my third or fourth wife," Odongo joked. But who could count a rich polygamist out?

"Your wife has a lot of enemies," Meg observed, not keen on challenging the handsome man to a verbal duel. They were sitting under a canvass shed near the canteen. She watched as Odongo drank his soda and egg-sandwich. She drank soda.

"They must be my enemies too," Odongo responded, wondering what else Aura's dreams had revealed to Meg about his home.

"Who are they?" Meg asked, attacking her own egg-sandwich.

"They perhaps think that I am a rich man," Odongo said, trying to throw Meg off her line of inquiry.

"No. Your enemies appear to be from your immediate family," Meg asserted, realizing what Odongo was trying to do. Work-place ethics prohibited her behavior, but Aura case was personal to her. She felt that no form of marriage should allow a woman to go through Aura's experience.

"Why do you say that," Odongo asked.

"There is the man who tried to kill Maria; he is the man you call your nephew, and she calls your son. Second, there is a reason why Maria distrusted everyone from your village after the encounter with the strange woman who posed as a nurse. I believe the 'nurse' is someone close to both Maria and you," Meg asserted, her eyes locked with those of the middle-aged man.

"Meg, don't look at me like that, you could turn the Kuja loose and end up drowning in its waters."

"I'm not tempted," Meg said, smiling. "I am standing on a firm ground, and my roots feed directly from a spring of fresh water deeper than the Kuja."

"The Kuja respects no living tree; its strength is in its tenacity," Odongo said. "Please, Meg, let's go back to Maria's safety; did she see the intruder's face?"

"I'm not sure. The woman was stopped before she entered the patient's room."

"The police will get to the bottom of it," Odongo said; he was greatly disturbed, though.

"I have to go before the Kuja sweeps me off my legs," Meg said, smiling. She was not tempted yet. "I hope you know your way back to Aura's Room," she said, walking away.

"Thank you for taking good care of Aura. When this is over, you should come to Thim Lich. I promise to slaughter a goat for you," Odongo said, wondering why Meg was giving him a second look; he wondered why she could disregard the crisis in his home and sail upstream with him in a leaky boat. "No. I'm too old for a new round of toddlers crying for my attention," he mused as she let Nurse Meg be.

What have I done to Atieno to raise her ire against Aura? Odongo mulled this question the whole evening. Before, he knew that the Atieno-Aura wars were over their sons' birthright! He wondered what had changed to release the full measure of Atieno's wrath against Aura and her son.

When he, Odongo, told Okulu to start a new home, he had done the right thing. Okulu was a grownup man, a young elder who deserved his own home. The land Odongo gave to Okulu to start a home on was the Ougos' ancestral land. Yes, the land was close to the home of Omulo (Atieno's father) but it was Ougo's land. If the move to resettle Okulu had raised Atieno's ire, he, Odongo, felt sorry about it, but a grownup man like Okulu needed his own home. He, Odongo, had not returned Okulu to Omulo's land as Atieno and idle pundits claimed.

As to whether Okulu was his biological son, he, Odongo, suspected he was, and the issue only mattered to him because of the shameful manner by which he must have passed his seed. It was a shame he walked with daily.

Is it Juma's academic progress, which has raised Atieno's ire? Odongo wondered in silence. As he pondered these matters, he fell asleep in his seat outside Aura's room where he had assumed guard duties the whole night.

It was about midnight. Aura was under a heavy dose of sleeping pills and was asleep. It was a day since he arrived at the hospital. Odongo who had been sleeping in a chair outside Aura's room woke up to soft footsteps. Excited, Odongo stood up to stretch his legs as the footsteps and the sound of a trolley grew louder. Just then, a masked woman in a nurse's dress entered his room. The woman was pushing a trolley of medical supplies toward Aura's room.

The woman stood still on seeing Odongo, but only briefly while she rolled her eyes about to adjust to the dimly lit room. Odongo was watching, scared. He saw that she wore a yellow glove on the left hand; her right hand was free, leading him to conclude that she could have been left-handed. He could see that the other glove was on the tray. Odongo looked on as she resumed her journey toward the door to Aura's room. At the door to Aura's room, the woman turned on the light, allowing Odongo to see familiar things about her. He saw strikingly familiar features about her: the way she walked, her height, the nails on the exposed hand, and her upright gait. Even with the mask on her face, the woman resembled Atieno, his wife, except the woman was far much younger.

My own daughter is a killer! Abich is part of the plan to finish off Aura, Odongo shouted in his heart. He was certain the woman was Abich, a local resident of Migori town by way of marriage to a local schoolteacher. Odongo trembled in fright as the reality of how widely Atieno's tentacles of hate for Aura had spread.

So Atieno has recruited her children to join her in her murderous schemes, Odongo wondered in silence. He could have fainted but for his solid health and a heart that had gone through life fighting every day as his wives schemed against each other. Even then, he was greatly disturbed, and he was close to his emotional breaking point.

The woman stopped at the door, pretending to read the nametag on the patient chart hanging on the door. Then it occurred to her that she had challenged her father enough. So judging, she made an about-turn to leave the room, pushing her cart.

Now seeing her, head on, Odongo was certain as to the identity of the nurse in a mask: he knew she was Abich, his lastborn in Atieno's house. Odongo shook visibly, almost losing control of his bowels as the woman turned to give him one last look.

Remembering how her father had reacted after she turned on the light, Abich knew that he had recognized her, but she dared him to stop her and blow up the mess in his home in public; she was prepared to scream loudly.

Stop me at your own peril; you have treated my mother like a spare wife for too long, she said in her troubled heart. She judged that, because she wore a mask that left only her eyes, she had caused enough uncertainty in her father's mind.

At the exit, she gave her father one last glance, saying, in her deranged mind, *Odongo, we are coming for your favorite wife and her son, then you! You can't treat Okulu like a dog and expect us to let you live in peace.*

Odongo thought of shouting for help, but he could not muster the courage to go through with it. He was not going to expose another scandal in his home. He sat down, wondering how many of his children he had fathered with

Atieno were part of the conspiracy against Aura and her children.

Is Juma alive? Odongo wondered, a chill running through him, remembering the image of his lastborn daughter dressed and behaving like a killer nurse.

Just then, Nurse Meg walked in with a trolley of supplies. She found Odongo crying silently in his seat. "Are you okay?" Meg asked, wondering whether Aura's condition had worsened.

"No. I have a fever," he muttered looking down in shame.

"Are you sure?" pressed Nurse Meg.

"Yes. It is just a little headache. Some Aspirin will do for me," Odongo lied.

"I will have the doctor-on-call examine you," Nurse Meg promised, even as she believed something new had disturbed Odongo.

"I'm not leaving this seat," Odongo said.

"He will come and examine you where you are," Meg said, entering Aura's room.

The patient had woken up. In fact, she had seen the head of the masked nurse of minutes before.

"I have to leave tomorrow," Aura said. "I feel well."

"The doctor says that you will leave in two days," Meg responded.

"Did he eat well?" Aura asked.

"Who?" Meg wondered.

"Did my husband eat well?" Aura clarified.

"O yes; he ate very well; we talked much, even arranged a future date," Meg said smiling.

"You have not changed your mind about him?" Aura asked, smiling.

"No. I don't want to get involved; he has too many enemies," Meg observed.

"That is why I need you by my side. Won't that be nice, with you and me, two girls from Kowak, taking care of their husband?" Aura joked back.

"I wish you were that nice in your home," Meg said, smiling. "Your food is here."

"I'm a nice person," Aura said, while Meg helped her sit upright without disturbing the intravenous tube.

"Here are your pills; you must take them before you eat."

"Yet another pill?" Aura asked. The pills were red whereas the previous ones were purple.

"The doctor changed your pills; one dose tomorrow and you will be ready to go home."

"Seriously, I have a son you could marry."

"I'm too old for your Juma," Meg said smiling.

"Have you met him?" Aura asked.

"He is the leading boy in KCPE in the whole Kenya," Meg informed Aura.

"How do you know that?" Aura asked.

"His name and age are in the papers."

"He is a man already; you should know that," said Maria to keep the conversation going, but deliberately saying nothing in praise of her son.

"I love you, Maria; have a good night," the nurse said, and she was about to leave the room, when Aura called her back, saying, "Meg, get someone to help my husband; the woman, the masked nurse, was here again. I don't know if my husband saw her."

"I will let security know," Meg said, walking out.

"Meg, I'm serious. My husband can confirm my account," said Aura.

"Odongo, is it true that some nurse came here in a mask?" Meg asked.

"Yes. She stood at the door, as if she were lost, then left pushing a tray like yours.

"Odongo, take care of your wife; you will get your pills soon," Meg promised, even as she knew none was coming.

Odongo entered Aura's room immediately Meg left.

"So you know the woman," Aura asked.

"Yes."

"Who is she?" Aura asked; she too had recognized her masked stepdaughter.

"I'll let you know after we leave this place tomorrow. Goodnight. I'll stand watch outside," Odongo said, trying to avoid the subject of Abich. It was too painful on him to acknowledge that his own daughter had joined her mother's scheme to harm Aura.

"Have you heard anything about Juma?" Aura asked, changing the subject, having realized that Odongo had recognized Abich.

"No."

"How was your journey in Tanganyika?" asked Aura.

"I didn't like the girl your brother wanted Juma to marry," Odongo said.

"You went to look for a wife for Juma?"

"Yes."

"What is wrong with her?" Aura asked; she was not happy that Odongo had not divulged to her the nature of his mission before he traveled to Tanganyika.

"She cannot read," Odongo said.

"Can she write?" Aura asked.

"No. She is not blind, Aura. If she can't read and write, how will she communicate with Juma, who would be in school in Nairobi most of the time?"

"You must go and look for Juma; I could be here in the hospital trying to stay alive, while my son is rotting elsewhere," Aura said, tasting a spoonful of the rice sauce that Nurse Meg brought.

"Don't say that Aura," Odongo cautioned.

"It is the dream I had the first night I spent here that is unsettling," Aura volunteered.

"What dream?" asked Odongo.

"In the dream, I saw Juma in some river; he was trying to cross over to the other side, with Okulu behind him. Juma stopped wading across the river. For some reason, Okulu turned around, Grace, Juma's dog, behind him. Then it was dark and I couldn't see Juma; then it was light again, and I could see Juma struggling to pull a big cow out of the mud before he disappeared again," narrated Aura.

"I'm not good at interpreting dreams, but your dream could be saying that he could come home with a woman," Odongo said.

"Well, that is what you want him to do, you want have him to marry some woman before he goes to school," Aura said mournfully because her son could be in danger, and marriage was not in the list of things her son needed to do soon. Moreover, she did not intend to give away her little son to some woman yet.

11

Strange Justice

OKULU AND GRACE WERE NOT COMFORTABLE with each other during the night chase. If John and Judas held some hidden doubt about the claims made by Okulu over Juma, Grace the dog was, for some reason, openly hostile to Okulu. Each time Okulu separated from the group to answer to one of nature's calls, which was many times during the night, the dog would snarl at him. It was as if the dog had observed what Okulu did to Aura her benefactor. During the same night, Grace never allowed Okulu to handle her.

The unease between Okulu and Grace came to a boil early morning. The members of the chase team were in retreat but still deep inside Bwai land. Grace was leading the way home. Whenever she hit Juma's scent, she would reverse course, briefly, before resuming her southward journey. She had a sense that she had left her master (Juma) behind, even as she was anxious to return to base. She was not a happy dog. She was hungry and cold from having waded through many streams while chasing after her master's scent. She was constantly annoyed because of the uncertainty over her master's whereabouts. Every few hundred yards, she would hit Juma's scent, search among the bushes, and hit a dead end every time; he was nowhere within sight, yet teasingly everywhere to her sensitive nose.

If Grace was depressed and annoyed over her master's whereabouts, her greatest problem was hunger. She had left Thim Lich at dusk, before her benefactor served her dinner of milk, ugali and bones. In fact, she left when her benefactor Aura was writhing helplessly on the ground, groaning in pain.

During a night spent on chasing after Juma's scent through water and dry land, Grace had to do with some small-bird-and-eggs meal because the team was in constant motion. That was no meal for a hungry big dog at work. It was a moony night; dawn was still a few hours away, and the rabbits were still up grazing on a patch of short grass in a bushy area, somewhere to the south of Got Kojowi. She was on a trail her master had left hours before. As was her practice, she made a quick detour to check the trail, looking for her master. Suddenly, there ten body-lengths ahead of her were a number of rabbits eating some wild tomatoes. Grace froze; she lay down slowly to take strategic cover in the grass. She knew she had a golden chance at getting a good meal. She was ahead of the team of Okulu, Judas, and John, and so she had ample time to fine-tune her attack strategy. Moments later, she landed amid the herd, pinning one member underfoot. The rabbit was crying for help, but none came from the other rabbits; Grace was too big for them to have attacked.

The team heard Grace growl angrily. At that time, she was tearing into the small prey. The three men of Kadem hurried to find out what the dog had encountered. Okulu, with his imagination on a wild run, reached the dog first. It was difficult to imagine what he wanted to achieve in hindsight, but realizing that Grace had pinned down a rabbit, he raised his club threatening to hit her, saying, "Let go, Grace!"

"Gr . . . !" Grace growled angrily.

"Let go the rabbit, Grace!" he repeated, reaching down to grab the hind legs of the rabbit.

If Okulu had chased Juma across the land like one chasing a dog that had bitten a mother-in-law, he was not going to bully Grace into surrendering her meal of opportunity, not on a night when eating had been a luxury to the whole team.

"Gr...!" Grace growled, but Okulu, driven by greed and hate, did not retreat. In Grace's growl, he heard a defiant voice like that of Aura's groans of the evening before. In Grace, he saw Juma, her owner.

Then something warm splashed his face. He knew it was blood. Even in the partial darkness, he imagined it trickling down from the punctured jugular vein of the rabbit. *This is warm fresh blood! This is unacceptable; a dog cannot dare me to a fight!* Okulu exclaimed in his heart, but it was the rave for the blood, which had taken over his faculties and was driving him deeper into the fight with the dog. He needed to wet a finger just to taste the blood. "Let go, Grace!" he shouted again, and Grace greeted him with an even louder-and-more-menacing growl.

A larger splash of blood landed on Okulu's left hand, helping spike his thirst for the taste of blood. "Grace!" he yelled, threatening to hit the dog.

"Okulu, leave the dog alone! She will follow us; it is soon daylight, and we haven't reached Kiwiro yet," yelled Judas.

"Mind your business, Judas. I do not want a child giving me orders. You brought this dog along, and it has led us on a wild chase. Do you know that we left Juma in the pastor's house?" Okulu chastised Judas.

"You are wrong; we left Juma in the river where we stopped the chase!" Judas yelled back.

"You two, stop the quarrel; we are far from home, traveling in the land of our in-laws. Save me the shame!" John called out; he indeed had married two women from Bwai the land of warriors

"Grace, let go the rabbit!" Okulu shouted, his heart raving for the taste of raw blood. Blinded by the desire for blood, he reached down and grabbed the rabbit carcass.

Reacting to the violation of her hard-won meal, Grace grabbed Okulu's intrusive left hand and twisted it at the wrist.

"Help, Judas, the dog is breaking my arm!" cried Okulu. He felt his left arm go numb almost immediately.

"Grace stop!" Judas ordered.

Grace let go the left hand, and in a flash, she knocked Okulu down and was biting into his right hand, apparently intent on ensuring that the man remained with no hand he again could use to touch her rabbit carcass.

"Grace stop!" Judas shouted.

"Judas, hit the dog; she is breaking the other hand; I have children to feed," Okulu cried out in pain.

"Stop it, Mayor Grace!" Judas said, trying to sound like Juma, the dog's master. He at the same time stroked her back. Mayor Grace stopped the fight and started walking homeward, her rabbit carcass left in the grass, forgotten. She walked on, as if she never had been in a fight moments before; she only was thinking of his master, home, and good food.

"Are you alright, Okulu?" John asked; he had joined the action rather late, having watched it unfold from a distance. His opinion of Okulu had always been low, and we already know why. It was about his unchallenged access to Juanita, Okulu's wife.

There is the impotent man overreaching and demeaning himself, John had said in silence, watching in amusement as 'the impotent man' fought a bitch over a mere rabbit's carcass.

Combined with Okulu's deadly cowardly act against Aura the previous evening, this latest theatre of the stupid and the absurd convinced Okulu that impotence perhaps came with irrationality and anger at the helpless. Except here, Grace the dog was not helpless; she could bite and mangle hands.

I'll give Juanita the child she has been asking for, John Odemba said in his heart, spitting in the general direction of Okulu.

"I have no feeling on my left arm," Okulu mourned.

"Are you left-handed?" John asked, knowing that Okulu was right-handed.

"No," Okulu said, feeling worthless. Why was John asking about his handedness, as if they were mutually alien to each other?

"That is good. Can you walk?" John asked, smiling.

"Yes," Okulu said attempting to stand up. However, he realized he needed help.

Okulu winced in pain, while Judas held him by the chest, dragging him to his feet.

"Isn't it funny that all people will learn from this event is that I lost my arm because I was fighting with a dog over a rabbit carcass?" Fallen, suddenly helpless, Okulu had a sense of humor to joke about his situation, which was worse than he expressed. Without both arms, one of which had thrown the stone that nearly had killed his stepmother, Okulu suddenly was a man who could not clean after himself.

"I don't think so. You know that you have greater issues you have to confront. This chase was unjust," Judas said, nailing his humbled cousin.

Okulu looked at Judas lugubriously. He was not surprised that Judas would support Juma Odongo. The certainty of the boy's indictment of Okulu was so loud that when it stopped, the groans of the dying woman he, Okulu, left in Thim Lich immediately returned to haunt his mind.

Okulu realized how shallow he had sounded in everything he had done in the last ten hours. Instead of taking a leading role in easing Aura's pain, he, the oldest man in the Odongo home, in the absence of his father, was jumping up and down the home, pointing at an innocent boy, as the early respondents took charge of the suffering body! Okulu realized how shameful his actions were. Simple, he realized that every responder had concluded that he had tried to kill his stepmother. Then he set on a path to capture the innocent stepbrother, hoping to kill or maim him before the latter talked. Now, Okulu had confirmed that Judas had brought the dog along on purpose, and that was to warn Juma as to where he, Okulu, was every mile of the chase. Now, the pain of a lost arm haunted Okulu; he perhaps never would go fishing again.

He looked at John's face, pleading for a voice of support, but it was not coming. Okulu wondered if all along, John, a junior village headman, had come to arrest him at the opportune moment. Armless, he felt vulnerable for the first time in his life; John already had the spear he, Okulu, had wielded the whole night to intimidate his cousins. Even in the partial darkness, Okulu felt John's sympathetic look that said, *Okulu, my cousin, now what do you want to do? Why not surrender?*

"Okulu, can you walk?" John asked.

"Yes," Okulu responded, even as he doubted how fast he could walk, with two arms badly abused by the dog.

Judas, the youngest man in the group, and a trained scout, had removed his shirt and was wrapping it around his older cousin's maimed hand, as he designed a cross-shoulder sling to support it.

"You need to get a tetanus shot and anti-rabbis vaccine

as soon as possible. We are three hours from Ndhiwa; the journey is shorter by bus. I know the morning buses will be in Got Kojowi in an hour; we can catch them after a thirty-minute walk," John said.

"No. I can't go to Ndhiwa," Okulu protested.

"Why?"

"I'm going to Macalder where my wife and children can visit me in the hospital," Okulu said. He had decided that he was better off if arrested among his people in Macalder than in a distant alien place like Ndhiwa.

"Let's go then!" John ordered.

"I'll follow you from a distance," Okulu said.

"Why? You don't trust us?" John asked, wondering when Okulu was going to own up and testify that he had attempted to murder Aura; John wondered when Okulu would apologize for having wrongfully accused Juma of the same offence.

"No. It is the dog; I don't want it anywhere near me," Okulu said.

John looked at Judas, who appeared to have understood what he, John, was thinking.

"Okay, we will go ahead with the dog; if you need help, please shout. The road to Macalder is ahead; you can hitch a ride from the occasional motorist, if you need to," John instructed Okulu. He did not want to be the man who brought back a fugitive only for the latter to face a murder charge and hang.

"Judas, your brother who is behind us tried to kill Aura. You should know that. I believe, she saw him, and Juma must have seen him, but it is not in our Luo character to pay for a life with another life. Let us go home; if he wants to escape, let him do so. If he wants to come back and face his clan, let him do so," John argued.

"What if Aura dies?" Judas asked. He never had seen his brother in such a testy mood.

"The law of the land shall take over," John asserted, walking homeward.

"But as an assistant headman, you are part of the law of the land," Judas observed.

"Even then, I have to excuse myself; Okulu and I are too close; someone else will arrest him. That is our Luo way. Judas, the man's wounds are of his own making; he will find his way home."

"He is injured; something could harm him, if we left him behind," Judas argued, wondering what had entered his elder brother's head. He always thought of Brother John as a cool-minded man.

"No. We are giving him a chance to resolve the issue himself," John said.

"He sounds so helpless he could die of the wound, or even commit suicide," Judas observed, bothered by John's cold-blooded ruthlessness toward Okulu.

"Well, he tried to kill a woman, but we are not handing him a rope with which to hang himself; you can see that we have taken his spear," John argued.

"When the dog attacked him, why did you stand aloof?" Judas asked, daring his brother.

"He is a murderous fugitive, Judas. We do not hang a man who has killed his kin; however, we cease to care about what happens to him. Do you get that? We let him struggle with the guilt and its consequences; we tell him to take away his wife and children (only if they are willing to go with him). All kin wish that such a man chose to go to a place so far away that that they would not reach him easily. We let the killer go never to return and share a plate with his kin. That is our way. Judas, we return a killer woman to her people," instructed John.

Judas kept walking on in silence, realizing that there was a cultural reason why John suddenly was treating Okulu with much contempt reserved for a cheap alien he was treating the latter the way the Luo treat killers.

"Judas, thou shall not beat your mother, your father, your stepmother or stepfather, so say the Luo. The consequences of disobeying this law can be severe and unpredictable. It also means that you should not enter an argument or put yourself in a situation that could force you to touch your parents or stepparents. A man must walk away when mother and father enter an intense argument; mother and father should limit their disagreements to the bedroom, in the depths of nights, and away from their adult children. A man who hangs around when his father and mother enter quarrels could find himself dirtying his hands against his father, and he could risk his father hitting back with tragic consequences. A man with grown-up sons must learn to drink less, lest alcohol leads him to act in a way that angers his sons and invites their wrath. A man with daughters-in-law must know his bounds; he cannot call the daughters-in-law names, because they can react, call him names, incite him to violence against them, and risk an all-out war between father and sons. Judas, our elders caution our sons and daughters to give their parents space, whenever the parents quarrel. In the same manner, they caution the parents to respect the spaces of their children. You get me, Judas?" John asked in conclusion.

"Yes," Judas said, looking back, but Okulu was out of sight. The latter man had left the road, having opted to take no beaten path.

His pain getting worse by the moment, and avoiding any beaten path that could attract unnecessary attraction, Okulu walked across the land, his pain lessened only because he tried to recollect his thoughts over some of the events in his life.

Okulu grew up listening to words of caution from his father and uncles; and where the cautionary words rang hollow before, now that he had beaten his father's wife, they now echoed hauntingly in his ears, reminding him of his failing to say no to his mother's claims of bias from his father.

Okulu believed that Aura, his victim, had seen him through the veil of dusk as he hurled the rock at her. The matter weighed heavily on him, and he believed the curse had caught up with him. Now, as Okulu trailed his cousins, John and Judas, he wondered what exactly had driven him to knock down Aura, his father's first wife, beyond the oath in blood his mother had administered on him.

Now in crisis, Okulu acknowledged growing up hearing that he perhaps was not Odongo's biological son, but he could not recall an instance when Odongo treated him any differently than any of his siblings. Second, Odongo never told Okulu that the former was not his son.

Okulu grew up a child of privilege. He went to a good elementary school, and qualified to join the famous Homa Bay Secondary School. If he had graduated with a mere pass, it had to do with overindulgence of a rich man's son and not because his parents neglected him.

When Okulu would not go beyond high school, he

married a boyhood friend, Juanita, with Odongo paying the requisite animal price. As Okulu matured as a man, his father gradually transferred herds of cattle to him. By the time he had his own home, he was a wealthy man by the standards of Kadem in 1980.

If Okulu's childhood and later adult life were troubled, it was because some mysterious hand made him virtually impotent early in childhood. He would recover partially but not enough to give Juanita a son or daughter. He recalled that his mother had blamed his condition on his grandfather. As a married man, he continued to watch painfully as Juanita raised John Odemba's sons. That was the most depressing feeling in his life, and now that he was hurting in the bush, he did not see how he could have blamed it on the Aura house. However, Okulu since avenged himself, stabbing back at Odemba's heart by siring a fortuitous daughter in Odemba's home.

If Okulu were to blame anybody about his mental condition, it was his mother who raised him on a diet of constant blame, drumming what she believed to be his illegitimacy, and warning of those people out to exploit it. Then there was the issue of his birthright, which his mother had spent a lifetime fighting to secure, even when tradition said otherwise.

Then there was a flashpoint: Okulu recalled that, a few years before the tragic event, Odongo mooted the idea that he, Okulu, should have his own home. Okulu eventually would get his home, a move that Atieno, his mother, detested. Atieno wanted Odongo to build a new home for her and her son; the new home would still have been Odongo's home. However, Odongo wanted his son to be a free man in his own home, doing his own things, and walking with the burdens and demands of his own home.

Okulu recalled that Atieno saw Odongo's action as an attempt to throw away Okulu from the former man's home and finally cut off any lingering links the duo shared.

Gossipers would revisit the word 'illegitimate' in reference to Okulu. 'Odongo ejects the illegitimate son,' said idle-talkers. That Okulu's home was close to his maternal grandfather's home would help to add fuel to the toxic gossip. Okulu listened to the gossips, and he became a firm believer in his mother's claims of a biased father, who perhaps was not his.

Okulu recalled growing up, hearing these venomous messages about a father who was not his, and a stepmother who was out to deny him his birthright. Then Aura gave birth to Juma, and Atieno saw Okulu's world crumbling before her eyes. Okulu recalled that on the day Juma was born, he already had joined Form 1 in Homa Bay High School. Atieno traveled all the way from Kadem Thim Lich to Homa Bay just to break the news about the damning development in the Odongo home. *'The inheritor of the Odongo stool is born!'* That was the gist of Atieno's message to Okulu as mother and son sat under a flowering Nandi flame tree by the school gate.

Okulu was not amused about the visit, but he could not have said so. Atieno was talking about the child Juma being Odongo's firstborn son; she was saying how, if Juma survived, he would take away Okulu's privileges. Okulu felt so depressed by her mother's hateful talk that he bade her bye right there by the school gate. Even then, Atieno's trip was not an exercise in futility; she had succeeded in planting the seed of hate in her son.

Okulu recalled that Atieno would be in a constant state of war against Aura and her young son, and that would be the state of things until a few days ago, when Atieno ordered Okulu to stop Juma from joining Alliance High School.

Okulu recalled the events of the darkest days of his life, while he sat, in pain, under the huge deciduous tree on Mikumu Ridge. On the fateful day, Atieno wanted to prepare some blood meal, and she had called him to return to his father's home to tap some blood from some heifer or bullock. He remembered that he entered his mother's house just before sunset, picked up a sizable pot, and entered the cattle shed to bleed some heifer for his mother's blood meal. He recalled enlisting Nyerere, Odongo's Tanzanian herdsman, who helped him wrangle, knock down, and tie up the legs of a heifer (from Atieno' stock) that was about to invite bulls to her shed. The pressure rope in place around the heifer's neck, and with Nyerere holding the heifer by the horns and jerking her head up, Okulu remembered tightening the rope a little more to isolate a specific pressure point on a specific vein his expert eyes identified. Then bow and arrow ready, Okulu hit the vein, drawing blood into the collector pot.

Okulu recalled relieving Nyerere from the stressful duty at the horns. He recalled Nyerere picking up a reed and inserting it into the heifer's mouth. Immediately, the heifer was chewing away as she donated blood painlessly, quickly yielding enough blood to fill the jar; the pressure too had fallen. Okulu recalled remaining at the horns as Nyerere secured the jar of blood, proceeded to remove the pressure rope around the heifer's neck, untied the knot on the rope around her legs, and set her free.

"O these arms never shall draw another drop of blood with a bow and arrow," he muttered, rubbing his mouth against his right shoulder to fight off a couple of gathering flies.

Back to the previous evening's scene, he recalled entering his mother's house with the blood in a wooden jar, as Nyerere escorted the heifer from the bloodletting health routine only lucky cattle occasionally experienced.

He shuddered at the thought of what happened next; Okulu recalled obediently kneeling down before his mother; she then gave him some porridge, which he drank, while Atieno mumbled some words, dipping her longest finger into the animal blood, and used the bloodied finger to mark an X on his forehead.

Okulu shuddered, worsening the pain on his right hand, blurring his memory as he hurtled across the rugged savanna grassland. A couple of yards later, a startled deer took his attention away from the pain. He soon was back to his thoughts as he crested a small ridge down which the land was under the plough; he avoided catching the attention of the ploughmen and their oxen by keeping a westerly bearing over the ridge until a small forest separated him from the farmers. Then he headed down the ridge to regain his southward progress.

He was back to his thoughts, while he scaled the next ridge, recalling his mother telling him to take desirable action against Aura and her son. He recalled the darkest moment of his life when his mother told him to kneel down, held a small calabash, and ordered him to drink its contents; he recalled his mind going blank as he sheepishly drank from a small calabash of warm blood adulterated with what smelled like alcohol. Okulu recalled how his vision improved several folds thereafter. He recalled feeling edgy and testy: Whatever else Atieno had doped the blood with had opened his mind's eye to the dangers Aura and Juma posed to him.

He remembered wiping off blood from his mouth before he hurried away from his mother's house, only thinking of reaching his home as fast as possible. He had gone through the main gate, when he looked back and realized that he had just passed his two targets at the center of the home. There, behind him, at the center of the home, Juma and Aura (Juma's mother) were arguing over food, work, and undesirable endless parties, in which the boy regularly engaged.

It was dusk and darkening by the moment. Aura was cooking *ugali*, at the center of her home, while sitting on a low stool, her light-skinned face a glow in the light from the logs of wood feeding her three-stone fireplace. Straining his ears, Okulu heard the boy asking for food, and the mother was saying "No" to his demands.

Okulu remembered that he made a detour, headed east and uphill along the euphorbia fence and soon was at a small gate, which Odongo and his wives used when they had to respond to nature's calls. He recalled carefully opening the gate, passing through it, and stopping to listen and watch his targets. Aura was hardly twenty steps away and focused on her cooking. Okulu recalled moving to his right and taking cover behind a granary to get out of her view. Okulu remembered thinking of making a few quick steps and hitting the boy with a club, he was carrying, and then knocking down Aura. However, he shelved the idea for it could have meant running over Grace the dog, which was sleeping three steps on a direct line toward Aura. Okulu was surprised Grace the dog had not barked at him, maybe because the wind was blowing toward him and away from her.

Okulu recalled seeing a pile of rocks, picking up one that filled his fist, intending to aim at Aura's head with the stone, and then clobber the teenager with the seasoned club as the latter reacted in awe. He remembered that he was hardly ten yards away, when he heard the argument between mother and son become more intense, with the boy shouting, "I want food!"

Okulu recalled seeing Aura stand up and swing her cooking stick toward Juma's head. He recalled taking advantage of the confusion, instantly jumping two steps and releasing the stone, hitting Aura on the head. He recalled how he quickly moved back to take cover by the granary, because the boy had jumped back a few steps and was not available for easy attack. Then Aura was down, groaning loudly.

"No! I didn't intend to kill her!" Okulu shouted, crying in the fast-fading dawn, awakening to the fact that he was in an alien land.

He was about to pass by a large deciduous tree, when he stopped, still crying like a kid as Aura's loud groans revisited his mind. He collapsed in fits, a giant of a man beaten by his burdens. When he stopped crying, he was at peace for a while; he even caught some sleep.

Hours later, Okulu woke up to his new reality: invalidity. He was a wounded man, suffering physically and spiritually. In pain, he now realized that the mother's message he had listened to over the years, as his parents engaged in internecine quarrels, had poisoned his mind. He realized that, much as Odongo had tried to take extra steps to please him, Atieno, his mother, always saw such steps as half measures. Whether it was paying school fees, buying clothes, or working in the fields or paying dowry to his in-laws, Atieno always told him that Odongo was not doing enough, because he, Okulu, was not his son!

Okulu was becoming emotional again in the middle of an alien land, unable to stand up. His mind drifted back to the present. Having lost the functions of his hands, he was in danger of losing his life. The pain was too much to near, and the morning heat was catching up with him, increasing his discomfort. Okulu knew that to reach home before late evening, he had to walk faster, but he could not even stand up from under the huge deciduous tree that was beginning to put on new leaves. Beaten, he lay down on his back to rest.

A mating pair of lizards teased Okulu's mind. Yes, he had a wife with three children, but he found it odd that the future of his wife and children had not featured at all in his thought process since last evening. Now leaning against the huge tree, watching birds and lizards at play, he thought of his wife and children and their future. Okulu pinched his left hand; yea some pain detectors were still there, but he believed that he would never use it again. That meant no swimming, no fishing, and no handling of the plough. What was he going to do to protect and provide for his family? Who would be there for him, a man who had beaten his father's wife to death?

"Odongo! I know that when you come from Tanganyika, you will want to kill me. You should do that. I need it," Okulu found himself shouting. "If only I had a rope, I would . . . ! No, I won't do it! If I had the strength, I would fight Odongo. No, I cannot do that. My sisters would disown me. My mother says he is not my father; so what? The so-called stool does not belong to me, if he is not my father. If he is not my father, then why has my mother led me along this path to destruction? Atieno, my mother, can you tell me who my father is?" Okulu rumbled on, angry with himself and a mother he now saw as the betrayer and a liar.

Realizing how odd that he was talking to himself in the wild, his mind wandered more toward the natural around him. His attention came to rest on a pair of mating lizards up the baobab tree. As he watched, a brightly colored, bigger and more-rugged male lizard subdued the rival male lizard in the mating pair. The victim's lost-tail dropped to a spot a few feet from Okulu's feet. "What a barbaric way to settle sex disputes!" Okulu cried out, as the victim tried to run away from the villain on hormones, only to lose his balance and tumble down twenty yards, falling on a rocky patch, a foot away from Okulu's right leg. The disfigured male was all right; a few seconds later, it was climbing back, his destination was another female on a lower branch of the tree. The new female was not amused at his lack of a tail. However, tail or no tail, the male youth insisted on courtship, trailing the female up-and-down the same branch before they fell down and continued their business toward a smaller tree twenty yards away from the deciduous tree. The lost tail continued to twitch, for the moment living a temporary life away from its owner.

"No. Not now!" Okulu protested, the scene reminding him of Aura twitching and groaning on the ground the previous evening. He had watched all that, looking for something akin to his situation; looking for some lessons he could hold onto as an invalid.

"Odemba ran over me in my home, when I was still whole. Now that I am an invalid, how daring are Odemba and Juanita going to be? Life and war for territory; my mother has been fighting for them for as long as I can remember. 'Do not eat that woman's food; she has doped it with Tanganyika charms,' she often warned me. I never listened to my mother. How could I have listened to her, when Aura cooked the best fish and meat and vegetable meals? How could I have avoided Aura's nice meals as we ate with my father in the anonymity of his command hut?" Okulu rumbled on, talking to lizards in courtship and other creatures of the wild.

"Then Juma was born, and you, Atieno, changed the line of hate toward Odongo and Aura and the baby boy: 'Okulu, I told you before, and you didn't listen to me; now, here he comes; the inheritor is here. You are doomed, Okulu. You have no future chance at anything; pray Odongo gives you animal wealth. I don't think he will give you any wealth if this boy Juma lives.' What a lie, Atieno my mother! Look at how I look: I am a one-armed fool. I am a man who beat his father's wife because he had taken a blood oath administered by his mother. Then she fed him more of the blood meal and alcohol and made him lose his head; while on a head running on alcohol, he chased his innocent brother across the land without any success. Defeated, he turned homeward, only for a dog to bite him, as he struggled with the canine over rabbit meat. How ridiculous! Here is a man whose father has many heads of cattle and goats fighting a dog over rabbit meat, while his cousins looked on in amused awe," Okulu sarcastically ranted in third-person, looking at his useless arms, beads of tears streaking down his face. He hated himself.

Some small sleep overtook Okulu's mind in the warm noontime, but his rumbles would continue in his half-sleep; he talked loudly as he fought the urge to sleep. "Mother-beating glutton, that is me; the son of wealth fighting a woman who never intended any harm against him; a man fighting a father who gave him all the wealth he needed!" he cursed. "'Okulu, it is about your birthright; he is running away with it,' Atieno, my mother, you often prodded me to anger. What a lie! What a lie! Atieno, tell me who is my father. You say you do not know who my father is; how can you fail know, when you kept singing that the man I feel is my father is not my father?" Okulu rumbled loudly in his half-sleep.

"Hi, Are you dreaming?" a voice asked, shaking him awake.

"Who are you? Do you want to kill me?" Okulu asked, struggling to sit up, with the huge tree as a prop, but he could not muscle enough strength to stand up without assistance.

"I have no enemies in this world, mister. The One I work for cannot allow that," Pastor Aaron said in his familiar pastoral voice. "Here, I'll give you a hand," Pastor Aaron added, offering a hand that the man could not take.

"Mister, I'm here as a friend willing to help you," Pastor Aaron declared, thinking that the man was hostile. He looked into the man's pained face and saw a drop of tears rolling down. Pastor Aaron saw a remorseful soul that too was hurting.

"I'm hurt. These hands cannot do anything," Okulu muttered, choking in pained emotion.

Aaron stepped back in shock; he also wondered how he was going to lift up the heavier man who had one limp hand and a heavily swollen one. Pastor Aaron bent over and held Okulu by the armpits, and was ready to assist him rise and sit on a rock. "When I pull you up, join me in the effort, and we will be fine. Here we go! Good," Pastor Aaron said, as he helped Okulu sit up.

"Thank you, Sir! I'm badly hurt," Okulu said, feeling grateful for the pastor's help.

"Is it snakebite?" asked Pastor Aaron in awe, now that he had time to examine the man.

"No. I have to go," Okulu declared, even as he could not stand up. He reasoned that the man could turn him in to the authorities. He, Okulu, had been sleeping under the tree for most of the morning. It was about noon, and the bushes were abuzz with insects and birds, all singing, producing an incoherent music into his disturbed mind.

"Easy! Relax whoever you are! You need urgent help. Look at that arm; you need a tetanus shot. What happened to you?" asked Pastor Aaron, concerned for the man's health.

"A dog bit me," Okulu said.

"Rabies! Do you know what that means?" Pastor Aaron asked

"Yea, I know what rabies is; I graduated from both

middle school and high school," Okulu said, finding something about which to boast, even as he felt that he was in danger.

"I'll take you home; you have to follow me!" Pastor Aaron declared

"What home?" asked Okulu, remembering that he had quarreled with the pastor the previous night.

"My home in Kadem."

"Who are you?" Okulu asked.

"You'll know. I work for the Lord and none other. So feel free; no one can harm you while you are in my hands," Pastor Aaron said, believing that he met the man the previous night.

"My name is Odongo from Thim Lich in Kadem. If something happens to me, you need to know where to take my body," Odongo said. He had realized that his survival would depend on the generosity of any other living soul. He could trust his life in the hands of a pastor of a church.

Pastor Aaron thought he had heard the voice and the name "Odongo" and the words "Thim Lich" from the three men of the previous night. *What luck! He must be the man who harshly talked to me last night. What change of luck for him; our God of today never allows the vengeful to see a peaceful sunset,* Pastor Aaron rumbled in silence, revisiting a familiar sermon line.

"We are not far from my home; you can sit on this bike and I'll wheel you home," Pastor Aaron offered to help Okulu, who had no choice but to oblige.

12

Abich, the Odd Seed

TWO MORNINGS AFTER ODONGO'S ENCOUNTER with a masked Abich, Hospital Security came to pick him up from Aura's ward. The Hospital Administrator wanted to consult with him over a matter concerning his wife's safety at the Hospital.

"I can't leave my wife alone after what has been going on here," complained Odongo to the man in a white lab coat. The man was a Clinical Officer of Health (COH).

"Corporal Odek (a Security Officer) here will stand guard while you are away," the COH said reassuringly. The issue of Aura's safety was a concern to all within the hospital administration.

"Okay then," Odongo said, picking up his walking stick to follow the Clinical Officer of Health for a short walk to the Hospital Administrator's office. Odongo wondered what was afoot.

The scene he confronted in the Hospital Administrator's office shocked him. *What has Abich done this time?* Odongo asked in silence, trembling, as the medical staff looked on blank-faced. Abich looked at her father defiantly. There was no love in her face, only hate.

"Mr. Odongo, do you know this woman?" Dr. Otago asked. He was the Head Medical Officer of Migori Hospital.

"Yes," responded Odongo, chocking, his tremulous voice hoarse with emotion and shame.

"Who is she?" Dr. Otago asked.

"My ... She is my . . ." Odongo struggled to make a sentence.

"Mr. Odongo, help us to keep your wife safe here in the hospital. What is her name?" Dr. Otago asked.

"You know her name," Odongo whispered, threatening to hit Abich with his walking stick, but the guard who had escorted him held the stick.

"Mr. Odongo, if you want to cane your married daughter with a stick, go ahead and do it," challenged Dr. Otago.

"How dare you, a married woman, plant a curse in my home?" Odongo whispered, threatening to use his stick against Abich, with the guard shielding the woman.

"Is she part of the group that conspired to harm your wife back in Macalder?" Dr. Otago asked. He had some background information on the strife in Odongo's home, having talked to Owinyo and listened to some of the patient's dreams.

"I don't want to talk about that in my daughter's presence," Odongo protested.

"Take her away," ordered Dr. Otago."

"Where do I take her?" asked the guard?

"Call Migori Police; they should be responsible for this investigation," Dr. Otago instructed before he turned to Odongo and asked, "Mr. Odongo, what did you do to your daughter that she has taken it upon herself to kill your wife?"

"Dr. Otago, the children of today often take domestic disagreements a little too far," Odongo attempted to justify the general discontent in his home. He was a disappointed man. It was one thing for turmoil to engulf a home, but here Atieno and two of her children were on a mission to kill Aura. Why? What had he done wrong to elicit such outrageous responses from his children against their stepmother? Odongo wondered.

"You are a polygamous man; find away to quench the anger in your home before it kills you or someone dear to you," advised Otago.

"These things happen, Doctor Otago. This is an eye-opener to all of us who are husbands and parents."

"You can go back to your wife but remember that she needs a peaceful home, otherwise, she won't recover fully."

"Thank you, Doctor Otago; tell them to let the misguided girl free; she has learned her lessons."

"That is a matter for you to explore with the police. Mr.

Odongo, bye," Dr. Otago dismissed Odongo.

My Luo people and their wives! Dr. Otago wondered, a sense of guilt and melancholy crowding his mind. Guilt because he, Dr. Otago, had two wives whose coexistence was not peaceful and he remained sane only because he kept the wives in two cities that were scores of miles apart. He was melancholic because he considered himself a victim of a polygamous system that taught him to hate his father and some of his stepmothers when he, Otago, was still a young adult in middle school. Had it not been for the intervention of his elder sister who would be properly married in cash and cattle wealth, he could not have made it to college. His father had ten wives, a couple of whom were always at war of words on any day.

"Damn! The poor woman is a victim of her father's messy home!" Dr. Otago cursed, pressing the intercom. "Greta, can you give me security?" he buzzed his secretary.

Moments later, Major Okowa, head of hospital security, was on the line.

"Major Okowa is here!"

"Major Okowa, can you do me a favor?" requested Dr. Otago.

"Sure I can help, Doctor Otago? I guess you are calling about Rita Abich; I can't blame you if that is the case. Doctor Otago, she is quite a catch," boomed Major Okowa's voice at the other end of the line.

"Major, if your men have not escorted the misguided woman known as Abich to Migori Police Station, have her released. We don't want to be the ones who set her foot firmly on a criminal path. Do you see what I mean? Prisons change petty convicts into criminals," Dr. Otago went to great pains to defend his decision to release the woman.

"She still is here. I was about to call the strong men (meaning Kenyan Police) to come and pick her up, but I have not. I concur with you; and I perhaps have a soft spot for her, but I must say she looks so innocent and delicate that she would die in a jail cell," the Major said mournfully, genuinely touched by the woman's strongly feminine physical features, including her long and delicately vanished fingernails.

"I hope she does not feature in the occurrence book

yet," Dr. Otago said.

"Well, she does, but I have just recorded that she was a victim of mistaken identity. She will be in your office in a few minutes," Major Okowa said.

"Can you tell your people to escort her to my office? They should avoid the Emergency Wing," Doctor Otago instructed. He did not want to risk the 'bad girl' bumping into her father so soon.

Minutes later, Abich again was sitting before Dr. Otago inside his Office, where she had been in handcuffs moments before, wondering what the doctor was trying to achieve.

"Abich, go back to your children, your father pleaded that we release you. Promise me that you will be of good conduct," Dr. Otago said, looking at the young woman in sympathy, who looked anything but innocent.

"Thank you Dr. Otago. Just a correction, I am not what they say. I did what I did, so that I could see my stepmother, something they had denied me," Abich lied.

"I wish I could believe you, and if we arrested you by mistake, forgive us," Dr. Otago said.

"Another correction . . .," Abich tried to say something, but the doctor signaled her to stop.

"Abich, you can go back to your children," Dr. Otago ordered.

"There you go again: I have only one child. Second, I am a woman; call me Rita for a change."

"Regardless, Rita, go back to your husband and child, and forgive me if I sounded rude or demeaning to you," Dr. Otago said, wondering what the woman was trying to achieve. But even in one of his best moods, she was not the kind of woman with whom he could entrust his back, thanks to what he knew about her.

But Abich already sensed that his hostile arms-length attitude toward her could change, the longer she hangs about his office. His darting eyes started to focus on her chest up.

"Doctor Otago, I am Rita Abich, an independent woman; I'm not some lost property that must urgently return the owner known as my husband."

"I said forgive me if I misspoke, Rita," if I may.

"I missed marrying a doctor by a day!" Rita observed, cheering up.

"Ah! You did?" Dr. Otago said, raising his eyebrows.

"Sure; though the teacher was just too fast for him on the dance floor," she pushed, smiling.

"The teacher; who is the teacher?" the Doctor asked, not believing that the gem before him was married to some teacher who had beaten another doctor, like him, to the prize woman. *That should not have been*, he said in his heart.

"Doctor Otago, you seem not to be listening to me, or you are convinced that I am a killer on the prowl among your patients," charged Abich, trying to be the victim of Migori Hospital Administrators—the principal among whom was Doctor Otago.

"Now that is an unfair accusation; I am listening to you, Rita," Dr. Otago confessed. He wondered why the woman of dubious record was beginning to tempt him. Was it her gutsy approach to dialogue? Here he was, a doctor, attracted to a woman he knew to be a criminal impersonator. Why did he ask hospital security to bring her back to his office? He wondered in silence.

"Can you examine me?" Abich asked.

"Examine you for what ailment? Are you unwell?" the Doctor asked, wondering if the woman was mentally stable. *Why am I conversing with this woman?* Dr. Otago wondered in silence.

"A friend told me that a woman should get a physical examination every year," Abich said.

"What friend told you that?"

"A white nun; she was my teacher in high school."

"You graduated from high school?" the doctor asked, realizing that he was dealing with a woman with a relatively informed mind in the 1980s Kenya.

"Yes."

"If you want a physical examination, go and book with the reception, pay twenty shillings, and they will assign you a doctor," explained Doctor Otago, trying to extricate himself from Rita Abich.

"I'm here, why not examine me, Doctor?" Abich asked in a seductive tone.

"Rita, my dear, hospitals don't work like that. If you died as I examined you here, inside my office, and I dumped your body in River Kuja, the hospital should have away to account for your body in order to satisfy your husband. That is why the hospital demands that we track your movements while you are here. Go and register right now and let's see which doctor attends to you," said Dr. Otago, amused, but his heart told him that Rita was worth knowing in detail.

After another round of arguments on the unrelated matter of "life in polygamy," which Rita Abich won by arguing that weak men are bad for polygamy, she left Dr. Otago's office with the understanding that she would book an appointment, and that she insists on seeing him. She booked an appointment and became Dr. Otago's patient. Rita hence started a relationship with Dr. Otago that would blossom in an unexpected way. This story is not through with them yet.

Abich was the last of the four Atieno daughters with Odongo. Odongo had since given her away in marriage to a man within Migori area. She had reasons to be angry against her father, and the reasons had accumulated in her lifetime, thanks to her mother's constant complaints against her father and his "other wife," the loved one, meaning Aura.

In the last year, Atieno's complaint was that Odongo had treated Brother Okulu like a child relative to the juvenile son, Juma.

"Odongo has returned Okulu to my people. My children, your father has located Okulu's home hardly a step from my father's land. Odongo has returned Okulu to his mother's birthplace," so Atieno told her daughters. In this act alone, Odongo has made a public declaration that Okulu was not his blood," so Atieno told her visiting daughters.

The Atieno daughters had come to see their brother's new home, which was built on the Ougos' ancestral land, though close to a piece of land the Ougos had sold to Omulo, an alien from Sakwa, and the father of their mother, Atieno. This visit occurred hardly a month before the tragedy that nearly took Aura's life.

"Is Okulu not our father's son?" Alal, Atieno's eldest daughter, had asked; she was thirty-two years old.

"I conceived Okulu the night I stepped inside the Ougo home; I would deliver him seven and a half months later; he was small, though," Atieno had strained to explain the circumstances that had surrounded Okulu's birth. Atieno's daughters never heard the explanation before.

Arua, the third born, and Atieno's second daughter, was grieving within in shame, having heard from her late paternal grandmother how her mother, Atieno, was "clearly pregnant and spitting saliva like a cobra" the evening she walked into the Ougo home.

Among his children, Odongo's blood was thickest in Arua; she defended her father relentlessly whenever her mother cast him in bad light.

"Arua, my daughter, I want you to stay in school, but when you decide to marry, never walk into a man's home with a child. It means trouble; if the child is a boy he becomes an instant reject," Odongo used to warn his favorite daughter. Arua was seeing a regular boyfriend, something her father detested, while her mother had abetted. Therefore, as Atieno revisited the issue of Okulu's ancestry, Odongo's direct caution to Arua gained more relevance to the latter woman.

Yet at no time in Arua's life had she seen or heard her father act in a manner to suggest that he regarded Okulu as none other than his son.

Arua could see that Okulu lacked all the features his siblings shared with Odongo: a hairy pimple-like scar was on every child's left cheek; even the half-siblings from Aura's house walked with it. So listening to her mother that evening, Arua was beside herself in rage, wondering why her mother was making things up, but she deferred any word about it.

Olga, Atieno's fourth-born and third daughter, had no opinion, but she found her mother's attempt to explain how their brother was born thirty-five years before intriguing. Second, she loved her stepmother's children like her siblings. To her, having another mother within the Odongo home was the best thing to have happened. Aura, her stepmother, was a better cook than Atieno, her mother. As a child, Olga ate from whichever pot was ready first. Now a teacher in Gwasii, and a mother of a son born to a monogamous man, she found her mother's complaints about how Odongo had treated Okulu depressing.

"Arua, are you escorting me to the bus-stage in Macalder? I should be in Sori at sunset, and I have to stop by Aura's stall at the market; she promised to give me some millet flour for my morning porridge at school," Olga had said, standing up, inviting a harsh look from her mother. With that, Olga and Arua left their mother still complaining about their father and his favored wife, Aura.

Alal followed suit, even as she empathized with her mother's concerns. She had the farthest distance to travel; she had to reach Homa Bay via Migori. She too could not recall any instance when his father showed open bias toward any of his children.

Sure, Juma is a spoiled child. Nevertheless, is he not the lastborn in the Odongo home? Alal posed in silence. She grouped the rest of her mother's complaints, such as how often Odongo visited her mother's house, as normal. Alal believed that issues about access to a husband were issues every woman must struggle with as her youthful luster goes south every day. She, Alal, had started seeing those signs in her own relationship with her husband.

That left Abich, the youngest Atieno sibling, alone grieving with her mother. Unlike her older siblings, Abich believed in her mother's word that 'Odongo had mistreated Okulu, as if he were not his seed.' She felt that her father had mistreated her mother when he married Aura. Abich believed that Aura had been the source of all of their mother's problems.

Therefore, when Abich would hear rumors that Aura was dead, she rushed from Migori, where she was married to a local schoolteacher, to come and give Aura a deserved farewell. She had intended to mourn and ululate loudest.

However, when Abich alighted at Macalder Bus Stage, she met Alal who told her, "Abich, Aura is not dead but badly hurt. Some unknown assailant hit her on the head with a big rock. Some people claim that Juma was responsible for the attack."

"Really? Will she live?" Abich asked anxiously.

"She could not talk when she left here on a stretcher," Alal said.

"She could survive?" wondered Abich.

"Yes. Why not?" Alal asked, visibly angry at her younger sister's attitude toward Aura's fate.

"Nothing, I thought my source was reliable," Abich said, sounding disappointed.

"Aura was rushed to Migori Hospital. She was badly

hurt," said Alal. "You are from Migori, have you heard that she died at the hospital?" Alal asked, surprised at her younger sibling's tone and body posture. Alal thought that her sister was smiling. Abich's black dress had not made her image any milder; it was inappropriate given that Abich was fighting for her life in Migori.

"No! Where is my mother?" Abich asked.

"Our mother is home," Alal said.

"Where is Okulu?" Abich asked.

"We heard that he went after Juma."

Thus filled in, Abich left Alal without saying goodbye. Abich rushed to the Odongo homestead to find a mother who kept talking to herself.

"Mother, what is the matter?" Abich asked after she was inside her mother's dark house, where the only window remained shut, even though it was broad daylight.

Atieno stopped talking and willed her tortured spirit to enable herself to stand up. "Abich, that must be you," she asked in a hoarse voice.

"Yes, Ma."

"Thank you for coming. Alal was here, but you know her type; she was more worried about Aura's health than the problem Okulu faces in this home."

"I met her in Macalder. She was on her way to Homa Bay onward to Migori, where she wished to see Aura."

"Ignore her. Your brother could be in trouble; he left here last night, going after Juma, and he is not back yet," Atieno whispered.

"What do you want me to do?" Abich asked.

"She must not live! I pray Aura must not live. Okulu would be in trouble if she lived."

"She must not live!" Abich added in refrain.

"Go back to Migori and see her, that is where Owinyo took her," Atieno said.

"Why should I bother to see her, if she is alive?" Abich asked.

"Abich, use your head," Atieno whispered anxiously.

"Where is Odongo?" Abich asked, calling her father by his middle name.

"What do you think? He, as always, is traveling in Tanganyika, visiting with his wizard friends. Twenty-six years and counting, Odongo still takes bride price to Aura's people. I don't know what magic they fed him,"

Atieno spat out the words in anger.

"I have to go," Abich announced.

"Take this money for your lunch. Go. Make sure you visit Aura immediately, but be careful. I love you," Atieno said, hugging her favorite daughter.

Atieno always said that, if Abich were a boy, she could have straightened her father's ways. By what means Abich could have achieved such a feat, Atieno never declared, but Abich hated her father to the point where she never cooked a meal she understood to be specifically for him. When her husband tried to give Odongo, her father, more than ten heads of cattle in bride price, she stopped him. Since she started living with her husband, she made sure that any gift from the man to her parents went to her mother directly.

Abich was so unflinching in her hate for Odongo and Aura that Atieno believed that her young daughter was capable of devising the means to finish the job her brother had left unfinished the previous evening.

13

Intent to Kill

ABICH LEFT MACALDER for Migori at a time when a drowsy heavily sedated Okulu was halfway to Macalder. Okulu was approaching Thim from the north, in the caring hands of one Pastor Aaron of Mikumu Ridge in Bwai, who had served him some painkillers he had come by in the course of his ministry to nurses. Okulu was badly hurt, thanks to a fight with Grace (Juma's dog) over a rabbit's carcass.

About the same time, Juma was waking up on top of the Sinai in Bwai North, adoringly watched by one Elizabeth Ochieng, the young woman he had rescued from a volcanic quicksand; the young woman, who called him "my superman."

The other Odongo female siblings were still in the dark about the tragedy unfolding in the Odongo home. They were the Atieno daughters Olga and Arua, and the Aura twins, Leah and Rachel.

Odongo was on the way from Tanganyika; he would be getting the information about the tragedy in his home in a few hours.

Once in Migori, Abich gathered the necessary equipment for her project. She had a neighbor, Jane, a single woman and a nurse, who often aired a lot of wet nursing apparel on their shared backyard. Abich disapproved of Jane's behavior, believing that the latter was showing off her trade. Jane's professional garbs and clothes angered Abich greatly; Abich saw Jane as her competition and threat to her young marriage Philip. When Jane aired the apparel prominently on the line outside the townhouses she and the Philips shared, Abich routinely locked her door to the backyard so that the clothes remained out of view of Teacher Philip. Abich saw the airing of the nursing clothes and other apparel as Jane's effort to remind Teacher Philip (Abich's husband) that he married a homemaker with no professional prospects, except "bearing children and cooking," to quote a phrase from Abich's rumbling deluded heart.

One morning, Filgona, Abich's elderly house help, complained about having to walk around the house to go and air wet clothes in the backyard. In response, Abich retorted, "Filgona, I lock the door to the backyard to ensure that my children don't get exposed to dirt from the nurse's uniforms." She would then be talking while all over Philip, as she served him tea.

"I didn't know that a nurse's uniform is contagious," Philip remarked.

"I don't want you to inject yourself into my instructions to my maid, Philip dear," Abich had cautioned her man.

Filgona never again would complain about having to walk around the building with wet and heavy washings. On his part, Philip religiously avoided talking with Abich's housemaids. Even then, the Philips residence saw many housemaids each year, and whenever a maid left, for whatever reason, Philip always bore the blame, and he could do nothing about that.

So Abich always had a maid, because, like most modern women married to modern men, Abich needed a maid to take care of the children, wash clothes, and cook food.

On the day Abich returned from Thim Lich, ready to embark on her lynching mission, Philip was traveling somewhere between Migori and Nairobi. He would be away for a week.

Reaching home at a time when she knew her neighbor Jane was asleep, in anticipation of a night shift at the hospital, Abich picked off the set of apparel she needed for a trial run at the hospital.

Abich was at the hospital within the hour and had no trouble inquiring about the ward wherein Aura was recovering. It was after the surgery and Abich could only view her from outside. Moreover, she, Abich, did not want to record her name anywhere. She met Owinyo outside the wards, and the latter narrated to her how Okulu could have harmed Aura terminally.

"Where is my father?" Abich asked, pretending to be concerned.

"He is traveling in Tanganyika," Owinyo replied.

"Where is Okulu?" she asked.

"He has gone after Juma," Owinyo replied.

"Why is my mother not here?" Abich asked, faking concern.

"She is the only one at home, handling Aura's friends, who are coming in to console the family," Owinyo said; he was lying.

"You need something to eat, my uncle," Abich said. She took Owinyo to a place to eat. Owinyo appreciated the gesture. He had had a long day and night, handling questions from the doctors; he even had signed the form authorizing the doctors to proceed with the emergency operation that saved Aura's life.

"I'll be back," Abich had reassured Owinyo, who had opted to visit a bar and restaurant instead of a traditional food-only joint. He had nothing to worry about; his sister-in-law was, according to the doctors, out of danger. Owinyo would drink too much, and would not return to Aura's ward. That gave Abich all the time she needed to study the traffic patterns around the ward where Aura rested.

Aware that Owinyo was in the hands of some night crawlers of Migori Town, Abich entered one of the Ladies Washrooms on the Emergency Floor, and quickly changed into the nurse's uniform she had "borrowed" from her nurse neighbor. At a supplies room, she had identified, she picked up a trolley with some basic supplies, which was all she needed. She was on her way to finish off Aura; how she was going to finish off Aura, she had not decided, but she had seen a nurse go into the room and adjust some things hooked to tubes that entered the patient's body in the belly and neck. If disconnecting the tubes became a problem, she would suffocate her. Abich had the time to execute her plan. By her estimation, Owinyo would not be back soon. When she last saw him, there was a woman all over him, as he drowned himself in beer, to relieve the stress of the last twenty-four hours.

Abich opened the door. Bad luck greeted her; there was a doctor and a nurse looking at the patient's record; the nurse and the doctor saw her before she could retreat.

"Jane, give us a few minutes, then you can see the most famous patient in Migori," Dr. Gagi said.

"I'm sorry, doctor," Abich said, happy that she was believable, but she was not coming back tonight. Abich thought she saw the patient blink when she talked.

The patient had recognized her voice.

Abich made a quick turn at a corner, left the trolley, where she had picked it from and left the hospital through the main gate. The maid and her child were asleep by the time she returned home ten minutes later.

She served something to eat. "I hope tomorrow will be a better day. It has to be tomorrow night," Abich whispered, clearing the last crumbs of food from her plate.

Back at the hospital, Aura, the patient, was trying to tell Dr. Gagi something the doctor could not understand. She had not only heard Abich's voice, but also saw her face. Aura felt scared.

The intensity of Abich's hate for Aura only compared with the intensity of her mother's hate for Aura. Aura understood that. Aura knew that Abich was the only child in the Odongo home who never ate anything she, Aura, cooked. Even Okulu, the man who had assaulted her, still asked for her food whenever he came to see his mother or father.

Seeing Abich, Aura remembered what had happened to her twenty-eight hours before.

"She is a killer!" she finally whispered to Dr. Gagi.

"She talks, Meg!" Dr. Gagi shouted, thrilled that the patient had spoken for the first time since she arrived in the hospital on a stretcher. However, what Aura had uttered, and the frightened face Dr. Gagi saw on her face, made a chill run through his spine.

"I always thought she understood everything happening around her. She always dreams audibly," Meg said, leaving to look for the intruder.

"Who is she, Aura?" Dr. Gagi asked.

No response; she was peacefully asleep again, or she was pretending to be asleep.

"Aura! Aura!"

"Yes, Doctor."

"Who is she?"

"I'm tired," Aura said. She did not want to share her experiences with the doctor.

"Okay, Aura; you are safe; I love your voice. We are here to protect you," Dr. Gagi said, pressing the patient's left hand.

"Dr. Gagi, she has disappeared," Nurse Meg announced, reentering the ward.

"But you called her Jane," Dr. Gagi said.

"The badge she wore read JANE. She is not the Jane I know. This one was darker-skinned; the Jane I know is lighter-skinned and taller," Meg said.

The following night, Abich hit the wards around eleven o'clock. On this evening, she wore a mask. Anybody watching her enter the ICU would have understood why a nurse working in the ICU would be in a mask, because, occasionally, doctors put some patients under quarantine.

Stepping cautiously, Abich met the shocker of her young life: there, slumped in a seat, half asleep, was her own father. She visibly shook, rattling the loaded tray she was pushing. Then she relaxed on realizing that the mask had covered the whole of her face, except the eyes.

No, he does not know me; he can't recognize me! she said in her heart, before resuming her forward progress.

Then what? Abich wondered, approaching the entrance to the patient's airtight room. Through the see-through glass door, she could see machines around the room, with an array of colored lights blinking in sequence, treating her to a whirring musical sound and a rainbow of colors. As a mother who had experienced a difficult childbirth, the machines fascinated her, but they never made her feel intimidated. Abich understood that her target was on some kind of support to breathe in air and eliminate water.

Abich pretended to read the name on the patient sheet clipped to a clipboard hanging on the door. She had decided not to enter the room. She judged it too risky.

Even if the old man were not Odongo, my own father, he could have been a guard, and he is not going to stand idle as I disconnect the machines or strangle the patient. Damn you girl! Abich judged, cursing in silence. She turned around and purposefully wheeled her supplies out of the room, even though she was tense.

Underneath her mask and skin, Abich was in panic. Once outside the ward, she literally ran, pushing the trolley down the corridor. In the women's room, she entered a washroom and changed into her civilian clothes, trashing Jane's uniform into a waste bin. She had not removed the nameplate JANE from the uniform, an error that would return to haunt her.

Someone had been watching Abich as she entered the ICU and out. A security guard had seen her. Walking briskly, the guard left his companion by the ICU and rushed toward the Ladies Washroom. The guard waited in the corridor for her to come out of the Ladies Washroom. She never did; she had used an emergency exit into a bush behind the hospital.

An hour later, she was back to her house, where she would remain awake until morning, anxiously waiting for a knock on her door. However, no one came for her.

Meanwhile, at the hospital, a female sanitation supervisor had saved the male guard the embarrassment of having to enter the Ladies Washroom.

"Some suspicious masked nurse entered that room an hour ago, can you check if she is okay?" requested the guard.

"I will check."

Moments later, the sanitation supervisor came out saying. "There is nobody in there, but there is this bin with a nurse's garb. Yea, the nametag on the garb is Jane."

There was a Jane working in the hospital; the guard would confirm that in the morning. Jane had been on night duty in the Children's Ward the previous night when the fake Jane visited the emergency ward's ICU.

Hospital Security called Jane to their office late morning.

"Were you at the ICU Wing last night?" probed the guard.

"No," Jane replied

"Is this your dress?" the guard asked Jane.

"I lost a dress from my airing line two days ago," Jane explained.

"There is someone going around the ICU in your name. You need to know that," cautioned the guard.

"Thank you," Jane said; the incident worried her. She had her job and name to defend, except she did not know how to go about it.

"You can go, but we have to retain your uniform and badge for dusting for dusting and fingerprints. We will call you back should we need your help with the investigation," the guard said, talking big, knowing that that was the work of specialized police units.

The duo parted, with the guard headed toward the Canteen, the uniform locked in his office, and Nurse Jane headed back to her station at the children's wards.

Jane had a long day, anticipating security calls that never came. In the evening, Jane met Filgona, Rita Abich's housemaid, in the backyard as they collected clothes from the airing lines.

"Filgona, how are you?" Jane asked.

"I'm fine, Jane."

"I need a worker like you," Jane said, for lack of what to say to Filgona, a woman who was old enough to be her mother.

"I'll look around; I need company now that Abich works at the hospital," Filgona said, not knowing that she was passing a vital clue to Jane.

"What does she do at the hospital?" Jane asked all ears, thanking her luck for the fortuitous information.

"She dresses like you. She must be a nurse," Filgona said.

"I believe you, Filgona. But has Abich trained as a nurse?" asked Jane.

"She never talked about it," replied Filgona.

"Have me in mind, I need a helper," Jane said, hurrying into her house, believing that her neighbor was the one who had adorned her uniform at the hospital. *But why?* she wondered in her heart.

"I will look around, Jane," Filgona said, wondering why Jane had quizzed her over Abich's work at the hospital.

Later in the evening, before Jane could report to her bosses about her suspicious neighbor in a nurse's uniform, hospital Security guards caught Abich, while she was scaling a wall dividing the ICU and the Children's Ward. In her possession were a rope and a knife. Abich showed no remorse; she maintained her innocence and never confessed to her criminal intentions.

If Abich had made it to the ICU wards, she would have met an empty room. The doctors had moved the patient into a recovery room. Aura was out of danger, but she still needed to remain under watch for another week. What the doctors feared was that, if they released her, she would return to menial routines of a rural woman and risk her recovery. Second, there had been an attempted murder on her, and the police had yet to investigate the case in order to assign responsibility for the crime. In short, the assailant was still at large in the patient's rural home. Even then, hospital authorities had arrested a woman (Abich, a member of the victim's family) whom they had set free after Odongo, the patient's husband and the suspect's father, had declared that the guards must have misunderstood the suspect's intentions.

14

Daughters Unite a Grieving Family

ON THE THIRD DAY since Aura's admission into the Intensive Care Unit at Migori Hospital, she received her daughters, Leah and Rachel, and stepdaughters, Alal, Olga, and Arua. That Abich had refused to accompany them to the wards depressed the Odongo daughters. Though Atieno was a self-declared foe of Aura, the Odongo daughters did not understand why Abich, their sister, had joined her mother in the never-ending battle over their dad.

"My children, your mother here (Aura) is a victim of some of you. You can see that both of your brothers are not here; none of them followed Aura here. You can see that Atieno your mother is not here. That should not have surprised me under ordinary times because Aura and Atieno always fought their endless war, even as they ate from the same plate unprompted. Their war is over my soul and it will continue until I die, and even after. However, my children, these are no ordinary times; Aura tasted death; she knocked at death's door. She told me that if death had opened the door to her, she couldn't have gone in without knowing where Juma went."

"Dad, you don't know how a woman feels over her lastborn child," Alal cautioned. She was sitting on the patient's bed, with Aura resting her head against her. Alal was Atieno's oldest daughter. After Aura set root in the Ougo home, Alal grew up seeing her stepmother as her big sister, and so would the other Atieno daughters, except Abich who would arrive a decade later and turn out to be an unusual seed.

"I don't know, Alal; Atieno has not made it here, yet she was home when Aura got hurt. Why? Well, she is still at war, even with her co-wife in her deathbed," Odongo replied.

"Alal ignore your father's words. I'm in no deathbed. Atieno is the only one taking care of the home, with Nyerere the herdsman in her support," Aura observed, trying to believe in what she was saying. She was willing to live beyond the incident; she was willing to forgive the assailant and his accomplices and move on with her life.

Even then, the incident had left Aura stunned. That a man who often came home to her hut to demand food, when his mother had not cooked, would attack her, face to face, with the intent to kill her, continued to haunt her. The image of him stepping into his step to deliver the blow to her head with a rock still caused her to shriek out of her sleep. Nevertheless, she hoped to move on and treat friends and foes fairly; she hoped to be stronger in church; she hoped to raise Juma to be an accomplished man, and like his father, a man who is fair man in his dealings.

"Out there in the wild, your brothers may still be hunting each other like Cain hunting down Abel in the old land. However, let me assure you that whoever attacked your mother is walking with the curse of kinship. You do not kill your kin and find peace thereafter; you do not beat up your mother or father and still live in peace.

"You have a sister living in this town; her name is Abich; she knows Aura is here hurting, but where is she?" Odongo posed.

"Pa, Abich says that Aura hates her," Olga said.

"You indeed went to her home?" Odongo asked.

"Yes. She was alone; she talked about a misunderstanding with the hospital guards and her recording a statement with the police about the misunderstanding," explained Olga.

"How was she when she talked?" Aura asked.

"She just talked the way she always talked; she talked as she cooked for us," Rachel said.

"There was no remorse, no sorrow," Olga added.

"Did she say what the misunderstanding was?" asked Odongo.

"No," Rachel and Leah said in unison.

"Well, we are family, and in every family there are odd ones. Any family can live with the odd thief, glutton, or moron, but it is hard to live with killers because they tend to want to bloody their hands repeatedly. All of you are young, but we the Luo do not live by an eye-for-an-eye; we let a man who has killed his kin go then burn down his house. Burning down the house with all its secrets, to us, is killing the killer and wiping him off from our collective memory. I am sorry to talk in these terms, but I have to because one of your brothers will receive severe sensor from the Ougo family because he beat his mother to near death. However, as a family, we have to stand aside. All of you, my daughters, have your own homes in distant places; if the errant brother stumbles into your home tomorrow, give him food and drink, and politely tell him to go. Don't quarrel with him."

"Aura, you don't want to reveal what happened?" Alal asked.

"No, I'm not well enough to revisit what I saw before I fell down unconscious only to wake up in blinding pain. I will let the people who schemed against my life talk first. How can I talk about my life when Juma is not here, perhaps still running for his life? Okulu is not here. They each will talk," lamented Aura.

Rachel and Leah freaked out and were in tears on hearing their brother's name.

"Rachel! Leah! Juma is well; you don't need to mourn him!" Aura said to her twin daughters.

Just then, Judas and John walked into the visitor's area. An antsy spell fell in the room as the duo approached the patient's bed, which already was overcrowded.

"I told you, Rachel and Leah, Juma must be well; Judas wouldn't be here, if Juma were in trouble," Aura reassured her daughters, yet within, she was burning with angst just to know about her son's fate. She knew that Judas and John were part of the team chasing Juma, and she believed they knew his fate.

"Aura, how are you?" John Odemba asked.

"You can see that I'm well; we from Tanganyika are made of diamond rock; no stone can harm us," Aura joked.

"I'm happy to hear your voice; the last time I saw you,

I'd lost all hope of ever drinking your special porridge again," John added, trying to be funny. He could see the patch on Aura's head, but there was no swollen hump even under bandage.

"I didn't know that many people loved my porridge; Judas, welcome to the Ougo clan meeting," Aura said, injecting humor into her words.

"Thank you, Mama Juma," Judas said; he was happy to see that Aura, his friend's mother, and favorite aunt, was well.

"John, where is Juma?" Olga asked. She had baby-sat Juma. Her stepbrother was special in her heart. It was significant that she had enquired about Juma's wellbeing and not the health or otherwise of Okulu, her brother.

All the girls were all ears; they eyed John intensely as he, their eldest cousin in the Ougo home, shifted in his seat, in discomfort. Running across rugged terrain, while going after Juma in the night, had been tortuous enough on John's mature, if not old, body, but the call to narrate the tale with strange twists and turns bore down heavily on his soul. Worse still, John believed that Juma was well, wherever he was, but he had no direct evidence for his belief. Shifting for the second time in a minute, John wished that the responsibility had passed on to the boy Judas. He looked at Judas. Judas looked back on a blank face, knowing that the onus of narrating his friend's fate was on John, who was two decades older than he was.

"John, where is my baby?" an anxious Aura whispered.

"Aura, relax. It is a long story, but what is important is that we didn't catch up with Juma," pleaded John.

"You did not catch up with Juma? Do you know where he is?" Alal asked, holding Aura down.

"We think we knew where he was, but we stopped the pursuit before we reached there," John said.

"Why, Odemba?" Odongo asked.

"We had his dog, Grace, which helped us track his movements up to a river between the land of Bwai and Nyamwa," John said. "At that stage, we thought it wise to leave him alone."

"Why?" Odongo asked, dismayed.

"You see, we were three people, including Okulu who was armed with a spear, and we were not armed. I am sorry to say this in the hearing of my sisters gathered here, but we did not know what Okulu could have done had we caught up with Juma," John said, with obvious unease. He was uneasy because he had just accused Okulu of having contemplated harming Juma in the presence of the former man's siblings.

"John, my brother, what led you to the conclusion that Okulu could have harmed Juma had they met?" Arua asked.

"Arua, my sister, on the fateful evening, when I reached Odongo's home, having heard Okulu shouting, 'Juma has killed his mother,' Aura here was lying down, groaning in pain. However, there was no one from the Odongo family around her. Juma was nowhere in sight. Okulu, who had alerted us to the tragedy, was still shouting, 'Juma has killed his mother,' as he ran in and out of Atieno's house. We still do not know why he never stopped by Aura to help in doing fast-aid," John pleaded for understanding from his cousins.

"Where was Atieno then?" Olga asked.

"She came out once, a club in her hand and saw Owinyo and Judas standing around Aura's body. She made a quick about turn and entered her house, the club still in her hand," John narrated what he saw.

A damning silence fell upon Odongo, his sick wife, and grieving daughters. They all shared in their kin's actions and guilt. They understood that Atieno and Okulu had conspired to harm Aura. *Shame; shame; shame;* each member of the family must have heard the same damning unspoken judgment. The girls were struggling to hold back tears. With Alal leading the way, they knelt down holding hands and prayed silently, each person mumbling her own prayer.

After a few minutes, Odongo asked, "Mm! Aura, is that true?" He appeared amused, even as a very tragic situation was under review. For so long the women had fought with words and nerve-racking deeds. However, the image of Atieno coming out of her house with a club in her hand ostensibly to finish off her helpless co-wife, who was then writhing on the ground and groaning in pain, sounded farfetched to Odongo. Yet he knew it had happened because he knew Atieno was capable of executing the alleged scheme.

"What kind of question is that, Pa?" Olga asked. "How

could Aura have known what was going on around her while lying down, with every second moving her closer to her death? You must be growing old, Pa," Olga fumed. "Olga daughter of Odongo, I have a mad mother, a murderous brother, a hurting stepmother, and here a father who has lost his mind. To whom will I turn, with Juma still out in the wild?" Olga sharpened her rhetoric in wonder. She feared the tragedy was threatening to tear her family different ways, and she believed that her father had allowed the situation to get worse by trying to be nice to everybody.

It is true. A woman I married well and gave very beautiful-and-responsible daughters, all of whom (except one) are here with me, propping up their recovering stepmother in love, has gone rogue and ready to dispatch her co-wife by all physical means! Worse still, she has recruited her son and my daughter to help her achieve her murderous objectives! I must stop her, Odongo raved within his heart, keeping everyone in suspense, each person wondering how he would react to Olga's strong challenge.

Odongo turned to look at Olga, in sympathy, and said, "Olga, old age has many advantages, but it has the key disadvantage that it is slow in confronting danger. Over the years, I always hoped that your mothers would cease their battles over things you, my children, cannot see. Like the River Kuja that overflows with water, even in the middle of a drought, bringing floods, disasters, crocodiles, and, fish to unsuspecting people downstream, your mothers overflow with ruinous jealousy and mutual mistrust, even in the middle of a peaceful spell, creating turmoil in the souls of us their relatives or blood. Their jealousy reserves are inexhaustible like the Kuja's angry muddy waters that come from as far as Kericho and Kisii Highlands. We are but their helpless victims. Olga, you are right, your father has lost his mind. What man, in my shoes, wouldn't have lost his mind?"

"Odongo, you are scaring the children with your jealousy talk; you chose the life of a two-wife home, enjoy its fruits: some are sweet, a few are bitter, but you can't spit them out, it is too late. Had you listened to your father and married a third wife, you could have doused the raging flames of jealousy between us," Aura said, even enjoying the verbal exchange between father and his daughter. "Olga, my daughter, you never chose your parents, bear with them; when they become unbearable, like now, seek refuge among your children and husband," Aura advised.

"Aura, my mother, I can hold on my own; don't strain yourself yet; you are not well," Olga said.

"I know you can, Olga of Thim Lich," Aura praised her stepdaughter and friend. She was happy that, even amid the crisis, the girls remained united as family.

"Judas, you have not spoken; why?" Rachel asked.

"John has explained things; we know where we must have left Juma," Judas said, fidgeting.

"And where is Okulu?" Leah asked.

John looked at Judas; Judas nodded his head in agreement. The truth was that neither of them knew where Okulu was at that moment. Then there was Okulu's injury after the fight with Grace, Juma's dog, an event neither John nor Judas wanted to revisit yet.

John understood that Judas would support whatever storyline he wove, but he was not going to reveal that Okulu was hurt.

"What happened to Okulu?" Alal asked, sensing that John and Judas were conspiring to lie about Okulu's status.

"He must be in his home," John said.

"Is he okay?" Alal asked anxiously, as all the women listened in anticipation, their hands still linked.

"How can we tell? We have not seen him since we came back from Bwai, but Thim Lich Village is abuzz with his name," John replied.

"How?" asked Arua, believing that something was not right with her brother.

"Owinyo has reached home, and he is talking about how Aura, in her moments of trouble, had shouted for Juma to run for his life; he is talking about how Okulu never went near Aura as she groaned in pain; he is talking of how Aura was taken out of the home without Atieno ever coming out of her house. People are talking about bad blood in the Odongo home; they are talking about bad blood between the house of Aura and the house of Atieno," John said, adding, "When I see you, my sisters, all hand-in-hand, praying and consoling Aunt Aura, I am relieved that Odongo's children are together against one or two bad ones."

"John, my son, why don't you advice your uncle to build a home for Atieno?" Aura asked, broaching a subject that the whole Ougo home had for years demanded, and Odongo had ignored, chasing an elusive unity, believing in a one-home family.

"I believe time is ripe for that; I believe that even after their separations, they will still exchange dishes and hot barbs over their husband," Alal observed.

"He has heard," John said. "Owinyo has concurred with you over the matter."

"I'd love to have a dog like Grace, she kept barking, whenever we were closing in on Juma. I know she helped Juma escape, whenever we drew too close to his hideouts," observed Judas, unprompted, inviting a stern look from John.

Hands untangled as the women looked from Judas to John, with eyes that said, 'What else have you not revealed?'

"Judas, do you want to see me dead? I don't want to hear such talk, not while Juma is still out there," Aura complained. "How close were you to him?"

"At one point, a pastor and a village headman had stopped us somewhere around Apuoche in Bwai. We then were at the pastor's gate. We believe the pastor's wife had allowed Juma to escape from her house under cover of darkness, while Okulu argued with the pastor and headman at the gate."

"Aren't you hungry, boys? Odongo, go and buy food for this mob," Aura said. She could not take it anymore. "Then take Judas or John to Bwai and search for the boy. Don't cane him, if you get him; go by bus," Aura ordered her husband. She imagined that Okulu was still on the trail of Juma out there in the wild. She wanted Juma found in whatever condition.

"Ma, do you think that Juma is still at the same place where John and Judas stopped the search?" Rachel asked.

"Yes. There is a woman confusing him there. I have seen it in my dreams," Aura said. "No more questions!"

Everyone laughed.

There indeed was a unique woman confusing Juma, a woman he could not and would not touch.

15

Atieno, a Troubled Soul

EARLY MORNING on the third day since the tragedy that nearly killed Aura, Atieno finally decided to go and bathe in River Kuja, having had three nights full of nightmares.

When Atieno was not dealing with lingering echoes of Aura's loud groans in her head, she had nightmarish dreams about her son, Okulu, and last daughter, Abich. Atieno had reasons to be worried about the dreams: she had recruited Okulu, her only son, and daughter Abich, the lastborn, to execute her schemes to eliminate Aura. Second, the firstborn and lastborn children are two children of special significance in any woman's life. In a polygamous home, the firstborn child perhaps reminded a woman of a period when she thought the man loved her, and the lastborn child could have marked the last time she, accidentally, saw the man in her bed.

In one dream, Atieno saw an image of Okulu she had not seen before: Okulu was walking home as one-armed amputee. As he neared the area of the home where Aura usually cooked in good weather, Grace the dog started barking at him, threatening to attack him. In the dream, Atieno saw Okulu swing his stick at Grace only to miss the dog and fall on his back. Moments later, he was fighting the dog over what looked like meat.

The dream troubled Atieno. She could not sleep. *It is not good to see meat in a dream*, she said in her heart. As she mulled over the dream, sleep overcame her, and her troubled mind eased into another dream: In the new dream, coming late into the night, Atieno saw Okulu in

Macalder Hospital, his body swollen from toe to eyelids. Next to his bed was a woman in white, pleading with and restraining his wife from even touching him.

Antsy, Atieno jumped out of her bed, and for the first time in close to seventy-two hours, she wondered whether Okulu was safe wherever he had gone chasing after Juma. In the contest of might, she was confident Juma was no match for Okulu. So reasoning, Atieno left her house and went behind the home for nature's call. Coming back, she passed by Grace, wondering where the dog had been since Juma left home, with Okulu in hot pursuit. The dog grumbled as Atieno entered her house.

Back to her bedroom, Atieno started a fire to brew some herbal tea to drink; her body craved the tea to fortify her disturbed mind. The cocks were crowing for the third time as she sat down to warm herself by the fireside. Atieno emptied her tobacco pipe, stuffed it with fresh tobacco from a recycled beauty pomade pouch, broke off a flint from a firewood log, lit the flint, and used the flame to light her pipe. A moment later, she was puffing off a stream of white tobacco smoke as she pondered her future in the Odongo home. She considered all the alternatives and concluded that the day or night Aura would come back would be the day she, Atieno, would leave for her brother's home. If Odongo needed her back, then he would have to build her a new home.

As Atieno continued to imagine a future in which the whole village would be calling her a killer or witch, sleep caught up with her in the eerie orange glow of the slow-burning firewood logs. She had forgotten her brew. She soon was dozing on and off, her forehead and pipe barely kissing the top of the bubbling herbal teapot.

A short moment into Atieno's sleep, her troubled mind wandered off and paid a visit to her familiar antagonists, Aura and Odongo, in the warm glow of her bedside fireplace. Atieno had an apparition of Aura and Odongo. In the apparition, Aura and Odongo were talking and laughing in the middle of the home as the former cooked fish at her outside fireplace. Enraged, Atieno ran toward them (in her dream), but as she threw a punch at Arua, the latter dodged, and she punched Odongo instead. She woke up cursing her luck; she had punched an empty stewpot by her fireplace, sending it tumbling on the floor.

"Aura is beating me whichever way I turn," she loudly cursed, nursing her aching fingers, scalded fingers.

Next, Atieno tried to pump her tobacco pipe, but drew in wet ash mixed with tobacco dust, for her pipe had dipped into the boiling teapot as she fought Aura's apparition.

"Leave my pipe alone, Aura; I surrendered Odongo to you," Atieno said loudly, wondering whether Aura already died. The thought of a dead Aura set Atieno's spirit to torment her terrestrial enemies. Atieno's tobacco pipe had taken in some of the teapot water she had been heating up. She emptied her pipe in disgust, dried it over the bedside fire, and refilled it with tobacco from her pouch. She lit the tobacco pipe up with a splint, and she soon was smoking again, her bubbling teapot forgotten in the rush to get some tobacco smoke.

Thanks to the numbing effect of the fire and the tobacco-smoke chemicals, she was dozing again. The winded dreams were not over with Atieno yet. Moments into her sleep, she saw Abich, her fifth-born child, dressed in red prison garb and in chains. Escorting Abich were two stern-faced female correction officers. As the correction officers frog-matched Abich, Atieno screamed, in her sleep, saying, 'Leave my daughter alone!' Animated, still in her dream, she reached out to grab Abich, but she drew blank, fell facedown, and awoke in shame, lying over her hot teapot.

"Aura, leave my daughter alone; fight me instead," Atieno mumbled, smarting from a scald from the hot brew. She was fully awake. She cried silently inside her house, rolling on the dusty floor in anguish. She was a broken-hearted woman; she understood that her harmful activities against Aura and her son had come back to haunt her.

As the sun rose above the Suna Hills, on the third day since Aura's near-death situation, Atieno picked up her pot to go to the river. She needed to bathe, but had she looked at herself in a mirror, she could not have left her house. She looked strange. Now, as Atieno walked toward the gate, the herdsman the villagers nicknamed Nyerere (because he was from Tanganyika) emerged from a shed where he was milking Aura's cows, his wooden milking jar (*wer*) in his left hand.

Nyerere was shocked at the image that greeted him. The woman he saw was not the woman he used to call adoringly "Mama Okulu." He almost dropped the milking jar he was carrying. Regaining his composure, Nyerere asked, "Mama Okulu, to which hospital did they take Aura?"

"Nyerere, I don't know," Atieno whispered harshly.

"I heard that Juma nearly killed Aura?" Nyerere asked, lying, testing Atieno's knowledge of events around her.

"Nyerere, your work is to milk Aura's cows and herd Odongo's livestock. I don't want to hear anything from you."

"I am sorry, Mama Okulu, but what has happened to your skin?" Nyerere asked. Atieno's skin was ashen gray, and the inquisitive boy had noticed.

"Nyerere, you ask too many questions, someone is going to hurt you," Atieno warned the gadfly.

"Mama Okulu, you cannot go to the river like that," pleaded Nyerere.

"I am an old woman. Who cares how I look?" an exhausted Atieno said for lack of what to say to the nuisance, thinking that she should not have responded to the boy's first question.

"Mama Okulu, I am a child, but I know that people will start calling you names, if they meet you like that," Nyerere made a stinging observation.

Atieno stopped where she was, just to look at the boy; he could have been twenty. Like other women in the village, Atieno considered Nyerere to be some half-wit who knew nothing going on in the Odongo homestead. It had not occurred to her that Nyerere was just doing what aliens always did for generations before, which was to work for food and shelter, get up on their legs, and even marry the employers' daughters.

Now, Atieno was seeing Nyerere the herdsman as a dangerous witness to her deadly schemes and therefore a threat to her children's future.

Has Nyerere heard some new information? Where was he, when Aura fell down? Atieno wondered in silence.

"Nyerere, milk the cows; let me hurry to the river before the village wakes up. You must be hungry, aren't you?" Atieno posed moments later, attempting to get the nasty boy off her back.

"No, I'm not hungry. Aura cooked a lot of food before she left for the hospital," Nyerere said

Is it possible the Tanganyikan boy never saw or heard of what happened to Aura? Or is he enjoying my predicament? Atieno wondered in silence.

"Milk the cows; if you don't mind, milk mine too," Atieno said, attempting to leave. She had hardly moved since Nyerere met her.

"Mama Okulu, if you have not heard, Owinyo is back from Migori; he says that Aura is recovering well; he says the doctors had to cut open her head," Nyerere streamed a batch of new information on the prognosis on Aura's health, taking Atieno by surprise.

"Where did you hear all that?" Atieno asked, trying to sound as normal as possible, but she was angry with the boy and the news update on Aura.

Damn! Aura was not supposed to live; where was Abich? Atieno raved, her inner demons threatening to get loose.

"Owinyo has spoken to some people, and Judas and John are back. They brought back the dog (Grace) and Okulu's spear," Nyerere said, enjoying Atieno's situation, wondering why Atieno was in the dark over the developments since Aura left home on a stretcher.

"Nyerere, if you don't move out of this home now, I'll bash your head with this pot," Atieno threatened, her mind darkening with rage.

"I won't leave before Aunt Aura comes back," Nyerere said.

"Do you know who you are talking to?" Atieno asked angrily.

"I won't leave. You hit my aunt in darkness; I won't allow you to touch me," Nyerere threatened, saying what he wanted to say all along.

"Child, watch your tongue," Atieno shouted in rage, hurling her empty water pot toward Nyerere.

Nyerere dodged the pot, spilling the milk he was carrying in a wooden milking jar (Luo: *wer or were*). As if to perpetuate the battle between Aura and Atieno, a battle that had always been more spiritual than physical, the pot landed on Aura's three-stone cooking place and split into several pieces.

Atieno had not failed to notice the irony and torture;

she had lost her pot to Aura, simple. In Atieno's mind's eye, Aura had won another round of her (Atieno's) internecine assaults against her. *Witch! Aura you are a witch! Even your cooking stone fights in your absence!* Atieno cursed in silence. Thus in extreme inner anguish, Atieno redirected her fury at Nyerere, saying, "Child, I am going to kill you!"

"I won't allow you to kill me," Nyerere said, standing his ground; realizing that he was nearer to all the locations than she was, in the home, where Odongo kept his weapons. Moreover, he could run away at any time of her attack.

"I am going to strip . . .!" Atieno said, reaching down to gather her skirt by its base.

"Atieno, what is happening here?" Owinyo asked, entering the home through the front gate. His words caught Atieno, who had reached for the base of her skirt, by surprise.

Atieno could not speak; she trembled in fear and anger; she trembled in fear because she guessed Owinyo had heard the full exchange between Nyerere and herself; she was angry because she had missed a chance to eliminate a noisy witness to the events of two nights before.

"Nyerere, go back to you duties!" Owinyo ordered.

"Baba John, she is going to kill me," Nyerere said.

"I'm here. She will not touch you. Go back to your work," Owinyo reassured Nyerere.

Reassured, Nyerere left for the shed to milk other cows, having wasted a whole gourd of milk.

"Atieno," Owinyo called out once Nyerere had left for the shed. He was approaching her.

"Yes, Owinyo," Atieno responded. She thought that she was trembling, which was a normal reaction on a number of counts. First, Owinyo had found her, in a precarious situation, executing a violent act on a helpless herdsman, only a few days since Okulu nearly killed Aura. Second, she respected Owinyo as a fair senior brother-in-law and the late Ougo's principal representative, and she suspected that he had concluded that Okulu was responsible for Aura's injury. Third, Owinyo and Atieno shared some uncomfortable family secrets involving Okulu; she therefore was beholden to Owinyo.

"What is going on in this home?" Owinyo demanded, finding an opportune moment to confront Atieno with the demons she had set lose to wreck havoc on Aura and her seed.

"What do you mean?" Atieno asked, going defensive.

"The other day, someone felled Aura with a stone on her head. As she groaned on the ground, struggling to breathe, you never came out of your house, even as your dangerous son screamed at the top of his voice, blaming Odongo's little boy for having killed his own mother. What are you up to this time?" Owinyo challenged.

"Owinyo, I don't know what you are talking about," Atieno retorted, looking away, overcome with shame and guilt, yet her pride could not allow her to face to her crimes.

"You should know; look at your face when you reach the Kuja, then drown, if you have some pride left in you," Owinyo said in a demeaning tone, spitting out the words.

"Owinyo, I won't do what you wish; this battle has just started; you know you are lying."

"Stop, Atieno! I have never lied to you! I have never failed you," Owinyo said, hurting. What had he not done to correct the injustices in Odongo's home? Had he not given Okulu's wife a new life as the mother of two boys where before she had none? Owinyo wondered. "You don't attempt to kill your co-wife over love."

"Who does not know that Aura is my enemy? Why did it take me decades to figure out how to kill her? I have no obligation to visit a woman who took my husband away decades ago. Owinyo, do you know that your brother has never spent a whole night in my bed since that woman you took to Migori entered our lives? Go and ask Aura which of her boyfriends, you included, stoned her on the head because she suddenly changed her mind about him," Atieno mouthed an astounding claim whereas her guilt was as loud as Kuja Falls and its thunderclaps during the rains. She was playing victim of a bigamous relationship, essentially saying that she did what she did because her male lover had abused her for too long.

"Since you want people to fight with, I want you to go to Macalder Hospital; if you have a holy book, carry it along. Ask for the room where Okulu is dying. Carry a rope; you may need it on your way back," came Owinyo's ruthless response. He didn't like Atieno's attempt to play the chronic victim game.

"What happened to Okulu?" Atieno asked anxiously.

"Well, he is confessing his sins on the Bible. Please wash your face; you look like a witch. You no longer are the long-necked bird all of us wanted to dance with the whole night not so long ago," Owinyo weaved a stinging sarcasm amid a dire situation, taking a shot at the romantic side of his odd sister-in-law, who was a woman he always admired for her tenacity against adversity. However, on Atieno's role in the current crisis, Owinyo found her utterly disagreeable.

"O Atieno, will this pain ever end?" Atieno mourned, bending down to sit on a stone under her granary. She was shedding tears. She wondered who had hurt Okulu. Her mind went to John Odemba, the man who, by her own request to Owinyo, volunteered and entered Okulu's house and seeded Juanita's field on two different occasions. *Had Odemba hurt Okulu after a fight over Juanita?* Atieno wondered.

His delicate mission accomplished, Owinyo joined Odongo's herdsman in the shed, leaving Atieno to suffer alone.

An hour before, Owinyo was in Macalder where he had stopped to visit with Okulu. Leaving the hospital, Owinyo had decided to do what he knew Odongo would not: and that was to confront Atieno with her criminal acts. Now, he had done his part, and he was relieved.

Owinyo had witnessed what happed on the fateful night. He was there as Aura writhed in pain, groaning like an animal under the knife of the slaughter man. He so far had played innocent bystander for the sake of a peaceful resolution. What he did not want was for the case to end up in a court of law. He had succeeded in browbeating Atieno, verbally. He would work on Odongo next.

Owinyo, was yet to know whatever happened to Okulu during the latter's chase after Juma, but to have seen a man who had been healthy a day before live as an invalid who could only feed from a helper's hands, had shaken him to the core.

Okulu had told Owinyo that a dog had bitten him. However, Okulu never revealed under what circumstances the dog bit him. He found the circumstance too painful to narrate to Owinyo.

Okulu had not admitted to having hit Aura on the head, only saying, with tears rolling down his face, "The God of my day punishes the errant in his day."

"What happened to your hands?" Owinyo had asked.

"A dog bit me," Okulu had muttered, wincing in pain.

"What dog bit you?" Owinyo asked.

"A wild dog bit me," Okulu replied, telling a lie.

"Where were Judas and John when the dog bit you?" Owinyo asked.

"I was with them, but by the time they reached me, the dog had done the damage," he said shedding tears.

Owinyo was tempted to ask if he, Okulu, had hit Aura with a stone, but he decided to leave Okulu alone.

I have just seen a man under a curse! Sure, no man ever beat his mother or stepmother and lived without blemish, Owinyo would reflect moments later, walking out of the hospital gate.

16

Dreaming on the Sinai

JUMA AWOKE to an unfamiliar voice. There was a young woman humming a familiar tune, while sitting next to him on the mat.

Am I dreaming? Juma asked in wonder, his scrambled mind recalibrating time, reorganizing events, and scanning the place for anything familiar. He could not tell the time, he was slow to remember recent events, and he recognized nothing around him.

"Stranger, how are you?" the woman greeted him, touching his left eyelid, looking into his face adoringly. Juma looked up the ceiling and the paraphernalia he saw warned him that he was in an alien land. The only source of light was a small window to his left and a door at the six-o'clock position.

"Who are you?" Juma asked finally, his voice hoarse from dehydration; he was thirsty.

"I am the woman you saved last night. You need to go and bathe. I have new clothes for you," Elizabeth said, believing that the alien could remember the events of the previous night.

"You've bought new clothes for me? How did I reach here? How is my mother?" Juma asked, his mind clearing up; he could recall that his mother was hurting the dusk before.

"You are far away from your mother; you should remember that," Elizabeth teased.

"O poor Juma, I'm still alive," he said feeling about a body that ached all over and was rough with scratches and dried-up mud. He sat up on the mat, facing Elizabeth.

"Oh, you are Juma?" Elizabeth chirped excitedly. She was happy that the man was voluntarily opening up. She had heard his name through his mumbled words during his many dreams and nightmares, but now the man was willing to say who he was.

"Yes. Is that funny?" Juma asked, wondering what the woman knew about him.

"Cool down buddy; you are among friends. You need to bathe, and then drink some late tea. That should help you start your day."

"O boy! I am a mess, my body aches; what a journey; the dog barked in my head the whole night," Juma said, stretching his arms, yawning.

"What dog?"

"My dog, Grace; she barked the whole night."

"You must be in love with your dog; you called her name the whole night," Elizabeth said teasingly, but she was relieved finally. She had watched over him as he slept, anxiously waiting for him to wake up; she had listened to his loud dreams, refusing to leave his side, even when her mother chastised her to "behave like a decent educated woman." Elizabeth now realized that Grace, a name the stranger named Juma had mentioned repeatedly during his nightmarish sleep, was a dog and not another woman. She was relieved; Grace was not part of the potential competition with whom she would have to contend for his heart and mind.

Elizabeth understood why early morning, the man known as Juma had looked in the direction of the ridge yonder whenever some dog barked. She realized that Juma's pursuers had missed him by only a few hundred yards; she realized how lucky she was the previous night. She realized that had Juma's pursuers seized him before he reached the river, he might not have been there to save her! Thinking thus, a chill ran through her spine.

This boy must live; I'll protect him, Elizabeth promised in her heart, tempted to move closer to him and bridge the one-foot space separating them on the mat. Her heart was weak, but she was not going to do anything stupid in her late father's home. Moreover, she was still mourning and out of bounds to any man.

"You are shedding tears," Juma observed, reaching

across to wipe off the tears with the back of his left hand. However, Elizabeth moved aside, dodging the hand of empathy, saying, "It is because I love you." Saying so, Elizabeth stood up. She was not going to spoil the innocent boy, so she resolved. She had been all over him last night, but that was during a time when she had been lost in joy, and the person she had kissed was 'the savior' and not 'the man' now tempting her heart.

Juma stood up and sat down again on realizing how sparsely dressed he was.

What a tall and skinny light-skinned innocent thing! O the scratches; they must be painful, wondered Elizabeth, struggling with the physical evidence for the ordeal Juma went through during his escape from the lot of his pursuers. Then her mind wondered back to the boy's troubled dreams. She associated the wounds all over his body with the nightmares he continued to experience in his sleep.

'Mama! Mama! Aura, Mama! I did not hit you! He hit you,' he had mumbled the words throughout his sleepy day.

He variously mentioned other names, like Okulu, Odongo, and Atieno. 'Okulu, you are the killer; you killed her! Okulu, don't call me a killer!' he had mumbled several times, making Elizabeth wonder whether the boy had killed his mother.

Of course, he is a sweet boy; he couldn't have done such a thing to his mother! Elizabeth's heart would exclaim, dismissing such thought several times over, while watching over him as he slept.

He is a sweet green thing that still needs training in the ways of the world of women and men. He is sweetly young; I will not leave his side, whatever his circumstances happen to be! she mused in her raging heart.

Then as she continued looking at his baby face as he slept next to her on the mat, he clearly would say, 'Okulu, you killed my mother. Don't lie. You killed her!' making Elizabeth wonder who Okulu was and what relationship he shared with Juma.

'I'm sorry, Mama; you must live. I'll be a nicer boy. Tomorrow, Mama, I'll be in Alliance Boys High School. Are you happy, Mama? Uuwi! Uuwi! Uuwi! Okulu, you killed my mother!' one rather long dream session went, tempting

Elizabeth to take notes, but she could not keep up with him, as his dream hit fast crescendos and slow rumbling doldrums randomly.

Alliance Boys High School; the boy is heading to Alliance Boys. O poor Elizabeth, I knew it. The boy has assertive airs! It is about Alliance Boys, Elizabeth's heart raved in joy. She had to make his bathing arrangement.

"The water for your bath is ready, my Juma," Elizabeth said, tickling him. She was surprised as to how readily she had warmed up to him, a stranger who definitely had some heavy baggage behind him.

"Okay, stop it. I am a wake, and I want to know where I am."

"You are on top of the Sinai Hill in Bwai North," Elizabeth said, using the name members of the Legion Maria Christian sect had assigned Oriwo Hill.

"And who are you, the girl from Sinai?"

"Elizabeth Ochieng."

"How did I reach here?" Juma asked.

"You saved my life, last night; that is all I know," Elizabeth said.

"Now, don't be a little girl," Juma joked, believing that the girl must have been at least a year older than he was.

"Let me be serious here; you saved my life. I was drowning . . . . I was sinking into volcanic quicksand, if you understand, and then came this man, God's Angel, from nowhere, and before I knew it, I was free," Elizabeth said bubbling with emotion. "Then I realized you were coming to this home all along! I daresay, in hindsight, that the spirit of my father had directed you to this home. Now I realize you were running away from some danger, with some people hot on your heels, with your own dog Grace leading them. My late father's funeral fire directed you to this home."

"I'm sorry!" Juma said, but he desisted from wiping off her tears, remembering her earlier protests.

"Okay! If you allowed me to stand up, I will put on the clothes you have bought for me, bathe, and then pour out my heart to you, but only after I will have listened to your tale," Juma said, begging for some space for privacy.

"Okay! Do not run away while I am looking the other way. I love you like food!" she said turning to look away from him.

"Hold it, baby! I'm a young man, but I am old at heart; I was born to be the elder in my father's home. I'm as old a man as you will get. Be careful, this little puppy can bite you, the Girl from Ogande!" Juma staked his credentials, as he changed short trousers, remembering the name of the school the girl had told him about early that morning. The romantic angling of his response surprised him. *I definitely had matured overnight,* so he thought.

"You sound too wise, stranger! How do you know that I am girl from Ogande Girls?" asked Elizabeth, refusing to challenge him over the "puppy metaphor."

I'm not going to encourage a romantic talk here. This home is in mourning; is still a compromised shrine to quote Grandma, argued Elizabeth.

"I read the badge on your shirt!" Juma said. "You can come back."

"Love you! Let's go! I want you to bathe then eat, then my grandmother and mother will hear your story," Elizabeth said, stepping into the house.

"I need water to drink," he said.

She served him a large calabash of water she had drawn from a black earthen pot. He drank most of it. Moments later, she led him to a large pond one hundred yards away toward the northern end of the hilltop, and drew some water for him to bathe. He bathed in a bush at the northern end of the pond.

Half an hour later, she came back to pick up the basin; he was sitting on top of a large rock, enjoying a panoramic view of the landscape to the north and east.

"Which place is that to the north?" Juma asked, pointing in the direction of Homa Bay Town.

"That is Homa Bay. You can see Asego Hill, beyond that is the lake, in blue, and Huma Hills and Kendu Bay. In the distance is Kisumu, which is more visible during the night because of its many streetlights. Turn and look southwest; the hills in the distance are Nyarandi and Rachar; looking farther west, you can see Tigra Hill and beyond that is Lake Victoria, which extends south into Kadem and Tanzania. If you look carefully past Tigra Hill, you will see two islands in the lake: one is Aluru Hill and the farther one is Migingo Island. The nights are more beautiful here, because then you can see more urban centers and boats fishing for *Omena* (sardine-like fish), with their lights on," Elizabeth explained leaning on Juma.

Juma was surprised how comfortable he was around Elizabeth. He too had time to recall the circumstances surrounding their meeting the previous night. He wondered how much she knew about him already. However, she was a woman he would welcome home, if Odongo, his father continued to push him to marry.

Thinking about women and marriage, Juma's heart rushed to the memory of his mother's condition the previous evening, but the girl's warmth and mild perfume immediately whiffed away all that. He was living for the moment, thanks to the ability of the youthful mind to engage in many contradictory activities at the same time with hardly any regard to priority.

"Where is Rusinga Islands," Juma asked, but his attention was on the girl; he loved to hear her singing voice.

"Beyond the ridge yonder to the northwest is Ruma Game Reserve, but we can't see it from here. The hills in the distance are Kaksingri Hills, beyond that are Rusinga and Mfang'ano Islands, which we can't see from here," Elizabeth explained. She loved local geography as a subject; she particularly loved the way Miss Hill of Ogande Girls taught it.

"Olisa! Olisa! What is wrong with you? That man you are holding like a piece of juicy sugarcane must be hungry. Bring him home," Grandma Atigo called out. She was standing on a rock at the southern end of the pond.

"I have heard you, Grandma," Elizabeth said smiling.

"Who is that?" Juma, who had stepped away from Liz, embarrassed, asked.

"That is my grandmother Atigo. Why step away from me?" Elizabeth challenged Juma.

"I just realized that a strange woman was leaning against me as she taught geography," Juma joked.

"Don't be naughty. Tell me something before we go home. Who is Okulu?" Elizabeth asked; she was leaning on him, while he sat on the same rock as before.

"Did Okulu come here?" Juma asked alarmed, standing up.

"No, don't be alarmed. I know you ran away from trouble; your dreams told it all."

"*My dreams?* What didn't I say in my sleep?" Juma asked; he was genuinely concerned.

"Honey, relax. People dream loudly at times. I know Okulu tried to kill someone dear to you. Do you want me to say her name?" challenged Elizabeth.

"Is my mother alright?" Juma asked, ignoring the challenge, believing that Elizabeth perhaps had some news about his mother.

"I don't know, but I want to know how she is fairing soonest possible. She is dear to me just as she is dear to you. Know that, even if we separated, because I am in Ogande and you are in Alliance, I would travel with your heart."

"I hope she slept fine," Juma said, tears rolling down his face. He felt ashamed that the girl knew he had run away from home, leaving his mother in danger. Thus, bubbling with emotions, he shed tears before Liz, violating his father's caution to him that men do not weep!

"It is okay, honey!" she said, wiping off his tears, and Juma felt nothing unusual at all from her touch.

What is it with this girl that makes her touch feel like that from my sisters? Juma wondered in silence.

"I have to return to my mother soonest possible. Can you accompany me to Macalder tomorrow?" Juma observed

"I don't think my mother would agree to that request, but I love you and don't want to leave your side. Let's go, you are hungry. You will know who Okulu is soon," he said, touching her lips with his hand.

'Don't do that, Grandma may be watching."

Side-by-side, they walked home to her grandmother's house.

17

Dorca's Angst

TWO DAYS LATER, DORKA WATCHED from a distance while Elizabeth brought Juma home after another scenic view of the land from the hill, which the locals called the Sinai. When Dorka first saw the boy and Liz walking instep, a chill ran through her body. They shared the long, lazy steps. Dorka noted that the boy was lighter-skinned than Lisa, but the way they frequently touched their noses, as if there was a constant stench in the air, had scared Dorka. She looked intensely as they approached the middle of the home, walking side by side.

"Dorka Adhiambo, what has just happened to me? That boy from Kadem could be Betha's brother or cousin. I hope nothing has happened between Betha and the boy she calls 'My Juma,'" she whispered, chuckled then served herself a shot of *chang'aa*, hoping to get a clearer view of the boy from Kadem. Moments later, Elizabeth and Juma entered Grandma's house, and Dorka's take of the situation had not changed: the boy was likely to be Elizabeth's cousin or stepbrother; Dorka resolved to stop their romantic relationship. But how would she do it? She was in a predicament.

At the time, Elizabeth had mentioned to her mother that the man who saved her life was from Kadem. Now, Dorka wanted to interview the young man, but she could not because she was still mourning the loss of her husband and could not have risked talking to a man who could become her son-in-law.

An hour later, Dorka was talking to Grandma Atigo,

who had been dosing under a tree near the latter's house.

"Grandma Atigo, when you talk to the boy, you must try to get all the details about his parents; I don't want to risk my only child walking into a home of wizards. If the father has many wives, the boy's relationship with Elizabeth is over, because, one day, the boy too could think of marrying many wives. Also, I want to know what happened where he came from, before I risk the life of my only daughter around him," Dorka had briefed Grandma, hoping to use her to gain useful intelligence on the boy.

Now, Grandma had no idea that the man who fathered Elizabeth was from Kadem, though she knew that Dorka was pregnant when she prepared the first bed for the late Ochieng'. And because Elizabeth was a girl, there would be no issues of legitimacy, birthright, and inheritance involved in her relationship with Ochieng (Among the Luo, girls brought wealth and inherited none). Even Ochieng,' died without having demanded to know the name of the man who fathered Elizabeth, though he knew that the man he had denied a wife was from Thim Lich in Kadem. Moreover, the late Ochieng' loved and trusted Dorka so much that he never would have asked such 'irrelevant' questions about the name of Elizabeth's biological father. Elizabeth was his daughter, full stop. He too loved Elizabeth dearly, for she was the only child to have survived from his lover's womb. Finally, few in the family knew that Elizabeth was an illegitimate child.

Having listened to Dorka's briefing, Grandma Atigo entered her hut; she was ready to complete the assignment of unraveling the alien's family background, unaware that Dorka intended to use her to establish whether Juma was the son of Odongo Ougo of Thim Lich. Grandma unknowingly was on a mission to establish whether Juma was Elizabeth's stepbrother.

Elizabeth and her alien guest were through with their late lunch of *Tilapia* soup, which they had enjoyed from the same bowl, an experience Juma found a little romantic, because, since the age of eight years, he never ate from the same plate with a female. Juma always ate either alone or with his father, who kept stressing that he, Juma, was a man who needed space to do *men things*!

"Elizabeth, I want some privacy with this man,"

Grandma announced, having taken a seat in her ageless three-legged stool by her bed.

"But don't ask him embarrassing questions; I don't want to lose him," Elizabeth joked.

"If you lose him, I'll have him," Grandma Atigo joked back.

"Then don't talk to him," Elizabeth protested.

"Okay, deal; you go and draw water from the spring for me, and I promise never to mention your name when I talk with him," Grandma Atigo said.

"Deal, then," Elizabeth said, leaving Grandma Atigo's hut, a clay water pot in hand, knowing that her grandmother would extract some mutually useful pieces of information from the troubled man from Kadem.

Even Elizabeth needed to know more about the man who had rocked her heart since extracting her from a muddy quicksand the night before. Beyond his rare genius, which had cracked the gates open at Alliance Boys to let in a boy from Southern Kadem, Elizabeth believed that there was something more special about the boy that made her shudder whenever she touched him. Even as she declared her love to him, she felt as if he was something unreachable, something holy; he was like a mirage she never would catch up with, however hard she tried.

One hundred and thirty yards later, Elizabeth was at the soft-water spring toward the southern end of the hilltop, and she already was drawing water.

It perhaps is love; maybe that is how real love feels like to the loved, Elizabeth wondered, dipping her calabash into the spring water for the fifth time to fill Grandma Atigo's three-gallon pot. She was a hundred yards to the south of her mother's house. Minutes later, just as Elizabeth was ready to lift the pot of water and put it on her head, she realized she was under the shadow of her mother, who was standing forlornly behind her.

"Ma, you scared me!" Elizabeth said.

"Betha, what else do you know about the boy that saved you?" Dorka asked. She indeed was interested in knowing more about the boy who resembled her daughter. Dorka hoped her mother-in-law would bring to light any hidden relationships, but the latter needed time with the boy. She, Dorka, intended to divert Betha's attention and hold her at the well until Grandma Atigo would have had enough time with the alien boy.

"What else do I know about him? Well, he saved me last night. I know that there is trouble where he came from; I also know that a relative hurt his mother," Elizabeth said.

"I want to make sure that the man my daughter dearly loves, and the one she sheds tears for, is the right man," Dorka said, looking at her only child in the eyes.

"Ma, you are cruel! I am not madly in love with the boy; he is just a boy who saved my life," Elizabeth protested.

"I want to believe you, dear Betha. Uncle Thomas would be mad at you, if you were to drop out of school because you have mistaken your teenage feelings for love," Dorka spoke matter-of-factly, invoking the name of her elder brother and Elizabeth's benefactor, who met her daughter's school-fees obligations.

"Ma, I love the man. But I am not going to drop out of school because of that; in fact, the love for him is the more reason I'll remain in school," Elizabeth said.

"Betha, I want to believe you, but there are eyes watching for any sign of scandal; the sooner the boy leaves for Macalder, and you leave for school, the better."

"Ma, you know that I have four more days left before I return to Ogande."

"Good. Keep a decent distance from the boy."

"Ma, I'm not a loose girl!" Elizabeth protested.

"I didn't say that, Betha. Here, is your calabash," Dorka said handing over the calabash to Betha, who already had the pot of water on her head and already was walking home. "I love you, Betha."

"I love you, Ma!"

"I know you are emotional now, but watch where you step; I am not ready to replace Grandma's pot again," teased Dorka.

"Ma, I am a grown up woman!" Elizabeth said. On any other day, she could have invited her mother's wrath for referring to herself, a mere child, as a woman. But this was Betha's special week; she had survived an accident, and the fugitive who rescued her was still her guest.

"I know, Liz," Dorka acknowledged, letting her daughter be. Dorka even chanced a smile as her daughter walked on like a "town girl," even among the rocks, while precariously balancing Grandma's earthen pot of water on her head.

"Sure, Betha is a woman already! Our daughter is a woman! How I miss you, Ochieng; how sad that you won't be there to receive Betha's suitors!" whispered Dorka mournfully, tears rolling down her face. Yet she was able to suppress the urge to sing out audibly, solely because Elizabeth's guest was still around. Moreover, the prospect of meeting Odongo, her daughter's long-forgotten biological father, was tweaking her heart every moment, threatening to outlast the late Ochieng' in the duel for space in her mind.

"Odongo, why tease me now? Leave me alone!" she found herself muttering, while twenty yards ahead, Elizabeth turned the corner and entered home through the front gate.

Moments later, Dorka entered her all-female home, uttering no more word. She pushed off her dueling male lovers from her mind, took up her guard position a few steps away from Ochieng's grave, and anxiously awaited Grandma Atuka's feedback on the boy from Kadem. Dorka dreaded every moment of the wait, fearing that Grandma would confirm her (Dorka's) fears.

While Dorka engaged Elizabeth at the well, Grandma was interviewing Juma.

"Young man, what is your name?" Grandma had asked after Elizabeth had left for the spring.

"My name is Juma Odongo," Juma responded, wondering why Elizabeth had to be absent during the interview.

"Where do you come from?" Atigo asked.

"I come from Kadem?" Juma replied.

"Which part of Kadem do you come from?" Grandma asked, trying to be as precise as possible.

"I come from Thim Lich in Kadem."

"Who is your father?" she asked, though she knew no one in that part of the world.

"My father is Odongo son of Ougo," Juma replied, giving a more detailed answer than requested; but there were many Odongo's in his village hence the need for a more explicit answer.

"Where was your mother born?" Grandma asked; she

knew Luo men to be proud of their maternal-ancestral roots.

"She was born in Tanganyika, among the Kowak of North Mara," Juma replied, again offering a more detailed answer than Grandma had requested.

Grandma knew no one from Kowak in Tanganyika, but she was impressed with the boy's candor.

Having established mutual trust with Juma, Grandma jumped to the more important question of why he ran away from his village. She needed to be tactful and friendly to the boy, and so, calling him by his name, she asked, "Juma, what happened where you came from?"

Silence; Juma kept fidgeting with his fingers, looking down.

"Juma, you had a sleep full of nightmares; you kept dreaming loudly, even crying and calling names. Tell me what happened before you left your father's home," Grandma pleaded.

"I can't remember if I dreamed or what I dreamed about," Juma responded; he did not want to share all the bad things he had experienced over the last day.

"I believe there is serious trouble where you came from," Grandma insisted. "Who is Okulu?"

"Was he here?" Juma asked, standing up, looking agitated.

"No. Sit down. You kept calling Okulu's name. What did he do to you?"

"He is my half-brother. We are both sons of Odongo. Our mothers are different though," Juma said, avoiding a narrative of the tragic event of the night before.

"Your dreams tell me that there is no peace in your father's home," Grandma said. "If you don't open up and talk about your troubles, how could I help you? Moreover, how can I entrust the life of my granddaughter with a man who is always on the run from his past. Open up and speak about the person you are. We don't know you well, though we know that you are a brave man," grandma pleaded, even praised, dangling her granddaughter as an enticement for Juma's candor and cooperation.

"It is true that some *bad thing* happened in my father's home yesterday," Juma acknowledged, looking away.

"It looks like you don't want to say what bad thing happened in your father's home. I want to warn you that you should not go back there. Even you have stated that some bad thing there. It is not good that you go back there," Grandma said, her hand on Juma's head.

"You can feel that?" Juma asked, trembling, thinking that the woman was a prophet or a psychic.

"No. Your loud dreams show that your father's home is at war. Something tragic could happen to you if you went back immediately," Grandma said, keeping her left hand on Juma's head. She realized that the boy was about to yield some useful information.

"Ah!" Juma exclaimed, wondering what else the woman knew about him.

"I suppose that your mother is still alive?" Grandma Atigo asked, tapping from the content of Juma's nightmares, in which he appeared to say that his mother was in trouble.

"I hope so," Juma replied in a more tremulous voice; he continued to tremble, as if he had a fever.

"You hope so? Is your mother alive or not?" Grandma Atigo kept pressing her victim.

"I ran away from home when she was hurting badly," Juma said, shaking in fear; the images and sounds of a mother groaning in pain revisiting his mind.

"Juma, What happened to your mother?" Grandma Atigo pressed on, her hand still on the boy's head. She genuinely needed more information, so that she could try to help the boy's unfortunate mother, who was not even in the room.

"She was badly hurt; someone hit her on the head," Juma said haltingly.

"Tell me why there is war in your father's home," Grandma Atigo asked, lifting off her hand from Juma's head.

"I am too young to explain why my mother and stepmother are always at war, Grandma," Juma stated, careful to project the right posture a young man growing up in a polygamous home is required to maintain. He too was relieved, now that his interviewer had removed her nerve-numbing, hair-raising hand from his head.

"You are right; a young man like you is not supposed to be preoccupied with digging up the dirt in your parents' bedroom," she said. "Yet they continue to fight over your father. O poor child of polygamy, what are you going to do?" she lamented rhetorically, expecting no response from Juma. "You are safe here; no one will harm you. Now, Juma, promise me that you won't leave this home until your father comes for you," Atigo asked, pressing the boy to promise compliance.

"I promise," Juma affirmed. If he feared for his safety, that was not reason enough to hang around Sinai Hill. Elizabeth remained the key source of the soothing music that kept him from thinking about his mother and his turbulent past.

"Thank you Elizabeth, you can have your man back," joked Grandma, tickling Elizabeth, who entered the house, just as the former concluded interviewing Juma.

"I can have him back, if you found him uninteresting," said Elizabeth, lowering the pot of water. The duo always took healthy jabs at each other's "ugly boyfriends," real or imagined. In so doing, Grandma taught her granddaughter personal respect and the need to be discerning while choosing a boyfriend. And the younger woman kept the older one mentally and sensually engaged in the latter's increasingly shrinking social world with its long list of dos and don'ts.

18

The Untouchable Pearl

LATER THAT DAY, WHEN ELIZABETH AGAIN was out with her catch (Juma) for a tour of Sinai Hill's centuries-old stone hedges, Grandma Atigo joined Dorka for a meal. Atigo would share the intelligence she had extracted from Juma with Dorka. However, Grandma was unaware that the information she would provide to Dorka had a hidden value to the latter.

"The boy has a father and a mother. He ran away from home after a fight that left his mother struggling for her life," Grandma said to Dorka what she had found out from interviewing Juma.

"Who hurt his mother?" asked Dorka.

"I think it is his stepbrother; his name is Okulu son of Odongo. This boy's name is Juma Odongo. His father's name is Odongo from Thim Lich in Kadem," Grandma said.

"What do you think about the boy? Does he look like someone who could harm somebody? Would Elizabeth be safe around him?" asked Dorka, worried about what she was hearing. She did not want her daughter to walk into a home at war. Even then, she still needed to find out which Odongo fathered Juma.

"Why not? He is a cable boy," Atigo said.

Dorka wanted to say, "He is a curse to her," but said instead, "There is trouble in his father's home." She prayed that Odongo arrived soon and unwound the mess he created years ago, when he confused a young girl using his livestock wealth.

"If you are thinking of him as the future husband of Olisa, I have no objection; he is a man I can give Olisa to; and who doesn't want good cows from Kadem?" Grandma said.

"Grandma, you can't be that willing to throw away Olisa to just anybody," complained Dorka.

"The boy is not just anybody. He is brave. He saved Olisa's life. Or do you doubt that he saved Olisa's life?" Grandma challenged, believing that the boy should stay in her house until his father appeared, and Olisa was the key attraction that would keep the boy around.

"No. I do not doubt that he saved Olisa's life. But Olisa is not going to marry a man from a polygamous home," protested Dorka, laying grounds for separating Elizabeth from Juma. She was beginning to believe that the duo shared a father.

"Not every man becomes a polygamist because his father had many wives. Besides, who said that Olisa wants to marry him?" asked Grandma.

"Grandma, look at the way Olisa looks at that boy; she could marry him."

"That may well happen," Grandma said, smiling.

"Cattle wealth or not, my only daughter cannot marry a man from Kadem. Kadem men tend to turn polygamous," protested Dorka, offering a believable reason why her daughter could not marry Juma of Kadem.

"Dorka, you know that, as a mother, you cannot control where, when, and whom your modern daughter of books marries or runs to for comfort," cautioned Grandma.

"As a mother I can offer guidance," Dorka countered.

"When you regain your freedom to go to the river, I want you to visit the spot where the earth almost swallowed Olisa. I went there and could not speak. The quagmire is so wide, I cannot imagine how the boy was able to reach out and bring out Olisa to safety without himself going under. Watch out what you say about this Juma Odongo; he could be an Angel," Grandma cautioned her daughter-in-law.

"I'm sorry, Grandma, but you don't understand how I feel," countered Dorka. She had lost a dear husband; now she walked with a troubling fact of her daughter's ancestry that was about to become public; then Juma was threatening to claim Elizabeth's heart, yet they were stepsiblings. Dorka knew that she would have to blow the whistle against the intensifying romantic relationship between Juma and Elizabeth, and she had to do it soon or risk an uncomfortable scene involving the duo.

"I know you are grieving over the same man I'm mourning. We should stop talking about what two young people may or may not do with themselves in future. However, when Olisa decides to go to a man she has chosen as her husband, you'll have to step aside and let her will prevail," cautioned Grandma.

"Grandma, tell Olisa not to get anywhere near that man; she still walks with her father's curse," Dorka said in resignation, having failed to justify to Grandma why Olisa could not marry Juma, without risk of revealing that they likely were stepsiblings.

"Olisa knows that she still walks with her father's unresolved curse. She is a good girl," Grandma said; then she soon was on her feet. Even as Grandma left for her house, she wondered why her daughter-in-law was that agitated against a man who had save Olisa's life.

The matter had rested there. Dorka would continue to watch the boy and her daughter with a mixture of joy and pain. In a short while, and she felt it would happen anytime, the boy's relatives were likely to arrive in Korondo village, looking for him. According to her daughter, those who had followed the boy had come as far as the Nyogunde. They were bound to come back, if they trusted their dog. The boy had been talking, saying that he was bound for Alliance High School. Dorka had a sense of pride in Juma, no longer as a possible suitor to her daughter, but as part of her daughter's close family.

I have no regrets; the man whose hand I skipped for Ochieng's hand is sharp; has he not sired my daughter, Elizabeth, who already is in Ogande High School? Now, the same man's son is bound for the venerated Alliance Boys, Dorka judged, believing that the anticipated reentry of Odongo into her life was a good omen, his family troubles notwithstanding.

The world is a small place; that would be increasingly true with better communication, but even in the nineteen fifties Colonial Kenya, buses already plied routes in rural Nyanza, and young men traveled long distances to party with young women. One such partying "young man" of great wealth named Odongo Ougo of Kadem traveled tens of miles to date a one young woman named Dorka Ochieng' from Gwasii. The year was 1952. The Emergency was on in the White Highlands; around Lake Victoria in Luo Nyanza, pre-independence politics already permeated the land, but social life continued, and boys and girls were partying as before.

Odongo Ougo was not a boy then; he was a young man with two wives he had married within the previous decade. Even then, he still was partying and toying with the idea of marrying a third wife, with his mother (Apudo) cheering him on. In Apudo's well-considered theory of stable polygamous homes, a three-wife home would have offered a more stable environment in Odongo's home than that which existed between Atieno and Aura, Odongo's dueling wives.

Initially, Dorka hedged her bets on Odongo as a suitor who would take care of her. The initial conversation had gone so well she lost her head, and more, in just one night. After the first meeting, she had wanted to meet him again. Their meeting point was Sori Center. She was from Gwasii, and he was from Kadem, two clans that shared no ancestral roots. Moreover, Dorka and Odongo were not blood relatives, and so there were no cultural marriage compatibility issues.

However, Dorka had one issue with the free-spending older man. He was a polygamist. If she had listened to her heart, she could have married him regardless of his marital status. However, two dates later, and a mention of the marital status of the man to her mother, the courtship stalled. Her mother was not going to have her youngest daughter marry a polygamist, full stop.

"Dori, it doesn't matter whether he brings countless numbers of bulls and cows; I will not welcome him, and if you insist on marrying him, you will be the only outcast among my children," Akelo, Dorka's mother had threatened.

At the third date in Sori, Dorka heeded her mother's call and declined Odongo's hand and wealth, returning a generous bundle of jewelry from Tanganyika. Their last meeting was so brief and dramatic that it left Odongo stunned for words.

"Owinyo, my brother, what just happened to me?" a stunned Odongo had asked, stammering.

"Odongo, you are old; it also is a warning to you that the modern girl values no wealth. You have two beautiful wives; you do not need another. I know our mother thinks otherwise, but a third woman of the modern type will not stick in your home. Today's youth have new ideas from church schools; they have no eyes for our polygamous type," Owinyo had cautioned his brother.

"You may be right," Odongo said. "Let's sell the cattle we brought here and go back to Macalder. Sori is no place for *old men*," a disgusted Odongo had said, having decided to dispose of the cattle and walk back home with money in his pockets rather than confront the shame of going back with the rejected animal wealth. He was not old by any standards; at thirty years of age, he was a young wealthy man. Yes, he had two wives, but no girl had a right judge him on that, and he would not try to marry again, so he had resolved.

Well, Dorka rejected Odongo's hand because her mother did not want her to marry a polygamist. Unfortunately, things had happened "in the bush," and Dorka walked with Odongo's seed as she hurriedly eloped with one Ochieng' of Bwai before Odongo's livestock wealth could bribe its way into Gwasii. Moreover, it was in her interest to settle with Ochieng' before pregnancy became publicly visible.

Ochieng' of Bwai would marry Dorka; she was pregnant as she made her matrimonial bed for Ochieng'. Dorka would give birth to Elizabeth in Ochieng's home. Elizabeth would grow up knowing that she was the daughter of Ochieng.' Even back then, girls born out of wedlock were very acceptable to the conservative Luo mind that valued bloodlines. Girls were a promise of wealth. Therefore, Elizabeth grew up in a very welcoming environment. The subsequent children Dorka would have, with Ochieng', never survived beyond the age of five years: malaria, malaria, malaria and malaria killed Dorka's children before five years of life; they were two boys and two girls. Then Ochieng died after eighteen years of married life.

For close to two decades, Odongo would let his encounter with Dorka fade from his memory. Then in a strange twist of fate, Juma, a fugitive running for his life, already had staged a successful rescue of his stepsister Elizabeth. In a strange twist of fate, Ochieng's funeral bonfire was the source of the light was the beacon of hope that had attracted the young fugitive, Juma Odongo of Kadem, setting him on a nighttime course to the home on the hill.

Now, eighteen years later, the reality of a shared blood relationship was hurtling toward two young people joined in love by fate, and they knew not its existence, except Dorka was seeing it coming, and she was determined to smother its impact on her daughter's life.

Dorka was a two-week widow, and Odongo, the "polygamist" she had rejected, was reappearing in her life. She was thirty-six years old, the man could have been in his fifties, and she was a widow in clan other than Odongo's clan. How was she going to violate the vow she made to Ochieng', her late husband? Was she going to leave a home that housed the graves of her children in pursuit of a man from another clan? *I belong to the Bwai, full stop*, Dorka resolved. But would her resolve hold against the torrent of emotions that likely would sweep her to Kadem?

What about her daughter, Elizabeth, who had grown up believing that she was the daughter of Ochieng'? Was Dorka going to reveal to Elizabeth that the latter's biological father was not the late Ochieng' but someone else?

Would Odongo, when he reappears in recognize Dorka? Would she reveal herself to him should he fail to remember her? What was she going to do about her daughter? Would her daughter have a filial feeling for Odongo? Dorka wondered.

Dorka faced a more urgent matter: how would she, Dorka, stop Elizabeth from claiming Juma, the man who had saved her life? Who would break the news to the doting duo?

Dorka knew she was weak, human, and still a young woman who still desired another child: That begged her to answer the following question: Who would be the father of her next child? Dorka knew her womb still had a promise.

Like most women who had buried the children of one man, she was determined to try another man, now that she was a widow. Before the boy arrived in her home and reminded her of Odongo, she was thinking of marrying one Ogola, her husband's distant cousin. Ogola had not proposed to her in words, but she had seen it in his body language. Now that a previous lover, the man who sired her only surviving child, was coming back into her life, what would she do?

Dorka would retire from Atigo's briefing, struggling with many questions, but without finding any obvious answers.

"Let Odongo come, if he is the Odongo I know!" whispered Dorka in the solitude of her house, believing that she would make the right decisions about her daughter and herself. She decided to separate her life from her daughter's life, at least for a while, if that was what would prove best for her daughter. Even then, Dorka had the interest of the dead husband to protect. "Ochieng', I'll always love you," she whispered, hoping that dead heard the living, her mind more conflicted than ever.

19

Battle by the Graveside

IT WAS THE FIFTH DAY since Juma walked into the Ochieng home. Dorka was sitting in front of her house early afternoon, when she saw two men walk into her home through the front gate. Her heart missed a beat the instant the older of the duo removed his hat, revealing dark hair that had hardly grayed. *It's you, Odongo,* her heart exclaimed. She watched as the older man led the way to the late Ochieng's grave. The moment and the man Dorka had dreaded had arrived.

Elizabeth, who had been idling in her grandmother's house, waiting as Juma caught some sleep, quietly slipped out of the house and joined the two strangers by the graveside. Elizabeth stood next to Grandma, who had beaten her to the graveside. Looking at the man, Elizabeth saw a replica of Juma, except the latter was younger and lighter-skinned. She had no doubt that the older man was Juma's father.

Odongo led in prayer.

Dorka was not required to join the guests because she was "unclean;" she remained seated and continued to watch her daughter and Odongo intensely. She analyzed the way they stood, each left arm bent at the elbow and hand back, with their heads held high; their resemblance was unmistakable. *Yes, the man, known as Odongo, is the Odongo I dated; he is father of my daughter,* Dorka declared, leaving no doubt in her mind about the identity of the man, even before he identified himself.

Odongo concluded his prayers to the fallen alien he did

not know, except he knew that his son had spent nights in the home in mourning. *But where is Juma?* Odongo wondered.

Grandma greeted Odongo and Judas in that order. Then Elizabeth greeted Judas, smiling, displaying the little gap in her upper set of teeth. Judas smiled back, mumbling something about the resemblance between the girl and Uncle Odongo.

Then came the moment Dorka was waiting to witness: She always wondered how Odongo was going to react on greeting a daughter he never met and never knew existed, and here was the moment. Since both Elizabeth and Odongo always held their chins up, in a defiant posture, their eyes locked instantly. Odongo thought he was seeing a younger version of Apudo, his late mother. Then their hands interlocked, and they could not contain their mutual friendly yet reverential filial feelings.

Elizabeth trembled visibly. She tried to say something, but she could not because an uncontrollable well of emotions was building up in her chest. Elizabeth betrayed beads of tears, and she did not know why.

Odongo was examining the facial features of the younger woman next to him and concurrently stealing a side view of the older woman sitting not faraway from the grave.

What have I walked into, Odongo son of Ougo? That is Dorka; she is the woman who returned my love beads, and here is our daughter. Yes, she must be my daughter. Juma, you have led me into a trap, Odongo rumbled within his heart.

Odongo turned his head, looked at Judas, as if asking the young man whether they were seeing the same thing. Judas shifted uncomfortably more out of discomfort in the presence of the alien girl than her resemblance to his grandmother (which he had noticed). Odongo let Judas be and turned to face the girl whose sweaty hand remained glued to his.

Grandma was watching the man intently, wondering what she was seeing. She was one of the few people who knew that Dorka already was pregnant at the time she entered Ochieng's bed. The other person who knew of Dorka's compromised prenuptial condition was the late Ochieng. However, it was something each never discussed with anybody. Ochieng' had died with the secret; he died without broaching it to his wife. However, he mentioned to his daughter (Elizabeth) that she had close relatives in Kadem she would have to look for as an adult.

Now, here was Grandma Atigo, whose son had died, and she was looking at the man who remarkably resembled Elizabeth, her granddaughter. Grandma knew that Elizabeth had sensed a shared blood in the man, and the poor kid did not know what it was she was feeling. These thoughts worried Grandma.

Grandma chuckled, moving away. Her heart went to her late son, wondering whether the dead, like him, perceived events like what she was witnessing. Halfway to her house, she stopped to look in the direction of her daughter-in-law, who remained seated, emotionless and expressionless. Grandma read nothing from her daughter-in-law's facial expression.

Maybe it is my age playing with my mind, Grandma said in her heart, moving away to her house.

Two minutes since their hands interlocked, Odongo finally whispered to Elizabeth, saying, "I am sorry that you have lost your father."

"Thank you, sir! Juma told me about the trouble in your home," Elizabeth said, taking Odongo aback by how she diplomatically summarized his domestic situation.

Judas looked at Odongo, then at the girl. He was hearing two similar voices, except the man's voice was deeper; of significance, they shared that tremulous sub-note. Judas was a younger person, but he remembered the way Apudo, his grandmother, and Uncle Odongo's mother, used to talk. The girl talked and sounded like Apudo.

"Come this way," said Elizabeth to the two men, leading them to a mourning tent that was still up, wondering why the man, Odongo, had made her weak to her bones. She felt weak, where she thought she had recovered from a great loss and was ready to move on with her life. *What was it?* Her heart sang out,; she anxiously was searching for meaning.

Dorka, who had watched everyone's reaction, was pleased. She had ceased to care. She knew Odongo had looked at her from the corner of his left eye, when he saw Elizabeth and realized what had hit him.

Back to her house, Grandma shook Juma awake, saying, "Get out of the house, your people are here!"

"My people?" Juma had exclaimed in fear, still thinking of Okulu's violence on Aura, his mind revisiting the wounds he incurred as Okulu chased him across the land.

"Yes. Your father is here!" Atigo said.

Hearing the mention of his father, Juma became so excited that he shot out of the house in shirttails.

"I'm sorry, father, I left my mother to die!" Juma said, sobbing, embracing his father.

"Your mother is well," Odongo said, bringing instant relief to Juma's heart.

"I was a bad boy that evening," Juma said sobbing, trying to explain what had transpired the fateful evening five days before.

"No. Don't cry. You did not hurt your mother; someone else did. The good news is that she is well and should be home this week. Don't say anything more. You should get ready to leave with Judas. I have friends to visit around Oriwo Hill," Odongo ordered his young son.

Elizabeth was watching, and what she saw was Juma turning into a child in the presence of his father. But she had resolved that, child or not, he was going to be her husband someday.

"No way, he is not leaving me here; he saved my life," Elizabeth said.

"Whoever you are, young lady, I'll not leave you here; you protected my son. Tell your grandmother to count the number of cows she wants, but Juma must hurry back to Kadem to prepare to go to Alliance High School. Here is your letter to Alliance," Odongo said, hading over the letter to Juma, not caring if he hurt any feelings with his boastful speech. Moreover, other than Grandma, the rest of the people in his audience either were familiar to him or were his blood.

"He will not leave me behind. Congratulations, dear Juma. I told you that this would have a good ending," Elizabeth enthused, jumping up and down excitedly.

"Thank you," Juma said, reading the admission letter, his hands shaking as the tremor of joy ran through him, and tears of joy rolled down his face, blurring his vision.

Elizabeth too was sharing in his joy. She had an Alliance Boys' man in her hands; she was tempted to reach out, grab him, and kiss him hard and long, but she understood her culture well and desisted. Then competing tears started to roll down her face; tears of loss mingled with those of joy: the images of her late father flashed by; but then, within her grasp was Juma, the man she considered her future husband, holding a letter to an elite high school.

Looking at Elizabeth reassuringly was Odongo, the man who had overwhelmed her hardly minutes since his arrival. He wondered how his daughter would react when she finally learned about her true ancestry.

Dorka had not stood up since Odongo and Judas arrived in her home. She had enjoyed the unfolding scene. She knew Odongo understood what was going on. She was happy for Elizabeth. Seeing Elizabeth jumping up and down, even for the wrong reason, thrilled Dorka for the young woman would know the truth soon; she'd soon learn that she still had another father she never knew existed. Dorka felt a mixture joy and worry for her daughter, but for now, she eased into a relaxed mood, thinking that she could raise Odongo's expectations, if she wanted. However, in her calculation, that would be years later, after Elizabeth would have advanced in the academics and even married. *Don't be stupid, Dorka, you are an old woman and widow*, she rebuked her audacity to imagine another marriage to a man she once rejected.

Amused at her daughters changing situation, Dorka lit a cigarette, the last from Ochieng's stock, and soon was smoking away. "Even a widow like me has a right to amusement. This cigarette is in your honor, Ochieng'. I won't smoke another cigarette after this one," Dorka muttered. She felt like having a strong drink, but that had to wait until sunset. For one, she had no supply of alcohol. Second, she did not want to ruin Elizabeth's day with her new father.

"I'll escort you to Nairobi, and then come back," Elizabeth was saying, leading Juma and Judas to her favored basking rock near Grandma's house, when Dorka called her, shortly stopping her celebration.

"Elizabeth, get hold of some chicken, your *kinsmen* must eat before they leave," Dorka shouted out an order, hoping that Odongo and Grandma heard and noted her "kinsmen" tease, a tease intended to warn Odongo that she knew him as Elizabeth's father. She too had fired the metaphorical warning arrow near Grandma, who had been looking at the Odongos and Elizabeth with enhanced interest.

"Yes, Ma," Elizabeth said, choking in emotion, thinking that her mother had just given her off in marriage to the men from Kadem.

Not to be outmaneuvered in the bonding game, Odongo ordered Juma and Judas, saying, "You boys, save this beautiful girl the trouble; stand up and round up the fowl. That won't disqualify you from getting a woman to marry in this village."

He is a man who knows how to take charge. But what will I tell Grandma when, one day, I decide that I have to follow my daughter? Dorka said in her heart. Dorka stood up, believing that there was no human law that would stop her from greeting the father of her only daughter. She resolved that she was going to greet Odongo, but she had to wash her hands, feet, and face to free them of Ochieng's dust.

Let traditions be! I was born a Suba before I became a slave to Luo customs! Grandma knows who entered this home today. Let her fret about it, if she wants to do that! Dorka said in her increasingly rebellious mind.

Yes, Grandma Atigo had realized who Odongo was. When Odongo spoke and Elizabeth talked back, Grandma knew Olisa (Elizabeth) had met her biological father. What Grandma was still debating was whether Odongo, the boy Juma, and Dorka had staged everything. Had Olisa faked her drowning? Had the boy staged his dreams? But why had Olisa insisted that she had a husband? Why had Dorka insisted that Olisa could not marry Juma? What was true? What had Dorka and the rest staged? If they had staged nothing, how was Olisa going to learn of her relationships with the Kadem people? How would Olisa react to the revelation about her identity? Grandma struggled with these questions of consequence to her late son's heritage.

Grandma Atigo let the evening roll on without saying a word. She watched as Dorka emerged from her house dressed in her best dress and spruced up. Then Grandma watched, without uttering a word, as Dorka walked across the compound to greet the people from Kadem, including

Juma. Later in the evening, she watched as the youngsters left to tour the hill, leaving Dorka and the man, Odongo, alone.

"I'm sorry that you lost your husband," Odongo said, once the youth had disappeared behind the hill.

"Thank you. I'm sorry to hear that you almost lost your wife to a family dispute," Dorka responded in kind.

"I feel humbled. You were right, and you are still right today; polygamy is not a good thing," Odongo broached the subject that had made him lose Dorka to the late Ochieng'.

"Who are you?" Dorka asked, feigning a lack of acquaintance with the man before her.

"You should know who I am. Your daughter felt the bond of kinship, when she first saw me," Odongo said.

"*My daughter?* Elizabeth cannot be my daughter alone. She had a father, whom she has buried," Dorka feigned protest, teasing Odongo's imagination. They were speaking in low tones.

"That maybe true," Odongo volunteered.

"I know that Elizabeth buried her father a few weeks back," Dorka faked a challenge.

"What do you mean? You are Dorka, and you were born in Magunga," Odongo said.

"It must be a mere coincidence. I am not the person you think I am," teased Dorka.

"Thank you for the meal. My name is Odongo. Thank you for protecting my son. You know that I cannot spend here. Mourn your husband, then you could consider taking up a piece of some land I saw on sale near Macalder Mines; we still mine gold there," Odongo proposed to Dorka, throwing in a wealth metaphor at the end.

"You are still the sweet talker you were many years ago. Back then it was cows; now it is gold," Dorka said, in admiration of the man who gave her the only daughter and child to have survived childhood.

"Don't make it sound as though I am ageless," complained Odongo pleasantly, but his actual message to Dorka was that he was still in good shape regardless of his age.

"Yes, that is what it is; ageless, old yet no grays, still

trying to ensnare a hapless widow he could not trap in her youth," Dorka challenged.

"Thank you for the compliment," Odongo said, standing up to stretch his legs.

"How are you going to separate your daughter from your son?" Dorka came to the more urgent matter after Odongo returned to his seat.

"Is she in school?" Odongo asked, though he was not worried about school fees, what with his extensive wealth.

"Yes," Dorka said, believing she had prepared a path smooth enough for her daughter to follow, if the latter wished to go to Kadem.

They talked on, knowing their limits, keeping a respectable physical separation between themselves. Odongo was not going to risk the wrath of Dorka's in-laws, so he let her be once their talk ended. He left the home to explore its environs, while she retreated to her station by the graveside.

Grandma Atigo watched from her verandah, as Odongo and Dorka talked alone at length. Grandma was amazed. She noted no readable postures in the duo's mutual body language. To her, they were just two strangers talking. Even then, Grandma knew that her Olisa was the subject of their talk.

Grandma was satisfied with what she had seen. She concluded that Dorka was not going to decamp from her home soon, not while she, Grandma, was alive. Even then, she was ready to fight for Dorka, and she was ready to do it so loudly that the whole land would hear her plea. Grandma waited for an opportune moment to interrogate Dorka and share her concerns, if any, with her. She got the chance during their joint supper.

"So he is the man?" Grandma asked during their supper.

"So you knew?" Dorka asked.

"Yes, when he walked into this compound, the resemblance between Elizabeth and Juma became so clear that I understood why you sent me to interview the boy a couple of days ago," Grandma Atigo explained.

"He is the man. I ran away from his animal wealth only because he was a polygamist," Dorka said so dryly she could have been talking about some local herdsman and not the father of her only child.

"Did he marry you?" Grandma asked.

"No. He spoiled me with earthly gifts. When I said No to him, and even returned his beads during an encounter in Sori, he was on the way to my father with many heads of cattle. He had to tell his escorts to go back with the cattle. However, he left Elizabeth in me. Ochieng' never wasted his time thereafter. I have no regrets," Dorka spoke with pride, her long neck up.

"Why didn't you say this before?" Grandma asked.

"I guessed you knew, because Ochieng' knew," Dorka retorted, warning her mother-in-law as to how far she, Dorka, was willing to revisit the past.

"That is true," Grandma grunted.

"You will have to let Elizabeth know that Odongo is his father," Dorka said firmly.

"Are you returning to him?" asked Grandma, studying her daughter-in-law, searching her face for a lie.

"No. I never belonged to him. I am a widow with an old daughter. I cannot leave Ochieng's fresh grave. This land still has my brothers-in-law," Dorka said in a mournful tone, mourning her dead children and husband, yet she felt Elizabeth tied her to Odongo, however long the tether.

"Never?" Grandma quipped, challenging her daughter-in-law.

"Grandma, you don't want me to start mourning now. I am a human being. I know I have buried my husband, but I don't know who will bury me," Dorka said, choking with emotion.

"I'll talk to Elizabeth, but only because the boy saved her life," declared Grandma, ending the talk.

20

You Never Will Marry Olisa

LATER THAT EVENING CAME THE TIME to release the guests for the night. Elizabeth was to return to Ogande, while the Kadem men were to head home the following morning.

After the Kadem people introduced themselves formally and Dorka introduced her daughter and mother-in-law, Odongo thanked his hosts for keeping his son safe. He then paid a token amount towards the purchase of "the sugar Grandma used to entertain her funeral guests," who continued to pass through the home. Dorka protested against the gift, but Odongo ignored her as expected.

Finally, Grandma spoke to the truth about the weighty matter she shared with Dorka and Odongo.

"Unfortunately, my young friend from Kadem, you never will marry Olisa. She is not supposed to marry a man from Kadem," Grandma declared, fingering Juma.

"Grandma? Am I dreaming?" asked Elizabeth, alarmed.

"Olisa, you cannot marry any man from Kadem. Why you can't do that, you'll know when you have had your children," Grandma said sadly.

"Ma?" Elizabeth looked to her mother for guidance, but Dorka smiled on and could have been high on the glass of the alcohol she had taken "to fortify herself for the special-and-challenging occasion."

When Dorka finally spoke, she said, "What do you want me to say? This world is a small place. I spent my life as a young woman enjoying life, the way you do now in the prime of your teens. I am sorry; but Elizabeth, you have a divided heritage. The embarrassment is the price you will have to pay as my daughter. You will not marry the man who saved your life. You cannot marry him because he is your brother," Dorka replied.

"Liz, what is going on?" Juma asked; he equally was alarmed.

"I don't know, Juma," Elizabeth said in anguish, struggling to believe her mother. But the echoes of her grandmother's original declaration reverberated in her ears, warning her that neither her mother nor her grandmother were spinning a tale.

"Elizabeth, the man who rescued you is your brother," Odongo said, further inflaming his daughter's wounded soul.

"Is that a joke, Ma?" Elizabeth challenged her mother.

"No. You were in me the day I arrived here. I was running away from this man's vast wealth; I was running away because he was a polygamist. Betha, we have said enough. Embrace who you are. He is your father; get to know him, but don't forget Grandma; never forget the man we buried outside," Dorka implored emotionlessly, as if she were narrating a distant event she observed some years ago.

"Grandma?" Elizabeth cried out, wondering why the three adults in the room were saying the same thing to her. She locked eyes with Grandma, seeking the truth, wondering who her real father was. Was he the man infront of her or the one several feet below the rocky soils of Sinai Hill?

"Elizabeth, when you greeted this man known as Odongo by the graveside, he was shaking and so were you, did you wonder why?" Grandma asked, challenging Elizabeth to think.

Elizabeth smiled, realizing that her life had changed. She turned and embraced her cousin Judas, who was closest to her. She turned to her right and embraced Grandma, before crossing the circle to embrace Juma, sobbing and saying, "I love you, my brother!" Her face glistening with streams of tears of joy in the setting sun, Elizabeth stood between Juma and Odongo, holding hands with each of them, smiling at her mother who too was smiling. She was home with her kin.

It is true; when I first greeted my father, the warmth

*from his hand felt familiar and reassuring; thence I felt cold,
as if I had walked into a shade after a period in the sun; I
could not explain why.* Now I know why, Elizabeth said in
silence, living her new reality. She knew her mother was
on alcohol, but the latter's smiles amid what could have
been a major crisis, had made the transition easy for her
(Elizabeth).

"When you talk, you sound like your father; then the
way both of you touch your noses often, as if there is rot
in the air, you share that with your brother too; Elizabeth,
you are your father and your brother standing next to you.
Listen to your voice, and then listen to your father's voice
and to Juma's voice, in turn, and tell me what you hear,"
Grandma challenged Elizabeth.

"Obeth (Elizabeth), what do you hear?" Odongo asked.

"Is this a game?" Juma asked.

"Grandma is right; Elizabeth, you are Juma, and you
are your late grandmother, Apudo, buried in Kadem,"
Judas observed.

"I believe that the man who saved my life is my
brother. My late father said something before he died,"
Elizabeth observed.

"What was that, Elizabeth?" Dorka asked. She was
more sober, thanks to the heightened drama of the last
couple of minutes, which, to her surprise, her daughter
had survived well.

"My late father said, 'Liz, when I am gone, you should
be free to go and search for your cousins in Kadem.' I
asked him, 'Dad, what cousins do I have in Kadem?' He
replied, 'Elizabeth, you'll know who they are when the time
comes.' It appears this is the time he meant."

"Say no more, child; you are a woman; you know not
where you will be buried; you are like a bird; you can fly to
any corner of the world. Whether they call you the
daughter of the Bwai or the Adem matters not. Because
you are a woman, the whole world is your home. Your
home will be where your husband lives. Know that I love
you," Grandma said, tears rolling down her face. She was
dreading the reality of losing her granddaughter and
possibly daughter-in-law, though both were remote
possibilities to her. She believed Elizabeth would always
remember her. She too believed that Dorka would not
walk away from the land that swallowed Ochieng' and

their children.

"I love you, Grandma," Elizabeth said, reassuringly. "I'll always do."

"Thank you, Olisa. Go to school," Grandma Atigo said, feeling relieved. She never before played such a delicate role in her long life.

Dorka too was relieved. Her daughter had embraced her dual identity without problems.

Whatever struggles remained for Dorka were her own fights. By law, she belonged with the Bwai people, whose son she had buried in love. She hoped to leave it that way, even as she set her daughter free to follow her own heart.

Reflecting on the near tragedy and drama that had been her life since she sunk into the Nyogunde only for Juma to rescue her, Elizabeth was happy that she had done nothing stupid during the brief period she viewed Juma as a future husband. About this matter, her mother would quiz her at length late into the night.

"Elizabeth, you never thought of doing anything foolish with Juma?" Dorka asked.

"No, Ma. He felt like an Angel to me; he was a person I could not reach for a while; he felt like a part of me, even as I tried to believe otherwise. Then this discovery of kinship, and I now understand why I felt that way about him."

"You will visit your father's home so that you know your many sisters, and even the other brother you have not seen. You know that when you marry, your husband must know where I am and where your father is."

"You'll never go to Kadem?" Elizabeth asked.

"Why do you think I would do that? Ochieng' married me fully; I have buried him, but I loved him, and I'll live through widowhood here on Sinai Hill."

"You'll remarry," Elizabeth said.

"I still have several months to think through that?" Dorka replied without further comment, when she usually would have chastised her daughter.

"You won't give me another brother or sister?" Elizabeth asked—introducing a theme, which her mother and she had revisited over the years.

"Don't take me back there, Betha; you always wanted a brother or a sister, and I tried but they wouldn't live,"

Dorka said, without raising her voice, though it was a very sad theme for a mother, like her, who had buried four children to Malaria.

"I love you, Ma; but maybe, if you tried your luck with another man in another place, a child would survive," Elizabeth argued resorting to her high-school biology.

"Now, you want to spoil my day with you book ideas," Dorka complained. "You will excuse me, Elizabeth; smoking and stress go together. Don't ever smoke," Dorka cautioned, lighting a cigarette.

"Love you the way you are, Mom," Elizabeth said; she was getting emotional again. Dorka's smoking and drinking habits bothered Elizabeth. She wondered how her mother would survive alone with Grandma.

"Go to school and feel happy that you have a father who is alive, even as you lost another father you loved, and who loved us dearly. Goodnight, Betha," she said, dismissing her daughter for the night.

"Thank you, Ma; take care of Grandma."

The guests from Kadem slept over as a courtesy to her mourning mother. Elizabeth knew that Odongo had talked at length with her mother. She was not sure what it was they talked over; but she was happy that they were in talking terms.

Later that evening, Odongo walked down the hill to visit with an old friend from the old days at Macalder Mines. Elizabeth slept in her grandmother's house, and so did Judas and Juma.

In the morning, Grandma released Elizabeth and the Kadem men with a word of prayer. As Elizabeth left Korondo Village that January morning, with Juma, who was carrying her suitcase, following immediately behind her, Judas leading the way, and Odongo closing the rear, she was no less proud of Juma the newly discovered brother than she was when he was, to her, the stranger who saved her from sinking into the depths of the earth. She now loved him the more as a brother who had led her to her father, a part of her she never knew existed.

The settled plan was that all of them would board a bus to Rodi Kopany, from where Elizabeth would catch a bus to Ogande Girls Secondary School. The Ougos would head south to Rongo and then Migori Hospital, but

Elizabeth changed her mind on reaching Rodi Kopany.

"I'm going to Migori to see Juma's mother," she told her Dad.

"You must go to school," Odongo said.

"No, I'm not leaving you before I see your home. Besides, I have to see Juma's mother and console her," Liz said.

"I understand your concerns, Liz, but rest assured that I will come and collect you from school during half-term break. That should be a few weeks away."

"Then take me to school, all of you, before you head to Migori; I want to see more of you, Dad," Liz said, mournfully.

"You get your wish; we will take you to Ogande," Odongo said. "Juma, check your admission letter, I could buy for you some of the required items in Homa Bay."

Liz was thrilled; it meant she would reach school well supplied with essentials; she also would have a brother to show around to other girls.

Therefore, Liz and her father, brother, and cousin ended up in Homa Bay. Dad shopped for daughter and son. Three hours later, the men left Elizabeth in Ogande and headed south to Migori.

However, Elizabeth Odongo had other ideas; like a snake entering a hole, her head was out of the school fence before she sat on her school bed.

"I have a mourning ritual I have to attend tomorrow. I'll be back on Sunday," Elizabeth explained to the Acting Headmistress, in a tremulous mournful voice, tears rolling down her face.

"Elizabeth, calm down. I understand what you are going through. It is perfectly okay to go and bond with your kin. Moreover, it is a weekend," the Acting Headmistress said, filling an absentee form. "Make sure you are in class on Monday morning."

"Thank you, Madam!"

"It is getting late, tell me how you will reach the road," implored the Acting Headmistress.

"I'll try."

"Give me ten minutes; I'll drop you at Kabunde Junction, before proceeding to Homa Bay for a school business.

Elizabeth's destination was Macalder; she hoped to

visit Aura in Migori. She had resolved to go and see the land of her paternal ancestors and know her kin before she could settle in school.

21

The Odongos, a Healing Family

AT MIGORI HOSPITAL, Aura was ready to go home, but not before the drama that saw Juma breakdown on seeing a thinner, clean-shaven mother with a head scar.

"I'm sorry for the trouble I have always been all my life; I have always been a bad spoilt child; I promise that I will act like a grownup. "

"Stop weeping, Juma. You are a man. I know who hit my head. God will pay him," Aura said reassuringly.

"The troubles I have seen the last week have turned me into an adult. I swam with snakes and slept in the bushes listening to hyenas," Juma mourned.

"Juma, what happened? You have scratches all over your legs and arms; what happened to you?" Olga, his favorite stepsister asked. She was one of the Odongo daughters still with Aura at the Hospital. The others were the Aura twin daughters, Leah and Rachel. The other Odongo daughters had left for their homes, passing through Macalder to see Atieno, their mother.

The news about Okulu had yet to reach the Odongos in Migori. In addition, Abich still had refused to visit Aura at the Hospital. All her sisters still went to her house to sleep, arguing that she was their blood, however odd and foolish her actions were.

"Okulu, Judas, Grace the dog, and John chased after me as if I was a killer. I ran through the creepers and bushes of Kadem, then ran through even thornier bushes of Bwai, and crossed many streams overgrown with reeds, following no particular path. Whenever I stopped to rest, I could still hear Grace barking. My brothers were using my own dog to track me down like a village rabbit. However, I am perhaps alive because Judas here had thought it wise to come with Grace. Whenever Okulu and his gang were close to me, Grace would bark, and I would change course, often following no beaten path to make it difficult for them to catch up with me."

"We caught up with him holed up in a pastor's house around a place known as Mikumu Ridge in Bwai," Judas said, inviting a cruel look from Odongo.

"Juma, is that true?" Aura asked.

"No. But I was in the pastor's house, as they argued with the pastor outside the gate."

"Juma, stop; you make my head spin," Aura complained. She could not imagine Okulu, armed with a spear, hovering around where her little son had taken cover to escape detection.

"Sorry; but I escaped as the pastor argued with Okulu," Juma said.

"What was the pastor's name?" Odongo asked, joining Juma's narrative.

"His wife called him Pastor Aaron," Juma said.

"I know him; his wife's name is Ada. He is a pastor of my church," Aura quipped.

"Ada gave me water to bathe and drink, fresh clothes to wear, food to eat; we even read Bible verses together. I must revisit her in good times!" Juma pledged.

"What happened to your own clothes?" Olga asked.

"When I reached Ada's home, I was tired, hungry, and aching all over from the scratches on my body. I hardly had any clothes hanging on my body."

"Juma, I don't want to hear more; my head still aches from the accident," Aura complained.

"Just one more thing, Ma; you have to hear this," Juma said, looking at his father, who nodded at him, authorizing him to continue with his story, even as he didn't know what the narrator would say.

"Around midnight, I was close to a river known as Nyogunde," Juma opened up, forcing Odongo to eye him sternly, as if saying, 'Watch your tongue before you open your mouth!'

"Where is the river you call Nyogunde?" Rachel asked.

"It is a river in Bwai, somewhere close to Kanyamwa,"

Juma explained.

"You reached Kanyamwa hardly six hours after you left home in Thim Lich?" Aura asked.

"I could have crossed the river earlier, but I had stopped to eat some groundnuts some farmer had left in the field," Juma said.

"Juma, you stole someone's groundnuts," Rachel said accusingly.

"No, that is not stealing, Rachel; that is meeting a human need, like when Jesus ate from the fields on Sabbath," Leah observed, taking an opposing view from her twin sister.

"Leah is right, Rachel," Olga observed.

"We hope he doesn't make it a habit of eating from people's farms!" Judas said, taking a shot at his cousin and friend.

"So I was eating these groundnuts inside a cassava farm, when suddenly, behind me, perhaps a mile away, a dog was barking, while ahead of me in the distance, some hyenas were laughing and giggling over some animal carcass," Juma said, pacing around like a tough man.

"Really, you aren't making up any of this, brother? Which direction did you go?" Olga asked.

"I went toward the hyenas because behind me were Judas here and Grace, both after my blood," Juma joked.

"That is not true, Juma. You know that Grace and I were there to protect you," Judas complained.

"We know that you love Juma," Aura said, smiling.

"So with Grace barking behind me, I ran toward the Nyogunde, which I would discover, had hot and salty quagmires," Juma explained.

"Really?" Olga quipped, doubting the tale of bravado with which her favorite stepbrother was entertaining them. "So what happened?"

"As I ran toward the river, I heard a voice of a woman crying, "Help! Help! Can someone help?" Juma narrated, looking at his father, as if asking for permission.

Judas held up his hand, as if warning Juma that the latter could be treading on delicate ground, if he narrated the story of Elizabeth and brought the full wrath of his mother on his father.

Odongo nodded in the affirmative, encouraging Juma to continue with the narrative, believing that the boy could judge what was safe to say. Moreover, it was only a matter of time before Elizabeth's story reached Macalder.

Aura looked at Judas and her husband, in that order, wondering what unpleasant thing the two were worried Juma could reveal.

"I was scared at first. One, the woman was making noise and could have given away my location to Grace and Okulu. Second, I asked myself, 'Juma, what if the woman calling for help inside the bushy river valley was at the mercy of some python that was crushing her to death?'"

"Juma, enough," exclaimed Aura, freaking out at the thought of her child encountering a python.

"'Help! Help! Whoever is out there, help!' she cried as I drew closer to her. She was hardly ten steps away. I could see her head in the moonlight," Juma continued his narrative, ignoring his mother's displeasure.

"*Her head?*" Olga, Rachel, and Leah screamed almost in unison.

"Yes! She was sinking into the weak ground. Even as she moved, I had realized that the whole river basin was weak and could sink one day. There was a smell of salt and decay everywhere. I could see that she was in a muddy area," Juma talked, demonstrating as he went.

"Juma is not imagining things; we passed the area with Judas. It is weak and hardly a foot from the narrow path. It spews hot water and gas. There is white salt on dry land all around. The ground shook as we moved along the path," Odongo said.

"Really?" Olga quipped not believing her brother and now her father. But would each of them and Judas lie? Olga wondered.

"Yea! Here I was in the middle of a moony night in alien land, walking on a narrow path, beside which was weak land. There, next to me, was the woman sunk deep to the neck in the quagmire, with both hands still above the ground. My first impulse was to reach out, grab her hand, and pull her out! 'But what if she sinks right in with me as the ground gives way underneath where I am standing?' so I asked in silence.'"

"Juma, I have stopped listening to your strange tale. All I know is that you are safe and with me here, and we should go home. If you continue with your tale, you will send me back to the emergency room," Aura complained.

"What else are you yet to reveal? It looks like, you are a man; you should have turned around and faced Okulu right there" Aura said, before asking, "Did the woman die?"

Everyone laughed, now that even the patient was willing to listen to the rest of Juma's story.

"No. Ma, understand that I was so involved in helping the woman that, for a while, I forgot that Okulu was chasing after me. I was only thinking of how to get out the unknown woman alive," Juma argued.

"If she survived, where is she? I need a helper," challenged Aura. She could have been serious. The issue of her son getting married had been a matter of constant debate between her husband and herself. Of course, her boy was heading to Alliance High School, but having his wife around her would have been a blessing. That had been Aura's attitude since her near-death experience of a couple of days back.

"Ma, don't jump ahead of my story; people need to hear it, after which we will go and eat," Juma said, brushing aside the issue of marriage that had brought much torment on him whenever he dined with his father.

"We want to hear it, Bro," Olga said in English.

"I learned a few things in the Scouts Movement! Do not panic while in danger! Think of your safety, whatever you do to confront the danger! So thinking like a scout, I told the unknown woman, 'wait a minute; I'll be back,'" Juma explained, bringing joy to Aura who felt that her child had become an adult.

"She has no name?" Leah asked.

"Please Leah, allow us to hear the whole story," Rachel complained.

"Her name is Elizabeth," Juma volunteered, opening another line of interrogation.

"Elizabeth who?" Leah asked.

Juma looked at his father, who nodded in the negative, hinting to his son not to call her an Odongo, wondering whether Juma would understand.

"She is Elizabeth Ochieng," Juma said.

"Why do you have to ask for permission from your father to say the woman's name?" Aura asked, unhappy that Odongo was encouraging her son to tell lies.

"The young woman is not here, Ma, so I thought it was

not proper to use her real name, and Dad agrees," Juma explained, leaving his mother wondering how fast her son had matured since he excelled in KCPE. She let the lie pass for the moment.

"What is h*er real name?*" Rachel asked, believing that her brother had lied.

"Please everyone, allow Juma to finish his escape story, then we can go home," Olga pleaded.

"I walked back to a bush I had passed by at the edge of the river, yanked free a sizable branch of a tree, and hurried back to the girl. Grace was barking again, but now she was to the east on the previous ridge. I breathed easy, knowing that they had missed my trail to the river. I knew why, but that is beside the point," Juma jumped onto Olga's suggestion and continued the narrative, leaving his mother amused, and his light-skinned sister Rachel enraged, even her skin was darkening a shade.

"Bro, you are an educated man, if you have a real story, tell it the way it occurred. Why do you think they missed you?" Rachel challenged her brother.

"They missed me because Grace had followed the path recently used by a group teenagers going to a party on the eastern side of what the locals call Nyamos Ridge," Juma explained.

"Judas, is that true?" Olga asked.

"Yeah! By the time we realized what was happening, we were behind the home where the party was in progress," Judas said, offering Juma a needed hand.

"Why didn't you join the party?" Olga challenged.

"One, Okulu was armed with a spear and was not in the mood of partying. Second, we were dirty and scratched and aching all over; we too were hungry," Judas said.

"You see; I am right?" Juma exclaimed.

"Continue. Bro," Olga pleaded.

"Back to Elizabeth: I told her, 'Hold this branch with both hands; I'll pull you out. Never hold me! I will hold you, if I need to, during the rescue!'" Juma said, demonstrating on Olga his favorite sister.

"So you were thinking of how to remain alive, if she were to sink, as you tried to rescue her?" Rachel asked.

"Yeah!"

"That is cruel, Bro!" Olga quipped. "Heroes don't think of their lives when they help people in danger."

"Anyway, she said, 'Whoever you are, I want you to know that I love you. I particularly love your voice. I want you to know that I love you, incase both of us go under as you try to save me,'" Juma narrated, choking with emotion.

"She really said that?" Rachel asked.

"Yeah! Then I replied, 'I love you too!'" Juma found himself uttering "the love phrase" he could not have uttered weeks before, not in the presence of his mother. The incident had transformed him.

"Juma, I love you! Now I know I gave birth to a wise and brave man!" Aura said, holding her son's left hand.

"Hi! Bro, why did she love your voice?" Olga asked, teasing her favorite brother.

"Olga, what kind of question is that? Our brother's voice is deeper than what it was the last time we met him over X-Mass!" Rachel said in jest; she then turned to her father and asked, "Baba, why are you shedding tears?"

"You people cannot feel how close Juma came to sinking into that dangerous river? If the woman had not cried for help, or if she never were there that night to meet her brother, Juma couldn't have realized there was danger ahead, and he could have sunk into the muddy river, without a trace," Odongo said mournfully, his tongue betraying his intentions.

"I know it is unlike you to cry," Aura observed.

"I cried because a lot of unusual things have happened in the last few days. Any hardened soul could have wept. You almost lost your life; Juma almost lost his life. I feel there is more trouble at home, where I have not been for a month," Odongo said mournfully.

"Dad, why did you say that the Elizabeth was there that night "to meet her brother"? Which brother was she to meet?" Rachel asked.

"She was to meet her brother there; we heard that. Juma finish the story," Odongo tried to hush things up.

"Wait! Wait! Dad, why are all the men smiling? What conspiracy are you in?" Rachel charged.

"None," Judas said to protect Odongo.

"So what happened next, Bro?" Olga asked, deciding to guide Juma along, though she was convinced that there was something special about Elizabeth. Why else were Odongo, Judas, and Juma keeping her real identity secret? Olga wondered.

"Anyway, I pulled her out in one attempt! She was crying, hugging me; calling me an Angel! Then she cleaned herself; then prayed!" Juma spoke innocently, not fully understanding that words could mean many things.

"Then what happened?" Leah asked.

"She took me to her home," Juma said.

"Talking for myself, I am hungry. We the Ougo cousins can go and eat something? It is not common that we are together like this. Olga here is married to a wealthy man; she should buy all of us food," Judas said. "Here is the doctor," Judas added, believing that it was the right time to let Odongo brief Aura about Elizabeth in private.

"Okay, kids, go and look for something to eat," Odongo said, dismissing his children and nephew. He wanted to brief Aura on the delicate matter of the identity of Elizabeth.

22

Aura Leaves Hospital

DR. GAGI HANDED OVER the release papers to Odongo, saying, "You are a lucky man; your wife could have died, if people had not rushed her here. I do not know how your home is now, but she needs no more tension in her life. Second, stand up; I want to shake your hands. I have heard that you are the father of Juma Joseph Odongo, the top student in KCPE this year."

"I am Odongo Ougo; they call me Odongo Hippo!"

"Well, you are a good father of many daughters; I am not sure you still have a single daughter who is old enough to marry me. If there is none, the way I have been told, then I can wait for the next!" Dr. Gagi said.

"Well, I'm an old man, and she is an old woman, where will I get another daughter to give you?"

"Now hear this; are you ready? My mother-in-law, here, may give me a daughter soon!"

"I'm too old, doctor," complained Aura, faking surprise. She had known that she was expecting a week before, but she religiously was saving the announcement for the day after Juma left home for school.

"Mister Odongo, why are you not cheering your wife?" wondered Dr. Gagi.

"Cheering for what?" Odongo asked, wondering what kind of stretch of good luck he was enjoying after a trying spell.

"O the Luos and their reverence over pregnancies. My mother-in law is pregnant, cheer her up," Dr. Gagi said, enjoying the old man. Turning to Aura, Dr. Gagi said,

"Have a safe journey to Kadem; see you back here in a month. Eat well and avoid any work; let Odongo cook for himself, if he fails to convince your co-wife, who has refused to visit you, to cook for him."

"Doctor Gagi, I'll give you a daughter, but you must wait until she is through with school. Now, I hope you are not joking about Mama's health."

"No. She has recovered, but she cannot work because she is pregnant with perhaps a girl," explained Dr. Gagi.

"Since when did I become pregnant, doctor?" Aura asked, still feigning ignorance.

"See you in a month, and may God continue to bless you. We noticed you were pregnant before we did the surgery last week. That allowed us to take measures to save the baby," Dr. Gagi explained, before he closed the door, leaving husband and wife lost in thought.

"Lord, thank You for giving life where man had schemed death. May Your hands continue to guide the hands of Your workers in this hospital. Amen!" Aura prayed, and was on her feet as soon as Odongo said Amen. "Daddy! Aren't we leaving this room?" she asked.

"The children have not returned from their meals," Odongo said forlornly, still grappling with the latest news about Aura.

"What a situation I have here, Aura daughter of Gor? You men have no shame. How will I explain to my grandsons how I got a baby?" Aura joked.

"Men cannot create babies in the absence of women. In my case, an excited grandmother asked for a baby, and God heard her cries," Odongo said, picking up his stick and hat.

"Tell me something. Is it true that Juma rescued a woman from a quagmire?" Aura asked, sitting back on her bed.

"Yes. I met the girl," Odongo said, shaken, his tremulous voice getting even more tremulous.

"Why are you trembling like that?" Aura asked.

"It is remarkable that you were dreaming about an event as it was happening," Odongo said.

"Isn't that strange?" Aura asked, but she knew he was lying about something.

"Well, women tend to feel what their children feel, even if they are separated by oceans," Odongo observed, espousing telepathy.

"Mine are too real," Aura said.

"What else have you seen?" Odongo asked.

"Did Judas tell you that Grace bit Okulu badly?" Aura asked.

"No," Odongo said, relieved that Aura had moved away from the question of Elizabeth.

"Well, she bit him during the chase. They had given up hunting for Juma. That was when she bit him," Aura explained.

"Why? Why? What did he do to the dog?" Odongo asked nervously.

"The girls who spoke to Abich said that Grace bit Okulu so badly that he lost feeling on his left hand. The right hand is swollen. She told them that the wound was spreading throughout the body," Aura explained.

"God help us! But what can we say?" Odongo said in exasperation.

"I will not take Okulu to court, but I'll not live in that home any longer than I need to. I know Juma is going back to school, and so we cannot start a new home until he comes back, but as soon as he returns in two months, I must be in my new home," Aura said, setting conditions to Odongo.

"Aura, look at me, I abused your trust, when I brought Atieno to my father's home before you could join me. I married you, when you were a mere child, but you have done well. I know you have suffered greatly because of the woman I brought home before you could take your place as my wife. Your daughters Leah and Rachel tell your story," implored Odongo.

"So you realized why I named them so?" Aura asked.

"I did back then. Those were the names of the Laban sisters, for whose hearts Jacob toiled for fourteen years, getting Leah after seven years, when he thought he had worked for Rachel's heart. He then worked for another seven years before he could feed from Rachel's heart. Then you named your only son Joseph, seeing yourself as Rachel, the younger sibling for whose heart Jacob's heart raved. Then you forced me to take a new name Jacob," Odongo explained.

"Now Joseph's trials have just began; Nairobi to me is old Egypt; Juma must stay there and prove himself, because his brother has caused hard feelings in the home. Now I have no one to send on errands," Aura said, believing that Nairobi was not a good place for her little son, and that he would not return to Thim Lich because of the corrupting ways of Nairobi.

"How did you become pregnant?" Odongo asked, teasingly.

"Things happen when a woman is happy. How many women send sons to Alliance High School? Juma success brought untold joy in my heart! I said, 'Why don't I try, now that I am happy?' And the Lord listened to me," Aura explained.

"I offered no help in any of that?" Odongo asked, jokingly, his fingers offering some dorsal massage.

"You did. Now, talking of help; I thought Juma should have brought home the girl he saved," Aura said, returning to the Elizabeth story.

"Men rarely marry women they have saved from water; such women are like untouchable bodies of the sea dead; they are like living curses," Odongo spun a believable part-psychological-and-part-spiritual lie to explain why Juma could not marry Elizabeth. Odongo was shaking and blinking rapidly as he spoke, wondering whether Aura would accommodate him, if he said the truth, which was that Elizabeth was a daughter he sired out of wedlock.

"You can't be serious? Why are you shaking like that?" Aura asked again, wondering what was so special about the Elizabeth that Odongo lied and spoke about her in fear. She could not call her husband a liar, but she could see his eyes, and they told her that he was lying.

Odongo could not respond.

"What is the truth about Elizabeth? Did she survive the accident?" Aura asked holding her husband, searching his eyes as if the truth lived in them.

"Yes."

"Was she some sacrifice to the rains?" Aura asked.

"No."

"O my God! So Alal was right," Aura said, remembering something her stepdaughter Alal once shared with her.

"She was right about what?" Odongo asked, knowing that he no longer could lie about the identity of Elizabeth.

"The girl Juma saved is his sister. Is that not so?" Aura asked, looking Odongo in the eye. She saw a scared man.

But why? What else was out there? Aura wondered in silence.

"How do you know that?" Odongo asked, wondering what else Aura knew about his past life with women.

"The mother's name is Dorka," Aura said.

"You are amazing!" Odongo exclaimed, jumping to his feet.

"When I could not conceive for seven years, your mother ordered that you marry a third wife. You almost married a woman known as Dorka from Gwasii," Aura explained.

"You knew all that?" Odongo asked for lack of what to say, looking away.

"Owinyo told me how, after several dates with the woman in Sori, you collected a few bulls and cows, claiming that you were going to auction them in Aora Chuodho Livestock Market. With Dorka slipping away through your fingers, because you were a polygamist, your destination was her father's chair, before which you had intended to dump the livestock Kadem style," Aura explained, enjoying the exposition.

"You lived all these years with that information in your heart?" Odongo asked.

"Yes. However, on reaching Sori, Dorka rejected your hand, even returning gifts, with which you had conferred her. Now we know that the only gift she would not give back was your baby that was growing in her," Aura said, enjoying her husband's past misery.

"Owinyo narrated all that to you?" Odongo asked, feeling betrayed by his brother.

"He said more; he explained how you decided to sell the animals, promising, 'Never again will I go after another young girl,'" Aura reported.

"I have kept the promise," Odongo said

"Isn't it strange that my child ran across the land in the night, with a mad brother behind him, only to end up rescuing his sister from certain death?" Aura wondered aloud.

"It is strange," Odongo said, enjoining Aura in appreciating the many twists and turns in the tragedy, which nearly claimed the latter's life. "Juma claimed how, after he had rescued the girl, she led him to a home on top of Oriwo Hill. He claimed how, all along, he had intended to reach the home on the hill because it had a prominent bright light that was visible miles out."

"Strange! Did I not tell you how I dreamed about Juma rescuing some woman from a river?"

"You did. Now when you dispatched Judas and me to go and look for Juma in the land of the Bwai, we reached the place where Okulu's chase had ended. We crossed the seasonal river known as Nyogunde, with the land shaking under our weight as we walked. Then we reached this very unstable area with hot springs spewing gas, salty mud and water. My heart sank, thinking the land could have swallowed my child. A few steps later, we saw a recently cut branch of a tree in an area that had seen some disturbance in the mud, as if from an animal that had struggled to get free from the quagmire. 'If it had been Juma sinking here, someone had saved him,' I said in my heart, a little bit relieved."

"So he indeed saved the girl?" Aura asked.

"Yes. They pointed to the place on our way out of the area today. Aura, let me finish this twisted tale. On the other side of the river, a herdsman directed us to the home on the hill, saying that he had seen "a light-skinned stranger" walking the plains with a girl from the home on the hill. He told us to ask for a girl named Elizabeth Ochieng, and that she should lead us to the boy."

"Did you say a light-skinned boy? Juma is not some Arab; he is your own blood," Aura complained.

"You will forgive me, but I didn't mean to ridicule our son or the color of his skin; I'm reporting what the herdsman told us," Odongo said, squeezing Aura's hand to emphasize that he did not doubt Juma's Ougo roots.

"I know he is your son regardless of the color of his skin," Aura said, hurting.

"Thank you, Aura. Back to Juma's story: We entered the home. Ahead of us, on the right of the house facing the gate we had passed through, there was a fresh grave and logs of wood burning nearby. A middle-aged woman in a man's coat sat not far from the grave. *A man died in this home,* I said in my heart, judging that the woman was his widow and the position of the grave relative to the main house in the two-house home. Then as Judas and I converged around the grave to pray, a young woman who kept touching her nose frequently and walked lazily like

Juma joined us."

"Whose grave were you praying around?" Aura asked.

"One Ochieng's grave. He was the one who had beaten me to Dorka's hand," Odongo said.

"This Ochieng died recently?" Aura asked all ears.

"Yes. The fire that had guided Juma across the land was the bonfire that was still warming the vigil keepers guarding the late Ochieng's grave," Odongo rolled out a message filled with symbolism.

"Hmm! I am scared," Aura said, sighing. She then smiled to reassure her husband that she was with him in his predicament, even as his indiscretion was unforgivable. *Let it be I'm not going to fight another woman because of Odongo. This man Odongo stung me before, and he could sting me again. But if Odongo were to bring Elizabeth home how could I prevent him from bringing Dorka home?* Aura wondered.

"What can scare you? You are a survivor of a mean scheme against your life," Odongo observed.

"I am scared of Dorka only because she is younger, but I am happy that Juma has saved his sister while running away from his brother's murderous plot. I'm scared only because I don't know how many more stepsiblings Juma is yet to discover in the bush. Odongo, yours is a story worth telling so that other cattle traders, who go about depositing children in the wild, may learn about the dangers of their folly. Juma could have married his sister, if you hadn't arrived in time," Aura said dryly, partly enjoying and partly mourning her husband's situation.

"Are you having fun listening to this tale?" Odongo asked.

"Why shouldn't I have fun with you? It is the best way to remain sane. Why should I not be happy? My only son is leaving home for high school, and the Lord has given me another life. Why should I not be happy, when the Lord took me away from the hand of an assailant who is my own stepson? Why should I not be happy, when Juma has stumbled upon and saved a sister he never knew existed? Only God can do that to a woman in one night," Aura spoke emotionlessly, but Odongo knew she was hurting.

"Are you sad?" Odongo asked.

"No, I am happy," said Aura.

"Dorka lost her husband. Her only child is my

daughter. Elizabeth is a Form Two student at Ogande Girls High School," Odongo said; even as he still was not able to read Aura's exact posture over Elizabeth and Dorka.

"So, is Dorka coming home?" Aura asked devoid of any emotion; she was beginning to convince herself that three wives were safer than one or two.

"No," Odongo said, but he knew it was going to be Dorka's decision to make

"Who can believe that?" Aura asked, hoping that Dorka would not leave her husband's fresh grave.

"She is a Bwai widow, and she is not leaving her late husband's grave unattended. However, she has allowed Elizabeth to visit us whenever she wants," Odongo said, thus rekindling Aura's fears with his talk.

"I know that if Elizabeth were a boy, you would have brought her home years ago," Aura said, imagining that Dorka could give Odongo many boys, where she, Aura, had yielded one.

"Only I didn't know Elizabeth existed," Odongo said.

"It sounds like Dorka is sending an emissary first. She must visit us," Aura observed. She was tempted to lobby for Dorka to join the family. If Dorka were listening to Aura's wishes, it was better the former formally joined the family. Otherwise, Aura foresaw a situation in which Odongo would be shuttling between Bwai and Thim Lich, his blanket always on his bike.

"You want Dorka to visit you?" Odongo asked surprised, because Aura was a possessive woman, only that her tactics were subtle and neither verbal nor physical.

"You know, I won't mind her as long she is the new target for Atieno to attack," Aura said truthfully, but her major concern was a husband who would be shuttling between Tanganyika businesses, Thim Lich, and the land of Bwai.

"Aura, let's go home. The hospital has changed you," Odongo said. He believed that the head injury had changed Aura in a more somber person, a woman who always was forgiving. He believed that her Christian faith had taken over her heart since the accident that nearly took away her life.

"And face Atieno," Aura said sadly, if not anxiously.

She did not know which face of Atieno she would meet. Would she meet Atieno's happy face that shared dishes or the angry one that sent her son to kill Aura?

"I believe Aura has left by now," Odongo said, trying to believe what he said. He was tired of Atieno's wars, yet in the new Kenya of his time, he saw no practical means of ejecting a middle-aged woman out of her house.

"I don't think so. She still is your baggage; give her a home," Aura said, encouraging her husband to do what he should have done a decade before.

23

Cigarette Dialogue

HAVING GIVEN THE DAMNING INDICTMENT of his sister-in-law a couple of days back, Owinyo routinely took up a seat in front of Aura's house during the day. That is where he was early afternoon Aura would return to Thim Lich. Sitting not faraway was Atieno who still passed her time at home with no particular project in mind, waiting for "things to happen" when her husband or Aura or Okulu or Juma—all her victims—returned home. In short, Atieno had a lot to worry about, but now resigned herself to fate.

His eyes on her rogue sister-in-law, Owinyo leisurely reached into his left-breast pocket, pulled out an in-use pack of cigarettes, and professionally tapped its top, ejecting one cigarette. He returned the pack to its source. Then holding the cigarette with his lips, he reached into his right-breast pocket and retrieved a box of impregnated matches. He partially pushed out the tray, pulled out a matchstick, struck its head against the impregnated surface of the matchbox, coddled the weak flame between his palms to protect it from slight sea breeze, and used it to light the cigarette. He pulled in the smoke into his lungs then professionally released the white fumes through his nostrils and mouth, sending the smoke in Atieno's direction. Owinyo repeated the smoker's drill a couple of times, all the while maintaining a worried look at Atieno.

Atieno coughed, after Owinyo had executed the third drill, reminding Owinyo that he was rude. Second, she was a smoker, and Owinyo knew that she was a smoker.

She wondered why a fellow smoker was discourteously puffing away into her face without offering her a cigarette. She coughed again, after Owinyo repeated the drill for the fifth time. Craving for nicotine, she anxiously shifted in her seat.

"When are you going to visit Okulu?" Owinyo asked. He received no verbal response from Atieno, who remained slumped in her seat in deep thought. Owinyo let her be for a moment, taking a long pull on his cigarette.

At Owinyo's seventh smoke drill, Atieno reached into her skirt pocket, pulled out her pipe and started pumping on it. She had no matchbox but the smell of tobacco gave her the peace of mind anyway.

Where did I go wrong? How many women out there had children out of wedlock and have since lived very happy lives? Should I have married at all after the anonymous man violated me? Was I to blame for the rape? Did Okulu turn out the way he did in life because he was a child of sin? Atieno wondered, reflecting on a life of constant stress.

Atieno tried to revisit the good times with Odongo; she tried to remember a time when Odongo called Okulu a bastard or illegitimate, but she could not name any instant. She tried to recall any time when either her mother-in-law or father-in-law called Okulu names, but she failed. Yes, Ougo was cold toward her and her son. Yes, Okulu would become a man of doubtful—a man who perhaps never would father a child! That was cruel, but Atieno had no evidence as to who had so radically changed her son's future. Yes, she was right in her judgment that someone within the Ougo family had played a dirty hand on her son, ensuring that he never would see his children. Yes, she was right to have been angry, and she was right to have suspected the Ougo's hand in her son's fate, because families tended to want to eliminate alien males seeds from their midst. Yes, the village had thrown barbs at her and her son, but the Ougo family had not. If they did anything that crossed her, it was their insistence that Odongo brought home Aura as the senior wife. Amid all these, Odongo remained disengaged and unassertive in every crisis, a fact that encouraged abuse of Atieno and her son. Atieno hated him for that.

Even then, Odongo had been a model father to Atieno's

daughters, and he had shown no obvious bias in the way he treated Okulu. Atieno recalled that, at time when few parents sent their sons to school, Odongo sponsored Okulu in boarding schools from primary through high school. He sponsored Okulu through Mirogi Boy's Primary School; he then sent him to Homa Bay Secondary School. Both were boys' boarding schools. Only the very rich sent their children to boarding primary schools; Odongo was none of that.

Had I misread my husband's motives when he relocated Okulu to a new homestead? Atieno wondered. After all, had Odongo not located Okulu's home on the Ougos' ancestral land? How would she reconcile with her husband, console Aura, and even apologize to her? Importantly, why was she, Atieno, at war with Odongo and Aura? Atieno struggled with these issues in silence.

Aura and her son denied Okulu Odongo's stool; that is why I must continue to fight, Atieno concluded, looking at Owinyo, who was on his second cigarette.

The scent of the expensive tobacco had diffused into every air passage in Atieno's lungs and had overwhelmed her sense of smell. Now that she had stopped reflecting on her tortuous journey in life, the smell of tobacco was too inviting to continue ignoring.

I want a cigarette and I don't care what Owinyo thinks about me, Atieno said, her heart raving nicotine. She again coughed; she looked in the direction of Owinyo, sending a signal that she needed a cigarette.

"Why are you pulling on an uncharged tobacco pipe? Here is a cigarette; it is free," Owinyo said, standing up to go to Atieno. Moments later, he was lighting up a cigarette for Atieno.

"*It is free?* Since when did I want any free thing from you?" Atieno said, snatching the cigarette from Odongo's right hand. "I guess you understand what happened on the fateful evening a week back?" she asked, ready to revisit the tragedy in her own terms.

"No," Owinyo responded, realizing that the rogue sister-in-law wanted to talk.

"I don't believe you don't," Atieno said then pulled on the cigarette, inhaling the smoke, before releasing a stream of smoke.

"I can only guess," Owinyo said.

"Your brother is to blame; he should have separated us years ago. He had chosen to confine two women, who hated each other, in a home, and one woman got hurt. Thank God, she is alive. Odongo turned my son into a criminal," Atieno confessed.

"How?" Owinyo asked.

"Have you been listening to me?" Atieno challenged Owinyo. He, a man who knew everything that happened in the Ougo clan, should have understood to what issue she was alluding.

"Yes," Owinyo responded, happy that Atieno was willing to speak about her life.

"Do you know how it feels to be rejected?" Atieno asked, surprising Owinyo with her unusual candor.

"Odongo never rejected Okulu," Owinyo said lighting another cigarette for himself.

"Why did he throw him out of his land?" Atieno asked.

"A man with a wife and children is old enough to start his own home. Second, the land in question is our land," Owinyo observed.

"Do you know how a woman feels when a younger woman plays the first wife's role over her head?" Atieno asked, revisiting another of her old wars against Aura.

"Atieno, for how long will we continue to litigate this same complaint you launched the day you arrived in the Ougo home? Can't all of us live in peace?" Owinyo pleaded.

"Aura denied me a life I had dreamed of when I married Odongo; that is why ours will be a war to the grave."

"Let the hostility rest," Owinyo said.

"Thank you for the cigarette; tell Odongo to give me a home," Atieno said.

"I asked you a question awhile back: when will you visit Okulu?" Owinyo asked.

Atieno did not answer. She instead picked up her empty water pot and started walking to the river. As she passed through the gate, the herdsman (Nyerere) was getting in; she looked at the boy angrily, believing that he needed disciplining.

Owinyo watched as Atieno moved on; he cursed Odongo's sour luck in having married her.

24

Elizabeth Teases Thim Lich

ATIENO'S FIRST JOURNEY to the river after a couple of days spent battling her inner demons would be eventful. Reaching the river, she met Melissa Genga, a young schoolgirl. Atieno passed the girl without uttering a word; she proceeded to the water's edge, and stood there, contemplating jumping into the swirling river, thinking of drowning.

What Melissa saw shocked her: Atieno's skin was ashen grey; she too had grown thin.

"Mama Okulu, what happened to your skin?" Melissa asked

"What about my skin?" Atieno asked absentmindedly, standing by the water's edge, her back on Melissa.

"Yes; it is dry and as white as ash," Melissa explained.

"Watch your tongue, child," Atieno threatened the girl for stating what she was seeing because it was not right to judge people by their appearance.

"Here, use my soap, should you decide to bathe," Melissa said, attempting to give Atieno a bar of soap.

"Child, I'm in no mood to talk to rude children. I must tell Agola about your conduct," Atieno warned. Agola was Melissa's mother.

"I'm sorry, Mama Okulu. But I must be going," the young girl said, her water pot on her head, leaving Atieno behind by the river's edge where she continued to stand precariously.

Atieno did not respond; she already was in her own world, lost in troubling thought, contemplating suicide. Behind Atieno was the weight of guilt of having colluded with her son to harm Aura, her co-wife. Ahead of her, she imagined the faces she had to confront soon. There was the disabled son she feared meeting face to face. What would she tell him? There was Aura, her co-wife: What would she tell her? Then there was her husband. How would she approach him? She felt wronged, but who would listen to her? Her heart darkened several shades of red; the river appeared to turn red to her. She was about to jump into the water with her water pot in her hands, when a voice called her out, "Mama!" jolting her back to the world of the living where reason ruled paramount over impulse.

"Mama, you are too close to the river's edge; you could get dizzy and drown in the water; move away from the water's edge," ordered the young woman (Elizabeth) with remarkably familiar features. If her tremulous voice was too familiar, her poise confounded Atieno.

"Child! Child" Atieno called out in shock; then she was awake, walking inland, the empty water pot still on her head. She realized that she almost committed suicide. "Child whoever you are, I'm okay; you can go home," Atieno said stumbling on her words.

"Ma, I shall not leave you here! Let's go home. Here, I will fill your pot and carry it home for you. I know your troubles," the young woman known as Liz said, prying away the pot from Atieno's hand. Atieno surrendered the pot after a brief feeble resistance, wondering if she was speaking to a reincarnated Apudo, her mother-in-law.

From Melissa Genga's reference to Atieno as Mama Okulu, Elizabeth realized the troubled woman was one of her stepmothers, unless there were many Okulus in the Village of Thim Lich.

"You sound so familiar; who are you?" Atieno asked.

"No, we never met before. You don't know me, and I don't know you, but I can see that you are not well."

"You can see that I'm not well?" Atieno asked

"Anybody can see that you are not well. If you could bathe, I'll carry this pot of water home for you," Liz said.

"No; I don't bathe in the river," protested Atieno.

"I insist that you bathe; after that we can get to know each other," Liz commanded.

"I'll bathe because I love your voice; it reminds me of somebody long gone from this world," Atieno said, still wondering whether she was not speaking with the spirit of Apudo, her late mother-in-law. "Before I bathe, you must tell me where you come from."

"I come from Bwai," Liz said.

"Where are you going?" Atieno asked.

"Bathe first, and then I'll put the pot of water on my head and follow you home," Liz said.

"Are you sure I don't know you?" Atieno asked, thinking that the woman could have been Owinyo's granddaughter by way of one of his older daughters, who had been long gone in marriage.

"No. You don't know me," Liz said, smiling for the first time.

"I'll bathe down there in the bush; after that we will go home," Atieno said, wondering who the young woman was. She believed the young woman had cast a holly spell over her; she no longer was thinking of suicide. Even her eternal enemies like Aura had ceased to bother her.

An hour later, the duo walked into the Odongo homestead, Atieno in the lead. Grace barked at them, waking up Owinyo, who was dozing under a large deciduous tree near Aura's house.

Owinyo looked at the young woman carrying the pot of water for Atieno; he wiped off cobwebs from his tired eyes in disbelief. He looked at her again; he did not believe what she was seeing. The young woman was an exact replica of his late mother. She resembled the mother who used to cook potatoes for him when he was a little boy, who still was too young to herd cattle alone. Standing tall and erect like a eucalyptus tree, the woman walked, smiled, and rubbed her nose frequently the way his mother used to do. Owinyo rubbed his eyes again, stood up, cleared his throat, and asked, "Atieno, who is this?" They were passing hardly five steps from him.

Liz smiled again, knowing that she had touched a nerve in the man who looked like her father.

"*Who is that?* Of course, she is my daughter. Can't you see that?" Atieno challenged Owinyo to help her solve the riddle.

"Which of your daughters is she?" Owinyo asked.

"There are only six Odongo daughters in this home; you should know them all," Atieno said, happy that she was not alone in seeing a young Apudo's double.

"No. I have not met this one. Yet I believe you," Owinyo said.

"She is Rachel," Atieno said then waited to enjoy Owinyo's mental suffering.

Owinyo kept quiet, watching intently as the young woman lowered the pot down into a depressed spot on the ground by Atieno's house. Owinyo judged that the woman was younger than Rachel and Leah by at least five years. She could have been in her late-teens.

"I have to go," Elizabeth told Atieno, sending the older woman's head spinning.

I could have been talking to Apudo's ghost, Atieno said in her heart

"Thank you, but who are you?" Atieno asked, sounding as serious as she could.

"My name is Betha," Elizabeth said.

"Where are you going, Betha?" Atieno asked, studying the younger woman's face.

"I'll talk to the man under the tree then go my way," Elizabeth said.

"Stop playing with me, child; who are you?" Atieno warned, suddenly becoming harsh.

"Do I look like someone you know?" Elizabeth asked, refusing to be cowed.

"Whoever you are, you look like someone I used to know," Atieno said.

"I have to go," Elizabeth said.

"You cannot wait for some porridge? You see, you carried my pot of water, and you cannot go without tasting my food."

Owinyo looked on, still standing, listening to the discussion between the two women. He was convinced that the younger woman was a relative of his late mother.

"No, I don't need food," Liz said walking directly toward Owinyo.

Atieno looked on, her curiosity aroused. Now, she thought the woman looked like Olga her daughter.

"Where is the man who owns this home?" Elizabeth asked, beating Owinyo to the first words; her lazy long strides had placed her hardly a step from Owinyo.

"I own this home," Owinyo said.

"I know that you are not Mzee Odongo," Elizabeth said.

"I may not know from where you hail, but my blood

flows through your veins," Owinyo said ponderously.

And what strong character and authority she possesses. This girl is Apudo's main branch! Owinyo exclaimed in his heart.

"Why do you say that?" Elizabeth asked.

"If you are related to Odongo, you are part of me," Owinyo said; he still was standing near his chair under the deciduous tree.

"I'm your daughter!" Elizabeth said; she was tempted to embrace her uncle, but desisted for she was a grownup woman.

"You are my daughter. I know you are my daughter. Now, pull that chair, sit down, and tell me your name," Owinyo said, taking his seat.

"My name is Betha," Elizabeth said.

"Elizabeth? How are you my daughter?" Owinyo enthused, knowing that Odongo had traveled out of the home and deposited his seed elsewhere.

"If I am Odongo's daughter then so am I. Where is my father?" Elizabeth asked, but the answer came in a different manner.

25

Elizabeth Graces Aura's Return

GRACE STARTED BARKING EXCITEDLY; then the dog was running toward the gate. There was no one in sight yet because the new arrivals still were behind the tall euphorbia fence. However, Juma, Aura, Odongo, and Judas were about to turn into the gate.

Atieno heard Grace bark, and she knew her moment of reckoning was nigh. She peeped through her door and saw Juma, who was having problems controlling Grace.

The boy is alive and well, she said in her heart, surprised at how normal she felt. Atieno had resigned to her fate, and her hostility toward Juma had thawed a bit.

Then Atieno saw a leaner Aura; her heart darkened for a moment. Atieno whispered animatedly, "Aura, welcome back. As long as Odongo is still a man, our fights live on. Welcome to your home, but I'll not rest until Odongo gives me a home."

Atieno thought of sneaking out of the home through a rear passage she used to go for nature's calls, but resolved to stay. She was not going to run away from Odongo and his lover Aura, with Okulu still down.

Resolute and prepared for the worst from a kinship she had put through a harrowing experience, Atieno came out and sat on the right hand side of her house. She watched as Grace greeted Aura, jumped on Judas, pawed Odongo, and came back to Juma as the latter neared Owinyo's seat.

Watching everyone's body language, Atieno realized that the Migori team knew Betha. They were all hurrying toward the new girl in the home.

"Elizabeth, we thought we locked you up in Ogande. How did you reach here ahead of us?" Juma asked.

"Welcome home, Elizabeth, my daughter," Aura said.

"You must be Aura, and you are Juma's mother?" Elizabeth asked.

"Yes, don't talk anymore; come into the house," Aura said leading the way. Inside her house, Aura prayed surrounded by Odongo, Juma, Elizabeth (on whom she leaned), and Judas. When they had said Amen, Judas left for his home, saying, "See you later, Betha."

Odongo emerged from the house and joined Owinyo under the big tree near Aura's house.

"Who is that?" Owinyo asked.

"You can't guess who she is?" Odongo said in response.

"No, but I know that my blood runs through her veins," Owinyo said.

"Many years ago, when we were hot-blooded men, we left this home with a few heads of cattle; our destination was Gwasii, but we aborted our journey in Sori, when the bird could not allow us to land in Gwasii," Odongo said.

"I remember how a bird rejected your song and pleasant beads," Owinyo said.

"Yes. She was pregnant then," responded Odongo.

"So this girl is our blood? No wonder she resembles Apudo, our late mother, in every way," Owinyo observed.

"Yes. The mother married a man from Bwai. The man died three weeks ago."

"So you knew all along that you had a daughter in Bwai?" quizzed Owinyo, eying his brother suspiciously, but saw no lie.

"No."

"So the girl sought you out, now that she has a man to marry her?" Owinyo joked, but that was a common story among the Luo. Adult kids always sought out their biological fathers when they become of age, often doing so for pride or as victims of rejection by men, they grew up calling their fathers.

"How we met is along story that will not recur elsewhere. But she is here. I wish I had allowed Juma to narrate to you his nighttime ordeal after the tragedy that engulfed this home and left Aura struggling for her life on your laps, and Juma running for his life across the land in darkness. I wish to hear this from Okulu's mouth, because I understand that he was the aggressor against Aura and my son. I also understand that he, Okulu, has lost the use of one arm, thus completing the tragedy. The only good thing was that, later the same night, Juma would rescue his sister, we never knew existed, from going under in a quagmire in the famous River Nyogunde in North Bwai," Odongo tried to paint a simple summary of an otherwise complex picture.

"Is this story true?" Owinyo asked.

"I doubted the story when Juma first told it, but having visited the scene in the Nyogunde, I have not slept well since. Juma could have gone under with her sister, Elizabeth; one man could have lost a son and a daughter to the river. I am a lucky man, Aura survived the operation and Okulu is still alive, though he is hurting," Odongo said humbly.

"So how did you realize that she was your daughter?" Owinyo asked.

"When I left Migori Hospital to go and search for Juma in Bwai, with Judas as my guide, I was relying on John's opinion as to where Grace had lost track of Juma. On reaching Oriwo in Bwai, a herdsman directed us to a home on a hill, saying that he believed he had seen a light-skinned alien dating a girl from the home."

"Juma was dating his sister?" Owinyo asked the obvious question given that Odongo reached the home after Juma had been there for days.

"I guess the herdsman had seen them walking hand-in-hand on the plains," Odongo said, avoiding a direct answer. "Now, on reaching the home, we met a fresh grave. I led Judas to it so that we could pay our respect to the departed. An old woman and a young girl hurried to the graveside and joined us in prayers. I led in the prayers. After I finished praying, the old woman shook my hands. Then it was the young girl's turn to shake my hand. First, our eyes locked, and what I saw on her face frightened me. She rubbed her nose with her left hand, and I instinctively did the same; then our right hands interlocked in a greeting, eliciting a chill that ran though my right hand. I trembled, and I could feel her trembling too. I was seeing and holding a youthful person of my late mother. After an odd emotions-filled moment of silence, I asked her, 'How are you?' She responded, 'How are you?' in a tremulous voice. I thought I had heard my late mother speak from the grave, except I could feel the warm hand of the youthful face speaking to me."

"Strange, isn't it?" Owinyo wondered aloud, lighting a cigarette.

"There was a woman sitting under a verandah, not far from the grave. She had all along looked at me intently, and she looked familiar to me. Taking it all in as we walked to the visitors' tent, with the old woman leading the way, my mind raced back to 1953 in Sori. That was the fateful evening nineteen years ago, when a girl refused my hand and even returned my beads as you watched," Odongo said, pausing for effect.

"I remember the shame that hit you on that day. You were so shocked that you could not come back with the cattle, and so we had to sell them. Had I not been there, you would have thrown the money into the lake in anger," Owinyo observed.

"The old woman led us to a mourning tent. When the widow would call her daughter saying, 'Elizabeth, get a hen to slaughter for your relatives,' the riddle that had played before my eyes and chilled my body unraveled immediately. I knew the woman was Dorka from Gwasii. I also knew that Elizabeth was my daughter. I knew Dorka knew who I was. I don't know how Elizabeth felt, but what was going through my mind and bones could have bothered her too.

"What can I say? Again, you reaped what you sowed as a young man. Her case is no different than Atieno's case, except with the latter woman, nobody knows who fathered her son," Owinyo said, a trace of sarcasm in his tone.

"I know. The old woman, who was Dorka's mother-in-law, must have realized that Elizabeth had met the man who sired her; her body language, as she looked from Elizabeth to me and back, told it all," Odongo said avoiding a comment on the Atieno-Okulu case that remained a sore in his heart.

"Strange!" Owinyo quipped.

"It is strange in deed. In Elizabeth's honor, we spent the night in that home, though I had to retire early morning to a friend's home on Ratil Plains," Odongo explained, aware that his brother was wondering whether he tried to bond with Dorka while she was still mourning her husband.

"You did the right thing to have left the home. Will Betha's mother follow her to Thim Lich?" asked Owinyo, smiling at his brother.

"No. She is a widow mourning her husband. That is what she told me," Odongo said.

"That saves you another trouble; you still have the ongoing war in your home; you don't need another battle. Several urgent things though: Atieno must have her own home soonest possible; whatever you think and feel about her, she is still your wife," Owinyo advised his brother, adding, "Our wise say that a quarrel with one's wife should not last for a whole night, otherwise there would be no children in the land. The Holy Book you read says the same: let not sunset find your sins against one another neither forgiven nor repented. Atieno's ways often seem outrageous, but most of the time, they send a message to you that you have ignored her," Owinyo reminded his fellow elder about obvious pitfalls in marriages that come when husbands and wives don't communicate.

"I have no problem with relocating Atieno; I should have done it earlier," Odongo acknowledged.

"Second, you have to reconcile your wives and your children," Owinyo challenged his brother.

"That will be difficult and unnecessary. Only Okulu, Atieno and Abich have problems, the rest of us are at peace. Moreover, Okulu has a lot of anger now that he stands out as a man who beat his mother, and to make it worse, he has a disability. We can show him love and compassion, that is all," Odongo reasoned. Even as he spoke, he believed that nothing short of his confessions as to why he believes that he is Okulu's father would bring Okulu and Atieno back to the fold.

"You have to do it; talk to the three individually, and tell Aura to forgive them. You must be the one doing the talking, because you are the common rope between your family members. If you, the rope, rot in the rain and snap in the noontime heat, your family will fall apart. You'll be in Aura's house tonight, and don't fail to visit Atieno's house tomorrow night," Owinyo rolled out his bonding plan for the Odongo family, taking charge as the elder in the Ougo family.

"You suggest that I visit Atieno's house uninvited?" Odongo asked, but before Owinyo could answer him, Atieno was closing in on them, carrying two calabashes in her hands.

26

Owinyo the Peacemaker

ATIENO PASSED THE CALABASH in her right hand to Owinyo; she then transferred the calabash in her left hand to her right hand, before passing it on to her husband.

"I see you still know who the boss in your home is," Owinyo remarked.

"You are always number one," remarked Atieno, but she had missed Owinyo's point. Owinyo had taken note of the fact that Atieno had transferred the calabash intended for Odongo from her left hand to her right hand before delivering it into the hands of her husband, which was a mark of good training and respect.

"I'll take that; I am indeed the boss of your house; if I had killed my mother at birth, Odongo couldn't have seen the light of day," Owinyo said, trying to draw Atieno into further dialogue.

"I know that, and if you have nothing more to say, I can leave you alone before your brother's temper slaps me with hot porridge," Atieno said.

"Who said he was going to slap you?" Owinyo asked.

"Well, he has not spoken to me since he came back," lamented Atieno, smiling.

"He is Odongo Rao, the hippo; he grazes by night," said Odongo, smiling, enjoying a moment of self-praise.

"I won't take that grunt from the unpredictable hippo as a sign of peace," joked Atieno; but her husband's racy remark was just perfect for her troubled soul that was still struggling to reestablish its bearing within the Ougo clan; moreover, there was no child around.

"The hippo never has been at war with anybody," Odongo observed.

"Am I still your third wife?" Atieno asked, now that her husband was available for her ears. She had concluded that the so-called Betha or Elizabeth was her stepdaughter.

"Why do you ask that?" Odongo asked.

"I want to know, while Owinyo is here, because as my elder brother-in-law, he is like my late father-in-law. If you have shown me the gate already, let me know," demanded Atieno.

"You still are the second wife; I know that as fact," Owinyo said. Atieno's improved emotional posture had encouraged him; she no longer was the beaten-up lunatic he had seen in the morning. He judged that her spirit was up, because Aura had recovered and was back in the home.

"What about the girl Aura calls her daughter?" asked Atieno.

"She is her daughter?" Owinyo asked.

"She could be her daughter, or even her sister's daughter," Odongo said.

"Why not just say that she is my daughter," Atieno pressed on, though she already knew who the nice-mannered-yet-firm-handed girl was. Atieno had heard Betha refer to Odongo as Dad. Betha's physical features had betrayed her; she looked like Apoda. Besides, Atieno loved Betha, only she didn't know how to insist that Betha operated out of her house. However, Atieno understood that such honor to host the girl belonged to Aura, who was the first wife.

"Well, she is my daughter," Odongo said.

"Thank you for the information. I must go now; I have not cooked yet," Atieno said.

""Where is Okulu?" Odongo asked.

Atieno wondered how lucky she was. She had been waging a fruitless war against the Odongo-Aura home, since Okulu established a new home, demanding a home of her own. She was surprised that the near-tragic event that almost took away Aura's life appeared not to have dumped Odongo's resolve at preaching peace in the home. "You know that he is hurt, hospitalized," she said, where she previously would have said, 'Do you ever care for how

Okulu is?'

"What caused him harm?" Odongo asked.

"Can't we discuss this in the privacy of our bedroom?" Atieno pleaded in as gentle a voice as she could. The question had shaken her, but she was quick enough to realize that she was still on trial and needed to be as gracious, in her dealings, as possible. She was not going to allow Odongo to complicate the path she had prepared to achieve reconciliation.

"Well spoken, Atieno!" Owinyo cheered her on, adding, "Your porridge is the best in the whole of Thim Lich."

"Are you trying to spoil me?" Atieno asked.

"No. Your porridge is the best in the village; and you are right too. If my brother had no reason to visit your house anytime soon, you just invited him, and he cannot avoid the invitation," Owinyo continued to cheer up his troubled sister-in-law.

"I always wondered why I married this man instead of you," Atieno joked said to Owinyo.

"Atieno, you made the mistake most of our young girls make; you were after a bachelor, and you got one," Owinyo said, trying to make his sister-in-law's evening lighter. He knew Odongo might not appear in her house for another week.

"Only it turned out that he was not a bachelor," Atieno said, making light of what turned out to be a marriage made in hell for her.

"I have to go to my home, now that Odongo is back. Atieno, pray that Okulu recovers fully, otherwise a lot of souls will be cursing you," Owinyo said, speaking frankly.

"Owinyo, you should have been one of those preachers of the Holy Word; with you, souls like mine would have stopped spreading the fire of hate; seriously," Atieno said, even as she could not remember when she last attended any church service. Even then, her satanic role in fueling the current crisis had left her wondering when to seek refuge in the nearest Convent for widows and old runaway women. Atieno feared for the life of the next man to enter her bed. She could have been delusional, but she already had a dream in which she was strangling a man!

"Atieno, you need to change; you can't be fighting for this old man's body for the rest of your life," Owinyo challenged his fighting sister-in-law.

"I thought my fight over him ended this morning, but I see that I won't be the last wife. The girl Elizabeth has a mother, and if her mother is coming, my demons are back. I have built this man's wealth, and I'll fight any woman who tries to dip her fingers into his pockets. I fought Aura because she displaced me as the number one woman in his heart, but I'll fight the next woman over wealth," Atieno said taking away Owinyo's empty calabash.

"Odongo, you heard that? That is your own fight; I won't waste any sleep over it," Owinyo said.

"There is no other woman coming here soon," Odongo said, then drained the last drop of porridge from his calabash.

"Owinyo, ask your brother whether he has forgiven me for whatever happened this week. I take responsibility for the actions of the man who now lies in Macalder Hospital without a working hand, because I raised and fed him all the venom brewing in this home. I have had many hours of prayer, spent days without food, and, until this afternoon, I had not bathed, and I only bathed because your new daughter forced me to do so. I know *Nyasaye* (God) has punished me. Where my mind sought war, I now want peace, because I have no reason to fight anymore. Worse, my son with a family to feed has lost feeling in one arm and is struggling to save the other, all because he was chasing an enemy I made up," Atieno lamented, pouring out what had tortured her soul for the last week.

Atieno had encouraged her son to eliminate her co-wife. She had drummed into Okulu's head the idea that Juma was threat to his future; she had drummed the illegitimacy of her own son to every willing listener, even as she was not certain as to who could have been his biological father. Now, the co-wife, who nearly lost her life in Okulu's hands, had recovered and returned to their husband's home. What was she, Atieno, going to do?

Talking to Owinyo earlier in the day had psyched, and prepared her for this moment with her husband. She was happy that her husband had eaten her food, and he even enjoined her and Owinyo in the three-person discussion. All that had helped her morale. However, she yet had to face Aura one on one.

"I have never been at war with Atieno; I have never been at war with my son, Okulu. Whether Okulu is my senior or junior son is a matter our ancestors left clear rules to settle. I believe the matter of seniority between my wives, and by extension their sons, will remain contentious in your heart. Only you, Atieno, can resolve that and live in peace," Odongo said.

"Well, Atieno says that she is willing to move on," Owinyo observed.

Atieno did not want to answer that for the battle between her and Aura will always be there. She gathered her calabashes to leave, pleased with how well she had advanced along the path to reconciliation with her husband in a short time. She wished to live in peace with her husband, even as she continued to duel with the other wife over matters of access to her husband and his material wealth, all of which were normal fights in a polygamous home.

"Atieno, I have not eaten fish in a long time," Odongo said, stopping Atieno in her tracks. She thought it was a teasing dream. She was pleasantly surprised at how fast things had moved; having her husband by her side hardly ten days since the tragic events would be something special.

"Where do you expect me to get good fish from this late in the evening?" Atieno complained, amid extreme excitement in her heart.

"I'll eat it when you are ready," Odongo said.

"Now that is a threat, isn't it?" Atieno quipped, smiling.

"Atieno, you are missing the point; you should surprise your hungry man with something he doesn't expect, while you still look for good fish; surprise him with something like fried crocodile eggs, and you should do it fast before he changes his mind," Owinyo teased.

"Owinyo, leave us alone; since when were you an expert in how to take care of hungry men?" Atieno said, her heart still throbbing with excitement.

Owinyo would not respond to the challenge because, just then, Elizabeth emerged from Aura's house, Juma behind her. They walked to the spot where Odongo was hosting Owinyo.

"Uncle Owinyo; Mama Okulu, this is my sister Elizabeth," Juma said, Betha by his side. He was executing a show directed by mom, who had instructed him to introduce Elizabeth to Uncle Owinyo and Atieno.

"How is she your sister?" Owinyo asked.

"Juma, don't answer that question," Odongo ordered, relieving Juma of the burden of explaining how Elizabeth was his stepsister, while the latter's mother still was a mystery to Atieno. "Owinyo, can't you see that she is my daughter?" Odongo asked.

"What don't you want Juma to tell us?" Atieno challenged her husband.

"How Juma met Betha is a winded story that scares even me, whenever it is retold," Odongo responded, adding, "Juma, look for John; I want him to help you slaughter some bull for your sister here. Be quick."

"Mama Okulu, Mama Juma says that she wants some of the porridge you gave Uncle Owinyo," Elizabeth said.

Meanwhile, Juma hurried away, anxious to pick up life in a village he understood, knowing that in a few days he will leave for Alliance School.

"Betha, let's go, leave those men and their meat talk alone. This is Kadem, if you stay around the men too long, you would be a cowgirl and a fishmonger before you know it," Atieno said, pulling Elizabeth away in the direction of her house, hoping to interrogate her further.

"Betha, don't believe any of that; Kadem men are none of what she says," Owinyo said, while Atieno and Betha disappeared into Atieno's house.

"Odongo, it looks like there is new room for peace in you home," Owinyo said, standing up.

"Perhaps, the peace shall last until Elizabeth leaves," Odongo said.

"She is going to leave?" Owinyo asked.

"Did you miss something? Elizabeth is a student at Ogande Girls High School," Odongo said, standing up.

"Well, you have deep pockets," Owinyo said.

"Deep pockets?"

"School fees for two people, one child going to Alliance and the other to Ogande; that means money from your pocket," Owinyo observed.

"Owinyo, I have led a life of trouble; this may be the next big one. Betha is such a strong character that I see her bringing along her mother soon. In the event that happens, I don't know how Aura would react," Odongo said.

"Aura?"

"Yeah! Dorka is younger than Aura," Odongo said, doodling with his walking stick.

"What haven't you seen, my brother? Talking of Aura, let me have a one-on-one with her," Owinyo said entering Aura's house.

Odongo remained outside; he looked on pensively as his herdsman, Nyerere, and another helper escorted the hundreds-strong livestock into the expansive kraal, with Grace chasing after a couple of sheep into their thorns-protected housing (*Abila*). Odongo mentally identified a few bulls he wished to sell in a few days to raise school fees.

"Good job Nyorere! The cattle look healthy and well fed. Thank you for taking good care of the home while we were away," praised Odongo.

"*Wasema, kidole kimoja hakivunji chawa* (One finger cannot crush a louse," replied Nyerere, speaking in *Kiswahili.*

"Well said, brother-in-law. Now, watch that black cow to your left; she could deliver tonight," observed Odongo.

"I will," responded Nyerere guiding the cattle into the pen.

27

Okulu: Wronged and Bitter

IT TURNED OUT THAT OKULU the villain, the man who
beat up his stepmother, was himself a victim on a number
of counts. He was not just a victim of his mother's
manipulative ways, but also a casualty of his father and
the Ougo clan. Okulu's kin even called him a *kimirwa*
(bastard), yet he was not one. Now an invalid and still an
inpatient in Macalder Health Center, Okulu was a very
angry man, and the immediate person to whom he
directed his anger was his wife, Juanita.

"Woman, here is what is left of your husband; he'll
never fish again," Okulu said from his hospital bed. His
right hand was heavily bandaged and in a sling. His left
hand rested limp by his side. He was in a sitting position,
with a pillow lodged between his reclined body and the
headrest.

"What happened, my dear?" Juanita asked mournfully.
"They decided to kill you this time around?" she asked.
She had gone to see him on his second day at the health
facility.

Juanita's controversial husband was always at war
with some member of his Ougo clan. In each conflict, he
always played victim. This time around, he was the
aggressor, even as he had shouted otherwise; he was not
sure his wife knew that already.

"Are you asking what happened to me? Are you serious
about knowing what happened to me?" Okulu asked
drunkenly.

"Okulu, I came in peace; I know a lot has transpired

between us, but I come as that young girl you dated many years ago," Juanita pleaded. She had heard rumors that Okulu was hurt while hunting for Juma, and then late the previous night, John came to report to her that Juma's dog had bitten Okulu and that Okulu was in Macalder Hospital. She also heard that he, Okulu, had hurt Aura, but nobody was willing to speak to her directly about that. When she finally reached her mother-in-law's house, what confronted her was alarming; Atieno, her mother-in-law, was talking to herself.

"Yea, she was beautiful; Juanita Akinyi from Shirati. Hahaha! She was beautiful, and her beauty continues to cause me a lot of trouble. Juanita, do you know that your beauty has caused me a lot of trouble?" Okulu said in unusual jest. He sounded convinced of what he was saying.

"Okulu, my husband, I want to know what happened to you since you left our home two days ago. I have to explain to your children what is going on, and I don't want them to rely on rumors from other people," Juanita pleaded.

"*My children?* Do you have no shame that you should call your sons *my children?* You know better not to call your boys *my sons.* Yea, they are members of the Ougo clan, so they are my sons. Yea! They are Okulu's sons; what a lie!" he spat out the harmful words, completely oblivious of their effect on his longsuffering wife, who had been nothing but his strongest supporter in a world that was particularly cruel to him.

"Spare me the shame, Okulu; there are nurses around listening to your mad man's shameless rant. People get hurt, and I know you hurt, but they don't lose their heads and turn against their wives over it," pleaded a tearful Juanita. "Yea, there are weighty issues in our marriage, but they are not of my making. You were the problem, before your problem became my problem, because where a man is impotent, those watching soon begin to call the woman barren. Then I heeded a call and followed a secret path to prove that you were a man with a wife and children," Juanita found herself confronting her husband in frank whispered words.

"Juanita, you of all the people should know better not to abuse me," he scoffed at her, smiling.

However, Juanita knew she had won, if only temporarily. "John says that a dog bit you. Is that true?" Juanita asked, starting another unintended flare-up.

"*John?* That idiot called John; does he care about what happened to me? Do you know that the idiot you call your lover looked on, amused, as the dog bit me and broke this arm, and then went for this arm?" he asked pointing at his arms with his chin, in practiced efficacy.

"Okulu, stop; you are hurting me!" cried Juanita.

"*John?* He is a snake; when he is not confusing men with beer, he is confusing their wives with sweet words. John? The man is a serpent out of Eden," Okulu said, his rant trailing off into an incoherent lament, as if he was drunk.

"Okulu, my husband, why don't you let the past be? Yes, things happened before I married you, but I chose you, and he lost. Why go back there now?" complained Juanita, even as her sanctioned affair with John started several years into her marital life. She was bitter, yet not bitter; her sons were there as proof; she still loved her husband, and she never thought of leaving Kadem for her father's home in Tanganyika.

When it was apparent that Okulu would not seed Juanita's field, Atieno advised her to cook special meals for John Odemba whenever Okulu was on a long safari. Colluding with Owinyo, Atieno sanctioned the affair behind Odongo's back. Owinyo, as the late Ougo's eldest son, was not going to allow Juanita to go back to her people and shame the Ougo house. Odongo would know about the matter when Juanita already had a son.

"This remaining arm is going to kill me soon, then John can dance over my grave and then dance inside my house. Okulu the eunuch and bastard; that is what they call me, yet I beat all of them to the sparkling diamond from Shirati. O Juanita, my diamond, what shame is this? Hi . . . i! Hi . . i!" he ranted on, breaking into a wail like a bereaved Luo woman, mixing up self-hate, loathing for his wife, and pride for his marital conquest over other suitors. He behaved as if he was drunk on strong pain medication.

"Okulu, stop pouring poison into my heart; I am not listening anymore! When the sun rises, I'll walk out of your home and leave you with your sons," Juanita threatened, wondering whether her husband believed what he said.

"*My sons?* Stop your ridiculous claims, Juanita. You know that they can't be my sons," Okulu, whispered vehemently, his voice substituting for his injured arms.

"Okay, I'll leave with my sons, if they are willing to leave with me," Juanita threatened. The fact that Okulu had publicly disowned the children he loved shocked Juanita. She wondered why her husband, who had known much abuse about his ancestry, was doing the same to his sons. She always suspected that her husband was aware of her activities, whenever she strayed away from his home to get a child. Now, the utterances of her husband over the last few minutes confirmed to her that he indeed was in the loop all the years she got her children clandestinely.

"Don't do that; I need someone to bury this body. You know that I love you, Juanita. I wish I were able to give you children; I would have given you many beautiful daughters, but you know that was not to be," Okulu mourned, aware that he had planted a daughter in Judi Odemba's house. He could not explain how he fathered a child out of wedlock, yet he could not seed Juanita's bed.

"Okulu, stop it. You are hurting me. I loved you the way you were, and I still love you as you are now; the boys love you. We will not run away from you; but stop talking for a while; you could make your situation worse," Juanita pleaded, highlighting a more important point, raising the criminality of what Okulu had done before the dog bit him.

"Ah, what are they saying out there?" he asked, trying to stand up, but he could not prop himself up without a functioning arm.

"What are they saying about what?" Juanita asked.

"What are they saying about Aura's accident?" Okulu clarified his question.

"Okulu, my lover, get well, then we will worry about what people say out there; they always said something about you; what new thing can they say about you?" Juanita lamented, avoiding saying anything about Aura's case, in which Okulu was a suspect.

"How is my mother doing?" Okulu whispered, wondering whether his wife understood his mother's role in the tragic events of two nights before.

"She is depressed about things; she talks to herself; I can't understand what she is talks about. She is mad. Then I come here, and you are just as mad," Juanita lamented mournfully.

"What was she talking about?" Okulu whispered back.

"We can't talk about it here," Juanita said

"I hope my mother doesn't see me like this. How is Aura?" he asked, still whispering.

"Owinyo took her to Migori, and he is not back yet. Your father has not returned from Tanganyika. Juma is nowhere," briefed Juanita.

"I love you, Juanita; when all this is over, I look to the day when I'll be able to hold you in my hands again," Okulu said with a forced grin. The pain in his right hand was getting worse.

"Please don't go there; it hurts you, and it hurts me the more. I have to go," Juanita said, smiling.

"Let me know if anything new crops up. I know Odongo will be in the village soon," Okulu whispered conspiratorially. "Let me know when the boy, Juma, comes back."

"Why don't we migrate to Tanganyika? The boys need peace, and they won't get it here," Juanita suggested.

"As it is, I can't walk," Okulu observed.

"We can hire some vehicle," suggested Juanita.

"We don't have the money to do that," Okulu asserted.

"You can sell some of the bulls," Juanita suggested.

"Go, I can hear the nurse coming," Okulu ordered.

"I wish to ask her a few questions," Juanita said. She in fact wanted to hear any prognosis from any medical official.

It was not a nurse coming into the wards. Opi, the Clinical Officer of Health, entered. "She must be your wife, Mr. Odongo?" asked Opi, upon entering the room. The hospital wards were largely deserted.

"This is Mrs. Okulu," Okulu said, grimacing in pain.

"You sound more upbeat, is it because of your wife's presence," the Clinical Officer of Health said, hitting Okulu's left elbow with a mallet.

"Do you want to break my elbow?" Okulu cried out, wincing in pain.

"What did you say, Mr. Odongo?" the COH asked, flexing Okulu's left hand.

"You are going to break my arm!" cried Okulu.

"So, feeling has returned to your left hand?" the COH asked.

"It does not feel like it can lift anything yet," Okulu said.

"Don't be too excited yet; it will take time to heal completely," the COH advised, before asking, "Are you left-handed?"

"Yes; why do you ask?" Okulu asked, reaching out to touch his wife's right hand with his left hand for the first time that morning.

"Pray that your left hand heals faster; you might have to learn to use it instead of your right hand, just in case your right hand does not return to its full strength," observed the COH.

"When is he leaving the hospital?" asked Juanita.

"Now that feeling is returning to his left hand, he will be out of here after a physiotherapist has worked on him," declared Opi.

28

A Victim of a Father's Silence

WHEN ATIENO GAVE BIRTH to a son, with her new in-laws whispering, 'illegitimate son,' her mission was to protect her marriage and more so her son. With her son's ancestry in doubt in the eyes of her in-laws, and with nothing to show that her husband cared any less about her and her son than when he first dated her, protecting her son from harm, intended and otherwise, became her major employment. She would bring in a younger sister to act as the boy's babysitter and surrogate mother. The Omulo daughters carefully watched what young Okulu ate, and when he slept, the babysitter was always by him. Atieno was not going to allow the Ougos an easy chance to eliminate her son. Her fears were neither exaggerated nor misplaced. Men of her time and of generations before them eliminated male children who were not their blood. Therefore, though Odongo had not cared about Okulu's ancestry, what her father-in-law, Ougo, and mother-in-law, Apudo, could do to harm the boy was a constant concern to Atieno.

Like most mothers of baby boys, Atieno watched her son each morning, and she examined him whenever she bathed him, and yes, she knew he was a man who would, in all likelihood, grow up and father his own children. However, something worrisome happened along the way. The boy was then an active four-year old; he already had a sibling, a girl named Alal. Okulu was old enough to start asking his parents uncomfortable questions, and so he already was sleeping in his grandmother's house. One day, as Atieno was milking her cows early in the morning, she saw her son come out of her grandmother's house to pee. He was flat: There was nothing to show that he was a boy; more so a boy who had slept well in a warm room and was ready to pass urine. She was alarmed as to what had happened to her son overnight. She later would interview her son, asking whether anybody had touched him in his sleep or whether he felt any pain as he slept. The boy answered in the negative.

Odongo had traveled to Tanganyika to visit with Aura's people, and so Atieno could not share her concerns with him immediately. Anxious to get any advice, Atieno approached Apudo, her mother-in-law.

"Ma, I don't think Okulu is okay," Atieno said.

"What ails him?" asked Apudo.

"He is not strong like a man early in the morning," complained Atieno.

"I don't believe you, but I too will observe him," Apudo had promised her daughter-in-law.

Apudo would watch the boy for a couple of days, even touching him during the night, and she confirmed Atieno's fears. She too was baffled because, like a good grandmother, she observed her grandsons for any signs of future reproductive problems. Likewise, she watched her granddaughters for any signs of delay in the onset of womanhood.

"Ougo, Atieno's son has a problem," Apudo had said to her husband a few nights later.

"What problem does he have?" Ougo had asked in a tone that indicated that he cared less about the boy he called, in the privacy of his heart, 'the stranger in my home.' But Ougo did not betray any sign of guilt.

"Unlike other boys, he is not stiff like a man in the morning," Apudo talked in pursed terms. A shy girl, she still was not sexually expressive in the presence of her husband thirty years and counting since she married Odongo.

"You women like to fuss over little things; Okulu is only a little boy; he will wake up in time to see his children," Ougo said, dismissing Apudo's concerns. If he was responsible for whatever would change the boy's life irreversibly, he was not showing it.

Apudo would report to Atieno that she had confirmed

the latter woman's concerns.

"Can Okulu get help from any medicine man?" Atieno asked wirily.

"Yes and no. He will get help when he reaches the right age, but . . ."

"But what, Ma?" an anxious Atieno asked, interrupting her mother-in-law.

"It may never make him a father of a son or daughter," Apudo offered the damning response.

Atieno walked out in silence. She wondered who had locked out her son from ever siring a child, making sure that he would die without leaving behind a lineage. "They called him a bastard, now he has the title of a eunuch," cursed Atieno, once inside her house.

"Something has happened to Okulu," Atieno told her husband when he came to her bed one night after his return from another extended visit in Tanganyika. He already had passed through Aura's house, spending a couple of nights there.

"What is that?" Odongo asked. Even though Atieno was speaking in whispers, he sensed that she was holding a devastating message.

"What do you mean by 'He is not a man anymore'?" Atieno whispered.

"How is he not a man anymore?" Odongo asked.

"He is not a man; your mother has made the same observation," Atieno restated her message, wondering why her husband would not comprehend what she meant by her son not being a man.

"What does my mother say?" Odongo asked. Meanwhile, the enormity of her message was sinking in, his heart beating faster, with his wife effortlessly slipping away from his arms in disappointment.

"She says that it can be reversed when he grows up," Atieno said choking in emotion, hoping that her husband appreciated her shock.

Atieno long had learned that her husband responded to her desires for children only when she demanded his attention and cried literally. Atieno blamed Aura for his attitude toward her; she blamed Aura for her status as the second wife whose house Odongo only visited as an afterthought; she also blamed it on her own age. Atieno often joked that there was no worse curse on a woman than being a second wife, who happened to be older than the first wife was.

She cried in his arms that night, and he stayed until dawn, when his exit would have been three o'clock in the morning.

In the years that would follow, Atieno gave Odongo Arua, then Olga, and finally Abich. The second boy she wanted never came, even as the ancestry of Okulu remained a constant concern for her. Atieno too was struggling with whether her son would marry at all and have his children and grandchildren.

Amid all the pressures, Atieno's mother advised her to live for her children and to lean on her good husband. Her mother too was of the opinion that Okulu's condition could reverse itself once he was a teenager.

Atieno watched as Okulu grew up: he would be six years; then he was eight years; then the boy started to ask questions.

"Ma, I'm not like the other boy's."

"How are you not like the other boys, Okulu?" Atieno asked, even as she knew what the boy's concern was.

"I don't know how to say, but when they pee, it comes out straight, mine doesn't," the boy of six said.

"Don't worry, Okulu; not everyone is born with the same body. You will be okay when you grow up."

At nine years, he did not want to swim in the lake or rivers with other boys, and he would not bathe when other boys were around. When he really was dirty and stinking and had become the subject of ridicule by the other boys and his teachers, he would bathe at home, using water meant for his father, which created constant quarrels between him and his mother.

Twelve years, thirteen years and fourteen years went by, and other boys' voices were deepening, while his hardly deepened. Then he could see them spotting pubic hair; he had none. Fifteen years: the other boys, some of whom were early bloomers, were beginning to spot immature beards that looked more like a caterpillar's hair than a Luo man's tough and coiled facial hair. Okulu had none.

"Ma, will I get beards like the other boys?" Okulu

would ask. He then was a senior in middle school and would be joining a boarding high school in a few months.

Somehow, Okulu had realized that his father was closer to his sisters and talked more often with them than he did with him. It was as if his father was avoiding him. When his father touched him, it was with a cane, demanding that he bathed, and it was always late in the evening. Therefore, young Okulu channeled all his feelings about his insufficient male anatomy through his mother, who was a kind of ally against the rest of a world that constantly ridiculed him about his insufficiency.

On top of the struggles with his unique physiology, Okulu was beginning to understand that his mother came with him; that he was born out of wedlock, and that his mother was already pregnant when she married his father.

"Okulu, you will be okay," responded Atieno, soothingly, presenting to her son a sample of hot finger millet bread served in hot ghee.

"No girl wants to dance with me," Okulu complained as he rolled in the hot easy-to-swallow oiled bread.

"Okulu, dress up well and bathe regularly, and the girls will run to you," Atieno would encourage her unfortunate son.

From that day on, Okulu always dressed well to impress girls. Months later, Odongo, his father, traveled to Tanganyika and consulted a medicine man who gave him some herbal prescription. The man was gracious enough to have directed Odongo to a locally available herb; Atieno would harvest it regularly, mash it in water, and serve it to Okulu. Atieno would serve it with every meal her son consumed. Okulu was fifteen-year-old teenager then. Whatever the medicine did in the body deepened Okulu's voice and made him feel like a man around girls. Okulu would raise a few beads and a flimsy moustache he never would shave, but he was a man anyway. However, just as Apudo had warned eleven years earlier, Okulu would be a walking dud. Atieno knew that he was a walking dud, and so did Odongo. Sadly, Okulu did not know that he had hardly any potent arrows in his bag, even as he ran around with playing with fellow teenage girls.

Okulu's treatment, which he took regularly as prescribed by his mother, came just when he was joining high school. Additionally, he felt better about himself, but he didn't know that his missiles were duds.

By the time he married at age twenty, Okulu's system had recovered so well that he took his medication only once a month.

Juanita, his wife, knew she married a real man, but three years into the marriage, she had not conceived. Then there were whispers from various people—mostly from young women married to her husband's cousins and brothers. Some of the women were saying to her face that her husband was impotent.

"Juanita, how is it that you don't know that your husband is like a flat tire? Everyone, who knew him growing up, knows that, and I wonder how you have survived him this long," Judi (John Odemba's wife) said in genuine wonder.

"Okulu never failed to deliver in bed?" Juanita retorted.

"Really?" Judi asked, genuinely surprised at Juanita's declaration. Judi promised to investigate Juanita's claim. She would become the proverbial curious cat, and she would become Okulu's victim as she investigated the much-maligned brother-in-law.

"Listen, Judi, I have not asked for your husband, and I'm not going to allow you the chance to test mine," an angry Juanita warned her family member.

The verbal exchange between the women had occurred only after a few months into Juanita's marriage to Okulu. The months turned into years, and she was wondering what was wrong. Juanita was beginning to ask Okulu's cousins questions, and each respondent was telling her that Okulu's was impotent.

Juanita took the next step and challenged her mother-in-law over the issue of Okulu's potency. Initially, her mother-in-law generally was noncommittal in her response, simply saying that she had seen no problem with Okulu when he was growing up. Then Atieno started to hint that Juanita "cooked for" and "talked to" Okulu's male cousins who knew him better.

"But Ma, Okulu never failed to satisfy me as a man," Juanita said, hurting, surprised at the audacity of her mother-in-law to have suggested that she, Juanita, looked outside the home for a man. Juanita wondered how she, a married woman, was going to discuss her husband's virility with another man and invite the man into her bed without endangering the future of her marriage.

"Well, once in a while, women marry men with whom they are incompatible, and they end up never having children together. If I had another son, I could have given him to you," Atieno lamented, yet pointedly suggesting to her daughter-in-law to invite another man into her matrimonial bed.

"Ma, I never would violate Okulu's trust," Juanita protested, even as her heart was warming up to the idea of looking beyond her husband's bag of arrows for a quiver that could crack her eggs.

Who could have blamed Juanita? Three years is a long time. The cacophony of voices shouting 'barren,' at her, and 'impotent,' in reference to Okulu, had reached a dissonant din, and Juanita had started to think along the same line her mother-in-law suggested a year earlier. *What should a woman do when a man met all her marital needs except a child?* Juanita wondered as her moral values conflicted with her desire to have children in her marriage.

"Juanita, my friend, you know that your husband has many enemies within the Ougo clan. Okulu's problems started with how and when I married Odongo. The Ougo clan felt that I had violated Odongo before Aura, his childhood bride, would reach his bed. Both Aura and I have not seen our sons since I gave birth to Okulu. We don't' know who is fighting so that Odongo sees no sons and grandchildren within the clan," Atieno lamented, making Juanita's problem part of a wider Odongo family problem. She argued that Okulu's problem was a special manifestation; where he and she had neither boy nor girl, Odongo's wives only saw girls, except the odd case, Okulu, who was having problems siring any child of his own.

Tactfully, Atieno had woven a believable conspiracy case against Odongo's home, except she had no name of the conspirators.

"I know that Okulu is not a favorite of many in the clan," Juanita observed, without raising the fact that Okulu could have been born out of wedlock.

"Juanita, you soon will learn that, in future, what will matter in your life are your children; how you get them may not count. That is what I have learned. Juanita, let me be frank with you because you are family. I came here with a baggage. That baggage was Okulu, and he still is my baggage to date, but he is more of your baggage now. Know that he *changed* after he was a child off my laps. Do everything in your power to protect him, but remember that you need a future and that future means land for your children. You have the land; you need a son on it. But respect Okulu, even as you want to see your fruits," Atieno said tearfully, hoping Juanita would heed the advice.

"Ma, I love you," said a tearful Juanita.

"Think about it, Juanita; I have to go to the market," Atieno declared, closing the subject.

But what man would knowingly walk the path of fatherhood with another man's wife without boasting about it after a glass of alcohol? Juanita wondered, searching her local male associations for a potential reliable client.

Juanita did not know that Atieno was doing some footwork for her already.

29

A Man Rules Okulu's Home

KEEPING HER HUSBAND out of the loop, Atieno visited with Owinyo, her elder brother-in-law, to explain her predicament over the lack of fire in Okulu's marriage to Juanita.

"Who is that?" Owinyo asked in response to a knock on the door to his rugged hut, dressing up; he had been having a late-afternoon siesta.

"May I come in?" Atieno asked.

"Isadora, just come in; you never knocked before, why are you knocking today?" Owinyo complained, thinking that he was talking to his second wife.

"You must be getting old, my brother-in-law," Atieno said opening the door.

"I am sorry; Atieno it is you? It is dark in here; may I open the window?" asked Owinyo, apologizing for the mix-up in names.

"I'm comfortable as it is, but it is your hut; you can do what you normally do in it," challenged Atieno.

"What I normally do depends on who is visiting me. If Odongo came here to share a joint with me, we close the window; when the boys are here to share a meal with me, we open the windows; for anybody else, I keep the windows and door closed," Owinyo said in jest.

"Well, treat me like anybody else," challenged Atieno.

"Take that seat to your right. Close that door; I'll open the windows," instructed Owinyo.

"Why should I close the door?" Atieno asked, surprised at the turn of events.

"I don't want a dog, rushing in here as we talk. Or are you just passing by?" asked Owinyo.

"I'll do as you wish," Atieno said, reluctantly closing the door behind her, knowing quite well that Isadora had seen her enter the man's hut.

What guts I have, Atieno Nyomulo, Atieno said in her heart, believing that, by closing the door, she had started a scandal before she even stated the purpose of her mission into Owinyo's den.

"Well, I can see your face better," Owinyo said, grinning, his yellowed teeth reflecting the light from a fishing lantern he hurriedly had lit, an act that Atieno found ridiculous. However, she judged that Owinyo fought in the Second World War, and his lot had a lot of leeway in anything that touched on public decorum. Their African brethren were quick to dismiss the miscues of war veterans as the behaviors of men who had gone through hell and back and, therefore, constantly struggled with the contents of their violent past.

Here is a war victim in action. Atieno, why did I get into this? Atieno wondered why her brother-in-law was lighting a lantern for her at midday. She had heard that white women and men light candles for their spouses, but she never saw one such man or woman in action. Yet here in the middle of a bright sunny day in Thim Lich, her brainwashed brother-in-law was reenacting the same white man's nonsense.

"Keep trying to impress," Atieno said, laughing.

"Having traveled the world over, I have learned that *all women* love the unusual. We learned the same in our village classroom," Owinyo said, grinning.

"*School?* What school did you attend?" Atieno asked for the sake of keeping the conversation going, having realized that Owinyo was in unusually good moods.

"We called it the Ougo home school; it was established before the white man reached Wath Ong'er, with a gun in one hand and a book in the other," Owinyo said, and then quickly changed the subject. "Now, tell me what you want before Isadora storms this hut," Owinyo said, taking his stool across from Atieno. His tone suddenly was businesslike; he had shelved the trash-talk.

"Owinyo, Okulu's wife could leave him. She wants a child so that she could be grounded as a wife in this clan,"

Atieno challenged her elder brother-in-law.

Owinyo kept quiet for a few minutes, shifting in his seat, scrolling something on the floor of his dusty earthen floor. He now understood why Atieno had invaded him in his command hut; his sister-in-law indeed had a weighty matter in her heart.

Why had Atieno not sent Odongo? Is it because Atieno still sees Odongo as the man who broke her heart, when he married Aura, and thus relegated her (Atieno) to the rank of second wife? Owinyo wondered.

"What are you suggesting, Atieno?" Owinyo asked, trying to buy time for a thoughtful answer, wondering as to who knew that she was to see him to discuss such a sensitive matter.

Not that men never before left their homes to rule their brothers' homes in the dead of night, but such sanctioned procreative cooperation occurred among sons of the same man and preferably the same mother. In the present case, Atieno was informing Owinyo, her senior-most brother-in-law, that Okulu had no brothers and stepbrothers and that, by continued inaction, he, Owinyo, risked inviting strangers to plant alien seeds in an Ougo man's home. Atieno was demanding that one of Okulu's cousins, from Owinyo's home, should step in to help seed Juanita's bed before her time expired.

"Tell Odongo that a man in the family will rule Okulu's home in absolute secrecy," Atieno said, invoking Odongo's name for political reasons. "I understand that it is a difficult matter, but that is why you are Ougo's eldest son. You own his stool. And now that your parents are no more, all our burdens must land at your feet," Atieno challenged Owinyo.

Owinyo saw through Atieno's veiled political maneuver. Yes, he could order a son to enter Okulu's home, but he could only notify Odongo if he, Owinyo, wished. That was the challenge Atieno presented to her elder brother-in-law. Owinyo realized that she also was telling him that, as the elder brother to Odongo, he could take action in his brother's home regardless of whether the latter, Odongo, was informed and on board.

Astounding as Atieno's demands were, she knew and Owinyo knew that she stood on a firm cultural ground, because Owinyo, as Ougo's eldest son, had powers to act in the interest of the Ougo sub-clan.

"Who is the man you have in mind, Atieno?" Owinyo asked, pulling out a pack of cigarettes; he was thinking hard and running low on nicotine.

"The man will be one of Okulu's brothers or first cousins," declared Atieno.

"You know that Odongo has no other son, who is old enough to rescue Okulu from Juanita's unyielding battlefield," Owinyo reminded Atieno. Juma was then a mere three-year-old boy.

"That is true, but you have sons; you have married sons," Atieno said, believing that the assignment required a man with children to his credit.

"Atieno, I never knew you had such guts. Do you smoke?" Owinyo asked Atieno, offering her a cigarette.

"You know that I smoke," Atieno said, picking up a cigarette from the pack.

Much as Owinyo tried to feel comfortable, he could not. They were talking inside his hut, which in itself was unusual. It was usual for his wives to visit his hut; otherwise, the hut was his place to commune with fellow men and sons. Yea, unattached widows could visit that hut. Yet here he was talking to his sister-in-law who still had a husband, and he was doing it in the middle of his home, inside his hut, and in broad daylight, with the door closed. *I am damned,* cursed Owinyo in silence.

"Atieno, if you were any other woman, I could have caned you, so that you leave here wailing loudly for all to hear, because then there would be no doubt that I found you disagreeable and undesirable," Owinyo joked, lighting the cigarette for his brave sister-in-law with unusual demands. A rugged man, Owinyo loved fighters, and he had always prayed that Atieno gave birth to an-Odongo son, because such a son would be a fighter. No such son had come, in Owinyo's judgment. He believed that Odongo never fathered Okulu, but he admired Atieno for her will and tenacity to fight against a system that tradition had rigged against her kind. Atieno was a woman he silently admired at a time when his father (Ougo) mother (Apudo) were breathing fire in her face because she had stolen her way into Odongo's hut, upstaging Aura, who was Ougo's chosen bride for Odongo.

Now, Owinyo's parents were long dead, and the

decision stool belonged to him. Now that he had thought about it, he realized that Atieno had hatched a brilliant idea: She had challenged him to have one of his sons sire a son in Odongo's home. The child would still be an Ougo blood. The child would be the commonwealth of Odongo and Atieno because they paid for Juanita's bride price, and yet he secretly would be an Owinyo blood.

"I am a natural fighter; my father comes from Sakwa, Kowak; you must know what that means in Kenyan," Atieno said enjoying Owinyo's top-brand cigarettes, though she preferred the stronger pipe tobacco.

"I know; who does not feel the weight of the Kowak in this land?" Owinyo observed. "You will get your wish. Don't push me; I'll do it my way; it will be between you and me only."

"I have to go before Isadora breaks this door," Atieno said; her sharp sonic detectors had sensed the sound of footsteps approaching the hut.

"Hi, My Jealousy, is that you?" Isadora greeted Atieno, entering the hut. She carried two plates of *nyoyo* (a cooked legumes-grain mixture) in her hands.

"Isadora, you know that my stomach does not tolerate *nyoyo*; leave it here for another of his many girlfriends. I'll go and eat whatever else your pot can offer. Moreover, I am not going to eat in my brother-in-law's hut like a love-starved, homeless widow," Atieno said jokingly, standing up to leave.

"You women never stopped your wars; why do you continue to fight over a lifeless thing like me?" Owinyo joked, standing up to go and stretch his legs. He was not in the mood for a late-afternoon *nyoyo* a woman had provided for no other reason than to investigate what Atieno was up to in his hut in broad daylight.

"That isn't for you to judge," Isadora said, turning to go back with her food.

"Don't go back with the food; I'd divorce you if you dared," Owinyo cautioned Owinyo. Moreover, it was in his interest to have all wives bring food to his hut, even if her he was full; he otherwise would risk starvation, should his favorite wife fail to cook for him.

Isadora returned her plates of food and left it on the table, annoyed that she had wasted her nice *nyoyo*, knowing that her husband would throw it to his dogs.

"Isadora, let's go; I cannot stand the smell in here anymore," Atieno said leading the way out of the hut.

Having brooded over the matter, and even consulted with a trusted friend in Sori to seek an unbiased opinion, Owinyo concluded that son John Odemba would be the most suitable candidate for the task, mainly because he already had six sons, and at least one with each wife. John too was a steady hand over his three wives, and he was a man of a sound mind and good character.

"John, you are the oldest grandson of Ougo, and there is a battle brewing in Uncle Odongo's home. The ongoing battle calls for your intervention," Owinyo opened up to his oldest son.

Father and son were talking in a freshly plowed field after the oxen-drivers had left the field to escort the oxen to the river to drink. The meeting took place under an old baobab tree inside the late Ougo's old homestead, but the duo kept moving around in the shade as they talked to make their meeting seem as natural as possible. If an observer had seen father and son inspecting freshly plowed ground for errors, he or she had missed a point of symbolic importance, which was that the two men were in an abandoned homestead. Second, they were talking under the old ancestral tree of religious significance.

"Atieno and Aura always battled each other. How could I be of help?" John asked. He had taken Owinyo's battle analogy literally.

"No; that is not the battle I meant; moreover, that is my battle because Aura and Atieno are my sisters-in-law. You as their nephew could not join that battle. You know that, John," Owinyo said, leaving John wondering as to what other battle his father was referring. John was not aware of any other battle in Odongo's home.

"Have I missed a major event in Uncle Odongo's home?" John asked.

"You have missed the battle; it is inside Okulu's house," Owinyo narrowed the scope of his hint.

"How can I know what happens inside Okulu's house?" John asked.

"It is what is not coming out of Okulu's house that is significant. Okulu and Juanita have been trying to light a fire but there is no evidence for that; not even smoke comes out of that house," Owinyo threw the riddle at John.

"Why should that bother me?" John asked, irritated at his father's audacity to suggest that he (John) entered Juanita's bed. Even then, John sobered up the riddle; he sobered up the more he thought about the challenge. That his father had chosen to talk to him about cousin's procreative issue inside an abandoned ancestral homestead became the more significant to him, highlighting the importance and enormity of the challenge. John read the bond of blood and the challenges of kinship in his father's challenge. *Yeah, Okulu has no brother of age who could raise his head; the matter should bother me as his oldest cousin,* John said in his heart

"You risk losing a sister-in-law; who knows who shall burry you? It could be Juanita and her sons," Owinyo challenged the feeling of kinship in his son, holding the old ancestral tree.

"But Juanita has no child," John observed innocently, after a lengthy pause, spent watching a trio of weaverbirds in ritual courtship play up the big baobab tree. *Even among the birds, life has to continue from one generation to another,* John said in his heart. He had gotten his father's point from nature's timely demonstration.

"Odemba, I'm done talking to you; I am getting late for the elders' meeting," Owinyo said, moving away homeward, feeling that his son had slighted him by talking lightly about a serious matter of life and continuity. But he understood that he had delivered a weighty matter to his son and that the latter needed to think about it.

"I'll think about it," John said.

"Be careful, son," Owinyo said firmly; he did not look back, believing that his wish would see the light of day. Never again would Owinyo revisit the matter with his son. Of course, he, Owinyo, was ready to take the blame should things get out of hand while the young man executed the order.

Several weeks had passed since Atieno's clandestine meeting with Owinyo. Then, on one particularly crowded market day, Owinyo approached her and whispered into her ears, "Enemy! Is your bird nesting already?"

"What are you talking about, stranger?" Atieno whispered back, surprised at Owinyo's courage. However, she quickly dismissed her concerns because, as her elder brother-in-law, Owinyo was someone like a father-in-law to her, with whom no one could have suspected a sexual scandal.

"I must be mistaken, but you were trying to buy a good cockerel for your hens?" Owinyo whispered back into her ears.

"Owinyo, I hate your jokes. The white man must have blown off part of your brain with *miruti* (dynamite)," Atieno joked, alluding more to Owinyo's military service than to his work at Macalder Mines.

"You know that I am not alone. Gold has done that to any man who ever went down the mines," Owinyo said.

"Well, the hen has prepared the nest," Atieno whispered back.

"I wish you luck; have this pack, you may need it when my brother is not around; it is better than nothing," Owinyo said, giving Atieno a pack of brand-name cigarettes; he then moved on, melding into the noisy crowd in the fish market. Only a keen listener could have heard what they had shared.

Atieno knew that Owinyo had prepared the ground for Juanita to approach one of his sons. Atieno waited until Okulu was away on his next international business trip to North Mara, Tanganyika, and then hatched her secret plan to Juanita. She did not know how her daughter-in-law would react.

"A man will talk to you today; where he will meet you, I can't tell, but he will not fail to show up. Beyond that, I do not want to know what goes on between the man and you, but I'll pray for you. Remember that you have the name of your house to protect, that includes your name, the name of your husband, and the names of your future children. Know that I'm fully behind you in everything you do."

"Will he not know?" an excited Juanita asked.

"Okulu should not know what goes on; you know that he travels a lot," Atieno revealed the last piece of the puzzle.

I'll do it because I love you; I'll do it to cover for my husband's shame, Juanita said in her heart, moving away to her house.

As Juanita left her mother-in-law's house, she (Juanita) felt less burdened. However, she was anxious and felt guilty that she was starting on a journey that could portend ruin to her name and marriage. She resolved to go ahead with the relationship, but only if the man coming her way was reliable and could keep secrets. She hoped it would be a man in a secure marriage, mature, perhaps with at least two wives, and definitely with children who preferably were boys. Juanita didn't want a weakling who would decamp from his home and leave his wife after tasting her (Juanita's) special dishes.

That day, Juanita trekked to Macalder Center and back, but the man at the center of the project did not show up. Her husband was away on his long safaris to Tanganyika. She felt like going back to her mother-in-law to complain, but desisted. She remembered that Atieno had declared that she did not want to know about any affair she, Juanita, engaged in, except Atieno wanted her happy with children.

Once back home, Juanita prepared food in her mother-in-law's house. They had their dinner in silence before she bid her tense mother-in-law goodnight. "See you in the morning," Juanita said.

Atieno did not respond immediately.

Juanita idled about tidying up, while awaiting Atieno's response, which was taking time.

Yes, there was unusual tension between Atieno and Juanita because of the dangerous mission on which the former woman had set the latter woman. Second, they forever would share the heavy secret they had agreed to keep.

"Juanita, I want to see your face sparkle with joy; you are still young, no one should force you to have a sad day," Atieno said, realizing that she had not shared a word with Juanita the whole evening.

"I just thought of Okulu, wherever he is tonight," Juanita said, genuinely missing her husband. The more she thought about the mission, the more the desire for her husband increased, making her wonder whether she would live through the clandestine mission.

"I believe that you miss your husband; that is how it should be, whatever the ups and downs of your days and nights," Atieno said, believing that her daughter-in-law had failed in her maiden mission to bait and trap John.

"I believe we have settled that already; why should I be sad because some spare shoe disappointed me?" Juanita threw a hint, believing that Atieno would understand her.

"Move on; it is only a spare shoe; if it pinches, discard it," responded Atieno, knowing that her daughter-in-law felt that she had cheated her.

'It does not pinch; I failed to locate where I last saw it," Juanita said.

"Well, keep looking for it, then," Atieno said. "Have a good night."

"Thank you, Ma, Juanita said, leaving for her house, imaging that the man perhaps was waiting for her in her house.

Juanita still didn't know how she would react to his presence, even as she opened her door and entered her lonely house. Once inside, she switched on a battery-powered spotlight that she always carried around, and thoroughly inspected every corner of her three-roomed house, her anxiety inching higher at each turn. He was not there. "Who is this man to punish me like this?" Juanita whispered, knowing that her house would continue to be lonely for a while.

Okulu came back from Tanganyika, but he would be on another business trip a month later. In between, John Odemba spent a considerable amount of time with Okulu, gauging his manners, observing him as they swam or bathed along the river and the lake. Other than the scarcity of hair in his armpits and private parts, he looked like a man.

So what is the problem in Okulu's house? Of course, the flimsy beard. That is it! However, a number of men are like that, and they have wives with children; so where is the problem? John mused, resisting the urge to approach the Juanita, Okulu's wife.

Another month would pass, as John struggled with whether it would be ethical for him to violate his vows to his wives and seed another woman's farm possibly with sons. Wives Naomi, Consolata, and Judi all had two sons each. John felt good, because it would have been imprudent of him to even dream about possibly seeding another woman's field with sons when one of his wives had no son. Even then, the guilt of possibly violating his cousin's house weighed heavily in his heart.

Then, one evening, John saw Okulu and Judi (John's wife) in very intimate conversation behind a corner fish-stall in Macalder Market. Since her caustic encounter with Juanita years before, Judi dedicated a lot of her time investigating whether Okulu was what Juanita claimed he was—a functioning man. She had investigated the matter to her peril; the man she called the "flat tire" was not exactly flat. Careless and infatuated with Okulu, Judi had become too public in her encounters with Okulu, and she now risked igniting the flame of ire in her husband's heart.

Seeing Judi and Okulu in intimate talk, John's imaginations went wild.

What is the mere child doing with my wife? his aching heart said. At that time, John was in the company of an older man, who had seen him flinch in reaction to what both of them were witnessing.

"Odemba, my brother, beat it! Judi and Okulu have every right to talk about whatever they want, and they can do it anywhere, including in her bed. Is Okulu not Judi's brother-in-law? If you went fishing tomorrow and failed to return from the lake, Judi would not wait long before she acquired a new head of her house, because Okulu is there," the older man, Oloo, was quick to correct and chastise John.

"Oloo, I was looking at that light-skinned girl by the stall. I never saw her before. Of course, Okulu has all the keys to all my houses," Odemba responded, smarting from Okulu's barb to his heart.

"That is how it should be. Back to the alien girl tempting your heart, you never can manage to pay for her skirt," Oloo challenged John.

"What do you mean?" John asked.

"She is the daughter of the chief of Gem," Oloo said.

"Do you believe that I can't pay for her skirt?" John asked.

"Well, you can try, now that Judi has gone back to her fish stall," Oloo said, having used his diversionary talk to give Okulu a chance to move on from Odemba's view.

John Odemba would not forgive Okulu for having

talked that intimately with Judi. *I'll teach him a lesson he'll never forget!* John raved within his heart.

John was ready to taste from Juanita's bowl, and he was going to do it as a punishment to Okulu, and not as a man of honor answering to an urgent call from his desperate sister-in-law in need of a child to suckle.

From that moment in the market, John adopted his father's challenge to visit Juanita's house, only now he saw it as a means to settle his own score against Okulu. He would make initial contact with Juanita a few days later, when he was certain that Okulu had left for Tanganyika.

I'll be your guest tomorrow night. J.O., read a hand-scripted note John serendipitously had slipped under Juanita's door.

"Okulu matured late in his teens; he was like a woman until he was fifteen. He could not bathe with us between ages eleven and fifteen years," John said, having dipped his probing finger in Juliana's pot.

If the soup had been sweet, it had not done John any good. He would learn, the hard way, that he had violated a key principle in dating someone's wife: never talk disparagingly of the woman's husband. John had talked disparagingly about Juanita's husband. Yeah, the woman could disparage her husband before her new lover; the converse is not always safe.

"John, I like you, but Okulu is not the man you are trying to describe," Juanita said to an astonished John.

"Then why did I come here?" John asked, sounding even more stupid than before.

"John, I said I love you, but don't you think it is time you returned to your wives?" Juanita suggested in a cold tone that should have quickened John's departure.

"None of my wives was expecting me back tonight; I am supposed to be on a three-day business tour of Tanganyika," John observed. He felt abused and misused, and he in turn was invoking his wives' role in the noble affair.

What stunning mediocrity! Juanita thought. If she had not gotten what she wanted out of John, something she believed she had extracted from him because of her perfect timing, she would not have retained him for another assignment. She began to have an unfavorable opinion of him. Juanita had expected a smart man like John to have sneaked into her house and simply returned home late, and not weaving stories about traveling to Tanganyika. She wondered where she was going to hide a man for three days.

"John, you are strange; why do you need prior permission to return to your home?" Juanita asked innocently.

"I must be mistaken, but I understood that you were expecting me," John said, grumbling, wondering whether to slap the woman, but thought otherwise, remembering that he was on a secret mission

"John, I said I love you, but I don't want the first cocks to crow while you are still here. Second, this house has its owner; that man is Okulu," Juanita said remorsefully.

Showing remorse was the natural thing she had to do. She had stubbed her husband in the back, and she was sorry about it. Her harsh tone toward John arose from her anger at both his mediocrity and the sense of guilt she felt for betraying her husband.

"I got your point, bye," John said, subdued, walking into the night. But he had not understood the joke the woman had pulled on him. He would be back in four years.

John would be a very bitter man. When he walked into Okulu's house, he did not know that Okulu was a functional husband, except for the procreative aspect of the latter's marital life. Even when he had seen Okulu in intimate talk with Judi, his wife, and had felt challenged, he had dismissed it with, "There is a "woman" having fun around another woman; what harm could he do to her anyway?" Now, John was walking out of Juanita's bed baffled and in shame because Juanita appeared not to have appreciated his effort. A child, Luke Okulu, would be born months after the encounter.

As young look grew up, John sulked for a couple of years while the village whispered and passed knowing winks that said, "John has a son in Okulu's house." Most annoying to John was that, amid all the whispers, Juanita flashed occasional smiles in his direction but shunned his public and private advances. He would become a periodic tool, kept in the shed most of the years like the modern seeding plough. Juanita would come back to him only when she was in-season.

Four years later, John found himself in a similar abusive situation, when the woman's web caught him for the second time; she quickly put him to use and would abandon him just as fast.

Now, the second time around, John understood the limitations of his role. Moreover, the woman already had a three-year-old son named Luke, who looked like his sons. Then in John's own home, Judi had a four-year-old girl, who looked like Okulu. There were whispers about the girl's ancestry, but John had dismissed the whispers as cheap village gossip, arguing that, if Okulu were that hot, why was Juanita still requesting his (John's) services?

After an affair that lasted a week, John was in the cold again, promising never to come back. When it was over, she pushed him into an early morning rain, telling him, "Your wives need you back home." The corks were crowing for the third time as John staggered through a gap in his fence, too ashamed even to attempt returning through the main gate.

Didn't our wise of old say that no man ever dodged a woman's cooking stick? Odemba would reminisce in wonder, whistling through his kraal, pretending to secure loose bulls, before he retired to his hut.

The love-hate-tussle between Juanita and John remained an ongoing affair at the time of Aura's tragic encounter with Okulu's stone.

Over the years, Okulu would grumble about the occasional affair between Juanita and John. But what could Okulu have done about an affair that only recurred for a couple of days in four years, and only when he was away? Yeah, he could strike back at John through Judi, but she burned herself once and was not coming back soon.

Thanks to Juanita's sense of family, and the love and respect for her husband, the one-week affairs only recurred when she needed a child (and she hated the affairs), and her victim, John Odemba, felt abused about it. There was no love between Juanita and John, and the only proofs of the ongoing project, Atieno and Owinyo had hatched, were the two Okulu sons, Luke and Mark.

Okulu loved Luke and Mark dearly. Regardless, they were part of his commonwealth. The boys would still have been his sons, even if their mother had left him while childless only to return with them. They were his sons because of the dowry he had paid to gain their mother's hand. They had a right to his land.

Now disabled, Okulu was hurting from the cumulative effects of the weight of the crime he had committed against Aura, the never-ending controversy surrounding his ancestry, and the shame of his manmade impotency. Okulu was an abused man, and his reaction to the abuse was threatening to turn him against his sons—two innocent byproducts of an injustice by one man, Ougo Ng'ech, their paternal great grandfather.

30

Abich Catches a Big Fish

ODONGO HAD DISPATCHED JUMA to Alliance High School. The uneasy peace in his home forced him to act in haste and save his son from any aftershocks from the tragedy that had forced the boy to run for his life. He had designated Olga to accompany the young man on his journey to Kikuyu. Elizabeth was safely back in Ogande, having spent a weekend in Thim Lich, where the Ougo Clan had welcomed her warmly, feasting over the duration of her stay. She had promised to visit again.

Other notable events in the Odongo home: The day Aura returned to the village, Odongo, in the company of Owinyo, traveled to Macalder Hospital to see Okulu only to have missed him. The hospital staff told them that, earlier that day, two women, a Doctor Otago from Migori Hospital, and two boys arrived there in a minivan and took Okulu away. Pressed further, the hospital staff revealed that the patient's destination was Migori Hospital. The description of the two women fitted that of Juanita (the man's wife and the taller of the women) and Abich, whom the staff described as the patient's sister. They described the two boys as the patient's sons (Luke and Mark). The staff described the doctor as the shorter woman's lover or husband.

The description bothered Odongo, because Abich, his daughter, was a legally married woman. Odongo had chuckled at the description, but Owinyo nudged him with his elbow, eying him sternly, warning him to abandon any further inquiry into the matter.

"Odongo, go back home and bear with your wives in one home for a while longer. Atieno may not want a new home until Okulu recovers," advised Owinyo as both men walked out of the hospital gate.

"I have to go and check how Okulu is in Migori," Odongo said.

"No. Let him struggle with his sins, alone, while he recovers from his injuries. He is, as of now, a very bitter man; you do not want to mix your anger with his rage. Have you forgotten that he nearly killed your wife?" Owinyo cautioned Odongo.

"I know," Odongo grunted.

"About Abich, be prepared for anything. Young women of today give their fathers a lot of constipation. When you, the parent of a bride, spend the bride wealth she attracts, remember that it could get stale quickly and give you stomachache," Owinyo cautioned his brother.

"True," Odongo said as they entered a bar to drink.

Owinyo's words appeared to have foretold what was to come before Odongo's seat. Two weeks later, Abich brought Dr. Otago to Thim Lich. As the visit unfolded, Odongo realized that the good doctor was not there to visit Aura, whose life the doctor and his team had saved.

Atieno broke the news about the doctor's intentions to her husband. "Your daughter wants to bring the doctor before your seat," Atieno said, after her husband drunk generous mouthfuls of the warm sugary porridge she delivered to his hut.

"Which doctor?" Odongo asked startled, even as he knew that Dr. Otago was in his home. Odongo had reasons to be startled: One, Abich was a married woman. Second, he could not imagine why Abich would want to marry Dr. Otago, a man who knew her as a woman walking on a criminal mind. Indeed, Dr. Otago was there to announce that he was marrying Abich, an aggressively beautiful woman and a married mother with a child.

Sipping from the calabash frequently, so as to cover for his extended silence, Odongo remembered the dark day at Migori Hospital, when Abich entered Aura's convalescing room in a mask, ready to do harm to the latter, only to turn back on seeing him. Then hardly a day passed before hospital staff hauled him into the humiliating scene before

Dr. Otago, in which Abich was on display in handcuffs. Odongo vividly remembered seeing his daughter in restraining handcuffs and guard like the dangerous criminal, she could have been.

Odongo recalled Dr. Otago addressing him, wanting to know if he (Odongo) knew Abich. He recalled pleading for her release, which Dr. Otago honored. Since then, Odongo had been praying that Abich avoided any trial for the sake of peace and reconciliation in his home.

Now, Odongo's prayerful posture had changed; in its place was rage. His anger at Abich stated after his visit to Macalder Hospital, where he discovered that Dr. Otago and Abich had spirited Okulu away, and that the doting duo had been in a romantic posture during their visit. He hated scandal and wanted Abich arrested and charged before she executed another shameful act against the doctor or violated her marriage bounds.

Now, this: Dr. Otago was proposing to the same Abich—a woman the doctor once arrested over criminal acts. Odongo quietly put down his calabash of porridge on a wooden cradle on his table, cleared his voice and then said, "Atieno, my dear. Do you know that Abich is a married woman?"

"I know that Abich married some abusive teacher; but she cannot continue to live with the *abusive* man," Atieno responded.

Odongo let her explanation pass, even as he never before heard of the claim that Abich's husband was abusive.

"How much do I owe Oduogo?" Odongo asked. Odougo was Abich's current husband.

"Ask another question; or if you have other reasons to want to stop their relationship, please say so," Atieno challenged Odongo.

"Are you saying that my concerns are not serious enough?"

"*My husband*, if I may, you are like a fisherman who is about to get a motor engine for his boat but still worried about what to do with his old oars, instead of dumping them overboard," challenged Atieno.

"Well, when the boat's motor engine fails, the oars could become handy on a stormy day," Odongo mused, enjoining his wife's wisecrack.

Ironically, Oduogo gave Odongo very few heads of cattle in dowry; Odongo could count four cows—a measly number by his standards as a rich man. Because Abich hated her father for the way he had treated her mother, she had instructed her husband to pay Odongo minimal animal wealth. Under Abich's directions, Odougo otherwise greased Atieno's hands with informal unaccountable cash payments that were recorded nowhere.

"Not in the middle of a storm with a load of fish on board," Atieno said to keep the conversation going.

"What is your point?" Odongo asked.

"I want Abich to move on beyond her miserable life with the *teacher.* You owe the man nothing; he has the child and that takes care of the few animals he gave you; you have nothing to refund Oduogo; that is the law," Atieno argued.

Why am complaining? Odongo wondered as the irony of the situation hit him. Of course, he had moral grounds on which to base his objection to the proposal, but he could not state them for fear of opening up recent scars that were still too raw in the hearts of many in the family.

If Dr. Otago wants a woman who could cook him alive, I am ready to swallow my pride and host him, and even welcome him as a son-in-law. And who am I to fight a daughter who is sailing home with one fat fish in her net? Odongo pondered his dwindling options. He would shake the doctor's hands.

"Owinyo should be here soon, we then will listen to the doctor from Nyakach," Odongo announced.

"Okay, drink the porridge," Atieno said; she was relieved.

"The day is still young, so why the hurry?" Odongo asked.

"I don't want to risk leaving my calabash here for Grace to lick," she said, opening an old warfront. In her view, the Ougo home had treated Okulu worse than they treated Grace, their famous female dog.

"Is that a joke?" Odongo asked. He always was too slow to match Atieno's scheming mind that thrived on conspiracies and counter-conspiracies against her and her son.

"Grace maimed Okulu, and nobody has had the

courage to kill her. She still walks around with germs. You know, this home is the only place where a dog is more valued that a man," Atieno spat out her damning charge, blitzing Odongo from all sides.

Odongo remained silent for a few minutes. He found the truth damning. *The dog is sick. How did we all miss that simple fact?* Odongo wondered, his eyes blinking rapidly. Fighting emotions, he cleared a lump that was starting to build in his throat and said, "Atieno, my dear, this world needs a few mad people like you to make it work for everybody. In the centuries past, we never buried the dead, until, one day, someone was mad enough to complain about it. Otherwise, we would not be burying our dead today. Atieno, my dear, no dog shall lick your calabash. Besides, I must have forgotten that Juma took Grace to the animal doctor before he left for school," Odongo said as emotionlessly as his tremulous voice could allow, remembering that Judas and Juma had approached him to give them money for the visit with the veterinarian.

Why did I fail to follow up on that visit? Odongo wondered.

"Is that an apology or not?" Atieno demanded.

"Atieno, my dear, we should be willing to move on," Odongo pleaded.

"I wish you had always been as nice as you are today, this old body could have given you many boys instead of one impotent bastard?" Atieno mused in as sarcastic a tone as she could muster.

"Thank you for the porridge," he said, having drained the calabash of the porridge in one long draught. "All I want today is to give Abich to the doctor successfully. This home needs a lot to celebrate about after the events of last moth. I hope that Okulu will recover fully as Doctor Otago has predicted," pleaded Odongo, avoiding a fight.

"Are you coming home tonight?" Atieno asked.

"I hope to give away my daughter tonight, after which I'll be so drunk that I won't know where I will sleep," Odongo said cheerfully.

"Is that a No?" Atieno demanded, believing that the prospects of having Dr. Otago as a son-in-law had increased her value in her husband's eyes.

"Atieno, you are losing your patience. Can you please allow the porridge to work the magic through my body?

Let's give away our daughter before we celebrate," declared Odongo.

"That means Yes," Atieno said, wondering why her old husband suddenly looked that young in her eyes.

What is it between man and woman that even age has to struggle to subdue? Odongo also wondered.

Atieno left the hut happier than she had been in years. She had reasons to be happy: Okulu was responding to doctors' medicine. Second, she believed she was pregnant for the sixth time. Moreover, her favored daughter, Abich, was becoming the most visible daughter among Ougo's granddaughters. *Aura can have her genius son!* Atieno said in her heart.

Since she survived Okulu's attack, Aura had been very nice to everybody in the Ougo home. She was happy that a doctor from Migori Hospital had remembered to visit her home, even if he was in Abich's company. When she saw the two alight from the doctor's rugged-terrain truck, she was a little jealous. *I wish it were Rachel getting out of that car,* she said on a heart inflicted with a bout of jealousy, but she beat a quick retreat as she remembered that daughters Rachel and Leah were happily married to caring men.

If the doctor could turn Abich into a good soul, it would be good for peace in the Odongo family, Aura reasoned, even as she doubted whether such a character transformation was possible. Aura of all the people knew that Abich walked on her mother's body, heart, and mind.

Then Aura saw Abich leave Juma's hut, wherein Dr. Otago had perched like a kingfisher awaiting the invitation to present his case before the Ougo Family Council. Abich stood tall and sparkled in the sun on here well proportioned body.

"Abich is beautiful, who can blame Doctor Otago for spoiling his hands?" Aura posed, whispering, fully acknowledging her stepdaughter's wholesome physical attributes.

Hardly a moment passed before Aura saw Atieno emerging from Odongo's hut, carrying an empty calabash, her face beaming in joy. Atieno's body language projected a woman having a good romantic day, sending Aura on an emotional spin.

"Whoever said that *'Ober ka nyar Jajuok'* (She is beautiful like the daughter of a witch) must have had Abich and her mother Atieno in mind," Aura muttered in disgust on seeing her rival.

Then Odongo emerged from his hut, walking towards Aura. Envy toward Atieno intensified in Aura's heart; she wished that it were her day instead.

Aura guessed why Odongo was coming to see her. She knew Odongo' wanted a concurrence of their opinion over whether Abich could marry the doctor, given what they knew about Abich's behavior in Migori a year before.

In fact, Odongo wanted to see Aura essentially to buy her silence. He wanted Dr. Otago's case to succeed before the Ougo Family Council that was to meet in Aura's house.

"Aura, my love, how is your day?" Odongo asked.

"O my dear, I don't know why I got into this again? I don't know what I am carrying this time. It is only four months, and I am pregnant like a bitch. If you allowed me to rest this leg on you, I will be okay. Then you can tell me what Abich and Atieno are up to this time," Aura commiserated, treating her old husband like a comfort toy.

"Juma wrote back about his life in Nairobi. He says he is missing home, particularly the food. They eat sweet potatoes in the morning, at midday, and at sunset," Odongo said, ignoring a feminine verse he had heard at least nine times before.

"They must be trying to turn him into a Kikuyu," Aura remarked, surprised at how little she thought about Juma since her pregnancy became obvious two months back.

"He will get used to it," Odongo observed, massaging Aura's left foot.

"O this old body! Why are laughing at me?" Aura said playfully.

"I want peace. That is all," Odongo said, wondering how he became a physiotherapist.

"You know that Doctor Otago and his team saved my life; are you giving him a goat to carry back to Migori?" Aura asked

"I could give Doctor Otago some animal to go and slaughter, but things are changing rapidly. He has his hands on my youngest daughter. That has changed things: he is the one who will give me some animals. What do you think?" Odongo asked, knowing what Aura knew about Abich's behavior at the hospital, where the doctor's men had arrested the young woman while she was scaling a wall on her third attempt to reach and harm Aura.

"If Doctor Otago wants to catch a turtle instead of fish from this vast lake, who are we to say no to him?" Aura said in a stinging metaphor.

"I'll be traveling to Nairobi to acquaint myself with the place where Juma goes to school," Odongo said, changing the subject, now that Aura was willing to play along.

"You could use the opportunity to visit Kijabe where Okulu is hospitalized," Aura suggested in the spirit of reconciliation.

"No. Owinyo says that we give him time to heal from within," responded Odongo

Later in the evening, the Ougo Council met and quickly approved of Dr. Otago's proposal to marry Abich. Most of them were learning for the first time that the doctor had taken Okulu to a rehabilitation center in a faraway place known as Kijabe.

For the occasion, Abich was dressed like a queen, and she aggressively protected her man from any questions she considered invasive. When John Odemba asked about the doctor's marital status, Abich mildly said that he was trying to marry her, and left everyone writhing in laughter. Odemba did not proceed further; he already had in his pocket a couple of the doctor's hundred-shilling bills for the purchase of the boys' goat.

Then things moved fast, once the Ougo Council approved of their highly visible prospective son-in-law: Doctor Otago left Odongo with thousands of shillings and twenty heads of cattle, all within a week. According to the doctor, Abich had filed for a fast-tracked divorce application in Subakuria, bypassing the Local Chief's Court. Moreover, he had no time to wait as Abich awaited a prolonged litigation against an abusive man.

Two days later, the divorced teacher, Mr. Oduogo, arrived in Odongo's home, pleading for his intervention. The teacher was literally crying that a doctor had taken away his wife, leaving him with a child, but no one was listening to him.

Atieno, Odougo's mother-in-law, naturally had immersed herself in Abich's tumultuous wind of passion.

Therefore, she was more direct in expressing her disgust at the abusive teacher. To highlight her disgust at Odougo, Atieno cooked *fulu* (a cheap small fish) for him.

Aura was nicer, though, she cooked salmon for Odougo, even as the latter's image among his in-laws had fallen drastically. Tradition demanded that Aura or someone else in the home had to play nice to the unfortunate son-in-law who had fallen out favor with the family. One, Aura was the head of the home. Two, Odongo was still the man's father-in-law because Abich had left the latter with a three-year-old boy. Therefore, even if the marriage was on the rocks, a sense of decorum had to prevail because blood relationships (through the children) continued beyond divorce. Oduogo's son would remain the link between the Ougos and Oduogos.

The teacher quickly realized the futility of his effort: Abich's cousins, with whom he previously bonded readily, were not available to entertain him. He knew loyalties had changed. During his lunch, he had Nyerere, the herdsman, for company. Women had locked up their daughters. No girl was visible, even as it was a Saturday; that, alone, encouraged him to sneak back to Migori quietly.

31

You Are Hurting Me!

ONE YEAR LATER, things had returned to normal in the
Odongo home, except Okulu was still on rehabilitation in
Kijabe. On this night, Odongo had honored his
obligations, as a husband, to Atieno. He had arrived in her
house just after nine o'clock in the evening, just after the
home had settled into the sleep routine. The night had
progressed well, and though it was well past midnight,
each part of the doting duo was still awake.

Atieno was in a smoking break by the bedside. Odongo
was in bed.

"Do you plan to visit Okulu in the hospital?" Odongo
asked to break the loud silence in the house.

"No," Atieno replied, her words muffled because of the
pipe in her mouth.

"Why?" Odongo asked, wondering about the schism
that had developed between Atieno and their son since the
latter nearly killed Aura.

"I realized for the first time that he should not be my
burden alone," Atieno said, her pipe temporarily out of her
mouth.

"How has he been your burden alone?" asked Odongo,
sensing danger.

"Let me make it easier on you and say that Okulu is
not your seed. That should bring relief to your soul
because then you are not the father of a man who
attempted to kill his own stepmother; but I remain his
mother," Atieno said, reopening a subject her husband did
not want revisited. Odongo believed that a touchy subject

not talked about eventually ceased to be an issue.

"Can you stop smoking until I leave your house?" asked Odongo, ignoring her comments.

"Thank you; you should have said so many years ago. I always wondered why you never spent any whole night in my bed. So it was about the smell of my tobacco and not about Aura's cleaner and warmer blankets?" wondered Atieno, dragging Aura's name into their bedside talk.

"The past is gone, let's look to the future. Now, if Okulu is not my son, then whose son is he?" Odongo asked, ignoring Atieno's barb targeted at Aura.

"Under no circumstance is he your son. When you paid bride prize to Omulo, Okulu already was born, and I know that he is not your seed. Do not feel bad, you are the father of the rest of my children; you have been nice to Okulu, something I never acknowledged before, and I do acknowledge today. Okulu was my burden because I fed him the filth that eventually plunged this home in anarchy," raged Atieno, not caring if her words hurt her husband.

"Whose burden is Okulu now?" Odongo asked, wondering to what end Atieno was revisiting old issues.

"Okulu has become your burden in other ways: he is an invalid, if what I have heard is true. He will need your support because he had sisters who gave you vast wealth," Atieno said, keeping Odongo wondering whether he was listening to sarcasm or a serious challenge from his wife to own up and declare that he was the man who violated her four decades before.

"I never disputed that," Odongo said, wondering as to what man ever paid his son reparation. He knew he had lived in denial and had wronged Okulu in a way that money could not compensate. Odongo now wondered whether his wife of decades had lived with the knowledge of his shameful past.

"And more; Okulu had other reasons to be bitter with the Ougo family," Atieno said, heightening Odongo's anxiety.

"What are those?" Odongo asked; he was getting worried about the direction Atieno's early morning bed talk had taken. Okulu was his blood but his tepidity and life in shame had allowed someone in the family to deny Okulu his seed. He wondered if that was what Atieno was interrogating.

"His children," Atieno said, and left the words hanging out there, testing what Odongo knew about Okulu's children.

"His children are his and my grandchildren; why should they be a point of contention?" wondered Odongo.

"You should know that your son Okulu is impotent," Atieno announced, wondering what Odongo knew and what he did not know.

The matter of the ancestry of Juanita and Okulu's son was the subject of much whisper in the village. Was it possible that Odongo believed that the boys were Okulu's blood? Did he believe that the whispers were just gossip, aimed at maligning Okulu? These matters bothered Atieno as she waited for Odongo to respond.

"No! I thought that we treated his condition?" Odongo said finally, not even believing his own words, again demonstrating a lack of engagement in matters affecting Atieno's house.

"Did you treat it?" Atieno challenged her husband.

"I believe you visited a man, in Tanganyika, who treated it," Odongo said lamely.

"Did I tell you about that?" Atieno asked, enjoying her triumph over the husband.

"I got to know that during some of my visits in Tanganyika," Odongo said. However, even then he was not sure whether he was the one who went to Tanganyika to seek medicine for Okulu's condition. He indeed was the one who made the journey to consult in Tanganyika.

"He is impotent, and now that he is hurt, he is cursing Juanita and the boys. He is a bitter man; his is cursing at everyone to have crossed his path. Be prepared for that when you first meet him," Atieno warned. She was surprised that Odongo could not remember a very important trip he made to Tanganyika to consult with a doctor about Okulu's condition. Even then, she thanked her luck. For the first time in many years, her husband had stayed in her house long enough for a talk that was more about him and his failures as a husband and parent.

"So, who fathered his children?" Odongo asked, mourning in his heart. *Shame on me; shame on me*, he raved in silence, searching for anything good he ever did to Atieno. He found nothing to boast of; his home was on trial.

"Well, I beg you to save Juanita any embarrassment. Unlike Okulu, the children are Ougo blood. That should give you and your clan some peace of mind. It too is a burden you have to walk with, knowing that your brother's seeds are growing in your home."

"Why did you do this to me?" Odongo whispered in suppressed anger, wondering where he had been, that in crisis after crisis in his home, his input had always been either absent or mediocre.

"Which is more painful, the grandchildren from the Ougo house or a son who is not your blood?" Atieno asked pouring hot salt into Odongo's inflamed open wound.

"Then, who are my people?" Odongo asked rhetorically, accepting that the woman had beaten him; she even had selected what man seeded her son's home.

"We don't know how many children, like daughter Betha, you have in the bush. Yet you treated me like a spare wife, just because I came to this home carrying some unknown man's blood," Atieno challenged her husband's already frayed moral fibers, leaving him wondering what else she knew about him.

"I wish we were young and were to start all over," he was saying, his left hand massaging the back of her neck when the bed talk turned violent.

She kicked him, saying "No. It is too late; all my eggs are stale. It would do everyone some good, if you kept your bloodied hand away from my grandsons."

"I never killed anybody," Odongo said, wondering why she kicked him that hard.

"Do you want to repeat that?" Atieno asked coldly.

"I never killed before," Odongo protested

"When Ougo castrated Okulu, believing that he was not his grandson, were you not there alongside your mother?" Atieno charged raising her voice.

"No . . .!" Odongo cried out. "My father couldn't have done such a thing!" Odongo whispered standing up. He was angry. He, his father, and his mother stood accused of complicity to deny Okulu the chance to plant any seed within and without the Ougo clan.

But if Odongo thought he came back to a mellowed and more subservient Atieno, an Atieno who would watch her steps and keep low, now that her murder scheme had instead left her only son invalid, he was wrong. Atieno felt wronged and believed she needed some vindication and public apologies.

Who castrated Okulu? Odongo wondered. For the first time, Odongo's eyes opened to the big question in his home.

In truth, Odongo had held no bias against Okulu, however, he had lived a life that embraced Aura's point of view, and in that point of view, Atieno and Okulu were intruders in their marriage. He saw Atieno's problems as secondary matters, to which he could give little attention. Even then, Odongo believed that he had to solve their problems because they were his responsibility. Odongo walked with the haunting guilt as the secret man who once violated Atieno in their youth, and he in that way he fathered Okulu out of wedlock. The product of the guilt was a general contempt toward Atieno, the victim. She reminded him of his youthful indiscretions. That his parents had contested Atieno's marriage to him only helped to advance his romantic aloofness and general disengagement from her.

The general contempt in which Odongo held Atieno, translated into largely children-only romantic encounters, in a marriage marked by a strange form of behavior, in which he routinely left Atieno's bed in the middle of the night, citing the same stale excuse other polygamists before him had used to disengage from one woman to another. It was always, 'A bull has violated the fence, and I need to round it up before it damages a neighbor's farm.' Moreover, Odongo knew that he would always get warm bathing water and a warm blanket from Aura at any time of the night.

Atieno's fate was not complicated due to any luck of natural beauty endowments or material wealth. Both women were rich, and each was beautiful in her unique way, but where Atieno applied aggressive tactics whenever she had a case to make before Odongo, Aura made her case quietly, softly, tactfully without even mentioning Atieno by name. Whenever Aura mentioned Atieno's name, it was on the positive side. 'You have been here for months; don't you think Atieno needs you by her side?' Aura occasionally had to remind her husband.

But who could have blamed Atieno for her combative

style? She arrived in the Ougo home with the words *pregnant* and *illegitimate* in everyone's mouth. Then she gave birth to a boy and everyone said *kimirwa* (bastard). Before the boy turned five, someone in the Ougo family had neutered him. Through all these, Atieno adopted a combative style because she had realized that it was her son and her against the Ougo family. That she had arrived ahead of Aura, Odongo's childhood bride, had not endeared her to the Ougo family. Beautiful, combative, and wronged, that was Atieno. Atieno knew the late Ougo had been against her and her son, Okulu, while the late Apudo always joined her in fighting some of her wars. Owinyo, her brother-in-law, the man who was combative like her, was on her side: they occasionally fought but always found common ground when the dust settled. Amid all these debates and crises in Atieno's married life, Odongo's voice was largely absent.

Now, the son Atieno had protected was not only impotent but also invalid and a criminal; and the blame over his condition lay with her. During her long bed talk with her husband, her combative nature warned her that she had precipitated a major civil crisis, and that she should not fold up without revisiting all the injustices against her and her son.

Atieno was due for a surprise vindication. She had lived with a wolf in sheepskin, and the wolf was about to shed the sheepskin.

"Who castrated Okulu?" Atieno asked directly. "I am tempted to leave out your mother. She was such a nice soul, whose interest was to train and protect all her grandchildren from childhood to the moment they married. That leaves your father. He never looked at me in the eye after Okulu's troubles became public. He was a snake," Atieno upped he challenge.

"What did you say? Atieno, what did you say?" Odongo shouted, but his reflexes were faster than his words; he already had executed a strange left-handed stranglehold around Atieno's neck, with the blanket adding further airflow complications to the unfortunate woman.

"Let go my neck! You are hurting me!" Atieno cried, breathing erratically, kicking about helplessly, and fearing for her life.

"Did you call my father a witch?" Odongo shouted

tightening the deadly noose. The accusation against his late father had inflamed a raw nerve; he had ceased thinking of his actions.

"Stop, Father of Alal! Stop, you are choking me!" Atieno uttered the haunting words from her past, remembering to refer to him by their eldest daughter's name (Alal) for effect, believing that by calling the man by their eldest daughter's name, he'd remember the good old days and relax his killer hold.

Touched by her pained words that lifted him back thirty-five years, Odongo relaxed the strange stranglehold on her neck. His breathing that had been heavy relaxed too.

The pressure on Atieno's neck dropped. She had survived again. Yet something she now recalled from deep in her past warned her that she had been living with the man who violated her in her youth. As the weight of her words, "Stop, you are choking me," sunk in her mind, she remembered the strange left-handed stranglehold a man used against her one dark night thirty-five years before. She remembered the strong hands that had snuffed the wind out of her lungs instantly; she remembered that when she came to, the man was finalizing his sordid act, and by the time she found a voice to utter the word "Stop," whoever he was had vanished into the night. Not far from her was her friend Amondi, who was giggling hysterically. Amondi had gone through a similar violation, and her assailant too had vanished, but why Amondi laughed hysterically still bothered Atieno.

Amondi, who was older, would advice Atieno to live with the shame in silence and say "Yes" to the next person to propose to her for marriage. Both women would elope with men in a short while. Atieno was pregnant when she next met Odongo in a dance party. She made a bed for him within a month. Amondi was not pregnant as she traveled across the land to marry a polygamist in Homa Bay. Both women would live with that shared shame. That shame was immediate and real for Atieno, who would give birth to Okulu, a man rejected by his clan.

Believing that Atieno had unmasked him as the violator of decades before, Odongo turned away from Atieno and remained motionless for a while before he again turned in bed, struggling with his thoughts. He knew Atieno was revisiting a very old experience in their past.

Atieno knew Odongo was thinking and regretting his dated violent action, something he had subdued throughout their marriage. *Where was Amondi now?* Atieno wondered. She wanted to get to the truth, and she knew that Amondi must have known their assailants, otherwise why had the latter laughed hysterically after the violation? Why had Amondi insisted that they lived with their shame in silence?

Her mind all over the place groping for answers, Atieno recalled that Amondi died a few years before. She wondered whether she should go public. But what was she going to gain in shaming the man who gave her four daughters? Now, she just realized he gave her one son everybody in the Ougo clan much maligned, the son the clan called *kimirwa* (a bastard)—the son who almost killed his stepmother. What was she to do to get justice from cowardly man who denied his son a birthright to conceal a criminal past? And who would believe her narrative? Atieno wondered.

'Atieno, live with the shame in silence and say yes to the next person to propose to you for marriage. This world can be cruel to a pregnant single girl!' the late Amondi's old words of caution reverberated in Atieno's mind.

Odongo again turned in silence, Atieno's creaking wooden bed silencing a lone cricket singing somewhere in the house..

"Why did you do that to me?" Atieno found the courage to challenge her husband in as damning a voice as she could muster after a long moment of mutual silence.

He did not respond, believing that Atieno had unmasked him after decades of him living a suppressed lie. He hated himself for having allowed his kin to harm and throw mud at his own son. Even then, he decided to continue to maintain a cowardly silence and let Atieno, the victim, be the judge. He knew Amondi was long dead; also dead was the friend with whom he had conspired to waylay the pair of young women.

It was first cockcrow! Odongo turned in bed, feeling that he better slipped out of Atieno's bed and left her hut. *Then what?* Odongo wondered. He tossed in bed for another half hour, his guilt weighing down on him.

What if Atieno went public with the shameful experience, she endured in my hands four decades before? Odongo wondered.

"Don't you have any reason to leave me alone? It is morning already," Atieno challenged him.

He did not respond, in words, he instead quietly slipped out of bed, groped around for his work pants, put then on, grabbed his shirt and stepped out of the bedroom.

"From now I would believe you, when you insist that Okulu is your seed. You appear to have had a better memory than mine all along," she challenged him, broaching the subject of the sexual violation that occurred thirty years before.

He said nothing, thou she knew he was still in the house, listening.

"I wonder why you stood aloof when they castrated Okulu, thus denying him the promise of seeding his gardens. What man deliberately would condone an act that ensured that he never would see his grandchildren? That was murder in your name," charged Atieno, completing her judgment.

Odongo said nothing, but her arrows were taking atoll on his heart. A tear rolled down his face; he wiped it off fast, as if someone was watching him in the dark. A heavy lump of emotion clogged his throat. He managed to stifle a verbal outburst for a moment, but the emotional pressure was so great that it threatened to blow up his lungs. He was suffocating; he let up and started whimpering like a child.

"Hey, my friend; I'm not dead yet. Stop mourning me," Atieno said in triumph, though it also was a belief that a man should not shed tears before his wife. "Be a man and confess to your sinful past," challenged Atieno.

Odongo quietly opened the door and slipped outside to attend to nature's call. She heard him close the door behind him.

On his way back from the bush, he thought of going to Aura's house, but found it unwise. He was grieving within, and he risked displacing his anger on Aura. As he weighed his alternatives, he saw a cow jump out of the fence. He rounded up the cow that had violated the fencing. After tethering the cow, by the fence, he stumbled back to his place beside Atieno in bed.

Atieno slipped out of the bed to attend to nature's call. She came back moments later, took her place in bed intent on keeping peace with the man who, after all, fathered all her children. She turned to face her husband, wondering what he would do next.

'Never in anger should you turn your back against your wife in her bed,' he said in silence, remembering the words from his late father, Ougo Ngech.

"You remembered to come back for the first time after thirty-five years of constant pain to my heart?" Atieno asked two cockcrows later. She was sitting up in bed, smoking her pipe, after a satisfying early-morning romantic duel, during which he said nothing.

He dressed up to leave for his hut.

Atieno watched him in dawn's light filtering through the eave. "Thank you for staying over, my husband, and the father of Okulu," Atieno said, deliberately planting the ancestry of Okulu in an otherwise complete sentence.

She watched him in the dim light as he turned around, looked at her, in silence, and then bent at the doorway to leave the house. He had not verbally confessed to his indiscretions as a youth, but his filth no longer was a secret to her; she felt relieved for the revelation that Okulu was Odongo's seed.

"The battle over you is a battle I will always fight as long as you and I are alive. I have a right, like any other woman, to fight it. When Betha's mother arrives here, I'll fight her too," Atieno said, but Odongo had left her house before she uttered the last sentence.

Odongo had just spent the first full night in Atieno's bed in ten years, but he was in mournful mood. As with previous emotional outbursts between them, there would be life a season and a half later, except here, Atieno presented two sons to her husband. She named the children Opiyo and Adongo because they were twins. Opiyo arrive first; he was a boy. Adongo, another boy, arrived an hour later. Adongo took a feminine form of the name Odongo to differentiate him from Odongo, his father. The twins left their old mother struggling to remain alive. She would live to welcome their wives.

32

All Have Changed

"PILOT, YOU CAN LEAVE ME HERE," the hot-tempered passenger said to the driver of the minibus named APOLLO 13.

"There is no stage here, Sir!" the driver of the minibus said.

"Pilot, I said leave me here; I know where I am going," demanded the passenger who shared the front cabin with the driver.

"Sir, if you know the home you are going to, I would take you there," the driver said, unsure whether it was right to leave the challenged man in the middle of nowhere.

"Young man, stop here; you couldn't take me to hell," shouted the caustic passenger.

Without another word, the driver stopped the minibus, opened his door and went around the front of the minibus to open the passenger-side door for the special passenger.

The passenger picked up his crutches and said to the driver, "I'll need your help."

Moments later, the driver, with the help of his baggage boy, successfully completed loading the challenged man on the hardly used crutches.

"Here is your money. Keep the change," the challenged man said, passing the fare to the driver.

"No, Sir! I'll give you your change," protested the driver.

"Young man, nothing is free in this world!" Okulu said firmly. He soon was hopping away across the grass, leaving the driver perplexed for words. A few steps later

Okulu was onto a narrow rarely used path, heading uphill and west.

Convinced the man could hold his own, the driver and his baggage boy entered their vehicle and were ready to drive on to Macalder.

All the passengers were saying something about the hot-tempered invalid.

"He is right! Nothing is free; he got that blemish for a reason!" a female passenger shouted above the sound of the engine.

Okulu turned around, looked at the woman angrily, but he was too far away to have been able to poke her with his walking-aid. In character, Okulu spat in the general direction of the minibus, but his sputum could not reach the bus, which already was speeding away southward toward Macalder.

Okulu was a bitter man, and his anger had not thawed even after eight months of rehabilitation in Kijabe. He was lucky to have had an aggressive little sister (Abich) and a new brother-in-law (Dr. Otago), both of whom had aggressively pushed for the rehabilitation of his hands. However, Okulu was unlucky; just when he thought he had recovered from the dog-bite-related wounds, he slipped in the bathroom and broke his left leg. The leg had healed, but he was still nervous about using it unsupported.

He had reached Mikumu Ridge after an overnight-bus journey that landed him in Ndhiwa Town. He could have gone home via Migori and Macalder, but he had fears. He didn't know how a home in which he nearly killed his stepmother would receive him. One thing had not changed; Okulu was the blood son of Odongo, and the latter had declared as much to the former man's mother.

So, Okulu returned to Mikumu Ridge to solicit help from Pastor Aaron, the man he collided with as he chased Juma across the land, only for the pastor to save his (Okulu's) life the following morning.

This morning, Okulu hopped briskly, even ignoring his crutches. Within a few minutes, he was going by the big deciduous tree, where he had rested on that trying morning. He walked on, entering Pastor Aaron's home a few minutes later. As if all confidence had returned to him, he hurried a cross the compound to meet the pastor, who was servicing his bicycle.

"The lost son, welcome! Ada! See who is here!" Pastor Aaron cried out, running to get hold of Okulu before the latter broke another leg in excitement. "How are you?"

"You can see that I am fine, Pastor Aaron," Okulu said; shedding tears as he embraced his host.

"Use your crutches; you still need them," Pastor Aaron cautioned.

"Okulu, welcome; I told you to have faith," Ada said, shaking Okulu's hands.

"You see, my hands are healed; I should be fishing again soon; thank God, Ada; you see He has listened to you too," Okulu said in reference to Ada's condition.

Ada grinned as she greeted Pastor Aaron.

"How is your morning?" Pastor Aaron asked. Since Ada became pregnant, he regularly had joked that the Odongo brothers had left some luck in his home.

"Difficult; it is as if there are several Pastor Aarons singing and stomping their feet inside me," Ada joked.

"Okulu, come into the house; we need to pray for Ada's health," Pastor Aaron said, following Ada into the house, with Okulu limping behind them.

Pastor Aaron prayed; Ada served them lunch, then Pastor Aaron briefed Okulu about Thim Lich. The pastor had been Thim Lich recently, and he had met Juanita and the boys; there were births in the Odongo home: Aura had a son; Atieno had twin sons.

Okulu already knew all that through Abich's frequent visits. He also knew that Juanita had given birth to another son; he had grieved over the news weeks before. The evening he heard about Juanita's new son, he fell down and broke his left leg. He had wondered why Juanita never visited him in Kijabe, the news about her pregnancy had explained why: She was not going to risk a fight with him in an alien land, so she had judged. However, the boy was Okulu's seed and Juanita had decided to withhold the announcement until he came home.

Okulu was determined to reach home; he had hoped that Pastor Aaron would accompany him. However, on seeing Ada's advanced pregnancy, Okulu realized that the pastor was unlikely to leave home.

"Pastor Aaron, I am going home, whatever the consequences it might have on my life," Okulu said.

"No one will harm you. Believe me, everyone in the Ougo Clan is preaching peace and reconciliation. Your mothers are too busy with their babies to engage in fights," Pastor Aaron said.

"What about my father? He could fight me," Okulu observed.

"No. He is willing to move on. He says he is the most blessed man on earth. He has seen three sons in one month," Pastor Aaron said.

"You prayed for him?" Okulu asked. He already knew that he had three "baby brothers" awaiting his arrival.

"Yes; we were alone. Like every man, he had burdens to unload from his soul. He is a changed man," Pastor Aaron said.

"He is a changed man? How Pastor?" wondered Okulu.

"Unusual events like what happened in your father's home often change people. If you are a good reader of the Bible, you must be familiar with David's ordeal after he ordered Abisai, his war general, to put a soldier named Uriah in harm's way in the battlefield. The general did that; Uriah died in the battlefield on the same day David violated his, Uriah's, wife. David would suffer to the bone for that sinful act. He never was the same after that. Your father and everyone in your home will never be the same as before. Events like that make people look back in search of what they did or did not do right to have caused the event. People will review their relationships; people will correct their behaviors; the brave ones, like David, will confess their sins because that is the only way people can reach a resolution and move forward in peace after a traumatic event," preached Pastor Aaron.

"Pastor Aaron, this man has many miles to cover before sunset, why don't you save your sermon for another day?" Ada said. She believed that her husband had spent too many months witnessing to various people within the Odongo family.

"Thank you, Ada for your kind words. Pastor Aaron, I might be having no friend left in Thim Lich," Okulu joked, even as the issue of his future in Thim Lich bothered him. He had thought of migrating to another land, but his poor physical shape demanded that he stayed where his sons would be available to help him. His wife wished that the family migrated to Tanganyika, a suggestion he had opposed. He had decided to return to Thim Lich essentially to confront the demons in his past.

"Okulu, you need that sense of humor. But you have more friends in Thim Lich than before, it has become clear that your father and mother wronged you many times," Pastor Aaron said. He wanted to say that Okulu was "a child of hate" but restrained himself because that could have been too direct, even if he were speaking from a pulpit.

"Thank you, Ada; I will remember you and the pastor for saving my life," Okulu said emotionally.

"Don't mention it; Pastor Aaron swore to serve fellow man," Ada said.

"Ada, I'll give him a ride until we meet a vehicle to Macalder. In case of trouble, blow the whistle," Pastor Aaron said, leading the way out of the house. He believed his wife's baby or babies would be arriving any moment.

"The day he or she arrives, you won't sleep for even a minute," Ada joked back.

33

Odongo Breaks His Cruel Silence

WHEN OKULU AND PASTOR AARON LEFT Mikumu Ridge for Thim Lich, Odongo had just seen off Juma to Nairobi and Betha to Ogande, and he was back home struggling with the question of Dorka who had been gnawing his heart soothingly.

Over the previous year, Elizabeth had spent most of her holidays in Thim Lich, where she had become a darling of the Ougo home. Her mother, Dorka, had met Odongo twice during the previous year. The venue was the same: Rodi Kopany. Betha had arranged both meetings between her parents. Now, Dorka had celebrated all of her late husband's rituals, even remarrying another clan member, whom she since kicked out. She was an available widow, and her heart was with Odongo, who constantly was tempted to bite the bait, but he had not gained enough courage to surmount the hill doubt and roll into the valley of lust. Moreover, he was worried as to how Aura would react to such a move.

The next issue bothering Odongo was how he would receive Okulu, when the latter finally arrived. Odongo knew he was going to be emotional about it. That Atieno had given him twin boys, Opiyo and Adongo, made his feelings tender toward her house. He had been talking to doctors, wondering whether medical intervention could cure a man's sterility, but all he got from consultations over beer was about improving sperm count and ongoing research into artificial insemination. Odongo felt devastated as Okulu aged without children, wondering how a man could pay a child he wronged, when such wrong was irreversible. This matter bothered him. He had confessed about his youthful indiscretions to a priest, but he had not said against what woman or girl he committed it. That left issues about Dorka and Okulu as the only unresolved matters.

Odongo was increasingly anxious to see Juma with a wife, but Aura was cool to the idea. Juma was a good student; his teachers were talking about Harvard and other places in America. Increasingly, Juma was learning to say No to the idea of early marriage.

Midday, Owinyo made an unplanned visit with Odongo in the latter's hut. They talked at length, their talk wondering across several issues, before Odongo brought up the matter of Dorka.

"Owinyo, Dorka is tempting my heart. Do you think it would be a good idea if Betha had her mother's house in this home?"

"Odongo, do you want to be called *jakowiny* (Luo: an alien man consorting with a widow)? Why not marry another virgin?" Owinyo challenged his brother.

"Well, I am prepared to pay bride price to her people," Odongo said, believing that paying bride prize to Dorka's people would solve the problem of compensation of the late Ochieng's estate for a wife lost.

"You'll still be her consort because she already buried a man. It does not matter how many livestock you were to pay, she will still be a widow," Owinyo, a man of vast experience said.

"Then let me be called *jakowiny*," Odongo said, believing that would be his fate within the year.

"Are you going to build her a home?" Owinyo asked.

"Must I do that?" Odongo wondered aloud.

"Yes. I will not allow you to destroy Aura and Atieno's houses through the dangerous game you are about to enter into with Dorka—a widow with spiritual burdens form her deceased husband. Remember, by law, the Bwai own her and could give you sleepless nights in a police cell," Owinyo cautioned his brother.

"Then I need a lawyer because of Betha; she wants her mother in this village," Odongo said in as serious a tone as he could muster.

"Good luck to you, but remember that she will need her own home," Owinyo restated his position.

"I'll take note of your concerns," Odongo said.

"Odongo, I have been a witness to a lot of things in your life. I am now an elder, and I need to confess some of them to you because some of the matters continue to bother you. When our father was dying, he confessed something concerning your home to me," Owinyo opened up, stopping for a moment to light his cigarette.

"Continue, Owinyo," Odongo said anxiously, opening the window to his hut. He was not a smoker, and so coping with the two smokers, Atieno his wife and Owinyo his brother, was a constant struggle in his life.

"I want to say two things about Okulu: You know that he is impotent?"

"We both know that," Odongo said.

"When Okulu was a little boy, he suddenly became impotent, and we all pained over it, and Apudo traveled the whole land in search of a cure that she would not find. Years later, my late father, speaking from his deathbed, whispered that Okulu would be strong enough to marry a woman and keep her, except he won't be able to seed her field," Owinyo said as emotionlessly as he could.

"Did my father say what made Okulu impotent?" Odongo asked.

"No. I could only *guess* that Ougo knew what had happened to the boy to have made him impotent," Owinyo said, leaving Odongo's question unanswered.

"Well, he has your son Odemba's seed growing in his house!" Odongo said, in pain, holding a distant gaze, his mind back to the night he violated Atieno. He cursed himself in silence, knowing that the said evil act produced Okulu—a son he had failed to protect against slander, contempt, and criminal schemes of his clansmen.

"From the same bed, he told me, "Animal of Flight, you are the Ougo left, you will carry my burdens, however filthy they are. Do not let Atieno's house end without warriors," Owinyo said.

"So you ordered Odemba to enter Okulu's house?" Odongo asked emotionlessly, yet hurting within.

"I did," Owinyo said gravely.

"You did not need to ask for my permission?" Odongo asked, his tremulous voice a pitch higher.

"No, it would have been too painful on you to have handled," Owinyo said, unmoved, smoking away.

"It hurts all the same," Odongo said, struggling to control his emotions, meanwhile blaming it all on himself and his reckless days as a youth.

"It should hurt, but Okulu is like a dead man. However, Juanita, his wife, walks with lives in her, and she is our commonwealth; her children are Apudo's great grandchildren. The children are Ougo blood; they are your blood and my blood," Owinyo justified his actions, writing it all in ancestral blood. He wrote the argument so intensely in scarlet that it jammed the gate to Odongo's heart of secrets, opening it wide.

"You should know that Okulu is my blood," Odongo said firmly, but he regretted his utterance immediately.

Owinyo remained silent for a while, taking time to collect his thoughts; he lit the cigarette whose flame had died due to disuse, pulled twice then released the smoke through his nostrils. His brother's statement was not new, but it was the confidence with which Odongo had just made the claim, that was different.

"Sorry, Odongo, I know you don't smoke. You said that Okulu is your blood?" he asked casually.

"Yes."

"Good, but how do you know that he is your blood, when the rumor then was that an unknown mine worker had seeded Atieno before you met her?" Owinyo asked, closely eying his bother through a haze of smoke. Indeed Owinyo walked with the Ougo family secrets.

"As a young mineworker together with another young fried, we waylaid two young women (both aliens from Sakwa) on their way home from the market. It was already dark. Each of us forced himself into his victim then disappeared into the night before the women could call for help," Odongo revealed. He felt better, having relieved his heart of the moral abscess he had had borne all his adult life.

"So Atieno was your victim?" Owinyo asked after a rather long spell shared with his cigarette.

"Yes," replied Odongo, volunteering, "The other woman died a few years ago and so did the other man."

"Did the young women know you?" Owinyo whispered coldly as the reality, moral significance, and enormity of the matter filtered through his nicotine-insulated mind.

"No."

"Why didn't you say this before?" Owinyo pressed on, trying to disbelieve his brother. However, building up behind the wall of restraint and his measured tone was extreme anger at his brother.

"I was ashamed."

"So you married Atieno to make up for your dirty violation?" Owiny whispered in anger, banging his clenched right fist.

"Yes. I have always lived in fear that she might recognize me by my breath," Odongo testified, maintaining his cool. If his brother was red-hot, Odongo was stone-cold. He mentally had rehearsed this scene for decades.

"No wonder, she always complained that you never stuck in her bed," Owinyo said, with much loathing, standing up to leave. He wondered why nature had seen it fit that Odongo would be his brother. "So you feared that she could recognize you?" Owinyo parroted, his heart darkening. As a veteran of a previous war, he hated those who challenged, through violations, a civil code of behavior. He was looking for a cane and there was none inside the hut. The only weapon available was a spear and the club he had in his hand, both of which could deliver mortal blows. Moreover, he knew Odongo was watching his every move. *Boy, he must have been getting ready for this meeting,* cursed Owinyo. He never saw Odongo that red-eyed yet collected in purpose. *It is his filthy life with women. Why should I care about it?* Owinyo raved still pacing about. He lit another cigarette to cool down his overheating nerves then sat down, his eyes on his brother through a haze of thick tobacco smoke. "Odongo son of my father, you are lucky," he warned.

"I have always lived in fear," Odongo said trembling, yet relieved that he had unburdened his soul of a lifetime of rot.

"You know what, my brother, in old times, the clan specifically called gatherings to cane people like you. You hurt so many people within the family that I see no reason why you should continue to live. In the army, we shot people, like you, who compromised missions or lives through their childish deeds," Owinyo said in disgust, trampling on a partially smoked cigarette..

"That is my life, my brother. I have died many times over the issue, to paraphrase Paulo the Apostle," Odongo said coolly, unwilling to pick up a fight.

"Listen carefully; if you bring the woman Dorka into this village, all the Ougo women will strip her naked and cane her while you watch! I have spoken." Owinyo warned.

"I'll think about that," Odongo said firmly. He long had resolved that he was his own man and would not allow Owinyo to play another game in his home. *You seeded Atieno's house behind my back. When will you stop? Dorka will be here this season, final,* Odongo declare in silence.

Owinyo looked at his brother through a haze of cigarette smoke, and he was quick to realize that he had had enough for the day. He abhorred mediocrity. He judged that staying longer could have precipitated a fistfight, or worse, between the two of them. Just then, he saw a lanky human form like that of Okulu hurtle past the window facing the gate on crutches.

"If you have not noticed, Okulu is coming through your gate," Owinyo announced, stepping outside, hoping that he never again would listen to the filthy stuff he was leaving behind. He promised he would live with his bother's dirty testimony, only because seniority-based birthright comes with its burdens, one of which is to keep secrets.

"Owinyo, close that door and come back here; let the women welcome their son home," Odongo said firmly, again surprising the tough-talking brother.

Odongo instantly was a man in charge. He had thought much about what would happen the day Okulu arrived. He would not beat Okulu, but would threaten him adequately to convince everyone present that, without some intervention, he could have thrashed the rogue son. Second, Aura would be the first to offer Okulu food because she was the first wife. Odongo believed Atieno already knew that he fathered Okulu.

Odongo knew that Okulu would return home in a position of strength. Okulu too had two sibling brothers and a new stepbrother named Ougo, and a son. Odongo appreciated that. The home needed some balance; he had started operating from the center, with Aura playing along, and Atieno had mellowed because of the burdens of late motherhood to twins.

Even then, Odongo greatest worry was how Okulu would react to the news about another son from Juanita! He, Odongo, had not known that the child was Okulu's blood, and neither had Okulu.

"I thought we were done?" Owinyo said, casually, as he resumed his seat.

"Now that Okulu is here, Atieno should get her home as soon as possible," Odongo said, announcing the final piece in the reconciliation strategy.

"Is she willing to move out?" Owinyo asked.

"She always wanted to move out," Odongo said.

"I read a new bond between your wives. Let them breastfeed their sons together, unless Atieno insists that she wants to leave immediately."

"I'll kill a bull tomorrow to reconcile with Okulu," Odongo announced.

"Tell him to get a second wife, and as a punishment to you, you will be responsible for the bride price," Owinyo ordered his prescription.

"Why put him through such pain again?" Odongo asked, hinting at Okulu's uncertain virility.

"Who knows? He may be strong enough to seed the younger woman," Owinyo said jokingly, but he knew something else he had sanctioned.

When Odemba first entered Juanita's house at the prompting of his father, he actually had done so in anger at Okulu, who routinely had visited with Judi, Odemba's third wife.

Now, Owinyo had a settled view that Okulu somehow managed to leave a daughter in Odemba's home. For a time, Owinyo had thought he was daydreaming, but as the girl matured and flowered into a teenager, she unfurled unmistakable facial features and body structure from Atieno, her *illicit* grandmother. Moreover, people were beginning to whisper about the girl, wondering what had hit them. Men whose wives were Okulu's comfort friends started inspecting their broods for any traces of the most-maligned breed in Thim Lich.

Looking at his brother in disbelief, Odongo recalled what Aura once told him about one of Odemba's daughters. Only back then, Odongo thought it was a joke because he understood that Okulu was impotent, but the Odemba girl looked like Atieno (Okulu's mother).

Searching for answers as to how an impotent man could sire a child, Odongo visited with some doctor who talked to him about sperm counts and recent advances in genetics and reproduction science. 'Yes, it is possible for a weak man to father a child,' the doctor friend had declared.

Aura must have been right! Odongo said upon reflection, now that his brother, who supposedly knew everything that transpired in the Ougo clan, was telling him to marry another wife for Okulu as a fine for the many wrongs he (Odongo) and his clan had committed against his son while he, the father, looked on in cowardly silence.

"I have listened to your orders, my brother. Owinyo, remember to join us tomorrow," Odongo said. He would act at his own pace.

34

Aura Charms away New Tension

WHEN OWINYO AND ODONGO EMERGED from the latter's hut, Okulu already was sitting under the big tree near Aura's house—his crutches resting against the tree. He was carrying his stepbrother Ougo Ng'ech (Aura's one-month-old son) on his laps and cooing to him.

Helena the babysitter stood idly next to the bonding Odongo sons.

Odongo and Owinyo walked briskly toward Okulu, their oversized walking sticks in their hands, their sights set on the sitting target and faces long. Helena stepped aside, thinking the two men would trample on her as they raced to kill Okulu. Okulu continued to coo to the baby unconcerned. He had opted never to challenge anybody.

Okulu's apparent insolence angered his father. Suddenly, a violent force took over Odongo's mind where he thought theatrics would suffice; Odongo wanted to draw blood and avenge Aura there and then. His steps became more urgent, his gait stiffened. Owinyo, who was close behind Odongo, was watching his brother's change of posture; he was ready to intervene should Odongo raise the heavy stick to hit Okulu.

Okulu continued to play with his baby brother. He refused to look up at his senior male relatives.

At the same time, Aura emerged from her house, carrying a tray of food, ready to play a good mother's role and scoop Atieno one more time. Behind her, a house help carried a small table for four. Aura looked from Okulu, who was playing a loyal babysitter to baby Ougo, to

Odongo, whose arm (right) holding the sizable club had stiffened, and she felt alarmed. She never before saw her husband so angry that his lips vibrated erratically, as if he had a fever. Seeing her husband's aggressive posture, Aura realized that he could hit Okulu and her baby, for whom the latter man continued cooing unconcerned.

Concerned, Aura looked at Owinyo, silently begging him to intervene.

Owinyo, hold that hand before it harms Okulu, she prayed. However, instead of a face in emergency mode, Aura saw a face that revealed nothing, even as Owinyo too was contemplating an intervention.

I have to act before that club lands on Okulu and Ougo my baby, Aura reasoned in silence.

Aura quickened her steps, plates rattling in her tray; she soon stopped somewhere between Odongo and Okulu.

Odongo stopped moving; he hardly was a foot from her position.

Aura stood still for a moment, pleadingly looking her husband in the face. What she saw was fear; his lips still vibrating feverishly, and it scared her.

"Odongo son of Ougo, give it up, this home needs peace," Aura whispered hoarsely.

Looking at his wife in the eye, Odongo realized that she was serious about what she had said; moreover, her message kept reverberating in his head. Then, Odongo began to relax as seconds ticked away; the strain from the building anger in his chest eased. Odongo began to see the broken, beaten, submissive man, the new Okulu, as the son he had wronged greatly and not as the villainous son who nearly killed a stepmother a year before.

As if the skies understood the thawing of tension among the human's below it, a dark cloud, which had covered Thim Lich all morning, moved on, ushering in sunshine.

Odongo took away a potato from the tray Aura was holding and started peeling it inch by inch, with Owinyo looking on amazed. "Welcome home, *Okew Kowak* (he whose mother hails from Kowak)," Odongo mumbled inaudibly moments later in welcome to Okulu, calling out (and praising) his son by the name of the clan and land of his mother's people. Even then, nobody heard what he said, thus dumping what would have been a hilarious message of forgiveness.

As if he wasn't part of the tension of the moment before, Odongo took up a seat on a foldable wooden chair close by and proceeded to eat the potato unconcerned, perhaps warning that he was a new person, a silent volcano that could erupt at any time.

Aura's babysitter put the table between Odongo and Okulu. The babysitter uploaded the baby from Okulu, who said "Thank you," to everyone's surprise for he was not a courteous man.

Aura placed the tray of food on the table, picked up a small kettle of water and served Owinyo to wash his hands.

"Thank you Aura, you are the only woman in this village who boils hand-washing water," Owinyo said in praise of his sister-in-law.

"My mother trained me well," replied Aura, before she moved on to Odongo, who declined her water saying, "I'm eating already. Moreover. . ." Odongo tried to say, but Aura finished the statement for him, saying, "My mother told me that a little dirt in a man's hands is good for his health." Aura had heard her husband recite that line countless times before.

"And she never was wrong," Owinyo said.

"Well, how can I argue against the wise words of my late mother-in-law?" Aura posed, handing over the kettle of water and a small plastic basin to her house help who proceeded to serve Okulu.

Okulu soaped his hands and then rinsed them thoroughly.

After Okulu had sanitized his hands, Aura said, "Owinyo, you can pray so that your brother and his son may eat in peace."

Owinyo crossed himself, mumbled a prayer and crossed himself again, and then greeted Okulu, hoping that Odongo would say something to the son. However, Odongo said nothing; he continued to eat in silence.

"May all of you eat in peace," Aura said, moving away, relieved, wondering how easily things had unfolded after the tense start.

Atieno had watched the pained arrival of her unfortunate son on crutches from the safety of her house.

For a few minutes, she wept silently for Okulu's misfortunes, her mind wandering off to the tragic evening when she administered an oath on him to go and kill, but she quickly blacked out that shameful episode in her life. She of late had decided to live a peaceful life for the benefit of her twin sons, whose births had left her with hardly any strength for domestic fights.

Atieno had looked on in awe as Aura took charge of and diffused an otherwise tense situation between Odongo and Okulu. She wondered how Aura had managed to bring the two men to eat together in hardly a blink of an eye. "She is a woman taking charge! That perhaps is what it is to be the first wife!" Atieno whispered sarcastically, even as she admired Aura's performance, battling to keep anger at bay on a day she should celebrate Okulu's return.

Now that Aura has done the hard part, how will I cope when Okulu walks through this door? Atieno wondered, retreating into her house to finalize the cooking she had started, having known that Okulu would be arriving during that day.

35

"Okulu Son of Odongo"

OKULU WOULD LIMP into his mother's house within the hour of his arrival. He was not alone. Abich, beautiful, pregnant, and delicately dressed in a simple loose-fitting, floral cotton dress, led the way in, having left her driver talking with her father and uncle under the communal tree. Abich had entered her father's home minutes after Atieno entered the house; she had a driver at the wheels of the Land Rover. She would spend a few minutes bonding with her male kin, and even Aura, before she led Okulu to their mother's house. Needless to add that Abich's hostility toward Aura and Odongo had thawed, perhaps because the duo held secrets about her criminal behaviors during Aura's days as an inpatient at Migori Hospital.

"Abich, why do you risk traveling the rough roads while still in your delicate condition?"

"I heard Okulu was coming home today and couldn't sleep over it; Ma, why are you unhappy to see *us*?" Abich asked taking baby Adongo away from her mother's arms.

"Okulu, son of Odongo, you made it back. Sorry for the misfortunes that have become part of your life, but you are here among your brothers," Atieno said, tears of joy on her face, as she addressed her much maligned son by his father's name, perhaps for the first time in decades.

"Ma, I stopped feeling sorry for myself; I have been called many things I am not; I am a curse to this home, and I understand why; yet my little sister here would not allow anybody to throw away my body to the dogs," Okulu said with vigor and rare zeal, handing over a black-and-white photograph to sister Abich.

"Who is that?" Abich asked, looking at the photograph of a woman with a child.

"The boy is my son, Allan; the woman is Wilkista Awuor, his mother," Okulu enthused.

"Who is she to you?" Abich asked.

"She is my wife. She is from Shirati, Tanganyika," Okulu said of the tall woman in her twenties. Atieno reached over and took away the photograph from Abich.

There was a period of silence, during which the two women wondered what had hit them. They both understood that Okulu was impotent. Atieno had looked wishfully at the Odemba daughter whom people had claimed to be her blood, but she had not believed her eyes because she believed Okulu was impotent. Yet here was Okulu telling her that he had fathered the boy. Atieno looked at Okulu and then the boy of three years in the black-and-white photograph. Atieno saw an unmistakable resemblance between her husband, and the boy who looked straight ahead defiantly, with his chin up.

That is a likeness of Odongo Rao, my husband, Atieno said in her heart, shaking feverishly. She felt dizzy as she recalled the dark night in her youth, when a man violated her. Then she realized her children were watching her. "So it is true; it was *him*?" she mumbled incoherently looking at the photograph. She was holding, in her hands, a photograph of human proof that Okulu was an Ougo blood. She almost ordered Okulu to leave immediately, go to Tanganyika, and bring home her grandson.

"Mama, are you okay?" Abich asked stepping forward to hold her mother.

"I'm alright now, Abich. I had seen the boy in a dream," she lied, thinking that her children had heard her mumble words that referred to her experience as a violated young woman.

"You did?" Okulu asked.

"Sure. O the twins took much strength from me. Okulu; lets sit down," Atieno said, signaling Abich to leave her alone.

"You better see a gynecologist—see a woman's doctor," Abich said.

"I will, now that Okulu is back. Abich of Thim Lich, I see you are fine, but how is my son-in-law?" Atieno asked, having successfully changed the subject from the sensitive matters of Okulu's virility and ancestry.

"Your son-in-law is doing well; he is busy today; that is why I came alone with the driver," Abich responded, before she turned and embraced Okulu, saying, "How I love you, my brother."

"Thank you, my sister; I had lost both arms, and you gave them back to me. Tell me something, my sister; from which water did you fish out that generous man?" Okulu asked laughing.

"If you knew what I eat, you wouldn't touch anything I've touched," Abich said, jokingly. She was alluding to where she was, and what she was up to, when she met her doctor husband. If there were people in Thim Lich knew the story of how she met the doctor husband, they were her father and Aura, and she hoped that they would keep quiet about it.

"I won't ask again," Okulu said, playing with baby Opiyo.

"Okulu, it is true that your Ougo clan wronged you many times before; I took part in some of the wrongs. Even then, remember that your father never said anything bad about you. Second, it is time to say 'I am sorry' before your clan and pay a fine.

"*A fine?*" Abich asked in shock.

"Yes. Okulu, you'll pay a fine. The clan will be here tomorrow, should your father keep his promise to kill a reconciliation bull for you tomorrow. Should the clan levy a fine against you, pay it and move on. Aura almost died in your hands; besides we humans are weak; a man does not beat his father's wife," Atieno declared, surprising her children, both of whom simply had carried out her instructions to eliminate Aura.

"Ma!" Abich exclaimed.

"Abich; I feel your pain; and you must be saying that Okulu did what I asked him to do, but we have to move on with our heads high. *Nyasaye* (God) knows that we have fought a just war, because Okulu was wronged, but our laws say that he must pay a fine."

"I'll pay the fine; it is fine with me," Okulu said.

"Okulu, if you have a woman you want to marry, go ahead and do it. You are a man with a home; don't be like Odongo, your father, who treated his wives unequally.

Never turn your back on Juanita, your wife. She has a son who looks like you," Atieno said, giving Okulu a calabash of porridge.

"My son?" Okulu asked, wondering why his mother was certain that the child was his seed.

"Yes," Atieno confirmed.

Okulu let the matter be, but he inwardly was happy.

It too was the happiest day of Atieno's married life. Abich had made her bed for Dr. Otago, and she was pregnant. Then there was her son Okulu, the much-maligned man in Thim Lich. It was clear that Okulu not only was Odongo's seed, but he also was a man, with sons, after all!

Who am I to continue to curse the man who fathered Okulu, never walked away from his responsibility, and became my husband? Atieno wondered, looking over the two adult children at meal before her. One was a man, who had lived a life of constant stress; the other was a young woman who had stuck with her amid times of crisis.

Atieno was at peace, yet she was troubled, knowing that both children understood, empathized with, and shared in her pain; beyond that, both children bore personal wounds they received while they fought her wars.

Joseph R. Alila, Schenectady, New York, December 2011

Glossary and Notes of Luo Words and Phrases

Amondi: a name given to Luo girls born in the morning but before sunrise.

Anete: a quagmire; muddy quicksand.

Ayie: Literal: I accept. In marriage, *Ayie* is a modern-day salutary monetary amount a son-in-law puts in the hands of a mother-in-law as away of saying, "I accept your daughter, and I thank you for raising a good girl."

Chira: a killer curse.

Duong': eldership earned through marital, parental, or ancestral seniority, with rights and expectations such as spiritual leadership and a leadership stool.

Fulu: a small fish out of Lolwe (Lake Victoria).

Jajuok; Ja Juok: a witch.

Kidole kimoja hakivunji chawa: (*Swahili* saying) *Literal* meaning: one finger cannot kill or crush a louse. Strength in numbers; a call to communal effort (team work) in tackling problems. It pays to work as a team.

Miruti: Swahili corruption for explosive; dynamite.

Ng'ech: a large lizard.

Nyako: a girl.

Nyanyuok: he-goat.

Nyar: daughter of.

Nyasakwa: a girl or woman born of a Sakwa man.

Nyatanga: a girl or woman born in Tanganyika.

Nyoyo: a cooked whole legume-cereal mixture.

Ober: she is beautiful; it is beautiful.

Ober ka nyar jajuok: Literal: she is beautiful like the daughter of a witch. Behind every beauty, there is a flaw. All that glitters is nor gold.

Oche: sons-in-law; male clan relatives of a son-in-law.

Or: a son-in-law.

Rao: a hippo.

Simba: a man's bachelor hut. (Note the related Luo word *Kiru:* a man's command hut, known for it rugged structure; a man's tent or tool shed).

Wer, Were: a wooden milking vessel.

ugali   blood meal

Other Books

by Joseph R. Alila

Fiction

The American Polygamist
ISBN-13: 978-144992798-1
The Choirmaster
ISBN-13: 978-144954199-6
The Thirteenth Widow
ISBN-13: 978-144951231-6
The Luo Dreamers' Odyssey: From the Sudan to American
Power
ISBN-13: 978-144148311-9
Not on My Skin
ISBN-13: 978-143825527-9
Sins of Our Hearts
ISBN-13: 978-143820013-2
Whisper to My Aching Heart
ISBN-13: 978-143820751-3
The Wise One of Ramogiland
ISBN-13: 978-143032554-3
The Milayi Curse
ISBN-13: 978-143032441-6
Sunset on Polygamy (PublishAmerica)
ISBN-13: 978-142416684-8

Poetry

Thirteen Curses on Mother Africa
ISBN-13: 978-1-4303-1592-6

Rateng' and Bride
ISBN-13: 978-1438251097

Made in the USA
Charleston, SC
26 December 2011